AN

INNOCENT

LIFE

By Ineke van Os

AN

INNOCENT

LIFE

By Ineke van Os

First Published – 2025
This edition published by Ineke van Os
Queensland, Australia

A catalogue record for this
work is available from the
National Library of Australia

The National Library of Australia Cataloguing-in-Publication

Creator: van Os, Ineke, author.

Title: An Innocent Life.

ISBN: 978-1-7635531-0-1 (paperback)

Subjects: Speculative fiction.
             Australian fiction
             Time-travel fiction

This book is a work of fiction and, except in the case of historical fact, any resemblance to actual persons, living or dead, is purely coincidental.

Content warning: This story of fiction contains descriptions that may disturb some readers. In particular, references to mental health and abortion may trigger strong reactions. Please read with care.

Typeset in Times New Roman 12pt by Donna Munro Book Design.
Cover artwork by Donna Munro Book Design.
Printed and bound in Australia by Ingram Spark.

CHAPTER 1

2013

'So, where to?' Emma said, as she slid into the passenger seat of the blue Mazda.

'I'm thinking it's nice to have some time with my sister.' Cassie leaned over and kissed Emma's cheek.

Emma smiled. 'Yes, it's lovely isn't it?'

'It's so good to see you again. Now let's go and see this guru, even if it is all rubbish. I'm only going because you're twisting my arm,' Cassie said.

'It'll be fun, you'll see.'

They found an old worker's cottage hidden on a large, overgrown block in a nearby suburb. It was painted a deep turquoise with a crisp white trim. Colourful prayer flags were draped from tree to tree alongside strings of fairy lights. Cassie imagined how pretty it would be at night. The house was set quite a way back from the road and would have been easy to miss, had it not been for a friend's detailed directions.

As Cassie and Emma scrunched along the path, the unmistakable fragrance of sandalwood and patchouli mingled with the sweet scents of the garden. A huge bougainvillea sat at the corner of the house, spraying tendrils of deepest magenta over the small verandah and the courtyard below. It emanated calm and peace.

Emma threw her arm over her sister's shoulder and took a deep breath, her blue eyes shining.

'This is absolutely perfect. I feel as if we are meant to be here.'

Cassie was sceptical. 'Hmmm, who'd have believed a week ago we'd be doing this?'

Inside was a small sitting room, admirably serving as a reception area. An elegant silky-oak table sat in one corner. On it, were a laptop, a unicorn-shaped container holding a few pens, and some papers scattered about. A moonstone paperweight caught Cassie's eye, shining like an oval rainbow on a small pile of paperwork.

No one was around so they sat down in a couple of wingback armchairs against the wall.

Emma sank back in the luxurious green velvet, picked up one of the New-Age magazines nearby, and started leafing through it.

A young girl came in wearing Doc Martin boots and a black boho dress patterned with colourful stars. Dangling amidst a shock of inky locks were bright-yellow hoop earrings. She radiated fun and fantasy.

'Good morning, you must be Cassie and Emma. We've been expecting you.' Her gaze was directed at Cassie.

The sisters exchanged quizzical looks.

She smiled at them both, turned and wandered out of the room beyond the curtain that separated the back of the house from the small office area.

'What's that about?' Cassie whispered.

'No idea, but let's just enjoy this.'

'Emma?' the young girl appeared again. 'Would you come through please? We can put you in Room 1. Cassie, perhaps you could wait here. Mrs Pendle will see you soon.'

Emma put back the magazine she had been holding. With a devilish grin she winked at her sister. 'This could be interesting. See you in an hour.'

Sitting alone, Cassie gazed at her surroundings, the motivational posters on the walls, the salt lamp glowing pink in the corner, and an array of crystals hanging from the ceiling, throwing colourful reflections around the room. She felt uneasy, a feeling of foreboding she couldn't explain. Her thoughts turned to her family. Her husband, Jeff, and their daughter Katy, twenty-three years old and studying physiotherapy at university. Cassie was thrilled Emma and her two nieces, Evie and Tamara, had come up for a surprise visit from Tamworth. The girls were home with her ageing parents. All these things jumbled into a mosaic of images and drifted into a warm mist of love and belonging. It brought such a flush of calm and peace that she was startled when a tiny, gnarled lady suddenly appeared from behind the curtain.

Mrs Pendle looked frail, hunched over and intense. Two piercing black eyes looked into Cassie's. Although the lady smiled, it was a little intimidating. She led Cassie down the hallway and into a room. It was a fairy realm, with colourful crystals and candles of every shape and size. Hundreds of figurines of fairies, elves, and unicorns decorated every available space. The sweet smell of incense hung in the air. Opposite a desk was a small round table with a deep-purple velvet cloth draped over it. Resting on a perfect disc of marble at the table's centre sat an enormous crystal ball.

When Cassie spied this, she shuddered. It was such a cliché. Next thing, the sorceress would be predicting a tall, handsome stranger entering her life.

The psychic's dark eyes bored into her. 'I understand you are a little nervous, but don't be.'

The break in tension gave Cassie a burst of resolve. She turned on her heels and headed straight back down the hall.

Mrs Pendle followed her out. 'Don't go. You must listen. Spirit simply co-operated by bringing you here today. You are carrying a huge burden of guilt and it's holding you back. It wasn't your fault Scott died, and I can help.'

Cassie froze. She'd never told anyone about Scott; not a soul apart from her immediate family. It was buried deep in her heart, safely out of harm's way. How did this old lady know? Who did she think she was? For years, Cassie had struggled with the consequences of her actions, and for years, she had managed to push the memory away. She wore her guilt like a permanent scar, hidden from sight. Occasionally she still had nightmares, and Jeff would wake her and hold her, helpless to assuage her pain.

'No. I can't do this,' Cassie said. She shook her head violently and strode towards reception. An image of Scott's tangled body lying lifeless in the car exploded in her mind's eye.

Mrs Pendle hurried after her.

'Don't go ... I know about the accident, what really happened. Don't rush away, we need to talk.'

But Cassie was having none of it. She had no intention of talking about it with this stranger. The very thought that this old hag knew such details made her skin crawl.

'Leave me alone, I want nothing to do with you.' It sounded more aggressive than she intended.

A scrawny spider-like hand grabbed her elbow. She turned and stared hard at her assailant, her eyes cold as steel.

Mrs Pendle softened. 'I'm sorry; I'm only trying to help. At least stay for the massage; you'll feel better, I promise.' Her eyes glowed amber and clear.

With resigned reluctance, Cassie allowed herself to be led into another room where a young girl stood waiting. *At least this one looks normal*. The masseuse was wearing a crisp white shirt and dark trousers, emanating professionalism. It was reassuring.

The therapist's hands skilfully kneaded and pummelled parts of Cassie's body she hadn't acknowledged for ages. Slowly the treatment started to work and she could feel the knot of anxiety inside yield somewhat. But still, Mrs Pendle's words hovered around her.

Afterwards, back in the sunlight, everything felt surreal. Someone had ripped open a sealed envelope in her heart, and the contents were spilling out.

Emma, on the other hand, was euphoric. She babbled on about how great she was feeling and how she'd wished she had done this more often and maybe they should have gone on and had the spa and hot stone treatments.

Cassie was quiet.

'You haven't said much, Cass. What did you think?'

'I could use a drink. Is it lunch time yet?'

'Come on, out with it' Emma said. 'She didn't hurt you, did she? She didn't try anything perverse?' Although she laughed as she said it, her eyes now softened into pools of concern.

'Not exactly, let's find a pub and I'll fill you in. It's weird.'

Later, wine in hand, Cassie told Emma what went on.' I shouldn't have gone. I was getting creepy vibes the minute we sat down in the waiting area.'

'Why didn't you say something?'

'Fair point.' Cassie shrugged. 'You were so looking forward to it, and I was just happy to be with you. I didn't want to put a damper on things.'

CHAPTER 2

Emma had been a kid when the accident had happened and she had no vivid memory of Scott. She knew he'd died, and how upset Cassie had been, but remembered no more. They hadn't talked about it since.

The things Cassie hadn't talked about sat on her like a lead weight, and she couldn't throw off the feelings of guilt. It was as if she was looking at it for the first time, even though it had been lying stagnant in her sub-conscious for years, colouring her life, adding extra layers to any challenges she encountered.

Watching her Katy grow up she couldn't help thinking of Scott's parents and the precious moments she had stolen from them. All Katy's milestones, her victories, were diminished because Cassie blamed herself for depriving other parents of the joys and triumphs she was so blessed to have. With those thoughts, the guilt grew; it fed on itself and grew bigger and stronger until finally she accepted it and wove it into her life. It was a part of who she was.

Had it held her back like the old lady had said? Not that she was aware of.

Outwardly, she carried herself with confidence and composure. Her family believed her story; they understood the circumstance and had long since acquitted her of any crime. However, they didn't know the truth. She knew who she truly was, even if no one else did. The memories drifted in—Scott getting drunk, their fight, her fateful decision to drive. The images started hammering at her; she was barely aware of her sister sitting opposite.

Cassie fell apart after the accident. She'd really cared about Scott, and the grief was unbearable at times, but there was also the guilt. She couldn't talk about it to anyone. She'd managed to get a scholarship to university but failed most of her exams in the first year. Her dream of becoming a vet melted. Without direction or ambition, she drifted from one job to the other. Nothing fired up her enthusiasm, nothing unearthed a passion.

It wasn't until she took the position as a dental receptionist that some sparkle came back into her life because she found the job interesting and challenging. Five years after the accident, Cassie was finally able to imagine some sort of future. She decided she wanted to study and travel, and repair the broken pieces of herself. She wanted her life to be better.

It was around this time that a new patient had swaggered into the surgery—a young man called Jeff with piercing black eyes and thick, wavy brown hair that just covered his ears. He was gorgeous. With his long, straight nose and sultry looks, he reminded her of Jim Morrison of The Doors, one of her favourite bands. Whenever he came in after that, she turned into a fumbling, ditzy mess and, when he leaned over the counter one day and asked her out, it was as if a skyrocket had exploded in her heart. Their date was the first of many, and the romance blossomed. His quiet confidence in the future made her feel stronger. Back then, he was a young technician at the local television station. Countless dinners, trips to the movies, art galleries, hikes and other outings later, he proposed, and Cassie Truscott became Mrs Cassie Foster. They went to London for the honeymoon and spent a glorious month exploring the places they had read and talked about for so long. It was bliss. On their return, they rented a flat in the inner city for a few years, saving hard until they were able to put a deposit on an old Queenslander in Wavell Heights, and they had been there ever since. The family they longed for hadn't come quickly, but after a lot of hoping and waiting, Katy finally arrived in 1990.

She sighed out loud at the memory.

'Cassie, Cassie ... hellooo.' Emma was snapping her fingers, shocking her back into the present.

***

The rest of the weekend flew by in a flurry. On Tuesday, Cassie dropped in on her parents on the way to take Emma and the girls to the airport. Gran was vibrant; she looked truly happy. Being with the family had lifted her spirits, and she was in fine form.

When they were gathered around the table for morning tea, Gran suddenly jumped up, muttering something as she headed towards the bedroom.

'Almost forgot. I've got something for you, Cassie...now you're home full time.' She was carrying an old shoebox.

Cassie grinned at her sister. She recognised that box.

Her mum plonked it down on the table. 'Old family photos, I've been meaning to ask you to scan them for yonks. My eyesight isn't what it used to be, and I'm so slow these days. You could do that for me, couldn't you love? Please.'

Emma and Cassie rolled their eyes at each other, understanding this meant a painful, time-consuming labour of love.

Cassie lifted the lid and peered in. There were hundreds of photos, all dumped on top of each other in no discernible order. *What a nightmare*. Then she looked at her mum's pleading eyes and realised she didn't have much choice.

'With no job to go to now, you'll have stacks of time up your sleeve and it would mean so much to me,' said her mother.

Cassie hugged her mum. 'I'll see what I can do. You're not in a hurry for them, are you?'

Emma was already into the box. 'Ooh I'd love to have a good look at these, it's been so long. I wish I had more time.'

'You can take them home if you like,' suggested Cassie, grimacing ever so slightly.

***

When she got home after teary farewells to Emma and the girls at the airport, the house felt hollow. All the corners where laughter and chaos had so happily lived that morning now lay quietly. Then there was the stuff—Emma always managed to forget something— usually a stray sock or maybe a T-shirt and the little bits of clutter that were her sister's trademark. She already missed her.

Cassie made herself a cup of coffee and meandered onto the back verandah, just to sit for a few minutes, to re-acquaint herself with the silence. She breathed in the warm air and listened to the magpies happily chirruping as they pottered about in the garden. She thought about her family and smiled, letting the comfortable feelings wash over her. Coco, a silky chocolate Burmese poured out from her favourite place beneath the shrubbery, stretching herself like a slinky. She half yawned and meowed her welcome, mildly irritated at having been woken. The cat padded slowly up the few steps towards Cassie, lifted her delicate face and pushed her elegant, smooth body against her calf, caressing it with the assurance of being stroked in return. Cassie bent down and picked her up, bringing the liquid creature close to her face, and burrowed into the smooth fur. She dwelt for a few moments in that empty space before jumping back into the present.

Sitting in front of the television that evening with Jeff she slid back into the banality of their life and, by the time she went to bed, Emma and the girls seemed far, far away.

CHAPTER 3

In the morning, the raucous cries of the birds stirred her. Daylight crept into the bedroom, the sunlight's sharp rays throwing patterns of light onto the carpet. Cassie woke slowly.

Jeff was in the kitchen mooching around, and for a moment she lay there listening to the comforting noises of domesticity. The soft clunk of the coffee cup on the bench top, the odd burps and noises from the coffee machine, drawers sliding in and out, taps flowing—all the sounds of her stable, congenial world. She swung her legs out of bed and padded into the kitchen.

'Good morning. Sleep in, did we?' Jeff said.

'Well, if you can call 7.30 sleeping in, I guess so, but it took me ages to drift off last night. All the excitement of the last few days, I think,' said Cassie, yawning.

She grabbed a cup off the drainer, poured herself a coffee and sat down at the table with a heavy thud. Jeff said nothing, but gave her one of his quizzical looks. He was still handsome, but in a mature, experienced kind of way. In place of his brown curls, his hair was now almost white and cropped close. He had an interesting face, which he wore in a habitual grimace that made one think he had the world on his shoulders, but when he laughed, it exploded into a mass of cracks and crevices that lit up his features. His smiles were worth waiting for. He was a no-nonsense sort of a guy, who suited her; it made him reliable and safe. Cassie sat and watched as he spread butter and lashings of Vegemite on his toast. She liked the way his cheeks crinkled as he took an enormous, satisfying mouthful.

'Hmmm. Now that everyone's gone I feel a bit flat,' Cassie said.

'Well, you're an enterprising woman. You'll find something to do.' He wheeled off and headed to the bedroom.

'You know what?' she was talking loudly in his general direction, 'I really don't feel like getting back onto the work treadmill. I might do some volunteering or something, or get to one of my projects.' She muttered this last thought to herself.

Before Jeff left, he gave her a hurried peck on the cheek then bolted out the door. Tidying up a little, she ventured into the study and booted up the computer. She looked at the files she had sitting on the table and decided none of them held any useful answers to the work issue. Unfortunately, the work had simply dried up for the company that manufactured components for venetian blinds and, just two weeks ago, she was given notice. It left her feeling quite empty. The prospect of finding another part-time job like it was slim.

Her eyes fell on the shoebox her mum had given her and she pulled off the lid. *This is going to take ages ... I might just sort them out a bit before I start the scanning.*

She carried the box into the lounge and plonked a pile of photos onto the coffee table. She picked up a handful and started looking through them one by one.

Moments later, she got that same sick, clammy feeling she'd had only a few days before. Her hand shook as she picked up the photo taken on the night of the Senior Formal. She looked gorgeous in her aqua off-the-shoulder evening gown, and beside her, handsome and confident, was Scott, his hand cradling hers. It was so long ago. She had just finished her Senior Examination and looked happy, glowing with the promise of the night ahead.

Scott was Maria's cousin. Maria was her closest friend who lived across the street, and she'd introduced them when he was visiting one day. She could still see herself the first time she met him. It was such a vivid memory. He had taken her breath away and everything else about that day had become a blur, but that moment remained strong in her memory. It was not in her nature to pursue anyone, but with Scott she had made it her business to be caught in the same space as him as often as she could. She was over the moon when she realised he liked her as well. He was a few years older, but she didn't care. After a lot of shy conversations and awkward moments, he'd finally asked her out. The formal was their third date. She'd been hesitant about asking him to escort her that evening, but none of the boys in class appealed, and besides, most of them were already taken.

How excited she'd been waiting for that big night. It was her first formal and she'd spent afternoons poring over magazines looking for the perfect dress and hours chatting to girlfriends on the phone, dreaming and planning in anticipation.

When the day dawned, she had been beside herself. Eating was out of the question and all afternoon butterflies frolicked in her tummy. Scott had risen to the occasion. At bang on seven, his car pulled into the driveway. He looked so confident and mature in his hired suit, and he'd bought her a white orchid corsage.

The photo quivered as she gripped it tightly, trying to control the waves of sadness. It had been taken by her dad, just before they left for the party. How her heart had leapt when Scott took her hand. Now, all these years later, she remembered his flushed cheeks, his azure eyes—moist and keen, so bright and open to adventure.

It had all gone so terribly wrong.

A great melancholy settled on her. Her temples throbbed as hidden feelings pounded to the surface.

'Damn that woman!' she said aloud, as if the psychic had conjured up the memory by mentioning his name. It wasn't fair; she wanted the stability of the present back again. Her life with Jeff was secure and predictable, and she treasured that. She was annoyed this horrible thing had been resurrected. Jeff knew about the accident of course, and that Scott had been her first boyfriend, but she'd never shared her guilt, the nagging conviction that it was her fault that Scott was dead. She felt too ashamed, and her bad memories had no place in their relationship.

She threw the photo back in the box and buried it at the bottom.

With an indignant snort, she stomped off, determined to erase the bittersweet memory tormenting her now. She couldn't think any further—she simply couldn't—if she pandered to the thoughts reeling in her brain she would never have any peace.

Digging around in the lawn locker, she found a spade, some gloves, and an old bucket and headed out into the garden. She fell to her knees and started attacking the weeds. It took a while, but through pulling and digging and tormenting the soil, she found some sanctuary. Eventually the murmurings in her head started to quieten. She managed to still her mind and kept the savage dog of anxiety at bay.

Once back inside, she showered and made lunch—a sandwich with some smoked salmon that was nearing its use-by date. She brooded about the morning's events, slowly turning things over in her mind. Coco lay peacefully beside her, stretching her lithe body in the warm sun.

This is ridiculous! Get a grip, Cassie. She'd promised her mum she would scan those photos, so she had better come to terms with any baggage that might be thrown her way. She wouldn't pussyfoot around. She pledged to be more pragmatic about the whole thing.

Her mobile rang and Emma's number flashed up on the screen.

'Hi Cass, sorry I didn't call earlier. We're home and settled. Thanks again for everything; I had a great time. Let Mum know, would you?'

'Of course. How was your flight?'

'It was good. Now I have to psych myself up to go back to work and juggling my life again. Still, it was wonderful.'

'It sure was. Thanks for coming. Look after yourself. Love you,' Cassie said. She heard Evie calling for her mother in the background.

'Ditto, byeee. Gotta go, sorry.'

Cassie sighed. Emma was four years younger, and unlike Cassie had been blessed with a beautiful complexion that took even more years off her age, but these days she always looked tired. With two demanding kids and working almost full time, she never stopped.

By the time Jeff and Katy came home, Cassie felt okay again. The corner of the garden looked better, she'd managed to put a meal on the table, and the physical effort had made her feel pleasantly tired. Tomorrow was another day.

CHAPTER 4

The next morning Cassie ventured into the office and her gaze fell on the shoebox, its lid balancing lopsidedly on the edge. She had to face this ... but not now, and she turned away.

Tea. Before I do anything. She shook her head. *This is stupid. They're only photos, deal with it.*

No doubt, there were other precious memories stuffed inside the box. Eventually she had to make her peace with it all. Confronted by the past and finding no sanctum in the present, she was forced to examine the details more closely than she had dared for more than thirty years. Nevertheless, here they were, strewn across her heart like corpses on a battlefield. She started to shake, wishing someone would come and hold her; tell her everything would be all right. She stared out the window and the empty wind rustled in the branches, the endless sky beyond gnawed at her insides.

The images came hard and fast. Cassie was mesmerised by their intensity. Scott at the dance. Scott drinking the bourbon he had smuggled in. His aggression. Her embarrassment. Scott out of control. Her innocence, her fear, not knowing what to do.

Her decision, oh, that decision, the ruin of it all! Staggering to the car, the fight, ripping the keys from his hand, hopping into the driver's seat, Scott passed out beside her. Driving, skidding, the sudden blackness as time stopped. The aftermath. The police. His parents. The grief, the lies—the dreadful lies. The realisation that she had killed him ... the interminable guilt.

She gasped suddenly, lurching back into the present by the ringing of her phone.

She couldn't speak to anyone now, instead she sat down. Coco skipped lightly onto her lap. Her softness was comforting and Cass hugged the cat so tightly she mewed in protest.

When she finally picked up her phone, a ripple of guilt swept over her when she realised she'd missed a call from Emma; the last call had been so brief.

Cassie found it almost impossible to keep past and present apart, so much had she been lingering in both worlds. Her thoughts weighed heavily on her. She wanted badly to share them with Jeff, but she had made a promise to herself that he should never be burdened by her guilt and remorse over something that happened before he changed her life.

'Sorry I missed your call, darling, is everything all right?'

'Yes, just had a lousy morning, and needed to hear your voice, that's all,' Emma murmured.

'I'm sorry, anything in particular?' Cassie's tone sounded flat and distant.

'Nah, all good now, I'm over it. But are you okay?'

'Yes, I think so. In the doldrums, that's all, been caught up in my own head a bit. Don't worry, it'll pass.'

'I'm sorry I have to run, dentist appointment, but talk later, hey?' Emma sounded fine.

'Yes, good luck. Love you.'

The silence again. Collecting her thoughts, she resolutely made her way back into the office. Let's do this.

She opened the scanner on the computer, ready to start the ball rolling. She would simply scan the photos into individual folders. Tapping away gently she created several, deciding the simplest way was to store the photos under the decade they had been taken and maybe some subfolders, such as 'family' and 'friends' and perhaps vacation photos. She sighed. It was more complicated than she'd planned.

She picked up the first photo from the box, placed it onto the glass bed of the device and pushed scan.

Palingggg.

She tried again

Palingggg. That dreaded sound when technology blows a raspberry at you.

'Damn, what's going on?'

Once more. She lifted the lid on the scanner, re-adjusted the photo, and pressed scan again.

Palingggg.

Bloody hell, I am not in the mood for this. Now she had no choice but to wait for Jeff to come home and sort it out. She really couldn't be bothered trouble-shooting herself. Not in her current mood. Then, thinking it through, she realised it was a selfish approach; she knew Jeff came home stressed anyway and didn't need her technical trials added to his workload. With a little patience she could sort it out herself.

Two hours later, after countless searches online, a few frustrating calls back and forth to the manufacturer, checking and rechecking her connections, a growling stomach, and the onset of an annoying headache, she gave up.

'Stuff it, I am just going out and getting a new one, they're only about fifty bucks. Maybe the poor old thing can't keep up with the computer.' Damn! She hated the way manufacturers coerced you into buying more stuff.

She grabbed the car keys and her jacket and headed off to the shopping centre up the hill. Thankfully, the kids were all back at school so she easily found a park.

Strolling through the entrance, she spied a small yellow postcard on the notice board.

FOR SALE
PHOTO SCANNER HARDLY USED $20.00
CONTACT 0432 786 499

Hmmm. It would certainly save all the tedious footslogging in the arcades. Standing there in front of the huge community notice board, Cassie stared at the card, wondering if it was worth pursuing.

Why not? I'm not busy.

She dug in her bag for her mobile. Then, as she started to hammer in the numbers, something strange happened. She felt a shiver as if someone had run a fingernail lightly down her spine. The yellow card started to flutter, then bounced from side to side like the pizza boards that fast-food juniors wiggled back and forth by the side of the road, offering cheap deals. She rubbed her eyes and looked around, slightly embarrassed, wondering who was watching. *This is crazy. There's no wind in here*, she thought. All the other notices sat obediently at peace, the way they were meant to, and the way she expected them to be. The more she looked the sillier she felt. It had to be her imagination.

Sheepishly she walked away and towards the department stores; it was all a little too bizarre. But curiosity got the better of her and she looked back. The yellow card sat perfectly still, nestled in amongst the many other bits of paper, cards and leaflets in a lifeless collage.

She couldn't find what she wanted and the thought of going elsewhere did not appeal to her at all, especially in the after-school traffic.

Feeling totally deflated and acknowledging that she had virtually managed to waste the whole day on this fruitless quest, she decided to go home and try again tomorrow. Heading back the way she had come, she slowed as she approached the notice board and couldn't help but peer sideways tentatively, as if drawn by an unseen force.

Oh, no ... there it was again. Gyrating and fluttering, standing out like a sunflower in the snow, the yellow note drew her like a magnet. Once again that semi-pleasant sensation ran down her spine, then all sorts of images started dancing in her brain. She blinked and shook her head, trying to knock sense into herself, but she couldn't walk away.

On impulse, she reached out and grabbed the card, relieved to feel it was just like any other piece of cardboard—no dancing, no fluttering, no hocus-pocus. Still, it was odd. This time she dialled the number on it without further thought and moments later, a voice answered. It sounded familiar.

So it was arranged: the following morning she would go for a drive into the hills to pick up the scanner. It was that simple.

Thinking about it that night, Cassie realised that her friend's house was virtually on the way. She made a mental note to give Maria a call first thing in the morning. She might be able to drop in for coffee and a chat.

CHAPTER 5

It was peaceful in the garden, and it was early enough not to feel caught up in the day's rush just yet. Cassie shivered involuntarily as her mind skipped to something unpleasant. She couldn't pinpoint it, just a vague menacing feeling; an irritating pebble in her shoe. This sense of foreboding made her feel uncomfortable. She had no idea why. She left her irritation in the yard as she turned and went inside.

She reset her focus as she stepped into the shower. The soft caressing water running down her body felt good. Everything was fine. *Everything would be fine.*

An hour or so later, she gave a friendly wave to her neighbour across the road as she backed her car out of the driveway and headed north towards the highway.

Damn, forgot to call Maria, she thought. With one eye on the traffic and the other on her phone, she scrolled down her contacts until she found Maria's number and dialled.

'Hi, Maria, it's Cassie here. I'm on my way up the mountain and it occurred to me that I'll be driving past your place and I wondered if you have time for a quick visit?'

'That'd be great. I have the morning free. What time do you think?'

'It's about 10.00 am. If I come over now I can be there in twenty minutes or I can get my errand out of the way first. What works best for you?'

Maria invited her for lunch and it was arranged.

Cassie found the traffic was quite effortless. The sun was shining and she was looking forward to the drive into the hills. It was quite pretty with great displays of cascading bougainvillea framing the route. Leaving the ugly industrial sheds behind Cassie felt at peace with the world. Any uncomfortable thoughts had been left in the dull back streets of suburbia.

The Mazda hugged the edge of the mountain, labouring a little under the steep incline. Here and there rocks lay scattered on the road, evidence of the heavy rainfalls a few weeks ago. Cassie admired the green and clean landscape below. Before she realised it, she saw her turn off to Francis Road, where she was to collect the scanner.

Cassie pushed aside great sprays of jasmine to reach the latch of the rickety old wooden gate. It gave a gentle squeak as she opened it, alerting a yellow labrador snoozing in the warm sunshine. He gave a few perfunctory woofs and ambled towards her slowly, swishing his tail from side to side. She reached down and gave him a gentle rub behind the ears, and he rolled over, offering his tummy in the hopes of a few extra belly-rubs from this stranger.

It was an old house and vines tumbled all over the place indicating no gardener lived here. In her mind's eye, Cassie conjured up an image of a studious, serious person more dedicated to books and indoor pursuits.

She knocked on the door, the firm rapping disturbing the peace, startling her a little. She heard hurried footsteps approaching.

The door opened a crack, and Cassie gasped. She steadied herself against the railings on the verandah and breathed deeply, trying to stop her mind from spinning out of control. There stood that weird Mrs Pendle from the massage place. 'Shit. Shit. Shit.' *This couldn't be happening.*

She thought she'd closed the door on that episode two weeks ago. How could it be? What was going on here?

'Hello,' Mrs Pendle said.

'I ... um ... sorry ... I must have the wrong house.' She began to back away. *No wonder the bloody voice on the phone had seemed familiar*. Oh, God. She wanted to be somewhere else. Not facing this again.

'Wait, wait ... you drove all this way, and I'm not going to eat you, for goodness sake!'

Cassie just wanted to be out of there. She would pay for the thing and run. After all, the woman was right, and she felt stupid enough already.

Biting her lip and fumbling with the car keys, she waited while the woman went inside to collect the device. *I'll bet it doesn't work anyway. What possessed me to drive all that way for a $20 scanner?*

Now she had no choice but to see it through. She just wanted the transaction over.

The woman brought out an older model scanner. It was a bit chunky, but didn't look too bad, and it was cheap. She pushed the unpleasant memories of their last meeting away and focused on the fact that this was a business deal, nothing more.

'You really need to come in so I can explain how it works. There are some important features you need to understand. This scanner is quite special, and it will serve your purpose admirably. Scanning some photos, are you?'

'How did you know?' Cassie shivered, fiddling in her wallet to get the money and be as far away as possible. 'Here's the $20. Sorry, must rush.'

'Don't go, I want to explain something. Don't you want to know how it works?'

'I'll be right.' Cassie snatched the scanner and spun around, almost tripping over the dog. She stumbled onto the path. She couldn't get to the car fast enough. 'Sorry, have to rush, thank you.'

Mrs Pendle called out instructions to Cassie as she hurried off. 'Remember the serial number; it's very, very, very important. And for heaven's sake, don't get yourself into a panic. Give me a call; you have my number.' But Cassie was already loping towards the car.

When she was sure she had left the old woman behind, she stopped. Her shoulders heaved and her breaths came deep and fast in rhythm with her pounding heart. This was no accident! She couldn't believe what had just happened and her fertile imagination was doing cartwheels.

All the way down the mountain, she hashed and re-hashed the scene. Even though nothing had actually happened, she was uneasy. She was almost at Maria's before she managed to gather her thoughts.

Maria welcomed her warmly before narrowing her eyes and frowning. 'You look pale and flustered ... everything all right?'

'Yeah, no, oh, I don't know ... something really strange happened. Let's go inside, and I'll tell all. Co-incidence is a funny thing isn't it? I just bought a scanner from a lady who I only met a couple of weeks ago. She said a few things then that unnerved me. What are the chances?'

Maria had lived through that dreadful time of the car accident with her, had seen Cassie lose her confidence and slide into a depression for years, but had no idea of the depth of her guilt and self-recrimination. Over lunch, she comforted her old friend, at the same time urging her to let the whole thing go and move on. As it turned out Maria had had some interesting psychic experiences of her own and they discussed related topics about magic, sorcery, and all things unexplained.

The hours flew by and at 2 pm Cassie drove off feeling a bit more at ease with the morning's events, a little more prepared to accept it was one of those things—synchronicity or destiny, or whatever. She'd still call Emma though; she really wanted to bounce this off someone else who understood just how intimidating that first meeting had been.

CHAPTER 6

On the weekend, Cassie pushed aside thoughts of scanners, psychics, and past memories to enjoy some time with Katy. They went for a long walk on Sunday morning.

Strolling along the bush path, Cassie linked her arm in Katy's and breathed in the cool fragrance of the eucalyptus tickling her nostrils.

'We're so lucky that you're still living at home with us, most girls your age would have fled the nest long ago.' Cassie snuggled into her daughter.

'I appreciate you guys putting up with me for so long, but once these final exams are over and I find myself a half decent job, I'll probably move in with some of my mates from college.' Katy said.

'We'd miss you.' Cassie replied.

Katy nodded, 'I'm twenty-three; I really need to get serious about my future. Here I am tending my little succulent collection; out for games night once a week ... it's so boring, mum. A couple of the other girls are into tennis, and I'd enjoy that. Besides, how am I going to meet people living at home with my parents?'

'You're right, and I know there's a wonderful world waiting out there for you.'

They walked on, chatting easily.

***

After a pleasant family meal on Sunday evening, Cassie suddenly remembered that she had planned to call Emma.

She went into the study to get away from the noise of the TV and called Emma. 'Hi! How are you? How was the weekend?'

Emma filled her in on the girls' exploits and brought her up to date with their family news. She sounded tired. The sisters shared their parents' dark hair and slightly olive skin, though the years had been kinder to Emma, Cassie mused as she stared and looked at her heavily lined, sun blotched face reflected in the hall mirror.

Cassie jumped in. 'You won't believe what happened last week. You remember that weird old lady that unsettled me when we went for the massage?'

'Of course, how could I forget? Don't tell me you ran into her again?'

'Sort of ... I ended up at her place by an uncanny *coincidence*.' She emphasised the last word so that Emma understood the implication of what she was thinking. 'It's spooky. It's creeping me out. I can't get it out of my head. I knew something was up when the postcard fluttered at the shopping centre.'

'What did you say?'

'You know those little cards people use when trying to sell something; the ones they put up on the notice boards in shops. It was an ad selling a second-hand scanner. The card fluttered. I know it sounds stupid, but it nudged me to pull it down and follow up on it. I'd been looking for a scanner and I felt compelled to call the number. I thought the voice was familiar and I had a *feeling* about it. The sensation was so strong ... It fluttered at me. It really did.'

'Okayyyy. So how come you went ahead anyway?' Emma challenged her, her scepticism echoing through the speaker.

'I was intrigued, I guess. You know me, can't resist a challenge. I swear to God it was beckoning me. Next thing I know, I am at her doorstep and falling over myself to get out of there. I had that same creepy feeling I had the first time. I grabbed the scanner and left.'

'So, that's it? You've got yourself a second-hand scanner, and the woman who sold it to you was creepy? Let it go.'

'Yeah, I guess so, but it is weird, don't you think? That it was the same woman from the massage place?'

'Yep, it's definitely weird, but I think your imagination is working overtime. It's a co-incidence, that's all, a co-incidence. Haven't you got better things to do than let some old woman get under your skin? Get those photos sorted. Focus on that and cut yourself some slack. Aside from the fact that you are totally fazed by your unfortunate shopping experience, and you are now unemployed, is everything else okay?'

'Yeah, I think so, just a little overwhelmed, that's all.'

They nattered on for a bit longer and said their goodbyes.

***

The following morning, Cassie ventured into the study and pulled the scanner out of her bag. It was in quite good nick. She squashed her doubts and congratulated herself on scoring a bargain. She turned the unit over and examined the manufacturer's plate underneath. A number was clearly written in crisp black print on the tiny silver identification plate.

'XPR2000079.' As she read it, the old lady's words about the serial number rang in her ear. Slowly she repeated it softly to herself several times, wondering why the woman had made such a fuss about it. She shrugged as she set it up on the cupboard behind her, plugged it in, and ensured the computer recognised the new unit. There was just a faint whirring sound for starters, then the little red light on the top panel started to flash. It stopped, turned green. She was good to go.

Cassie stretched across the desk behind her and pulled the box of photos nearer. They were in no discernible order and she reached in and picked up the first photo her hand touched. It was a slightly blurred image of two little girls, about eight and twelve years old. She remembered that day. It was Emma's eighth birthday and she had been given a new pair of baby-pink ballet slippers. They were silky, sleek, and shiny. She smiled to herself, remembering a hint of jealousy—a feeling so unnecessary and uncomplicated. Their world had been so much smaller then.

Smoothing out the yellowing edges, she laid the photo gently on the scanning bed, neatly tucking it into the corners marked and pressed START.

The room exploded.

A starburst of brilliant blue filled every corner and crack, the machine no longer visible in the vivid sapphire glow.

Cassie gasped. With unbridled horror, she felt her body explode. No pain, but her limbs flailed in the swirling nothingness, searching for something tangible, something familiar. She was being sucked away.

Somewhere in the distance, she heard a scream. 'NOOOOOO ...' It was her own voice—a disembodied thing, echoing far away. Her blood fizzed. The air crackled. A thousand sparklers fired in her brain. Her skin tingled, spitting tiny electric pulses into her being, and then everything collapsed into a black void.

***

Across the street, mouth agape, Mrs Parker watched and wondered. A phosphorescent shimmering light blasted from the window across the road, turning everything in her line of vision a glittering blue, just for an instant. It all happened so quickly, she barely believed it.

Was it an explosion? Her brain wriggled through the possibilities. There was no obvious damage. All she heard was a whooshing sound carrying voices on the wind. Was there a scream? She couldn't remember, everything was swallowed up. She wasn't even certain that she'd heard anything at all. It was surreal. She slumped back into her chair. Tendrils of fine grey hair clung to the tiny droplets of perspiration forming on her forehead.

She tried to distract herself by taking her knitting from the basket, struggling to focus. It looked quiet and peaceful at the Foster home now.

But all afternoon the image flashed before her. It was so odd. Needles clicking away, her thoughts strayed back time and again to the house across the street—Cassie's house.

In her eighty years, she had mellowed into aging, but her body groaned and crunched with her heavy movements. Day after day, her tired eyes stared out of the window, fixed on the passers-by and the small community that was her neighbourhood. One day a week she'd shuffle to the local shops to get a few essentials. But she still wanted to be a part of life's rhythms.

She was lonely, Ada Parker craved the company of her family, but they lived far away in Melbourne. The neighbourhood was the only world she knew. Lately she had noticed a lot of comings and goings at the house opposite. She envied them, this youngish family. Occasionally she would catch the eye of the lady of the house, but they'd never had a proper conversation. They seemed friendly enough, occasionally they would throw a neighbourly wave her way.

Pulling herself back into the present, she deliberated again on the scene she had just witnessed. She resolved to let it slide, but perhaps she might try to be a little more neighbourly. Maybe she should venture across the road and say hello? Age hadn't dampened her curiosity.

CHAPTER 7

1963

'Cassie, Cassie ... Wake up!' Emma was screaming at her.

Wading through the fog of consciousness, Cassie realised something was terribly wrong. The room was all blurry with wavy lines and shadows. She could barely focus. Slowly, she came out of her fug, her legs and arms tingling to life. She glanced around. Minute specks of sparkling blue dust seemed to be floating in the air, creating a fine gossamer web of cerulean crystals, which clouded Cassie's vision. They settled gradually, spinning in ever-decreasing circles until the air was crisp and clear once more.

'Cassie, Cassie!'

Voices tumbled at her—a cacophony of sounds, distant yet familiar. Vague images started taking shape. Her brain was a whirlpool, but the fact that she was alive provided a modicum of relief. The scene sparkled in her vision, but she could see!

She moved her fingers, wiggled her toes. What had happened? It was her body, wasn't it? She was enveloped in the strange sensation of being encapsulated in her own skin, like a chrysalis waiting to burst. She could move, but it was unlike anything she had ever experienced.

The voices, the shouting and screaming, were all directed at her and nothing—absolutely nothing—made sense.

People crowded around her. Cassie felt the gentle touch of her mother's hand on her cheek. She tried to say Mother, but nothing happened. Her mind was in a whirl. *This is ridiculous; Mum is home with dad, several suburbs away. Where am I? What happened?*

She grasped for the last thing she remembered. Was it a scanner? That's it! That's ... what? She didn't have any answers.

The soothing touch on her cheek calmed her. Whatever was going on, she was safe.

The voices spoke again, calmer, more measured, oozing compassion.

'Are you all right, darling? You fainted. Talk to me, Cassie.' It was her mother's voice, soft, strong, and ... and younger. *Huh?*

Very slowly, she lifted her head. She narrowed her eyes and squinted, and gradually things came into focus. Her mum! It was her mum! She was young and vibrant and beautiful, with eyes that spoke only of love and concern. Cassie lifted her hand and ran one finger gently over her mother's cheek. She was consumed by love. Tears swelled as realisation started to sink in. Her gaze swam around the room, taking in the details. She was in her living room. Not the one in Holt Street, but the one she remembered from her childhood!

She sat bolt upright. She scrunched her eyes shut for a moment, trying to make sense of things. Mum, only a much younger version of her, and next to her, Emma. Dear Emma, her little sister. Both were staring at her with concern.

She looked down, searching the ground in the hope of clearing her confusion. Another shock. Her feet were small. She had on white strappy sandals with daisies on them. She remembered them from her childhood.

'Oh, noooo,' she wailed. But before any words could come out her mother hugged her tight to her bosom, one hand on her long, dark hair, stroking it gently.

'It's all right, darling; you fainted, that's all. Come on, get up. Let's take you to your bedroom for a little lie down. I'll fetch you a cold drink. Come on.'

Timidly, Cassie found her feet and reached up to wrap her arms around her mum. Second by second, reality pinched at her.

She'd travelled back in time.

She was here, smack bang in the middle of the photo she'd held just moments earlier.

Overwhelmed by this thought, she snuggled in close, and together the three lurched towards her bedroom. Dizzy, she lay on her bed, nursing a flurry of emotions with nothing to anchor them to. Blood pumped through her veins. She felt more alive than she had for a long time, but it was as if her heart and body were separate entities. Despite feeling loved and intact, panic lurked at the edges. Her brain was Cassie's—sixty-two-year-old self, not the little girl in whose skin she now found herself.

Apparently all was well in this world. But something terribly big had happened. It was bigger than she could process. So that's what the old woman was raving about. Oh, she should have listened!

Her gaze travelled around her old bedroom. She'd forgotten so much; it was like she was seeing everything again for the first time in over forty years. On one wall was the bookshelf her Dad had made her. It contained her collection of favourite books. A poster of The Beatles graced a wall above her chest of drawers, and a dressing table full of bits and pieces of her childhood rested against another. They all bought back memories.

Reality stabbed at her again. Her eyelids fluttered and closed.

'Okay, Emma, let's leave Cass alone for a little while. I think she needs to rest.' Her mother shepherded Emma outside. 'I'll bring that drink back in a minute,' she called over her shoulder as she left the room, pulling the door closed behind her.

A weird mix of relief and anxiety gripped Cassie. Time to think. She needed to work through this freaky twist of time in her mind; work out what it meant. She wanted to grab the nostalgia and hang on to this glorious past, but right now she needed to think.

Cassie lay back on her pillow and studied the desk opposite, noticing the emptiness. Not a screen in sight, not a cable, no devices—nothing. She resisted the urge to jump up and run out into 1963. Fortunately, her family seemed blissfully unaware. Her mum was worried; she could tell by the forced calm in her voice, but otherwise, fine. The world here was fine. Would everything stay that way if she went back? Assuming she could get back. She squeezed her eyes tightly shut again, wanting normal...whatever that was.

Impotent and still, she lay there, following her thoughts as her mind tumbled and skipped through a web of complicated problems. It was sticky and unpredictable; there was no telling how this would end. What if there's no going back? What happens to Jeff and the family? *Oh, God, I wish I'd listened to that crazy woman.*

She loved her family and her life back in Holt Street; it was there where her adult-self belonged. She had to get back. Stay calm. If she allowed the python of panic to suffocate her, she was lost.

She lay there, plotting and scheming, trying to work out how to get home. There was no indication of how time had been bent out of shape. For all she knew, her family could be frantically looking for her right now, or she could be lying unconscious in her study. It could all be a dream, an altered state of imagination. But it felt *real*. The sounds were real; so were the smells. She ran her fingers over the chenille bedspread. It was all real. Solid. She had no idea how any of this impacted on this moment in 1963. That was another worry. Would going back leave a vacuum in this now? She had to go. The shorter the time here, the less damage done, she reasoned.

Her heart ached to think of her family worrying about her in the future, yet to see the younger version of her mum filled her with love and longing. Yes, she had to go ... and soon. But how? And when?

Not having a clue how to get back eclipsed all the other problems. All she had, and it kept ricocheting in her brain, were the old lady's words, 'If nothing else, remember the serial number; it's very, very important.'

That's all very well, but I am stuck in this other dimension. Telling me it was very, very important was an understatement, she thought. How could I have been so stupid? Cassie cursed her own recalcitrant nature. *If only I hadn't been so obsessed with getting away. Damn, I have to focus.* She punched her head in frustration.

She had to remember the number! It had something to do with human resources. But what?

After what seemed an eternity, something did come. PR. *That's it! Public Relations. There was another letter as well, one at the end of the alphabet. W? No, X ... that was it!* She felt sure the letters were PR and X, but what order?

There were also numbers. She remembered 20,000 was part of it—the first part. Then there were a couple of numbers at the end. What were they? Was it 2 or 3? That was the question; she couldn't be sure.

She got up and quietly slid open the top drawer of her desk. Rummaging through the paraphernalia of her childhood, little flutters of delight rippled with each new discovery, making her pause for a moment as the memories came flooding back. At last she found a pen; it had a transparent top that had a scene of Sydney Harbour Bridge with a little ferry that floated down as she inverted it ... another time. She grabbed a notebook lying on top of the desk. Inside were scribblings long since forgotten, but no doubt important in this now.

'Keep moving, Cassie. You have to do this,' she murmured.

'Cassie, Cassie ...' It was Emma. 'Can I come in?'

She leapt back on the bed, pulling the bedspread over herself to hide the notepad and pen clutched in her hand, and pretended to feel drowsy.

'Hmmm, yes ... okay,' she said.

'Cassie, do you want some birthday cake? It might make you feel better.'

'Nah ... I just need to lie here for a while.'

This is going to be tricky. How could she mesh back into her past? She didn't relish the thought of pretending. How could she possibly act normal? What a mess!

She returned her focus to the problem—the serial number.

Think, think, think ...

She wrote down XPR20000??? Her mind darted to all the possibilities, keeping the panic monster at bay. What were they? She sighed loudly in exasperation. Looking at what she wrote, her brain whirred, a master code-breaking machine, willing the last few numbers to appear. She scribbled a few on the pad, hoping the visual would prompt her memory. She tried two and three different numbers at the end, and starting to go cross-eyed with concentration and exhaustion, she gambled there were only two. It just seemed to look better. There was nothing but her gut to go by, and if it didn't work she could try three numbers, but she prayed that wouldn't be necessary.

Yes, two was easier; she could find them through a process of elimination. Just start counting to a hundred. Those last two numbers had to be in there somewhere. Cassie realised she had to be the heroine in her own adventure. It fortified her. It also brought her to the decision to repeat the full number three times to herself ... for no other reason than countless fairy tales and magic stories couldn't be wrong. Her stomach lurched at the thought of leaving her family; she almost couldn't bear to go without savouring this glorious opportunity to study them, commit their youth and beauty to memory. She would wait until bedtime when everyone was asleep to start running through the numbers until she struck the jackpot. It had to work. She had nothing else.

In the meantime, she would spend quality time with her parents and little sister.

CHAPTER 8

Cassie spoke very little, fearing her voice would betray her—she was floating, dream-like, trying hard to take in the nuances of her past. Every gesture, every show of tenderness, even Emma's impatience, was a treasured jewel. How lucky was she to have this chance? Her twelve-year-old self could not grasp any of it, but neither could the senior version, and Cassie was left feeling disoriented and confused, all her energy going into holding a tenuous grip on her sanity.

It was a reunion to end all reunions, but bedtime finally loomed, and feigning confidence, she followed Emma's lead in the night-time routine.

The television blared in the lounge room; her parents were watching *The Mavis Bramston Show*.

Burrowing deep under the covers, Cassie tried to still her mind. She needed to stay awake. Her head swam with the complexity. Nothing made sense, and she prayed she could leave as surreptitiously as she had arrived, hoping the 1963 Cassie would wake up the next morning as usual.

The room blurred as the tears welled up. Her chest was tight. She breathed deep and slow, trying to calm herself. She wrapped herself up firmly in the sheets to stop herself from shaking, trying desperately to focus.

The house fell quiet. Her moment had come; it was time to leave.

Cassie had the first few characters in her head, but working through the possibilities was nerve-racking. As she recited each number for the third time, the tension was almost unbearable. She whispered them one by one to herself. Was she supposed to address anyone? Was there some magic Porta Ghost waiting near the ceiling to teleport her to 2013? Her throat was thick, the whispers sneaking out in fragments. Even as the words left her lips, they exploded in a fountain of expectation and subsequent disappointment. When she was halfway, she stopped.

Keep breathing, keep trying. This is ridiculous. I have no idea how to get out of this mess. If she did nothing, she was compelled to stay, locked in a reality she both loved and cherished, but where she no longer belonged. This was not what nature intended; to relive her life went against nature. She had to get back to Jeff and Katy.

Once more, striving for calm and purpose, she started.

'XPR2000051, XPR2000051, XPR2000051.' She droned on to herself, pinching her thigh every now and then to stay awake and actively in the moment. Reciting the numbers was tedious. Lurking in the dark corners of her mind was a myriad of possibilities. This could all go terribly wrong.

'XPR2000079, XPR2000079 ...' Something was happening. Cassie's skin started to crawl; it was no longer her own, waves of pins and needles shot through her veins. She held her breath. Her fist clung tightly to the now-damp sheet. Her bedroom started to shimmer. The walls and ceiling sparkled. It was an Aladdin's cave. Barely whispering, she dared herself to repeat it one more time. Her universe exploded. Cassie was swept up into the inky sky. A million stars flashed around her. Another heartbeat and a black void swallowed her up.

***

2013

Cassie stirred. Her eyelids fluttered and squeezed shut again. Gradually the surrounding buzz settled, and she could make out a voice. Someone touched her on the shoulder. There was comfort in it. She didn't want to look.

'Cassie, Cassie.' A familiar hand clutched hers tightly. She melted into the feeling as Jeff leaned over and embraced her. She felt the roughness of his unshaved cheek against hers.

'Am I h-h-home?' Cassie whispered, opening her eyes.

'Of course you are. What happened? I called to say I would be late and left a message. Are you alright? You gave me a hell of a fright! Thank God, you're okay.'

'Um ... um. N-n-no idea. How long have I been out?'

'I don't know. I just came in. Coco was mewing and carrying on, and I assumed she was hungry, but she trotted off towards the study and there you were, lying comatose. It's nearly eight o'clock. I'm calling an ambulance.'

'No, no don't. I'm fine, probably just stress.' She loathed being the centre of attention. 'I don't want any drama.'

'Are you sure? No pain anywhere?' He brushed her cheek, his gaze sweeping over her whole body, looking for any signs of injury. Cassie heaved herself to her feet, leaning heavily on Jeff for support. He led her to the bedroom. 'You rest here and I'll get you something to eat.'

'No, no, I'm not hungry. I'd kill for a brandy though.

'Not sure that's a good idea hon; you were unconscious. How about a cup of strong, black tea instead?

'Okay, but I am fine, honest.' She lifted her leg up off the bed and twirled her hands to prove that all her body parts were in good working order. 'See, nothing bent or broken. No bruises. It's all good. I'll feel better after a good night's sleep. I might even remember what happened.'

Coco was now purring madly. She vaulted onto the bed and snuggled in close to Cassie, trying to weave into the contours of her body, but Jeff scooped her up instantly.

'Come on, girl, I'll make you some dinner.' He walked out of the room. 'Let's leave your mistress to get some well-earned rest.'

Alone again, Cassie rubbed her temples and buried her face in her open palms. 'What just happened?' She vaguely remembered the scanner in the study, but simply couldn't entertain the other thoughts zipping in and out. It couldn't be. Surely, this had all been some sort of vivid dream. In her mind, she could still picture the room she had just left, the room that had been her sanctuary in childhood. She'd been safe there. *I'm going crazy. It's impossible.* She was exhausted; her lids felt heavy. She started to drift off and Jeff walked in.

'Here you go. One strong, hot black tea for the patient. Do you think you'll manage to sleep tonight or will I go and get something from the chemist?'

'No, but I am absolutely worn out; I just want to sleep.'

Jeff stood at the door on his way out. 'I imagine Katy will be home soon'.

Cass had already closed her eyelids and was burrowing into the pillow.

Her head was swimming. Thoughts darted every which way like tiny fish as her mind wandered into murky depths. She groped for answers.

Finally she slept. But it was a night of strange hallucinatory dreams and images blending past and present in a conglomeration of reflections.

CHAPTER 9

2013

Judging by the colours that played on the walls in the pale morning light, Cassie guessed it must be about quarter to six. She longed for the sunlight to stream in, bathe her in its light and maybe give her some clarity. She focussed slowly, taking in the present. Had any of it been real? Rolling over and nuzzling her body against Jeff, she took comfort in his strong form; something she knew was true and solid in her now-shaky world.

'Grrrr ...' Jeff groaned in the half-light, stirred and swung his arm over her fragile frame.

'I love you,' she whispered, snuggling in tightly.

'Ditto,' Jeff responded with a squeeze and a moment later, he was asleep once more.

'I think I'll get up and go for a walk,' she muttered as she peeled herself away from her sleeping man and carefully slid out of bed. The clothes she'd been wearing yesterday were in a heap on the chair. Gathering them up, she tiptoed over to the dresser and, as quietly as possible, slid open the drawer, grabbed some fresh underwear and a pair of socks, and snuck out of the room, pulling the door gently behind her.

Morning light poured in through the kitchen window, creating a tangram of shadows on the benchtop. The sun wasn't quite up yet. Cassie hurried; she wanted to meet the sunrise, stare at it and ponder the universe, as if it might make sense of her experience.

Outdoors, heaving big deep breaths of fresh air, she paced wildly. She wanted to swallow the world, to break down all the components of reality and figure out this giant puzzle in her head. With each step she felt more grounded, more attached to the parts of her that had been scattered into the universe.

Could that machine really have helped her travel back in time? That card fluttering at the shopping centre had been the beginning of it ... or had it? Did it go right back to Mrs Pendle?

Great shafts of reds and oranges sprayed across the morning sky, but Cassie was too deeply engrossed burrowing into the labyrinth of her mind to notice. This giant juggernaut of ideas and choices was heading towards her and preparing to shatter life as she knew it. She shuddered knowing that nothing would ever be the same again, that all the tiny securities she had clung to were like porcelain, ready to be ground to dust at any moment.

Woven into her musings were sweet moments of euphoria as the memory of her childhood ignited her soul with pure joy.

'Good morning.' A passer-by jerked her back into the present. 'Beautiful morning.'

'Ah, yes. Hello.' She was pulled back into the day, whether she was ready for it or not.

She hated not knowing; not understanding what was going on. She had no idea how to process this information. *Show me things I can touch, can explain*, she pleaded to the universe.

When she arrived home, the house was empty. She picked up a scribbled note left on the table.

Call me when you get home.

X Jeff.

Normal. Guilt bit at her. There was no way she could share this with her family. She couldn't bear the thought of ridicule; who'd believe her? No, she would shut off this episode and pretend it never happened.

But there were tiny pulses of excitement as well ... this was her secret, hers alone. It was amazing. No, she didn't want to share it with anyone.

She picked up her mobile and called Jeff.

'Hi Honey, are you okay? Don't forget to make a doctor's appointment will you? I don't expect to be home too late tonight, so don't worry about dinner, I'll cook.' Jeff answered.

'That's sweet, thank you. I'm fine. I went for a long walk to clear my head. I'll be fine, probably just low blood pressure or something.' She hoped she sounded convincing.

'You need to get checked out, Cass. Why would you faint like that for no apparent reason? Don't ignore it.'

'Yeah, I will. It threw me a little. I'll take it easy today.'

She couldn't face breakfast, but a cup of tea would go down well. As she waited for the kettle to boil, a light veil resembling peace fell over her. She indulged herself, allowing her mind to drift a little, as she imagined the impossible and the improbable, dismissing common sense and rationality.

She picked up the cat. 'You are my lifesaver, Coco. Bet you didn't know that, did you?' she whispered, burying her face in the soft, glossy fur.

Coco purred loudly.

The kettle clicked off, and her thoughts flipped again. Her calmness escaped in a breath. She dumped the cat who responded to the indignity with a loud raucous meow.

Cassie grabbed her handbag, glanced in the hall mirror, noting she looked as drained as she felt, and scampered out the door. She jumped into the little Mazda and revved it into action, then zoomed up the street.

She drove into the hills and before she knew it, she found herself in front of Mrs Pendle's cottage.

She could barely recall the drive. Something had propelled her back to the very place she had hoped she'd put behind her. What was the past anyway? Her experiences of the last twenty-four hours pretty much made a mockery of everything she'd believed and trusted. Now, nothing was stable; nothing was a given. In her chest, her heart beat a tattoo of military proportions. Nothing made sense. Reason and logic dissipated as quickly as the fine blue mist that had detonated her into the past.

She rapped on the door, ignoring the slobbery labrador nuzzling her legs.

No answer. She grunted in frustration. She needed questions answered ... NOW.

Cassie beat on the door with both hands this time. The timber stung her sweaty palms. She slumped against it in desperation. Her pulse pounded in her brain and she was dizzy with defeat.

She was about to give up when she heard footsteps.

'I wondered when you would turn up,' Mrs Pendle said, after wrenching the door open.

Cassie couldn't read her features, but she didn't care. She wanted answers, and this was her best chance of getting them. 'Couldn't you just have told me what was going on? Why be so obtuse ... so cryptic?'

'Would you have listened or believed me?'

Was that smugness Cassie saw in her eyes? Not that she was bothered. She didn't give a rat's what this woman thought. If she had created this mess, it was perfectly okay for Cassie to use her to get information.

Mrs Pendle reached out a bony arm and took Cassie by the elbow. 'Come inside, we need to talk.'

'Too right, we do.' Her voice shook with emotion and trapped anger.

'Don't you be angry with me, lady. I tried to explain, and you didn't want to know.'

Cassie stared at her wide-eyed. Her chest heaved, but she was silent.

The silence lasted for a long time, only broken by the dog's collar rattling, the gentle tinkle of a wind chime in the garden, and the sweet call of the butcher birds outside.

'Fair enough,' Cassie said as she managed to breathe out at last.

'Have a seat, and I'll get you some tea. We can have that talk we should have had long before now.'

Cassie's fury subsided a little and she followed the old woman inside.

The room was dark. There was a salt lamp in the corner on a small round table, creating a pink glow. Great swathes of material were draped all over the place, creating fluidity and movement. Beautiful silks and velvets in magnificent colours glowed into the space. This was a peaceful place. Why did she still feel uneasy? She sat down in a wicker chair by the window and waited. The palpitations had stopped, but her guard was still up.

'Here you go.' Mrs Pendle padded into the room and handed Cassie a delicate porcelain cup.

Cassie started to relax a little.

'I know why you are here,' Mrs Pendle began. 'Nothing is accidental of course. Let me explain. I can't take the credit; I have help from my angels.' She glanced up reverently, paying homage to her silent guides. 'I have been using the machine for good. Darling, the instant I met you I could tell from your aura that you carried a burden. I wanted to help ... knew I could.' She eased back into the chair; its rich golden brocade seemed to envelop her, giving her an ethereal glow.

Cassie sighed. 'I was scared to death. When you mentioned Scott, I just lost it. I've never really told anyone how I felt about the accident, and until you said his name aloud, I'd buried it.'

'Well, it's obvious you haven't, isn't it, dear? And now I think you need to listen and, more importantly, have an open mind.'

'I'll try, but I wasn't too impressed with being knocked unconscious and wondering where the hell I was when I woke up. That was definitely not a good beginning,' Cassie retorted.

'It must have been frightening.' Mrs Pendle could afford to be patronising now; she held all the cards. 'Take some long, deep breaths, drink your tea, and pay attention. This is bigger than both of us, and if you can stop being so suspicious and fearful you may understand that I can actually help you.'

Cassie grunted. 'All very well for you to be calm and composed; you aren't the one who shot through the time barrier.'

'You think I haven't been where you've been? *Really?* You think I could have this power and not explore the opportunities for myself? Of course I have. I know the sense of panic at the total loss of control when you're whipped away from everything that feels familiar and safe.' She sipped her tea delicately.

'So, what are you saying?'

'I'm saying, the magic in this machine is a gift I've been given. The scanner is only a vehicle. It's just a scanner, but the gift is mine. My blessing is what gives it its magic. I can travel back in time whenever I want. I'm old; I know that the past holds nothing that can control my present. You don't. Not yet, at least, and I know you carry guilt over Scott's death. Can't you see I'm bestowing an amazing opportunity for you to revisit your past?' Her eyes zeroed in on Cassie, penetrating her doubts.

'I wish I could be as cool as you are about it.' Cassie finally picked up her tea cup; her hand wasn't shaking any more. 'All right then, suppose I admit this whole crazy thing really happened. What now?'

'Now ... the hard part.'

Time stumbled on as Cassie did her best to listen and take in the enormity of the whole premise while still concentrating on what Mrs Pendle was saying—instructions, directions, a hundred do's and don'ts. She didn't think she could possibly remember them all.

After several hours, she was almost as dizzy and confused as before, but eventually she had to concede that it sounded like the psychic was telling the truth. The scanner could help her travel in time. She didn't like it, but having released the genie from the bottle, she couldn't force it back in.

'So dear, have you got all that?' the old lady's voice broke her reverie.

'What did you say?'

'You haven't heard a word I've said, have you?'

How could she? Her mind was a pinball, zapping and bouncing off on tangents all over the place. It was impossible to focus.

'Well, perhaps you should have been taking notes, but as you haven't ... I'll just say this:

Remember, repeating the serial number three times out loud gets you home. You can save yourself all that drama of fainting if you simply relax into the process. This first time was a shock, but it gets easier, I promise. Most importantly, you MUST use it for good, because whatever you do will impact the present. Remember that.' Her voice was earnest and sincere; that much Cassie registered, but it felt like her brain was being frogmarched down a million corridors with closed doors at the end of each one.

She got up, thanked the woman, and headed for the door in a stupor of confusion.

As they stood at the top of the front stairs, Cassie was acutely aware of her surroundings—the brilliant azure sky, the soothing touch of the light breeze brushing at her cheeks, the fragrance of lavender from the garden. This was real. Her breath skipped as she tried to take it all in, sucking in the moment.

The old lady reached over and took Cassie's hands into her own. 'It's all right, dear. Be gentle on yourself and take all the time you need. It is a lot to take in. It's no wonder you feel fragile and perplexed but trust yourself. The choice is yours. I'm here if you need me.'

Sitting behind the steering wheel a short time later, Cassie wondered how she would get home. Both versions of herself lay clinging to each other. The world was still sitting comfortably on its axis, though everything seemed askew.

She drove to a national park nearby, its rolling lawns cascading into the hidden darkness of the rainforest. Here she could find peace.

She set off down the track, feeling comfort from the cocoon of trees in which she wanted to bury herself. The air was cool, the ground damp, and the sweet cleansing scent of eucalyptus and the woody detritus on the forest floor mollified her. The cold humus pushed through the soles of her sneakers. She needed to feel the earth. Impulsively, she sat down on a nearby log, the rotting bark soft, pungent, and brittle as it pressed into her thighs. She ripped off her shoes and socks.

Her toes found some mud, and she pushed them hard into its grimy surface. It felt good, a secure foundation of her being. Cassie knew that if she took the next step, life would never be the same. Arching her body to the heavens, she reached into the canopy, searching for the resolve she needed.

Overnight the world had become so complicated, so perplexing, that she didn't even know what the next step was, or how to find the courage to take it.

She sat for a long time, the shadows were getting longer, and when she looked at her watch, she was shocked to see it was four o'clock. She knew it was going to be tough, but sitting here wasn't helping.

I need to accept this is happening. I have to control it.

That was the thing she feared most—not being able to control these events.

She flew down the mountain towards home, conscious of the time, of her responsibilities, and of the new colossus that would now share her life.

It was nearly six by the time she got back. Jeff was preparing dinner. She hugged him, told him she'd been delayed. She wondered if she'd fooled him.

There was something bothering her. 'Have I got time to call Emma before dinner?'

'Sure, Katy's not here yet.'

Cassie wandered onto the verandah and dialled her number.

Emma answered almost immediately. 'Hi, Cassie. You okay? Mum and Dad alright?'

'Yeah, yes, absolutely fine, but I just need to ask you something. I was going through those old photos, and I came across the one of us on your eighth birthday. Do you remember that one?' She needed to see if anything had changed for Emma, that whatever craziness was going on for her personally was not affecting her family's memories.

'Vaguely, can't remember much. Can't even remember what my present was.' She laughed.

A sigh of relief escaped Cassie's lips. Her shoulders dropped and her white knuckles gripping the phone began to return to pink.

'I th-think it was the one where you got the ballet slippers, wasn't it?'

'Could be,' Emma said. 'Can you imagine me as a ballet dancer? What was I thinking?'

Cassie quickly skipped to the usual enquiries about the kids. They talked a bit longer, and then said their goodbyes.

Later in the kitchen, when she was tidying up, Jeff handed her a mug of coffee.

'You were quiet tonight. Did you get to the doctor today?'

'Yes,' she lied, shocked at how easily it rolled off her tongue. 'It was nothing, probably just stress; it's been an anxious couple of weeks, what with losing the job and the family visit.'

Jeff grunted. 'Yeah, well, we all know about stress. Speaking of which, it looks like they're letting a few people go at work. I should be fine, but I'm a bit concerned. There's talk of re-assigning our roles. I hate change!'

Cassie rolled her eyes at him. If only he knew.

CHAPTER 10

In bed that night, Cassie lay wide awake staring into the darkness as a thousand thoughts ricocheted through her brain. She needed to sleep so badly, but it evaded her.

She couldn't tell anyone, could she? If, and it was a huge IF, anyone did believe her, what then? There was no one she could confide in, anyway. Although she trusted Emma, how would her sister feel if she knew she'd been lied to for the last twenty-five years or so? What could she do anyway? Maybe her friend Maria? She was broad-minded, but that broad-minded? Jeff? He'd just laugh.

The town hall clock struck 3.00 am. It was a still night, broken occasionally by the sound of a passing car. She envied those souls making their mysterious journeys in the dead of night. They led normal lives. Shift workers perhaps, or insomniacs like her, but she reckoned none of them were faced with the enormity of dealing with a fantasy.

Eventually, exhaustion won. She fell into a fitful sleep, only to be woken early by the lorikeets chattering in the garden and muffled sounds in the kitchen.

Cassie dragged herself out of bed and ambled to the bathroom. She didn't want to deal with decisions. Her face looked like leftover pasta, with two stale, dark olives where her eyes should be.

'Coffee, I need lots of coffee.' She walked into the kitchen, sounding brighter than she felt.

'There's a fresh brew in the percolator, but I've got to rush, sorry love ...' Jeff threw her a casual kiss.

'Where's Katy?'

'Katy left early. Sorry, gotta run. Bye.'

Cassie was relieved that she didn't have to face Jeff; she didn't feel ready to be normal. Her secret was eating away at her and she desperately wanted to tell someone, but she wasn't sure it could be him. But who? She'd never been one to share her deepest feelings with anyone, and she wasn't inclined to do so now. She could choose to ignore it. It would certainly be easier. Or would it?

What if there was a possibility she could save Scott? What if she could travel back in time and prevent that car accident? Mrs Pendle said she must use the scanner's magic for good purposes. Surely, saving a life would qualify? For the first time since this whole bizarre episode had begun, Cassie's heart pounded with excitement rather than fear.

Outside, birds still squawked and twittered, flowers bloomed and traffic hummed as it always had. It was only her world that was in turmoil.

A shower washed away some of her fatigue and a coffee sparked her mind a little. She was tired of dithering. She made a snap decision. If she could prove to herself that she could manage her new-found 'gift', then she owed it to Scott to at least try.

She paced back and forth in the hall in two minds, struggling with her conscience. Either she took this leap or she didn't. Her choice. Damned if she did. Damned if she didn't. Was it an opportunity or an albatross? Furtively she looked into the room. Everything was exactly as she had left it.

Just do it. She'd start small: do a trial run, test the old woman's theories, test her own resilience. She had to discover how to control it now or she'd lose her nerve. She could feel her throat tightening already.

She strode into the office and upended the box of photos on the desk. She rifled through the pictures until she found one that would be suitable—a photo of herself in a pretty white dress, waiting backstage for her big moment. She wrote the serial number of the machine in ink on her forearm and memorised it, hoping that the shock of blasting into the past again wouldn't addle her brain.

Carefully, she placed the photo on the glass plate of the scanner. She stood for a long time, trying to slow down every thought and part of her body that wanted to run.

But the scanner unleashed its power before she could change her mind. There was the same amazing burst of colour, the same feeling of speed and disorientation. This time, she counted to keep herself focused and conscious.

***

1963

'It worked.' Suddenly she was in the back-stage wings of the town hall. She was ten years old and ready to perform at an Eisteddfod.

Her mother stood behind her. 'Do you feel nervous? Deep breaths, that's right.'

Nestling into her mother's bosom for a re-assuring hug, Cassie had to think fast. 'I don't think I can do this, Mummy. I can't go out there; I can't remember anything.' And she meant it; her mind was blank. 'I'm scared, I can't remember my poem.' She burst into tears like any normal ten-year-old whose nerves had got the better of her.

'It's okay, dear. You can do this. You've been practising for so long, don't throw it all away.'

There was no sign her mother had noticed anything strange at all. It occurred to her that this was a good moment. Young Cassie felt embarrassed and insecure; it would suit her perfectly well to get out of this mess.

'Do I have to, Mum, honestly? I don't want to go out there and face all those people. What's the point anyway? I won't win.'

'Honey, if that's the way you feel, I can take you home. I hate seeing you so unhappy, but you know you'll feel much better afterwards if you go through with it.'

Cassie's bottom lip quivered. She stared into her mother's eyes, crinkled with concern.

'Go on then, go and speak to your coach and explain. I'll take you home.'

She hugged her mum for an interminable time, breathing in the smell of her, touching the velvet softness of her skin, languishing in the safety of her protective arms.

Enough. Enough, she thought, remembering the pact she'd made with herself. She was not going to get hooked on staying in the past. This was a practical reconnaissance mission to test the process. Thankfully, she had already established that, however disoriented she might feel, there seemed to be no impact on those around her.

Finally forcing herself to walk away, she said the number twice under her breath and prepared to zap back to 2013, but not before she whispered a few inspiring words to her younger self. She trusted them to work and that the little girl she left behind would find the courage to go out there and give it her best shot.

***

2013

Coming back was easier this time. She'd steeled herself to the fact that she might return unbalanced and perhaps even out cold again. Taking concentrated breaths, she'd spoken the serial number one last time, shaking her fingertips lightly, willing herself to stay calm.

The world of 2013 hit her with a flash. She was back in the study. It had worked!

She dropped onto the floor where she stood, weak and spent, but relieved. Dazzled by the whole thing, nostalgic for the past, she nursed the bittersweet feeling of fleeing again so quickly. It would always be too soon.

She sat there on the rug for a long time, digesting what had just happened, trying to come to terms with holding the gift of time travel in her palm, but she was too exhausted.

Coco was sleeping peacefully on the settee and Cassie picked her up and meandered into the bedroom, threw herself on the bed, and cuddled her cat closer.

Moments later, just as she was dozing off, she was startled awake by knocking on the front door.

'Helloooo. Yoo-hoo. Anyone there?'

Cassie didn't recognise the voice, and as much as she wanted to roll over and ignore it, the calling persisted.

'Hello, I'm Mrs Parker. I live across the street.'

Really! Now? This is unbelievable. Cassie heaved herself up, ran her fingers through her hair, and lumbered up the hallway. 'I'm coming.'

She had a mammoth headache and was not feeling at all hospitable. She patted her cheeks to shake off the lethargy.

When she opened the door, an old lady stood there, smiling sweetly.

'H-h-hello. I'm sorry; I was just having a lie down. Sorry to keep you waiting. Why don't you come in?' Cassie said, cursing under her breath.

'Oh dear, I do apologise. I've been meaning to come over, but moving around is a bit hard these days ...' She trailed off as she leant heavily on her walking stick.

Cassie thought she must have been about eighty. Her fine grey hair was neatly tied back into a bun, and her dark eyes, nestled over her cheekbones, were as bright and alert as a meerkat's. Cassie couldn't quite read what they were reflecting—curiosity ... eagerness, maybe? Her skin was almost translucent. It stretched taut over her angular features.

'Anyway, I'm Ada Parker.'

'It's perfectly all right. Do come in. I'm Cassie. Would you like a cup of tea?'

The old lady cautiously stepped over the threshold. Her joints seemed stiff, and Cassie felt a bit sorry for her. She guided her to the living room, holding her elbow as they walked over the polished floors with its various mats.

'Sit down.' Cassie gestured in the direction of the lounge. 'This is the most comfortable. What will it be? Tea, coffee, a cold drink?'

Mrs Parker looked around, taking in the spacious, light living room with its pot plants scattered here and there. 'A cup of tea would be lovely, dear.'

As her visitor eased herself down onto the leather sofa, Cassie thought of her own mother, who she'd seen only hours before. Back then, she'd been fit and well and quick, but now, in 2013, she was so much closer to walking in this old lady's shoes. Cassie felt a lump in her throat.

'Milk and sugar?' she called from the kitchen.

'Yes, please. Only one sugar and a dash of milk, thank you.'

Cassie was still in a daze after the morning's events but found some biscuits and put them on a little tray together with the tea, then returned to her guest.

'It's nice to meet after all this time.' She was doing her best to be sociable. 'Do you live alone?'

'Yes. I don't really mind, but it's more by necessity than choice. It's difficult to get around. I tend not to go out much.'

'Do you have family nearby, Mrs Parker?'

'Call me Ada. Not really. My husband died four years ago, and my only daughter lives in Melbourne. We were originally from Kooyong and came up to Queensland when Jock retired; he disliked the cold. Patsy and her husband stayed down there to run the family printing business. She has two daughters and I don't get to see them very often; it's hard for her to get away.'

'I'm sure it is. You must get a bit lonely.'

'Hmmm. Yes, sometimes.' She stroked her knee, and again that far-away look as if pondering her situation.'

'I'm incredibly lucky,' Cassie said. 'My parents are both well and living just a few suburbs away.' Cassie sensed that Mrs Parker was withholding something. *There's a reason she's turned up today,* she thought, *maybe she saw something.*

'... and I find ... that the shops down the bottom of the street have most of what I need.'

Ada was prattling on, and Cassie realised she hadn't been listening. It jarred her back to the present. 'Well if you ever need anything from the supermarket where I do my shopping, just let me know.'

'Actually, and this is none of my business ...'

Here it comes.

'I'm concerned, that's all. Well, concerned and curious, to be honest.' Ada struggled to get the words out. 'A few days ago, I was sitting by the living room window as I do most mornings, and I saw what looked like an explosion in your front room. There wasn't a big bang or anything, just a brilliant flash of light, the likes of which I have never seen before. It was most peculiar. I was worried something had happened to you, but then you went out the next morning and I assumed everything was fine. Today the same thing happened. I'm inquisitive, and just couldn't resist coming over and asking you. Are you conducting some sort of experiment or something?'

'N-n-nooo, I can't imagine what it was. It was probably just the light from the copier I've been using.'

'Oh, no, no. It definitely wasn't that. I know what that looks like. No, this was different. It was blinding. It was a brilliant blue shimmering light that lit up the whole room. It sparkled. It was actually quite beautiful, almost celestial. I'm sure I didn't imagine it. Actually, it was also a little bit eerie.'

'I don't recall anything strange happening.' Cassie began fidgeting. 'I'm so sorry but I really should be doing something about dinner. Perhaps I can pop over and say hello sometime?'

Mrs Parker wrinkled her brows. She wasn't buying any of it, and Cassie had a moment of panic. She wanted to push the woman out the door, make her observations and suspicions go away.

Cassie flinched at Ada's penetrating stare. She looked away.

Ada hoisted herself up, snorting lightly. 'Well then, I had better be going, but I do hope there is nothing reckless or sinister going on.' She shuffled towards the door, and as Cassie opened it for her, Ada cast a single accusatory glance over her shoulder. 'I imagine time will tell. Goodbye, Cassie, nice to meet you.'

Step by arduous step, Mrs Parker made her way across the street, and it was not until she had shuffled into the house and closed the door behind her, that Cassie slammed her own door shut. She fell heavily against it, softly banging her head against the timber in frustration.

This was all she needed; another complication. She cleared up the cups and absent-mindedly moved about the kitchen, working on autopilot. Feed Coco, cook dinner, brace yourself, smarten up, and face the family as if nothing's wrong.

Her mind whirled as she carried out her chores. Cassie knew this strange ability might prove useful ... could help her. It would be amazing if she could go back and save Scott, but she'd have to approach it logically. It would take planning. Mrs Parker was only the beginning. Of course, her activities would arouse suspicion. What could she possibly do to prevent that?

CHAPTER 11

Jeff looked drawn and tense when Cassie arrived in the kitchen the next morning. 'Good morning,' she said, doing her best to keep her tone light.

'So do you want to tell me what's going on?' Jeff said bluntly. He wasn't happy—almost angry. 'Ever since you fainted you haven't been yourself. You did go and see that doctor, didn't you?'

She didn't answer straight away; she shrugged and looked away, and said, 'I don't know. I'm just not feeling well, I guess.'

'I think you should go and see the doctor again; maybe he can give you something to perk you up.'

Cassie grimaced.

He took a deep breath and pulled his shoulders up to his full height. He towered over her. 'The company is sending me to Perth for a few days. Perhaps you should come; the break would do you good. Anyway, think about it.'

Think about it, she did. Not about going to Perth or to the doctor, but about the opportunity that had just presented itself. If she could convince Jeff to go alone, she could use that time to go back and undo the horrors of that dreadful night. It was a plan, or if not yet a plan, a place to start.

It lifted her mood somewhat; it felt like a sign, a marker to get her to the next phase. Convincing Jeff wouldn't be easy; he'd be hurt, but if she could save a life, surely it had to be worth it. For the first time in over a week, she didn't feel the walls closing in and the floor wanting to swallow her. She had a modicum of power back. Bless the boss at Channel 4!

After dinner that night, Cassie broached the subject. Hanging up the tea towel to dry, she wiped her hands and approached Jeff as he was pouring milk in the coffee he'd just made her. She sidled up to him from behind and wrapped both arms around his middle that was a little less firm these days and perhaps a bit lumpy. She spoke softly to his back. 'I've thought about what you said about me coming to Perth.'

He turned around and took her in his arms, then stroked her long, dark hair, pulling her closer. She kissed him gently and looked at his face. The lines on his cheeks framing his sensual mouth were deeper now, but he wore the years with dignity and strength.

She spoke slowly. 'I'm all over the place at the moment, and I was thinking it might be a good idea for me to stay here when you go to Perth. It might do me good to work through a few things. Besides, I'm really poor company at the moment.'

'What things?' Jeff said.

'I don't want to burden you with all my self-doubt; I know the pressure you're under. It's something I have to think through myself. It's not you.' She stroked his arm and leaned against him, hiding her face and pushing away the tears pressing behind her eyelids. 'I just need some time,' she mumbled against his chest.

Jeff held her at arm's length and looked into her eyes. She still couldn't read his thoughts, even after all these years.

She pressed on. 'It's not that I don't want to be with you; you know that, don't you? I'd love to go to Perth, but just now I feel as though I would be taking this shapeless thing eating at me to another place without actually clearing my head at all. Does that make sense?'

'Not really, but, okay ... I need to think too. I'd love you to come. I'm worried about you Cass, but if that's what you want ...'

'I love you, Jeff. But I'm not who you need me to be right now, and I'm certainly not the person I want to be. I need a bit of time to think.'

He got up and slowly walked into the living room and turned on the television, effectively putting barricades up around himself and closing down the discussion.

Cassie felt miserable. Sipping her coffee, she stared at the kitchen table, aching for a way out of her conundrum. No point trying to talk to him now. She'd said her piece. He needed to mull it over and come to terms with it.

When Jeff came up to bed a couple of hours later, she was still wide awake, but she daren't say a word. He undressed quietly and climbed in, turning his back to her as he settled down to sleep. Tension hung in the air between them.

The next morning was not much better. Exhaustion made Cassie feel heavy and dull. If Jeff's mood was any indication, he hadn't slept much either. They moved about, tacitly avoiding intimacy and careful to keep their distance, locked in their own chagrin. When he was about to leave, Cassie murmured, 'I'm sorry.'

Jeff looked at her, then turned away and when the door closed behind him, she felt empty and alone.

Katy was coming out of her bedroom just as Cassie walked into the kitchen. She looked tired too; she'd probably stayed up late studying.

'Good morning, darling.' It felt like she hadn't seen her daughter for ages. Their schedules didn't always overlap and it could be days before they properly connected. They embraced.

'Hi Mum, how ya been?' She peered closely at Cassie's drawn features. 'Are you feeling better after you fainted the other day?'

'Yes, I'm fine ... a bit tired.'

'You've a lot on your mind right now: losing your job; entertaining your sister and her family ... not to mention Gran and Pops. Come on, I'll make you a coffee. I've got a few minutes before I have to go.'

'Dad has to go to Perth on business. He asked me to go with him, but I need to be by myself right now. He didn't react very well when I told him that. Am I being selfish?'

'No,' Katy snorted, 'of course not. You should book yourself into some nice little place and get away for a bit; after all you've been working without a real holiday for ages. I'll sort Dad out. You go ahead and make your plans. I think it's a great idea.' She looked at her watch, 'I should be going, I can cook dinner tonight.'

Cassie nodded. 'That would be lovely.'

***

By ten o'clock, she had been chewing things over so much her brain was sizzled, and the urge to run away consumed her.

On impulse, she grabbed her phone and tapped in Maria's number.

As soon as Maria answered, Cassie froze.

'Hello, hello ... is anyone there?'

'I—it's me, Cassie. Hey, listen, I'm sorry if I am calling at a bad time, but you're the only person I can think of to talk to, and I really need to talk.'

'Want me to come over?' Maria asked. 'You sound stressed.'

'I'm okay. Everyone is fine; I just need to talk.'

'I haven't anything special on; I can come now.'

'Are you sure?' Cassie whispered. 'I'd really appreciate it.'

***

When Maria arrived, Cassie suddenly didn't know what to say ... how to begin. The seconds dragged past. The only sound was a wind chime tinkling gently in the wind.

Maria hugged her, 'Let's sit down and you can tell me what's bothering you.'

'I have no idea where to start. This is ridiculous.' Cassie bit her lip and her shoulders drooped. Her eyelids felt tight, as though she was squeezing out the light, willing the darkness to swallow her. Tears slid in great heavy beads down her cheeks. She wiped them away as quickly as they appeared and taking a deep breath, summoned her voice.

'You know we talked about that weird old lady who sold me the scanner? There's more ...' Cassie buckled and wept as a bundle of unidentifiable feelings were unleashed.

Maria held her and stroked her back reassuringly.

Then words tumbled out of Cassie. 'The scanner, it's a time machine. I can travel back in time with it. I know it sounds like gibberish, but I can, and now I don't know whether to go back and try to save Scott. I've tested it and it should work. Maybe I shouldn't. I just don't know.'

Maria interrupted. 'Calm down. It's alright. Maybe you are imagining things; you've let this old lady get into your head.'

'It's no use. It's my problem. I've got to sort it out.' Cassie stared at her lap and went very quiet.

Maria saw her friend was deeply distressed. 'Why don't you try to talk to a professional? These people are much more capable than I am of helping you. You can't go on tying yourself in knots like this.'

They sat together in silence for a while, then Cassie sighed and got up. 'I'll be okay, I shouldn't have bothered you. Thanks for coming.'

'I'm sorry you're hurting Cassie, I'm glad you called. I just wish I'd been able to help.'

'You've been lovely, I'm okay, honest.'

***

When Maria left, Cassie felt shrivelled and wasted. Instead of feeling relieved and comforted by unburdening herself, she was more stressed than before. How could she be so stupid to think she could share her secret? She was all alone. She needed Mrs Pendle for the practicalities, but she'd get no support from her in manoeuvring through the emotional minefield.

CHAPTER 12

Jeff brushed past her with barely a peck on the cheek when he arrived home that evening. He was pleasant enough to Katy, giving her a fatherly hug as she was preparing a meal in the kitchen. His mood had improved. Cassie hoped he'd thought about her proposal.

At dinner, it was Katy who gently led the elephant in the room to the table.

'Mum mentioned you are headed off to Perth on business?'

'Yes, there's a bit of a reshuffle at work, and it looks like these trips might become a regular thing. Did Mum tell you I asked her to come along?' He glanced across at Cassie. A trickle of guilt flowed through her.

'Yeah, but I understand Mum's reluctance. I suggested she go away to a retreat for a break.

'Are you girls ganging up on me?' There was no malice in his voice.

'No, Daddy, of course not.' Katy knew how to hit his soft spot.

Cassie interrupted. 'Not ganging. I just thought it might clear my head.' That bit was true at least. 'A few days away at a retreat might be just what I need. It's not you. I said that last night.' Her voice had changed pitch; she was getting defensive.

'Okay. Okay.' Jeff said. 'It seems I'm outnumbered. There'll be more of these trips coming up, so perhaps you can come next time.'

'Deal.' Cassie smiled sweetly at him and cast a grateful glance at her daughter.

That settled, the conversation turned to other things.

At bedtime Jeff was still very quiet. Feeling a little braver, Cassie ventured into the subject once more. She needed to reassure Jeff and appease her conscience. A plan was starting to form. She was putting tiny pieces of a strategy together, convincing herself that abandoning her family would be brief and painless—for abandonment was exactly what it was. She always prioritised them, and here she was making plans to go on some crazy expedition of her own to put some ghosts to rest and resurrect others. The nagging guilt was another layer of worry on top of everything else, but the idea of a retreat was the best chance that her impossible idea might just work.

'I'm sorry if you feel let down about the Perth trip, darling.'

'Hmmm. It was just a whim. I'll probably be in the office most of the time anyway. I understand this is important to you, but I can't see how going off on your own is going to solve anything.'

'I can't promise it will, but I don't know who I am anymore. Some time alone being pampered might be therapeutic.' She cuddled up to him, her hand stroked his chest and she curled her body into his, kissing his cheek. She relished the nearness of him; it gave her a hiding place from all the chaos fluttering inside.

'I'll give you pampering,' he said, rolling towards her, taking her in his arms and gently stroking her back.

***

The following morning, some of Cassie's brain fog had lifted and the atmosphere was lighter, or so it seemed. Cassie's top was still spinning at a hundred miles an hour, but she was getting used to the feeling, becoming better at hiding it, so that, outwardly at least, the world looked more normal.

The minute the house was empty, she was back on high alert, managing the moments. She realised it had been a silly idea calling Maria. What could she have done anyway?

Scott dying was wrong. She could fix it. It was that simple. There was no choice. She had time, and opportunity, and the rest she hoped would fall into place. She couldn't waste more angst worrying about the ramifications and consequences. Giving Scott another chance at life was the right thing to do. Wasn't it?

Later that morning, she set off to visit a travel agent. Going through the motions of exploring options for her 'break' would provide tangible evidence.

Over lunch, she perused the brochures she'd picked up. She sighed. She could do with a real holiday. For now, though, she needed to find somewhere that looked convincing. She settled on a retreat in the mountains near the Sunshine Coast, only a few hours' drive from home. It was called Forest Escape and offered a spa, massage therapy, morning meditation sessions and most importantly, no wi-fi. Mobile phones were discouraged as well. From the images she could see on the web, it looked perfect—cosy cabins hiding in secluded spots amongst the piccabeen palms.

She promised herself she would take Jeff there when this mess was over.

She planned to leave immediately after dropping Jeff off at the airport. Then she could zap back to 1969, make good the terrible mistake, and be home again by the time he got back. What could possibly go wrong?

'Everything,' she cried aloud, 'everything.'

How she wished she could get this thing over.

She went into her bedroom and put on her runners. She hadn't been out for a walk since it first happened and she hoped it might lift her spirits. But the thoughts looped in her head. She was reluctant to leave the security and comfort of her life to take this giant leap into the unknown. It wasn't as if she had a Lonely Planet guide to a past life. She had no idea what she was getting herself into. The experiences she'd had already were irrelevant; she had merely popped in and popped out of the past and there'd been no great revelations or adjustments. She didn't know how her body would react if she stayed away longer or how the world would jiggle on its axis if she changed things around a little.

A little! That was an understatement. If the scheme worked, she would whip into the persona of her younger self, undo the damage done, and Scott would go on to live a long and productive life. What if he turned up in the present in 2013? Would that change everything for herself and her own family? She quickened her pace, trying to leave the doubts behind her.

She walked for hours, soaking up the sun and fresh air. When she arrived back home, Coco was curled up on her favourite chair on the verandah and Cassie lifted her off gently so she could sit down. The cat arched her back and, tail erect and head held high, strutted off into the garden with controlled indignation. As Cassie gazed out over the yard, she realised the problem wasn't going to go away. She would just have to stay calm, and somehow, navigate her way through the rugged terrain ahead.

During dinner that evening, Jeff shared the news that he was going to Perth the following Monday. Jeff rabbited on, but Cassie was distracted. No one noticed her push her food around her plate as she nodded in agreement with everything he said. It wasn't long for her to put her plan into action! She was standing on a precipice, preparing to jump into the adventure of her life. She wanted it over with.

A melancholy accompanied her to bed that night. Thoughts sped through her mind. Confetti in a wind tunnel.

***

Cassie stumbled through the few days, busying herself with constructing and deconstructing her plan a thousand times, constantly second-guessing herself. There were so many things that could go wrong; yet the chance to make things right became her obsession.

The evening before Cassie and Jeff were due to leave, she called her parents and Emma. She wanted to hear their voices one last time before embarking on her quest. She cooked Jeff his favourite— shepherd's pie. During dinner she reminded Katy there would be no phone reception where she was going and told her to call Gran if she needed anything.

After dinner, Jeff packed and Cassie did the same, making sure she took the clothes she thought she would need to look convincing. She also packed her favourite bath salts and toiletries, and a couple of good books. Lastly, her boots and some sneakers which made her feel wistful and sad for a moment. The guilt prickled in her pores. If only this was a real holiday. If only she was going away with her husband tomorrow. *If only*.

A sudden wave of panic engulfed her. She was leaving her family behind, and she couldn't be one-hundred percent certain she would get back. What if something went terribly wrong? She shivered involuntarily.

An idea flashed into her brain. She went into the study and booted up the computer to print out some photos of her beloved Katy and Jeff. Carefully she cut out two images that were small enough to place in an old locket she'd inherited from an aunt. They were barely recognisable, but it didn't matter. If she wore it when she zapped into the past, she hoped it would accompany her to the year 1969. Both times she had travelled back, she had appeared in whatever she'd been wearing in the photo. Finding plausible explanations for the practicalities was impossible. She couldn't even remember checking to see if her wedding band was on her finger last time, but it was still here now.

She was relieved to hear Jeff calling out from the bedroom. Something normal—he was looking for his favourite tie, and she had to burrow into the wardrobe to find it.

Then it was done. Their overnight bags stood packed and ready. No going back.

She took some melatonin at bedtime. She wasn't fussed on taking tablets to help her sleep, but needs must, for she knew that no matter how things unfolded hereafter, she would need to be alert and in control.

CHAPTER 13

Morning light streamed into the room as it had countless mornings before. Beside her Jeff slept, gently snoring, and at her feet Coco lay on her back, spreadeagled and totally relaxed in blissful repose. Cassie stirred, waking into consciousness. *It's today.*

Anxiety pushed her into auto pilot. Everything was surreal; she was destined to change the course of her own history and God willing, bring someone back to life.

She made a cup of coffee, had a couple of sips then, unable to sit still, she tipped it out.

Once Jeff woke up, the minutes flew by. Before they were about to leave, Cassie tiptoed into Katy's room and, leaning over her sleeping child, kissed her lightly on the temple. Katy stirred, rolled over and with eyes still closed, reached up with both arms and gave her mother a dreamy hug. Jeff followed and was treated to the same ritual.

Cassie fed Coco and then they were ready. Jeff put their bags in the boot of Cassie's Mazda. As she closed the door behind her, Cassie took one long, lingering look around, savouring all that was loved and familiar.

'You drive,' Jeff said. 'It'll save swapping at the airport.' He folded himself into the passenger seat. They were on their way. The traffic was slow because it was peak hour, but it didn't matter. It was generally only a fifteen-minute drive, so they had plenty of time.

At the airport, she pulled into the kerb and leaned over to give Jeff a farewell hug.

He held her tightly and kissed her. 'Stay safe, I'll see you on Wednesday night.'

Cassie hugged him then cradled his face in her hands and studied it, trying to take in all his features she held so dear. 'See you on Wednesday night.'

She drove off and glanced once more in the rear-vision mirror to see if she could catch sight of him. As soon as she had cleared the terminal area, she pulled over onto the gravel shoulder and sat for a while, breathing deeply, gathering her courage. She thumped the steering wheel and let out an exasperated howl before regaining her composure, then merged back into the traffic.

It had just gone half past seven, and she needed to fill in an hour or so to be sure Katy wouldn't be home. She drove in the direction of a long-term parking station where she'd booked the car in for two nights. Nearby was a little café where she could sit and wait. She pulled in and found a small metal table. She noticed the top looked a bit grubby and it wobbled, but she didn't care. A straggly array of people queued, all wanting their morning fix before heading off to work. She was glad ... anything to delay her moment of reckoning was a welcome interruption. She joined the line and ordered an espresso for herself then sat down in the shade. She watched the parade of strangers who milled about her.

After what seemed a wearisome amount of time, she finished her second cup and drove to the parking station. Having completed the necessary paperwork, she wandered over to the courtesy phone on the wall, picked it up, and called for a taxi.

At home, the coast was clear; Katy's car was missing from the driveway. Cassie fumbled with the keys, trying to open the front door. It was hard to concentrate, but at last, she heard the reassuring click of the tumbler and let herself in, ran straight up the hall into the bathroom and threw up. She clung to the sink, purging the vile, bitter reality of the lies, trials and the uncertainty of it all. She was still there five minutes later, her body empty, her mind blank, except for that one gargantuan thing looming over her like a hanging blade.

Coco joined Cassie in the bathroom, weaving herself fluidly in and out of her legs, softly mewing. Cassie stood hunched, leaning her elbows on the vanity and looked down at the cat. She grabbed a handtowel and wiped her face. She leaned over and stroked her gently, whispering, 'Thank you Coco. I couldn't have made it through the night without you.'

The soft comfort of the silky fur stilled her somewhat as she stroked her beautiful Burmese.

She picked up Coco and carried her to her favourite chair, patted her one more time and kissed her softly on the top of her head. 'Well, my darling, you'll keep my secret won't you?' Coco arched and pushed back hard against her hand.

At the door of the study, Cassie turned back, turned again, took a few steps, hedged and hesitated until finally she was there. She slowly pushed the study door open. Never had it been so hard for her to walk into that office. She tucked her handbag containing her watch, her mobile and personal paraphernalia into the deep drawer of her desk and took the locket she had prepared last night from its velvet box. Fastening the clip took forever. She was not used to jewellery and her hands shook badly. She twisted her wedding ring around on her finger, agonising about whether to leave it or wear it. What if she lost it? No ... she couldn't risk it; the locket had to be enough. She took it off and kissed the golden symbol of her promises to Jeff, admonishing herself for what she was about to do. She gently placed it in the box and slid shut the top drawer of the desk.

With slow deliberation, she picked up the photo of Scott and herself taken so many years ago on that fateful night and placed it on the glass plate of the scanner.

She scrunched her eyes closed tightly, her chest heaving, the blood curdling in her veins. Holding on to the side of the scanner with one hand to steady herself, she pressed start.

Her skin rippled in anticipation. One deep breath and the force took her.

The room shimmied and sizzled, stars sprayed, flashes of brilliant blues and purples ricocheted off the walls, and an instant later she felt the now-familiar pull as she was sucked into the darkness.

CHAPTER 14

From her vantage point by the window, Mrs Parker put her cup of coffee down and stared. She'd been watching closely ever since the taxi pulled up and Cassie had stepped out alone. She told herself she was being silly. The car was probably just in for a service, but it was strange, for she could have sworn she saw the two of them carrying out suitcases earlier. She couldn't tear her eyes away from the Foster's house.

Less than an hour later, she saw that brilliant blue flash of light again. Rubbing her eyes against the blinding light, she knew for certain this was NOT her imagination. The whole thing was over before it had fully registered and, afterwards, the house sat silent again, unchanged. Everything looked normal. She sucked her teeth, knotted her eyebrows. Concern was a tiny part of the current of excitement running through her, but curiosity was banging like a bass drum.

She shuffled into the bedroom. Moving like a spider, it took her a long time to get dressed, but finally she closed the bedroom door softly behind her, grabbed her walking stick and hobbled to the front door. Slowly and carefully, she lumbered across the street and clambered up the few steps to the front door of the Foster's house. She stood for a few moments to catch her breath then rapped on the door. Nothing. She waited for a little while then banged again, three times, loudly. No answer. Leaning heavily on her stick, she shrugged, and moved towards the window where she had seen the light earlier. She peered inside. There was nothing to see—no evidence of any explosion and certainly no evidence of Cassie. It was most peculiar. The house was as still as a lagoon. With a disgusted grunt, she made her uncomfortable trip back home, dropped the walking stick by the door, and walked, beaten, into the kitchen. Arming herself with another cup of tea and some biscuits, she went back to the lounge room, all the while curiosity nipping at her insides. She would wait.

The day dragged by.

With no further excitement and nothing to stimulate her senses, she eventually dozed off, only to awaken to a dark house.

'Damn!' she said to herself when she woke up. 'I can't go over now, not at night. I'll have to catch her in the morning.' She wandered over to her armchair, picked up the remote and turned on the television.

Stirring the next morning, she took a few moments to gather her thoughts and suddenly remembered yesterday's episode. She heaved her limbs out of the bed with renewed vigour. Sitting at the kitchen table, she scraped margarine on her toast and covered it with a thick layer of strawberry jam. She washed it down with a strong cup of tea and was ready to set off. It was 7.30 am.

The white car was still there so she was sure someone was home. Knock, knock, knock! Three strikes at the timber door. Surely someone would appear. She waited, shifting her weight from foot to foot, finding her balance with the stick. She looked around, listened, and waited a bit longer. At last, there were scuttling sounds coming from inside. Someone was coming. Suddenly, she was nervous; she didn't quite know what to say so that she sounded concerned and clever—not like a nosy neighbour.

***

Katy heard the knock on the door and peered out the window. It was her neighbour from across the road. 'Hello? Everything okay?' She ran a hand through her dishevelled hair as she opened the door.

'I'm so sorry. Did I wake you?'

'No, it doesn't matter; I'm due to go soon anyway. It was high time I got up. Do you want to come in?'

'No, no dear, but something's been worrying me, and I just thought you should know.' The old lady waddled over to one of the chairs on the verandah and dropped into it before continuing. 'Your mother might have mentioned that I was over the other day ... my name is Ada Parker and I live in the house opposite.'

'She may have. I don't remember. I'm sorry. I have exams coming up and I've a lot on my mind. Anyway, she's away at the moment,' Katy said with irritation.

'Is she?' The rheumy eyes lit up, opened wide in surprise. 'Is she really? Only that's not what I saw. The strangest thing happened yesterday.' She met Katy's gaze. She now had her full attention.

Softening a little, Katy pulled the other chair closer and sat down. 'What do you mean ... is she really?' Katy said, fidgeting with her dressing gown, smoothing it over her knees, doing her best to be patient.

'Well ...' Mrs Parker pulled her shoulders up to give herself height. 'Well,' she said again, 'I saw your mum and dad leaving together early yesterday morning in her blue car, but then a few hours later, she turned up back here in a taxi, alone. I didn't know what to make of it, I saw this strange blue flash of light coming from the window again, and I came over to see if she was all right and there was no one home.'

'Hold on, hold on. What are you saying? You reckon my mother came home in a taxi on her own, and then disappeared? And what's this about a blue flash of light; where does that come in?' Katy asked.

'Oh, I've seen it three times now. Your mother insisted nothing strange was going on ... still ... I wonder, you know.'

'Mrs ... Parker, there is nothing going on. Mum probably had car problems or something.' Katy frowned a little as she shook her head. 'I'm sure everything is fine; she'll be home in a day or two, and no doubt she will have a perfectly good explanation.' With that, she made her excuses. 'I'm sorry; I really do have to go. Would you like me to help you across the road? It can be busy this hour of the morning.'

'I'm perfectly capable of walking, thank you. I might be slow, but I am not clumsy.' The woman heaved her small frame up and clunking her stick on the floorboards, made her way back down the stairs, up the path and waited patiently for a decent gap in the traffic before she stepped out on to the road.

Katy watched her until she was safely at her own front door, then turned and walked back into the house. *Why would her Mum come back home in a taxi?* She couldn't imagine what the blue light was all about. Perhaps she was just confused. Old people tended to get confused quite easily, and she imagined that Mrs Parker might be lonely and bored. Probably just a vivid imagination, she decided. She had other things on her mind that morning and dismissed the whole matter as a demented old lady's ramblings.

CHAPTER 15

Katy's morning was punctuated by thoughts of the earlier conversation with her neighbour. There had to be a simple explanation, but it was perplexing. She thought back over the last few weeks. She'd had her nose in a book most of the time; perhaps she should have been paying more attention to her mother's moods.

Her parents had left together yesterday morning and, from memory, her mum was going to head up north directly from the airport. That made sense. What the old lady had said didn't. It was niggling at her. Bugger it! She dialled her mother's number. It went to voicemail.

Nevertheless, she was distracted all afternoon and made up her mind to head straight home when she finished at uni. As soon as the lecture was done, she raced to her car and headed home. Once there though, things were no clearer.

She couldn't sit still. Thinking about what Mrs Parker had said, she wandered into the study to have a look around. Everything looked normal. She mooched around, picked up a note pad from the desk and flipped through the pages. She could see nothing of value—a few phone numbers, some scribbled notes that she assumed related to her mother's work. All irrelevant. She pushed aside a shoe box with the lid partly off, closing it properly as she did so, heedless of its contents. There were various bits of correspondence, boring stuff mostly, but a coloured brochure drew her attention. It was opened at a page illustrating a variety of retreats. Right at the top with a black Texta ring around it, was one that sounded familiar. She read the advertisement, looking for clues, but there was nothing specific, although it did mention mobile phones were not encouraged. She put it aside. She opened her mother's laptop, then closed it again, blank on ideas. Then she pulled open the top drawer. The first thing she spied was a tiny velvet box. Picking it up, she flipped it open and saw a wedding band neatly placed on the black velvet cushion.

That's odd, she thought. It looked too delicate to be a man's ring; it must belong to her Mum. *Why wouldn't she be wearing her wedding ring?*

Her thoughts darkened and she grimaced, speculating about the possibility of an affair. Her mother wouldn't, would she? The idea gnawed at her, and like a woman possessed, she started opening cupboards, wrenching and slamming doors and drawers as she worked her way round the room, hoping to find a clue that she was mistaken. Her mum was not that kind of a person.

'That stupid old biddy; I wish I'd never answered the door!' she said out loud.

She'd been through all the cupboards and found zilch—no evidence, either incriminating or absolving her mother from guilt.

The desk drew her attention again. She looked down at the large bottom drawer and tugged it open with a fierce jerk. She felt sick when she saw her mother's favourite leather bag sitting on top of the few files at the bottom. Her hand trembled as she picked it up and opened it. It had all the usual junk her mum carried inside: her wallet, her phone, her pink plastic hairbrush, some make-up. Her mum had gone away for a few days and she'd left behind her bag? *What woman does that?*

She let herself fall into the chair and thumped the desk in exasperation. She ran into her own room, threw herself on the bed, and burrowed deep into the doona, trying to hide from the evidence and cursed the reality of what she had seen with her own eyes. She wished she hadn't seen any of it because now there were too many questions, too many explanations, and just as many excuses

It was starting to get dark. Coco was at her feet mewing and circling wildly, and Katy was lucky not to trip as she made her way to the kitchen, turning on the lights as she went. She took a food pouch from the fridge, and minutes later the cat was crouched over her bowl cleaning it up as quickly as she could.

Her phone buzzed. It was Dad. *Good grief, not now*. She ignored the call but moments later it buzzed again.

'Hello Kitten, how are you? Have you had any word from your mother? Her phone's going to voicemail.'

She wanted to tell him the phone was in her bag in the study and that she had found her mother's wedding ring. She wanted to tell him that the stupid woman across the road had thrown her a curve ball.

'Nah, haven't heard from her. She's probably lying back sipping a cocktail somewhere and the last thing on her mind is us.' What was the point in worrying him? Tomorrow they would both be home and they would move on from there, she assured herself.

'They booked me on a flight to get in at six. Will you be around if she doesn't get back in time? No, forget it, she'll be back. She said she'd be driving home after lunch and it won't take her three hours.'

'Okay, Dad, see you tomorrow. Call me if things come unstuck. Love you. Travel safe.' She ended the call and plugged her phone into its charger. She was distracted by thoughts about the ring in the box, her mother, wondering how tomorrow would unfold. She poured herself a glass of wine, and another and another until the events of the day softened and dulled to a point where she thought she might just get some sleep tonight after all.

When the soft dawn light started creeping into the room, Katy got up.

She wandered into her mum and dad's room, breathing in the atmosphere of her parents. Why had she been so caught up in her own world?

She turned and headed back to the kitchen. Passing by her bedroom she saw Coco still stretched out, languishing in the comfort of pure, untroubled slumber. In the half-light she opened the cupboard and rummaged about until she found herself a couple of aspirins for her headache then made herself a cup of coffee.

She had a shower and got dressed; sliding into the same clothes she had on the night before and was out of the house about an hour later. When she got into the car she just sat there. She turned on the engine then switched if off again. There was nowhere she had to be ... except home. She shook her head, hoping to dislodge the fog muddling her brain, and went back inside.

In her room, she unpacked her study books and scattered them in front of her in an attempt to do some revision. Just meters away sat the handbag, her mum's personal belongings—her presence, but no sign of her. Exasperated, she got up and marched back to the study. She poured the contents of the bag onto the desk. The ring, why on earth would she have taken that off? Leaving it behind was so out of character. She picked up the mobile and switched it on. She didn't know her mum's password. There was just the one icon showing missed calls. She opened Cassie's wallet, anxious to have some clues. There were a few dollars and everything seemed to be in its place. The credit cards, the Medicare, memberships ... all normal. In the side pocket, she found a small yellow card advertising a scanner with a number on it. She didn't give it a second thought.

She could only wait. There had to be a reasonable explanation, but it was nerve wracking. She was tired. She flopped back on the bed and allowed her mind to wander. She dozed off and for a few blissful hours, she was free from thinking about it.

CHAPTER 16

1969

Cassie lurched into 1969 light-headed, off kilter and disoriented. No sooner had she smashed through time than she became self-consciously aware she was supported by a strong masculine arm. She blinked. Again, testing, affirming. She was here! She focussed to see the beautiful, youthful face of Scott. The faint smell of Brut tickled her nose and the memories flooded back. But they didn't feel like memories; they felt like the present. It was the present.

'Whoa, what happened there?' Scott smiled at her as she came to her senses.

'I-I-I don't know, a dizzy spell or something. I'm fine.' The feeling was a little more familiar now, not as frightening. As Cassie leaned into Scott, she became aware of other people around her. Her dad, shouting instructions from the other end of the lounge and Mum watching lovingly from the doorway. She gazed around the room. Sadness, joy and every emotion in between fluxed through her in a crazy paradox.

Instinctively she clutched at her throat. The locket was gone! She gasped, then immediately coughed to camouflage the fact. *It's okay, they'll always be in my thoughts.* She had to get this done. It crossed her mind that all that she had worn, all that she was, floated somewhere in the ether.

Almost as powerful was the intense physical awareness of Scott. He was so handsome! She felt small and fragile and clumsy and awkward ... all at once, yet more potent and alive than she'd ever been. Her body sizzled. She'd forgotten what it felt like to be seventeen.

She walked over and stared at herself in the hall mirror. Her skin glowed with the luminosity of youth. Not a wrinkle dared mar its perfection. The mole on her forehead looked like it belonged; nothing like the ugly black thing of middle age, a fungus occasionally sprouting a beastly black hair she painstakingly plucked whenever it appeared. Gazing into the glass, she could see a likeness to Katy shining through, except for the hair. That big, dark, bouffant, glistening hair. Her delicate features were overwhelmed by its glory. Her limbs, like young saplings, felt supple and strong. It was a glorious feeling, and she immersed herself in the wonder and joy of youth. She ran her hand over her cheek, luxuriating in its velvet smoothness. For now, she was young and free with the whole world waiting for her—a blank canvas ready to be painted and worked to create a new future for herself and Scott. She silently sent kisses to Katy and Jeff, vowed to return, and prayed she could.

Scott took her hand, pulling her back gently, 'Come on, your father really wants these photos, and I don't want to get on his bad side.'

They stood close to each other as they posed for the photo. Cassie's knees turned to jelly when Scott squeezed her waist.

Her mum wiped her hands on her apron, adjusted Cassie's corsage and hugged her daughter, careful not to ruin the blossom. 'You look so beautiful tonight; I am so proud of you.' And looking over at Scott, she added, 'You look after my girl, won't you?'

Cassie felt deeply privileged to be having these moments twice in one lifetime.

'Yes, you be careful, young man. We want her safely home by eleven and no shenanigans, do you hear?' her dad chimed in.

Scott blushed and nodded. 'Yes sir.'

He took Cassie's hand again. With the other, she clutched the brocade evening purse and crossed her fingers and prayed that everything would turn out the way it should.

Her euphoria made her want to jump in and let the currents take her. This was now. She wanted to live this moment right now, with every part of her being.

Scott led her outside and opened the door of his Holden HR, which made her smile, but as she got inside, she was suddenly cold, frozen in panic at the enormity of her mission. She understood what was at stake and realised how much more she had bitten off than she could possibly hope to chew. She shivered uncontrollably, trying to get a grip on her emotions as Scott made his way to the driver's seat. She ran her fingers lightly over the bench seat; it was like meeting an old friend. It calmed her. The seat belts hung limply from their anchor points and Cassie had to stifle a groan. She reminded herself that couples cuddled in the front seat all the time, and it was the most natural thing in the world.

Scott interrupted her reverie. 'Hey, gorgeous, come over here; you're miles away.'

He pulled away from the kerb slowly and gave her a grin that sent her senses fluttering. She sighed and grinned back. Her heart was doing back flips, struggling to put all the emotions in the appropriate boxes. She reminded herself this was a mission. Now was all about Scott's life.

Her heart's conscience was hazier now she was beside Scott. She wanted to forget all she knew and be seventeen again, but with all the responsibilities just a breath away, she had no choice but to immerse herself in the task at hand. She slid across the seat and moved closer. She owed it to Scott and she didn't want to cheat herself out of this experience. Jeff would understand when she explained.

But this was going to be harder than she had anticipated. She thought she'd covered everything, but she hadn't factored in the powerhouse of teenage hormones pulsing through her like a wave pounding the edges of a cliff.

Scott filled the car and the universe. She wanted him and she wanted him to live for reasons way beyond altruism. Her body involuntarily sought out the shape of him, easing itself into the comfortable hollow of his shoulder. She felt the bottle in his suit pocket.

Another shiver. *Stay in control.*

When they turned the corner, Scott put his arm around her shoulder. It felt strange but fantastic. Cassie reasoned that she had to be authentic. She was relieved that it felt natural and good to play her part. They drove by the old bowling alley, past the road to the drive-in and their favourite milk bar. The world looked less cluttered—not a golden arch to be seen, no roundabouts, no huge shopping centres. It seemed less busy and narrower than she remembered. When they turned onto Enoggera Road and drove along the tramlines, another nostalgic wave flowed through her. The familiar 'ting, ting' of the tram approaching was music to her ears as it rounded the bend. About twenty minutes later, they pulled into the entrance to the school grounds, drove the short distance up the hill and parked in the car park.

Cassie's senses were overflowing. Every image, every smell, every detail brought back so many memories. No sooner did they emerge than they morphed into the present. Maybe they weren't memories at all. Maybe this was as solid and real and now as life got.

Scott turned to her. 'Wait here, ma'am. I am going to open the door for you. Let's make a grand entrance tonight.' He got out and opened the passenger door, then bent over in an exaggerated gesture, one arm sweeping towards the main entrance.

Slowly she got out. Her shoes touched the gravel and she teetered up, trying to appear elegant and sophisticated in the stilettoes she was wearing. She was a princess, but one with impossible challenges in an improbable situation.

Together they made their way to the door. There were a couple of teachers standing outside looking bored, chatting quietly to each other. Inside, there were a few more to manage the maelstrom of teenagers. Young people were huddled around the edges of the hall, and on the floor colourful couples twisted and shook to the rhythms of Tommy James and the Shondells.

Scott stood beside Cassie, fidgeting. He didn't much like dancing, but gallantly he led her into the crowd and threw his energy into his version of the Watusi. Cassie joined in, marvelling at her own nerve. She couldn't relax; the tension of knowing what was to come beat in rhythm with the music. Scott's forehead shone as beads of perspiration trickled down, and Cassie could feel her dress clinging to her as she too was starting to get uncomfortably hot.

Gently he pulled her towards the exit. He squeezed her hand and whispered, 'I'm going out for a few minutes.'

This was her cue; this was where she had let him go alone. What had she been thinking?

Scott patted his coat pocket and gave her a devilish grin.

'No, Scott, please don't. It'll spoil things if you start drinking. Please, please.'

'Don't be so boring. You can come if you want.'

Reluctantly she trailed after him as he walked towards the toilet blocks outside. 'Come back, Scott. The teachers will catch us, this is my school, remember?' Cassie grabbed him by the arm.

'No, they won't, sissy ... they're all too busy watching the kids inside. No one'll notice.'

'I can't Scott. Come back in, please, don't to do this.'

'You go back in. I won't be long, promise.'

Just then Cassie heard her name being called. It was her friend Maria.

'Are you coming in Cassie? They're going to do the Limbo ... you love that one.'

'Come on, Scott.'

Maria was pulling at her arm and Cassie reluctantly turned to join her friend. 'One dance, that's it. I can't leave him out there alone.'

He had already disappeared into the night.

After the dance, she explained to the teacher, now standing at the door, that she was looking for her friend. She walked the short distance in the half-light and started calling, picking her way across the uneven ground.

'Scott! Scott? Where did you get to?'

'I'm over here ...'

She moved towards his voice and saw he was in the company of two other boys she didn't recognise.

'Come and have a drink.'

'No, Scott. Not interested. Please, come back inside.' He'd only been outside for about ten minutes, yet Cassie could smell the alcohol on his breath. 'How much have you had?'

The other two retreated hastily. The music was thumping in the distance, voices echoed on the breeze, shards of light pierced the blackness, but they were alone behind a shed.

'Not much. Here ...' He gave her the flask he'd had in his pocket. It was almost empty.

'Good grief.' She couldn't believe she'd been so stupid ... again. He was being an idiot. Disgusted, she snatched the bottle away, upended it and peered as liquid trickled onto the grass, doing exactly what she had promised herself she'd do a million times before if given the opportunity.

Now she'd done it. She was in control; she would NOT let this night play out the way it had before. Scott would be alive.

She cursed herself and him. How dumb could she be? She had known the risks and what she was up against. He was leaning heavily on the corrugated wall, his head buried into his arm. Cassie knew he'd had some sort of spirit, but no idea what or how hard it would hit him. Besides, he might have had a couple before he picked her up for all she knew. She reached out and touched his face, roughly pulling his chin up to glare into his eyes.

'I'm really angry; you've ruined my night, and now you are too stupid to make things right. I've had enough. I want to go home. I'm going to get one of the teachers to call me a taxi. I can't trust you to drive home, and I'm not driving your father's car.'

Scott blabbered back, 'Good luck. What ya gonna tell the teacher?'

He was right. She couldn't tell the teacher without giving the game away, and that could lead to all sorts of consequences. The teachers wouldn't take kindly to a kid on school premises being drunk. She'd have to think of something else. She grabbed him around his waist and draped his arm over her shoulders. Together, they stumbled to a nearby seat.

'Sit there and don't move.' Cassie marched off towards the side door of the hall, rehearsing plausible-sounding explanations all the way there. She tidied herself up as best she could; tried to fix her beautifully coiffed hairstyle, desperately tucking the stray locks into place. At the door, she smiled at the teacher who had challenged her when she had left, as if to reassure her that all was in order.

'Is your friend all right?' the teacher asked.

'Not really, he probably ate something that was off. I need a taxi to get us home. Can I call one from here, please?'

'I'll have to get the key to the staff room from the main office, and that could be a bit of rigmarole. The nearest public phone is on the other side of the oval in the street behind. It's a bit of a walk but will probably be quicker. Wait and I'll get one of the male teachers to escort you; I don't want you walking out there by yourself in the middle of the night.'

Cassie pondered, rubbing her hands together as the anxiety mounted. There was no point in attracting anyone's attention.

'Actually, I've got my licence; there's no reason I can't drive him home. I just didn't want to drive his father's car, but I guess it would be all right under the circumstances, as long as I am careful.'

'Are you sure?' The teacher's face puckered with concern.

'Yeah ... I'll be fine.' There wasn't a choice really. 'Is it alright if I bring the car around the back to pick him up? I'll call my dad to come and collect me from his place when I get him there.' She said, wearing her seventeen-year-old skin like an old lady.

The teacher nodded, distracted by the noise inside the hall.

Cassie went to tell her friends she was leaving. They protested, but Cassie stood her ground, made her excuses, and left them in a disappointed huddle.

Then she went back outside to check on Scott. He was where she had left him, perched against the shed, staring ahead like a condemned man. She asked him for his keys and he dug into the pocket of his trousers and plonked them onto her outstretched hand. Clutching them, she made her way back to the car, walking outside the hall this time to avoid another confrontation.

Just seeing the car parked there brought it all back. She opened the door and slid into the driver's seat; sat there for a few moments listening to the Beatles in the distance and watched the silhouettes of her young friends moving about in rhythm to the music as they revelled in their youth and freedom. She rested her head on the steering wheel and allowed her pent-up tears to flow. It seemed her experience of years counted for nothing. She was seventeen years old, her boyfriend was drunk on the school grounds, and she had a mission to ensure he stayed alive. What had she been thinking to believe she could ever change history? Her thoughts wandered to Jeff and her 2013 family, and she wished she'd never come back to this mess. The longing to touch them and feel the safety of their closeness enveloped her.

It took her a long time to gather her spirit and feel strong, but at last she found the courage to put the key in the ignition. She had to.

Last time she'd driven too fast on the way home. The road was narrow and not well lit and when she took the corner, the wheels slid into the soft gravel shoulder and she'd lost control. The car slammed into a tree. The door had exploded open on impact and Cassie had been flung out onto the grass verge, landing yards away from the wreckage.

When she woke, she staggered back to the wreck. The driver's door gaped open and, venturing closer, Cassie had been shocked to see Scott's lifeless body lying on the seat. The front of the car had buckled when it hit the tree, and the metal was wrapped around him in a grotesque arc. In the dark, it was impossible to see where Scott began and where the car ended. And there was blood ... so much blood. In her panic, she had tried to pull him free, finding gargantuan strength as the adrenaline pumped and shock spurred her on, but he wouldn't budge.

Dazed and confused, she sat next to him, stroking his broken, battered body until a passing motorist stopped and offered help. The good Samaritan had driven the quarter mile or so up the road to a public phone box and dialled 000. Not long after, the ambulance came, then the police. It was all such a gruesome blur in her mind, but she recalled her panic at the thought of being found out. She told them she had been thrown out of the car, that she couldn't remember anything. She told them Scott was driving. She lied. She lied to save her own skin. She lied because she couldn't bear to let the people she loved down. So she claimed loss of memory and prayed she wouldn't be implicated.

Her conscience knew though. She had driven Scott to his death as surely as rivers flow, etching their way through the landscape.

Now here she was, about to do it all over again, to try to make it right. She had to make it right.

CHAPTER 17

2013

When Katy woke, the shadows were long and lazy ... she had no idea how long she had slept and was startled to see it was just after three. Coco was stretched out at her feet and looked up with irritation.

Where was her mother? She got up and padded into the kitchen. An ice-cold glass of milk and several Tim Tams later, Katy was wide awake. Fortunately, her dad was only a few hours away which made the wait bearable.

She tapped out a short message on her phone and sent it to him. *Mum not home yet ... let me know flight details. X K*

Sorting through the pile of textbooks on her desk, Katy found one and started leafing through it. It was useless. She kept reading the same passages, trying to take them in, hoping the information would stick. Her finals were coming up in a couple of weeks and she wanted to get a good grade.

A soft ping from the kitchen alerted her to a text message. Her first thought was her mother, but then she realised that was impossible. It was a short message from her dad. *Arriving 1845 QF556.*

That was it then, still two hours to go. 'Bahhhhh,' she said aloud. As if having her dad home would fix everything. Impulsively she dialled her aunt's number hoping she could shed some light on her mum's whereabouts.

'Hello Katy, to what do I owe the pleasure of your call? Is everything all right up there?'

'Yes, everything is fine.' Katy's voice was light. 'But did Mum give you any details about this retreat she went to?'

'What retreat?' Katy's heart sank. 'A while ago, she mentioned she'd like to get away for a while, but she didn't tell me any details. Lucky girl; I wish it was me. I could do with an escape from these two teenagers.'

Katy regrouped. 'Anyway, she's due back this evening, I'll ask her to call you. Gotta go, sorry. All good there?'

'Yeah, busy as usual.'

'Okay, love you.' Katy finished the call.

Another idea came to mind. She trotted into the study and found the brochure. Flicking through it, she saw the resort her mother had circled and checked to see if there was a contact number. There wasn't. She entered the name into the search bar of her phone, wishing she'd thought of it earlier. She waited impatiently for the page to load and scanned down. There it was. Her fingers were moving too fast and she fiddled around trying to hit the right buttons. Her spirits lifted when she heard the familiar ring tone.

'Good evening, Forest Escapes, Yvonne speaking.'

Katy was flustered. 'H-h-h-hello, my name is Katy Foster and I'm calling to see if my mother, Mrs Cassie Foster checked out this morning?'

'Just a minute.' Katy waited. 'I'm sorry; we've had no one here by that name. You must have the wrong place.'

'What?' she whispered. 'Thank you.' She hung up, discouraged.

If she didn't find something to fill in the time, she'd go mad. She rummaged in the fridge and found some vegetables and prepared a soup; a quick, easy meal for when her mum and dad came home ... if they came home.

Driving to the airport, she wondered what she was going to say to her dad. When she got the text saying he'd landed, she instantly wished it hadn't. She was worried about how he would react.

He was easy to spot in the jumble of people lining the kerb, he stood a head above most of them, and he was wearing his favourite leather jacket. He leaned over and waved to her as she pulled up. He tugged the door open, threw his overnight bag on the back seat and manoeuvred himself next to her.

'Good to be home.' He gave her a kiss on the cheek.

Katy eyed the traffic as she pulled out. 'So, how was the trip?'

'Okay. I've been trying to reach your mum, but she hasn't been picking up. Have you spoken to her yet?'

'No.' The crack in her voice caught her father's attention.

'What's wrong?' he asked.

Katy saw him frown from the corner of her eye. 'I've no idea why she's not back, and I'm a bit worried,' she said.

'Perhaps she was enjoying it so much she decided to stay another few days.'

The car fell silent. The atmosphere was suddenly heavy with concern. Katy wondered if she should mention the wedding ring. An affair was the only thing that made sense, even if her gut said differently. She let it go for now.

They pulled up and gathered their belongings.

'Coco has missed everyone.' It was all Katy could think of as she pushed open the door, and the cat trotted up and curled about Jeff in feline affection. 'I'll get you some soup,' she told him.

'I don't want anything; they fed me on the plane. I'll have a shower, I think.'

Katy walked over and hugged her dad. Suddenly she was a little girl again. Looking him squarely in the face, she voiced her concern. 'Oh, Dad, I'm worried Mum's not coming home tonight.' Hot tears welled up inside her, escaping on to her cheeks.

'Sit down. I'll make you a coffee. I'm sure there's a simple explanation. Let's not jump to any conclusions.' He was calm and composed, but his eyes hooded over, pinched and anxious.

Katy dropped into a chair at the table and wiped madly at her face, trying to stem the flow that wouldn't stop now that her father, her saviour, was home.

'So, what's worrying you so much? He placed two mugs of coffee on the table in front of them, reached out and placed his hand on her arm.

Katy picked up her mug and sipped carefully, unsure where to start. She heaved an enormous sigh.

'Start at the beginning,' her father said, urging her on gently.

'It's bizarre, Dad. This old biddy from across the road came over yesterday morning and told me she'd seen Mum come back here in a taxi after she'd dropped you off at the airport. That was odd enough, but then she went on with this other stuff about an explosion and a blue light. It didn't make any sense.'

He raised his eyebrows.

'Anyway,' Katy went on, sniffing and sipping, 'it really bugged me, so I came straight home from lectures yesterday and tried to get to the bottom of it myself. I didn't want to bother you in Perth. You understand, don't you?'

'Of course, go on.'

'When I had a look around, I found a brochure on the desk with the resort she had mentioned circled. That was something, but I was still curious. I pulled open the top drawer of the desk and there was a little velvet box with her wedding ring inside.' She started crying again.

Her dad jumped up and strode towards the study. Katy bounded after him. By the time she got there, he was holding the open box.

'It's her wedding ring,' he said. 'Why would she take it off?' His face twisted in a surge of pain.

'You guys were okay before you left, weren't you?' Katy whispered, now becoming the comforter. 'Like you said, we shouldn't jump to conclusions, but I also found this.' Katy walked around him and opened the filing cabinet drawer to reveal her mother's bag. 'Dad ... I have given this so much thought.' She was stronger now, fortified by the need to support her father. 'Mum wouldn't leave her handbag or her phone behind if she was gallivanting around with a new man, would she? There has to be more to it.' She went on. 'I rang Aunt Emma who didn't even know Mum was going away. I didn't want to distress her, so I said nothing. When I called the resort, they'd never heard of her. That's the worst of it. What'll we do?'

'I don't see what we *can* do. If she doesn't come home tonight, we'll get onto it first thing in the morning.' The false bravado in his voice broke Katy's heart.

It was late. Her father kissed her on the head and said goodnight.

Katy showered, wanting to clean the anxiety from her skin and soothe her frightened heart.

Hours later, she was still awake. She could hear her dad moving around in the kitchen.

CHAPTER 18

1969

Cassie felt her jaw aching and her hand shook as she stabbed the key at the ignition. The engine started. With one foot on the clutch, she carefully moved the gear stick into first gear. She wasn't used to a manual shift and practised a few times before she felt confident enough to move off. The car rolled, hesitated, and then did a kangaroo hop as it bounced forward. She slammed on the brake. Stationary again, she took slow, deep breaths, persuading herself she could do it. Barely at a crawl and with only the parking lights on, she eased the car around the school grounds to find the main driveway leading to the rear of the assembly hall. In the half-light she could see Scott slouched against the wall, looking sorry for himself. She stopped the car and watched as he ambled towards it. She didn't get out.

Scott clambered in, dropped his head against the seat and moaned. 'I'm sorry Cass, I didn't drink much. I didn't mean to ruin your night. I can wait here if you want to stay.'

'No, Scott, I just want to get out of here. When I get you home I'll call Dad to come and pick me up.'

Scott jerked towards her and she pushed him away. 'No, you stay on your side; I need to concentrate if I am going to get us both back to your place alive.'

Scott leaned up against the passenger door, sulking or maybe ashamed, but he did as she said. She shrugged, ignoring his belligerence.

Very slowly she drove down the gravel driveway and out through the school gates. This time she turned left, deciding to take the busy main streets rather than the back road which wasn't well lit. Besides, it was only a two-lane, one step up from a dirt track; it had been her undoing.

They crept along below the speed limit. A few cars honked at them as they passed, but Cassie didn't care. She was almost done.

Her knuckles were hard and white as she clung to the steering wheel, concentrating.

At last, she pulled into his street, then his driveway. She turned off the ignition and let out an enormous sigh of relief mixed with disbelief, exultation, joy, even smugness. She'd done it! Scott was alive! Unconsciously, she brought her hand to her neck, fumbling for the locket that wasn't there. Her destiny was decided. Now she had to leave and hope that one day Scott would find love and happiness too. She should leave right now, but she couldn't bear the thought of not saying goodbye to her family.

The house was dark. She hadn't expected that; he shared the house with three other students from the same year at university and she'd assumed at least one of them would be home.

He must have read her expression. 'They're out. They won't be home for ages.'

'I assume this is the key for the door?' She held a small key dangling from the keyring she was holding.

He had sobered up and was grasping at the shreds of his dignity. 'Yup, that's the one. I'm sorry I put you through this.' The more coherent he became the more apologetic and remorseful he was.

'No point worrying about it now, Scott. It's over. I'll call Dad and he'll be here in half an hour to pick me up.' Her voice had softened.

She got out and walked ahead, then turned and watched as he wriggled out of the car. It took a bit of fiddling to get the door open.

Once inside, Scott turned on the lights. 'You thirsty?'

'I'm okay. Where's your phone?'

He moved closer and put his arm around her waist.

'Don't Scott, I have to call Dad. Where's your phone?' She asked again.

He led her to the lounge room where it sat cradled on a tea chest with an old towel over it, next to the lounge. Cassie sank into the seat and picked up the old Bakelite phone and rested it on her knee. She lifted the handset and dialled her parents' number. There was a soft whirring sound as she ran her fingers around the dial. Hearing it wheel back to zero was like music. She hesitated in the pleasure of its simplicity. The number had come to her easily, which surprised her. It occurred to her that her future—her real future with Jeff and her family—didn't exist yet. But everything here felt familiar. She had slid into her past with the same ease as putting on her favourite T-shirt.

'Hello, Dad? We've come home early; I'm at Scott's place. Can you pick me up, please?'

He sounded grumpy; he didn't like being disturbed while he was watching his Saturday Night Movie. 'Okay. I'll be there soon. It's Laurel Street, isn't it?'

'Thanks, Dad.' She hung up, thinking how much she loved him and how she longed for time with her girlhood family before she said goodbye forever. She'd go tonight, while they were asleep.

'He's coming.' She eyed Scott, looking sheepish and dishevelled. Her anger dissipated; she was so happy he was alive.

He sidled up close to her and whispered into her ear, nuzzling lightly into the soft skin on her neck.

Jeff and Katy were far away, in another dimension altogether. They sat in a safe place in her heart. Yet here was the present pulling at her with a force she hadn't reckoned on.

'I really am sorry, Cass. Can't we make up? Please.'

She looked into his eyes and despite her wanting to stay detached, she lost her resolve when he touched her in that gentle way of his, when he spoke to her in that sexy, gravelly voice, and she felt his warm breath on her cheek. Her hormones were pulsing.

She nuzzled back and put her hand on his knee, and an instant later, he was kissing her hard on the lips. It was a beautiful, unhurried kiss, and Cassie felt herself drowning in the nearness of him, struggling against the potent lust. There was the faint tang of alcohol on his lips, a hint of aftershave in the air. That and the heady feeling that she had saved his life cast a thick and ominous cloud over her judgement, its opaqueness completely obliterating her good sense. She kissed him back.

She was seventeen again and her feelings were more powerful and urgent than she could remember. Her skin was tingling, her pulse racing.

His arms wrapped tightly around her, protecting, comforting, celebrating. She arched her body into his. When she felt his hand creeping towards her breast she couldn't stop him. Hell, she didn't want to stop him. All thoughts of missions and guilt and obligations were washed away in a current of sensations.

He groaned softly. She pushed her hips towards him, aching for his touch. He explored the curves and contours of her body and with every movement her fervour grew, her need became more urgent. He moaned, and there was nothing she wanted more than to feel him inside her. His breaths came in deep laboured pants. She could feel the heat of him as he touched her skin.

She couldn't. She shouldn't. She wouldn't. Yes, she would!

This teenage Cassie was a virgin. It meant something in the sixties but history told her the winds of change were blowing; she knew there would be a time when it didn't matter. The only thing she could think about was feeling Scott love her, allowing him to cover her body in tantalising caresses. He was breathing so heavily and he was so close she could see the veins in his temples pounding in rhythm with his grinding torso. She could taste him, smell his delicious body, nothing else existed. Cass took his hand and guided it gently under her skirt, leading him, coaxing him to the ultimate temptation. She felt him tug at her pantyhose and wriggled to help him so that she could feel the touch of his hand against her vagina. He pulled her closer and gently laid her down. She responded by stretching and arching her body to meet his embrace. It was delicious. She was floating in a bubble of surreal passion.

They fumbled and groped at each other fiercely, driven and eager. Scott's breaths were ragged and rasping. He found her earlobe and caressed it with his tongue, nibbling gently, softly moaning. 'Are you sure you want to do this? You've never wanted to before.'

'Yes, yes ... I want this.' Cassie squashed any voices she was hearing. This was beyond Jeff, beyond her experience; she had to do it. Anything less was denying herself the joy being thrust at her now. Their bodies merged, the earth stopped spinning. There was a sweet, sharp pain and then nothing except the intense, powerful feeling of their lovemaking.

Spent, exhausted, sated, they lay wrapped together in the calm after the fury. Panting heavily, her skin tingling and moist, she kissed his neck over and over. Sweet, lingering kisses that promised him tomorrows and ever-afters. For Cassie it was the culmination of months of angst and anxiety. Scott was alive. She was alive. Oh! She was so alive. She had devoured this opportunity and she had no regrets ... for now.

Scott raised himself up on one elbow and pushed back into a sitting position, hurriedly dressing as reality came crashing down.

'You'd better tidy yourself up; your dad's on his way.'

And then the realisation hit. It was a stupid, selfish thing to do.

'We should have used some protection, Scott.' Cassie bit her lip.

He shrugged. 'A bit late now. You wanted it, didn't you?'

'I did, and I'm not sorry, but I'll have to get the contraceptive pill from somewhere before it happens again. I'll have to find a willing doctor.'

'Yeah, I have a mate at uni who might know someone. We'll be right. Don't worry.' He kissed her on her forehead and squeezed her hand to reassure her.

She got up, embarrassed by her own passion, and walked up the hall and into the bathroom. She peered into the mirror. What a fright! Her hair was a mess, her make-up smudged. She buried her face in her hands, astonished that she'd let it happen. She'd completely lost her composure, lost all control over her silly seventeen-year-old body. She had behaved recklessly with total disregard for anything except her own desire. At least no one was hurt; that was the most important thing, but now she had complicated matters considerably. She couldn't go home now. *What if I'm pregnant?* She looked in the mirror to see tears running in dark rivulets down her cheeks.

They heard her father's car pull up.

She talked too much when her dad came in, chattering on about how Scott hadn't been well but the dance was boring anyway so they left early. He wasn't that interested. He'd done his paternal duty, and he was tired and a little irritated. Cassie breathed a sigh of relief that for now there would be no questions.

They rode home in silence.

Thoughts of sex and joy and commitment reared at her. She was ashamed. She was overjoyed at saving Scott's life, but she felt guilty about sleeping with him. How she had let herself be led astray so easily. She was technically a married woman. Officially, she had a husband and a beautiful daughter waiting for her in 2013.

At home, her mum greeted Cassie wearing her dressing gown, holding a cup of Milo. Facing her was harder. She would know. Mothers had that sixth sense.

'Hello darling, so the night finished early? It's only just gone eleven. What happened?' Her mother was a mixture of concern and curiosity.

'Scott started feeling sick, probably something he ate, but it got worse, and the dance was boring anyway, so I drove him home. That's all. He's fine now.' The lie fell so easily, her terse tone implying she really wasn't in the mood for questions.

'Oh dear. And you've only just got your licence. Those roads ...' she trailed off.

'It's okay, Mum.'

'I'm sorry your big night was ruined. Here, drink your Milo.' Her mum passed the mug to her. Cassie took it and had a sip. She tried to read her mother's expression. *Does she know?* Her mother reached down and took Cassie's face in both hands, looking very closely at her daughter. 'Well, perhaps you can tell me all about it tomorrow. Time we all got some sleep.' She hugged Cassie and went off to bed.

CHAPTER 19

2013

When dawn was only a hint on the horizon, Katy and Jeff were in the kitchen sipping coffee together. Neither had slept well.

'We should call the hospitals and police stations, Dad,' Katy said.

'No!' her father snapped at her, 'I don't want to go there yet; it's unthinkable.' In a gentler voice he added, 'What time does the old lady stir? Do you have any idea?'

He needed more detail; he needed to know exactly what the old lady had seen. They had to start somewhere.

'I've no idea, but she was here about half past seven the other morning, so I'm guessing she's an early riser ... maybe we wait until eight to be polite.'

'Good idea. I'll have another look around the bedroom. There has to be some evidence left behind. We just need to find it,' Jeff said, walking over to the sink and discarding his cold coffee.

'And I'm going through her handbag again. Is that snooping? I feel as though I'm invading her privacy.'

Jeff shrugged. 'I wouldn't worry.'

In the bedroom, he opened the door to the cupboard at Cassie's side of the bed. There were a few books, some night cream, pen and paper. Nothing jumped out at him. There were some phone numbers scribbled on a piece of paper by the bed—maybe that was something. He wished he'd paid more attention to his wife when she was packing. When he opened her wardrobe he couldn't tell what was missing and what wasn't. Her drawers told the same story.

***

In the study, Katy upended her mum's bag onto the desk. A lipstick and a compact fell out, a tube of mascara and a pen. It didn't add up.

If her mum was having an affair surely she would take all those things with her?

She sifted through the other bits and pieces: a chewing-gum wrapper, a little yellow card with neat, precise handwriting advertising a scanner for sale, a couple of bobby pins and a foil strip of Panadol tablets. She put the make-up back in the bag and swept the other bits into her cupped hand, then dropped them in the bin. Everything except the card, which she studied for a moment. She carried it back to the kitchen and dropped it into the basket on the table like a discarded train ticket, just in case it might mean something.

Cassie's phone was still on charge on the kitchen bench; maybe she could find the pin and see her mum's messages. She was distracted by the wallet lying next to it. She opened it again. All the important cards were there: two credit cards and a debit card, a few coins and about forty dollars in notes. She kept the cards out.

'Hey, Dad,' she shouted, rifling through the different compartments in the wallet. Can you get into online banking and see what sort of spending has been done in the last week or so? No, wait a minute. Just found something. Here's a receipt. Quick, come and see.'

Her father was there in a flash.

Katy handed it to him. 'It's dated Monday 21st September, just three days ago,' she said. 'I can just make out a business name at the top, though it's faint. Ken's Airport Parking.'

Jeff examined the receipt. 'I'll check the transactions online. You see if you can track down this company, Katy. We're on to something here.'

Their sluggishness from lack of sleep was replaced with a power surge.

Katy found a number for Ken's Airport Parking and called. It was only six in the morning, but what the hell; surely, they'd be open. People would be booking in for early flights.

'Hello, I am calling about Mrs Foster. She left her Mazda there on Monday, I believe?' Katy tested the waters.

'What's the rego?' the voice barked back.

'Just a minute I'll get it for you.'

She put the phone down and raced into the study.

'Dad, Dad ... what's the rego on mum's car?'

Her father shook his head and pointed at the filing cabinet.

Katy slid open the top drawer and plucked at the files. There it was. 'REGISTRATIONS – CARS' She reefed it out and let the contents spill on to the top of the cabinet, flicking madly through the few loose sheets to find the one she wanted. It flew up the hallway with her.

'Sorry to keep you waiting. It's 287-MPR.'

'I was about to hang up, love, haven't got all day.'

'She should be back by now,' Katy said.

'Yeah, she was supposed to pick it up yesterday afternoon. You owe me an extra twenty bucks for overnight parking.'

'Sure, sure. Sorry, we'll pick it up today. Can't give you a time, but we'll come before lunch okay?'

'Yup.' The phone went dead.

Katy marched back to the study where her father sat staring at the screen waiting for the little dots to stop circling as the details were loading. 'I got the parking guy on the phone. Mum did leave her car there on Monday. We can collect it later. He reckons she was supposed to pick it up yesterday. You know what that means don't you?'

He gave her a blank look. 'What? What does it mean?'

Katy frowned. 'It means Mum had every intention of picking the car up, so whatever has stopped her from getting home isn't her choice.'

Her father muttered, 'Maybe she's in trouble.'

All the accounts were displayed on the computer screen. He went straight into the credit card to see if she had spent anything in the days leading up to her disappearance. They found the last transaction, an amount of forty dollars to Compak Parking, Brisbane. 'That has to be it,' her father said. They checked the others while they were there but found nothing more. 'Is it time to go over and see the old lady yet?'

'It's only just gone six-thirty. We should have something to eat first; we missed dinner last night.'

It filled in the time, but they were anxious to talk to Mrs Parker and neither had much of an appetite. Katy put the receipt, the wallet, and the phone in the basket with the card. She still hadn't managed to work out the pin. Chewing absentmindedly on a piece of toast, she remarked to her dad that she hadn't had any luck.

He scratched his chin as though the stubble was irritating him. 'I know it's something to do with birthdays, but I can't remember the combination. Let's get this visit over and we can worry about that later.'

Together they crossed the road to the old lady's house. They waited on the patio as Katy knocked gently. Katy had to knock again before they heard footsteps scuffling behind the closed door.

It opened a crack. Ada Parker squinted into the light, taking a moment to work out who they were.

'Hello again, Mrs Parker. Do you remember me? I'm Katy from across the road, and this is my dad, Jeff Foster.'

'Of course I do.' Ada's face lit up, a big smile creasing her features. 'Come in.'

Katy and her dad stepped into the dim hallway. It smelt musty, and on the wall hung some neatly framed petit point works of old English cottages. They were rather pretty, but by the look of them, they'd been there forever.

Ada led them into her lounge room. It was small with only a floral lounge suite, a coffee table and a bookcase against the far wall which doubled as a stand for the television, filling up the space. They'd all seen better days.

One chair sat askew by the window. A small rectangular table with a few magazines stacked on top stood beside it. The blinds were open, and through them, Katy could glimpse her own house across the street; no doubt this was Mrs Parker's favourite vantage point. It was easy to understand how an old lady on her own might find pleasure in watching the world go by. It couldn't be much of a life, being on your own like this, bones all creaky and old age a lingering bad smell that would not go away.

'Sit down and I'll get you a cup of tea. I noticed your mother's car isn't back yet.'

'Let me help.' Katy followed her into the tiny kitchen where she explained their concerns about her mother to Mrs Parker.

'It's a bit of a mystery you have there, then,' Mrs Parker said as she and Katy returned to the lounge room with three tea cups.

Her father's voice was calm when he spoke. 'We're trying not to worry, but I have to admit it is not like her to go off and leave without telling anyone.'

'I suppose you've tried to call her?'

'Well that's what's so strange; she didn't take her phone with her, or any of her personal items for that matter. Her bag was in a drawer in the office—that room on the left at the front of the house.' Katy pointed towards the window and bit her lip. She'd said too much.

'Is that the room where the strange flash of light appeared, Mrs Parker?' Jeff asked. 'Tell us about it please, anything that might help give us a clue as to her whereabouts.'

Mrs Parker rubbed her hands together in a gleeful gesture. 'Well, I first noticed it a few weeks ago; I was just sitting here staring out of the window lost in my own thoughts when I saw this brilliant bluey-aqua flash of light. I was struck by how beautiful it was; it was almost celestial. No explosion, no bang. I tell you, it was all so quick, I wondered if I'd actually seen anything at all.'

'So what did you do?' her dad asked.

'Nothing. What could I do? I could barely take my eyes off the place waiting for it to happen again. I thought I saw another flash later in the afternoon, but otherwise it all looked perfectly calm and normal.'

'And that's all? Isn't there anything else you can remember?'

'Well, no ... like I said, I doubted myself. Mr Foster, I'm an old lady, living alone. I thought about it all that day, then the next, but decided it must have been my imagination.'

Katy and her dad exchanged perplexed looks before Katy said 'When you came to see me you said there'd been other instances. Can you remember when they were?'

'Well, only twice before that time on Monday morning. So it was that first time I just told you about and then a few days later it happened again. I'll see if I can pin it down to a particular date for you, but I have to think about it. I keep a list of phone calls I make to my daughter next to the phone; I'm getting a bit forgetful, you know, and it helps me keep track of our conversations.'

She got up, ambled over to the phone, and picked up a dog-eared notebook. She put on her reading glasses that dangled from a gold chain around her neck and peered at the page. Looking over at them she said, 'No dates, I'm afraid, but leave it with me. I remember calling my daughter the following morning. I just can't quite remember when that was.'

'Thank you so much,' Katy said. 'Perhaps you can give us a call? I'll write down our phone numbers in your book and you can let one of us know if you think of anything else. Anything at all would be helpful, anything.'

Her father stood up. 'Sorry to disturb you so early.'

Katy scribbled their numbers in Mrs Parker's book and followed him towards the front door. 'Thank you so much.'

Her father already had one foot on the step to the path when Mrs Parker called out. 'Wait a minute. I remember something else. After the second time, I was curious and I went over to see your mum. Remember I mentioned that when I came over on Tuesday morning, Katy?'

They looked at her with renewed interest.

'Not that I know her well, but she said she had been napping, and she was decidedly ill at ease. I implied that I thought there was something going on.' Mrs Parker sank her yellowing teeth into her lower lip and shrugged.

'Thank you ... not sure what it means but thank you anyway. Bye-bye, hope to hear from you soon,' Katy said, turning away and following her father.

Silently, they crossed the street. Once indoors, her father collapsed on the sofa and gave a deep sigh. 'Fat lot of good that was; we don't know much more than we did before.'

'It's all right, Dad, we'll get to the bottom of this, and it's early days. Don't you have to go to work?'

'Technically, yes, but I'd rather be here. I'll let them know I'm not coming in.'

'We have to pick up the car anyway. Come on.'

Katy got her keys and the pair set off for Ken's Airport Parking. The roads were busy; the lights against them, and neither were in particularly good humour when they pulled into the area set aside for customer parking. It was a tiny office, with barely enough room for three people. There was a water cooler in one corner and next to it a single chair and a tiny table with a couple of old magazines on it. On the opposite side, a counter stretched the length of the space. It was unattended. Katy brought her palm down on the bell with more force than she intended. Its loudness startled them both. They waited. Fortunately, it was air-conditioned; it was already getting warm outside. Neither spoke. They could hear the clunk of the minute hand of the wall clock ticking away the seconds, and they waited.

At last, a man in overalls pushed open the glass door behind the counter. He was wiping his hands on his thighs as he came in.

'Sorry to keep you waiting. It's a bit crazy this morning.'

Katy said, 'I rang about my mother's car. It's the blue Mazda, licence plate 287 ...'

'Yup, got the keys here.' He reached under the counter and pulled out Cassie's keys.' So how do you want to pay the extra twenty dollars?'

Her father was already opening his wallet and handed the man his card.

The attendant processed the payment then disappeared, 'Won't be long, I'll get your car.

Moments later the familiar blue Mazda pulled up beside the little office.

'I'll drive Mum's car home,' her father said as he climbed into the driver's seat. 'See you there.' And he drove off.

Half an hour later, Katy arrived home to find Coco pacing about, tail swishing fiercely. She picked the cat up and nuzzled into her fur. 'Sorry, we forgot to feed you.' She lowered the cat back onto the tiles and hurried to give her some breakfast.

There was a strange atmosphere in the house, even though all was peaceful and quiet. She sighed in exasperation. *There has to be an explanation.*

'I'm calling the office; I'll let them know I won't be in for a few days,' her father said as he appeared in the kitchen. 'If she'd had an accident, surely we would have been notified by now.'

'I'm not so sure, Dad. What if she had some sort of seizure or a heart attack? She's not carrying any identification; how would anyone know who to call?'

'Yes, I guess so, but my gut is telling me that's not the case. Maybe I'm just being hopeful.'

Katy picked up her mum's mobile, punching in numbers in all sorts of combinations in the hope of unlocking it.

***

Jeff ambled back to the office desk. He felt drawn to it as if he might fine some clue to the mystery. His eye fell on the basket wedged in between the wall and the cupboard on which the scanner stood.

He plonked into the swivel chair and put the basket on his lap. There was some old printed matter which related to Cassie's work, some pages with notes scribbled on them which he put aside just in case and, curiously he thought, a family snapshot with all the faces cut out. He scratched his head. The photo looked familiar. It had been taken on a family outing about four years ago. Katy was much younger. Funny that Cassie hadn't mentioned it. He kept the scraps and put them with the bits of paper he had collected earlier. He opened the jewellery box again and frowned. He took out the ring and rolled it between his forefinger and his thumb.

'Where have you gone, my love?'

CHAPTER 20

1969

Cassie slid into the room of her childhood, her sanctuary. She switched on the light and looked around, realising that this was the first time she could actually honour her time-travelling self. It defied belief or understanding.

How could she have forgotten all her good intentions, all the promises she made to herself, and betrayed the trust of those she loved most? She needed to go home, back to Jeff and Katy, who would be worried. But leaving young Cassie behind was a cowardly thing to do.

She fell on the bed and coiled herself around her pillow wishing she'd never seen the scanner. She had come here with all the wisdom of a sixty-something parent and, somehow, effortlessly shed all that knowledge and experience to jump into the skin of a naïve and passionate seventeen-year-old. How could she not have foreseen this?

She thought of Jeff, her stable solid Jeff, and she thought of Scott, the young, sexy Scott. Her thoughts were dominated by the latter. All the fervour and excitement of youth was pulsing through her. She felt guilty because she didn't really want to curb it. This energy and excitement of the world opening up was almost more than she could bear. She loved Jeff, and she adored Katy, but what about Cassie? What about her feelings?

She also felt grubby, ashamed of what she'd done. It might have been natural and accepted that a seventeen-year-old in 2013 was no longer a virgin, but unforgiveable to the 1969 version of herself. Her mum had made it very clear that nice girls simply didn't.

Hours later she groped under the pillow for her pyjamas and tiptoed out of the bedroom and across the hall to the bathroom, locking the door behind her. Slowly she stepped out of her beautiful gown. She stroked the delicate fabric lovingly. Its softness enveloped her, flooding her with feelings of nostalgia and love and regret all bundled up in its frangible folds as it slid onto the floor. For an instant she lost all sense of time and space. Sighing back into the present, she picked up the dress and hung it carefully from the hook on the back of the door.

She turned on the hot water tap, then the cold, fluttering her fingers underneath the running water to test its temperature. She discarded her underwear for the second time and stepped into the shower, allowing the warm water to consume her. She ran her hands over her delicious taut, smooth skin. Her heart lifted with the wonder of it. While she'd been overjoyed at saving Scott's life, the passionate sex and the warmth of family, this feeling was different. It was a miracle she was here at all, able to appreciate the wondrous gift of youth. With all the drama that had preceded this moment and the complicated challenges to come, Cassie was grateful for this poisoned chalice.

She towelled herself dry and slipped into her pale-lemon baby-doll pyjamas, glided back into her room and flopped down on the bed again. She looked at her desk. It was cluttered with schoolbooks and make-up. A hair dryer sat precariously on the edge of the dressing table, its hose falling limply beside it like some giant worm attached to the pink plastic hood. It'd been years since she'd even seen one of those. On a whim, she got up, placed the hood on her head and looked in the mirror. Her reflection made her smile.

The surface of the dressing table was scattered with the make-up she had used before going out. Cassie gathered up the bits and pieces and dropped them into the vanity tray in the top drawer. She sat down on the little stool for a long time, drinking in her forgotten world.

Cassie packed the dryer back into its case, climbed into bed, and laid her head on the pillow. It occurred to her that she hadn't properly slept for more than twenty-four hours. Her adrenaline had been pumping so hard, she'd had no time to think of sleep, but now her body was demanding it.

Tomorrow she would face the consequences and deal with the fallout. For now, she was exhausted. Her last thoughts as she closed her eyes were of Jeff and Katy. Scott tried to intrude, but she pushed him away. He was tomorrow's problem.

CHAPTER 21

2013

A lifetime away, Jeff was mulling over the options.

They had very few: a phone they couldn't decipher, the car, her wallet, and a garland of paper cut-outs from an old photo. It had to mean something. Why did she want photos of the three of them unless she was going far away and for a long time? Or was she just being sentimental and wanted them with her on her retreat; he still thought of it as a retreat. *She wouldn't just leave like that, would she?*

He swivelled back and forth in the office chair. He picked up the piece of paper with the phone number on it, but it meant nothing.

A squeal from the kitchen startled him.

'I did it! I did it!' Katy shouted.

His daughter appeared at the office doorway. 'I just kept juggling our initials and our birthdates and finally, voila!' She threw a note at him. 'Here it is.'

He read it and smiled up at his daughter. 'Brilliant. J10k17; you're a genius, child!'

Katy leaned over and showed him the screen of her mother's phone.

Jeff studied it for a moment. 'Lots of missed calls. Have you looked at the messages?'

'Yes, but they're only the ones we left for her.'

They examined the phone together as Katy scrolled back to see if any other numbers stood out. The ones to her aunt and her grandparents were to be expected, but there were a few they did not recognise.

Jeff laid the piece of paper he'd been holding on the desktop and Katy held the phone next to it as they cross checked the numbers dialled against the one written on the paper. One matched. Katy flicked back over the screen as she searched. It showed Cassie had called it several times over the past few weeks.

'Here it is; that number on the paper belongs to a Maria. Do you know who that is Dad? It looks like the first time she called it and I'm guessing it was around the time she was retrenched, I couldn't find any made earlier. There are three or four other numbers I don't recognise. They seem to be one-offs. Perhaps they have to do with work?'

'I'm pretty sure Maria is an old school friend. She told me she ran into her by co-incidence not so long ago and they picked up their friendship. I don't know a lot about her though. The others could be work related. Do you know when they were made exactly?' Jeff ran his hand through his hair while he thought. He pointed to the phone. 'There's a whole bunch of calls she made on the 14th of August.' His eyes brightened. 'You know, I think it was around the time she was retrenched. It was about a week after that when Emma called and said she was bringing the girls up.'

'That sounds about right.' Katy scrolled through the call list again. 'Yes, here's Aunt Emma's number. She called Mum on the 21st, exactly a week later. I'm going to call Maria.' Without hesitation, Katy dialled the number on Cassie's phone and waited.

'Hello, Cassie.' Katy didn't recognise the voice.

'I'm sorry, I'm not Cassie. I'm her daughter, Katy. Am I speaking to Maria?'

'Oh. Hi, Katy, yes. I'm an old friend of Cassie's. We were really close as children, and we've only just reconnected recently. Is everything all right?'

'That's actually why I'm calling. Mum has disappeared.' When Maria didn't respond immediately, Katy continued. 'She left her phone behind and we've just managed to get into it. Your number came up several times in the last couple of months, so I thought you might know something. Sorry if I'm sounding like Inspector Morse here, but we haven't heard from her in three days, and we are worried.'

'Oh, dear, I don't know what to say. I hope she's okay.' Maria continued. 'I haven't spoken to her in a little while, but we were old school buddies and about a year ago we ran into each other at the station and swapped numbers. I wrote down my number for her. We used to be closer than cling film way back then. Nothing happened for about nine months but, when she was retrenched, she must have had time on her hands and I got this call. We picked up the pieces exactly where we had left off. It was lovely. Then her sister came up from Tamworth and she invited me over so my grand-daughter, Hannah, could get to know the girls. Other than that, it's just been chats and coffee really.'

'Did she ever say anything about going away to a retreat?'

'Nope. Not a thing.' Maria's voice was clipped.

'It's just that we suspect something was bothering her, and I was hoping she might have opened up to someone, because we're in the dark here. We're at a loss as to why she would just disappear like that.'

'Have you tried her sister? They're close, aren't they?'

'Yes, we did, but she didn't know anything either.'

'Sorry I can't help. Your mum's no fool; there has to be a reasonable explanation. Have you rung the police?'

'Not yet ... sorry to have bothered you.'

'Could you ask her to call me when she gets back? I'd like to know she's safe.'

'Will do. Thanks again.' The call fell out.

'That was a dead end then, wasn't it, Dad? I'm going to keep looking to see if there are any other numbers we can check.'

They were interrupted by Jeff's phone buzzing in the kitchen. He went to answer it. Katy followed him out and hovered nearby. Listening, her father looked over towards Mrs Parker's house, at the same time gesturing for a pen and notepad on the bench. She pushed it towards him. As he nodded and scribbled, Katy dashed over to the table and picked up the basket containing the assorted paraphernalia they had collected. He was busy jotting things down on the pad.

'She likes a chat, that one,' he said as he pressed end call.

'She's probably lonely ...'

Jeff interrupted her. 'She remembered seeing the Care Nurses arriving at next door's house around 11.00 am, and they always come on a Monday. She'd know I guess.'

'But look dad, I thought of something in the meantime. Ada Parker reckons she first saw the flashing lights on that Monday three weeks ago.' Katy leant over the bench and unhooked the family calendar from the wall, laid it down and flicked back.

'Right, so that means ...' Katy was tracing back the days on the calendar as she spoke.

He cut her off. 'There's more. She saw it again a couple of days later, definitely on a Wednesday; she seemed certain about that. Things went quiet for a while, but then it happened a third time last Monday. So that ties in with what she's already told us.'

'We can work with that.' Katy gave her dad a thumbs up. 'And here's another number we need to check.'

She showed him the yellow card advertising the scanner. He took it and read out the phone number. 'Did she say anything about it to you?'

'No. Anyway, I'm going to ring this and any other numbers I can't identify to see if anything connects. Let's look at the dates ...' she muttered to herself, 'that was Monday, 2nd September, by my reckoning.'

'And that means ...?' Jeff gave her a blank look.

'I don't know yet Dad, but look at this.' She picked up her mum's phone again and opened the calls menu. She held the yellow card in one hand and peered at the list as she slid her thumb over the screen. There it is. 'Looking at this, Mum called about the scanner on Thursday, 29th August. Isn't that the Thursday after Emma left? She glanced over at the calendar again to check. And another thing, wasn't it the following Monday that Mrs Parker said she saw the first explosion?'

'It wasn't an explosion, remember,' her father corrected her.

She looked up at him, wide eyed. 'I think it's all connected, Dad. According to Mrs Parker, that's the first time it happened. It definitely ties in. September second—that's exactly three weeks ago.'

He looked at her blankly, mouth agape. 'So you're saying your mother's disappearance is somehow tied in with the scanner and her sister's visit?' He raised his eyebrows; his pupils shone large and dark. 'I think that's just wishful thinking dear. There is nothing to suggest anything untoward. It happens to be the number of the person who sold her the scanner. End of story.'

Both sat silently at the table, processing the information.

'Are you hungry?' He threw his arm over Katy's shoulder.

'Not really Dad. I'd rather get to the bottom of this.'

'Okay, well let's have a look at this scanner. I wouldn't know if it's a new one or not. I never use it.'

He marched back into the office and looked at it closely.

'Why didn't I think?' He lifted the lid.

There was a photo lying face down on the glass plate and he picked it up, muttering as he did so. Hadn't Cassie said something about scanning some photos for her mum? Turning it over, he was surprised to see an image of a very young Cassie on the arms of an equally young and good-looking young man.

He turned it towards Katy, standing close by, her expression a mixture of curiosity and apprehension.

'Who's that?' she asked.

'I think that's Scott, way before I was on the scene. Apparently he died in a car crash not long after, but it was so many years ago, I can't really remember. She must have been scanning it for your grandmother. Have a look in the shoe box.'

Katy leaned over, pulled the box towards her, and opened the lid. She looked at all the photos, scrambled together. On top lay one of her mother and her aunt Emma, and, spurred on by nostalgia and curiosity, she sifted through the others. There was nothing in them that gave her any clues, nor did she expect to find anything, but it took her mind off the problem for a while.

Jeff picked up the photo from the scanner. 'We'll ask your grandparents about it. Keep it out, just in case it's relevant.'

***

There was a knock on the front door.

'I'll get it,' Katy said.

What she saw when she opened it shocked her.

She couldn't find her voice. Katy stood there frozen, trying to stop her heart beating.

The taller police officer spoke first. 'Sorry, Miss, don't mean to alarm you, but my name is Constable Paul Burwood. We're here because one of your neighbours called the station on Tuesday concerned about what she described as an explosion. We called yesterday but you were out. She claimed the lady of the house had gone missing. Is everything all right?'

No, things were not all right, but for some reason Katy and her dad (who was now standing behind her with his hand on her shoulder), were disinclined to share their misgivings.

'The old lady across the road is a bit of a busy body, everything is fine.' Her father said.

Katy and her dad exchanged looks of solidarity.

'My wife's gone away for a few days. That's all. In fact, we were talking to Mrs Parker this morning, and if she had only waited and talked to us first, there would be no need to involve you at all. Everything's fine. Thank you.'

'Very well then. What about the 'explosion'?' He pointed to his left. 'She said it came from the room at the front over there.'

'Sorry, you can come in if you like; everything is as it should be. No sign of an explosion here. I have no idea what she's on about.'

'Fair enough. Here's my card with our number on it. Let us know if we can be of any help.' He gave them a conspiratorial wink. 'We'll leave it at that then.'

Katy closed the door and hugged Jeff. 'Thanks for taking over, Dad. I got such a fright. My first thought was that Mum had been hurt. I'm tired and jumpy, I guess.' She tossed the card in the basket together with the other stuff.

Jeff made a cup of coffee and produced a couple of biscuits, offering them to Katy, but she still wasn't in the mood for food.

'You know what?' he said. 'I am going to go to the office and put in a couple of hours to take my mind off this, and perhaps you should have a rest or something.'

'No, I'll stay on it. Perhaps we should call the hospitals, and the family should know.'

***

The door slammed and Katy was alone again.

She needed to run, get her blood pumping.

She ran for a long time. The feeling that the scanner and the photos were somehow connected nibbled at her. The clouds hung thick and heavy on the horizon, mirroring her emotions. The humidity rested on her like a wet towel, but she kept running— along the bush track by the creek, weaving through clusters of people meandering along at a leisurely pace. Wistfully, she tried to visualise herself a few weeks earlier and longed for everything to be just as it was. Eventually she came back home, had a shower and lay down. The sun was hanging low in the west. The promise of rain had not come to fruition. She was still as lost as before her run. Her dad wasn't back yet, and the stillness reminded her that she was alone, except for Coco. The cat bounced onto the bed, purring happily, and that's the last thing Katy remembered before falling into an exhausted sleep.

***

When Jeff arrived a few hours later, it was already dark. Opening the front door and walking into the black stillness, he felt the heavy atmosphere. He needed to see Katy's beautiful face, but most of all he needed his whole family back together. Cassie had been missing only one full day, and he didn't quite know how he was going to manage, but he had to stay strong for his family.

He walked past Katy's room to make sure she was there, and was pleased to see her sound asleep, Coco snoozing by her side. He dumped his briefcase on the bed, stripped off his tie and wriggled out of his clothes into shorts and a polo shirt, then headed to the kitchen. He sat down at the table with a cold beer, staring at the notes and everything they had collected, too exhausted to think.

Katy woke up and came and sat down beside him, dazed and disoriented. 'Hi ya. When did you get home?'

'Just now. Sorry I woke you.'

'It's all right.'

'You know what? Tomorrow we can start all this again. Right now we can do nothing.'

He ambled over to the fridge and pulled out the saucepan of soup left from last night. He heated it up on the stove, stirring in silence. Katy pulled out some bowls and spoons, then opened a can of cat food and fed Coco before sitting down. Casual conversation did not sit well; silence suited them better.

Afterwards, in the kitchen, Jeff hugged his daughter. 'We'll get through this, Kitten. You'll see, Mum will suddenly turn up and wonder what all the fuss was about. That doesn't mean we don't do what we can to find her, but we must stay optimistic and focussed. I promise it will all turn out.'

Katy growled. 'It's so frustrating; not knowing.'

He held her cheeks in his strong hands, peering into her eyes, his narrowed in fierce resolve. 'I know, and we'll keep on this, but not tonight. Okay? We need to try to let go for an hour or two to recharge our batteries.'

She nodded, her eyes shining with unshed tears.

CHAPTER 22

1969

Cassie slept more soundly than she had for ages.

It was Sunday morning, the voices and smells wafting from the kitchen roused her just after nine o'clock. She opened her eyes and was momentarily startled.

She was Cassie. Mother and wife. She was also 17-year-old Cassie, a young teenager who beckoned her into the present. She didn't want to get up to deal with any of it, sorely wishing she could go now and pick up life in Holt Street before everything unravelled.

Cassie in 1969 had no idea that women's freedoms were on the way. She was wedged in a judgemental and closeted idea of a woman's worth. In her world, last night was sinful and dirty. In her world, she had let her parents down, not to mention that she completely ignored her own moral code. She remembered her girlhood. That blissful time when sex and boys weren't a factor, when fun was going to the annual show with your parents, or playing outside with your friends.

Cassie was 14 years old when she got her period. She only knew what the girls at school had told her, but the first time was frightening. Her mum had given her a Modess pad and a narrow elastic belt still in its packaging, explained briefly what to do, and left her to it. The next day she had found a copy of *On Becoming a Woman* on her bed. It was not spoken about again. That was the extent of her sex education.

She was regularly reminded, however; especially as she got older, that nice girls didn't have sex before marriage, and if they did, they were in danger of getting a *reputation*. That was the last thing she wanted, and she felt embarrassed and slightly ashamed of her own sexuality. With the late sixties came the age of liberation and it had empowered her somewhat. It was that voice that had screamed in her ear last night as Scott heaved and panted on top of her. It was that voice that had made her cast caution to the wind. But now another voice nagged at her. What had she done? She couldn't possibly disappear leaving her young self with this guilt. She needed to know that Cassie in 1969 could be at peace.

First things first, she had to sort out some protection. But the subject was taboo.

And then there was Scott—gorgeous, handsome Scott. She had given him his life back, but how was he going to feel when she left? She cringed. Her heart melted again. The last thing she wanted to do was break his. Why had she been so blindly obsessed with trying to fix everything? She'd followed the yellow brick road and it had turned to gravel; she was sliding out of control.

By her calculations, she had two days to set this right, two days to settle young Cassie into a safe place in her soul and send Scott to his new destiny. After that, Jeff and Katy would start to get worried.

How was she going to pull this off? Of course, it was going to influence everything. The walls closed in, the confusion in her head crackled, over and over, cursing her stupidity. That stupid machine. She lay there for a long time, vacillating between fierce determinations and whimpering wistfulness.

There was a soft knock on the door.

'Cassie, Cassie ... you awake.'

It was Emma. Cassie rubbed her eyes and squeezed her head tightly in both hands.

'Yeah. I'm awake. What do you want?' she groaned.

The door opened a crack and Cassie felt a surge of love for her young sibling. At fourteen Emma was still gangly, but her short pixie-crop hair highlighted her beautiful cheekbones and she was so full of vibrant teenage innocence it made Cassie's heart burst.

Emma sidled up to the bed and sat beside her, patting her sister playfully on the hip as Cassie rolled over to face her.

'So, how was last night then? I'll bet you had the best time.' Emma said, eyes shining with enthusiasm. 'Scott's cute.'

'Yeah, he is, but the idiot had a few drinks on the sly, so we had to come home early.' Cassie said without enthusiasm.

She tried to find the words. She was elated Scott had been spared a horrible death, but she wasn't proud of her loss of control afterwards. Her wiser, older psyche understood that nothing was black and white—more of a blurred grey mess of ambivalence. How could she possibly explain that to her young sibling?

Emma's big round eyes examined Cassie.

She was here; it was real. The only way to get through it was to live it; it was vital to everyone, and that meant wading through this swamp of heavy thoughts and recriminations and getting on with it.

She smiled at Emma.

'Scott's lovely, I adore him, but we got a bit carried away when we were necking last night.' She pulled the sheet up over her head and hid under it.

Emma reefed it down again and peered at Cassie.

'What do you mean ... you didn't go all the way did you?'

'Welllllll ...'

'Ohhhh Cassie!'

'I feel so guilty this morning I don't even want to face Mum. Whatever you do, for heaven's sake don't tell her. I'm so sorry now.'

Emma bit her lip and reached out to touch Cassie on the shoulder. 'But you're nearly eighteen. Lots of girls do it at eighteen, you just have to make sure you don't get pregnant,' she said.

Both knew this was a big deal. In their secret conversations they had discussed sex, but with their limited experience it was pretty much fantasy and supposition.

'All I know is that I feel awful now. It wasn't worth it.'

Emma leaned over and hugged her sister, and Cassie allowed herself to relax deeply into its sweet comfort. They clung together. Cassie wanted to stay there forever in this safe hug, free of judgement or recrimination. It was a colossal task accommodating two personas. There was this constant feeling of being ripped apart, being drawn into the present; and at the same time clinging to a future she knew and trusted.

'Mum said I could go to the pool with Jess today, and her dad is picking us up at ten o'clock. You can come if you like,' Emma said.

'I don't think so.' Cassie grimaced. 'I'd rather stay here and wallow. Besides, you don't want your big sister hanging around. Just behave yourself, okay?'

Emma jumped up and skipped back to her room, leaving Cassie with her thoughts.

***

Later, she went in search of her mum, who was in the kitchen chopping vegetables for Sunday lunch.

'Hello sleepy head. How are you feeling?' Her mother's voice was gentle.

'It wasn't that late.' There was a hint of defensiveness in Cassie's reply.

'Do you want to tell me how the night was? You looked so beautiful. I'd love to hear all about it.'

Cassie was taken aback; this was not what she expected. She assumed her mum would see right through her and that this morning would be a harrowing game of deceit and guilt. She was guilty, no doubt, and maybe a bit deceitful by omission, but she was so relieved, she happily diverted her attention to entertaining her mother. Later, she would have to talk to Scott and deal with her bigger problem.

Being in her youthful skin for almost a day now, Cassie had already morphed into some sort of normality, ever mindful of her leviathan purpose. She lovingly embraced pieces of her past. She adored her agile, perfect body, revelled in its lithe, painless form. Yet, coexisting in this framework, like some Russian doll, was her other family, her future family. It was not something to dwell on; it was unnerving.

After breakfast, she told her mum she was going to see Maria. They could catch up on some serious gossip. Walking up the road to her friend's place, she mused that Maria's future had not been as blessed as her own. When she got there, the squeaking of the gate alerted her arrival and Maria appeared on the porch.

'What happened to you last night? How come you went home so early?'

Cassie grunted and rolled her eyes. 'Scott brought alcohol of all things, and I was afraid of getting caught, so we left early.'

'Well, you didn't miss much, though it got a bit exciting towards the end when one of the boys started flirting with Annabelle, the new girl. His girlfriend was really cheesed off. She stormed out and he went racing after her. They didn't come back in. I can't wait to find out what happened. That's about all. Turned out it was a bit dull in the end.'

They sat together on the steps as Cassie babbled about Scott but stopped short of telling her friend they had had sex. There was a limit to what Cassie was prepared to share.

'So when are you going out again?'

'I don't know,' Cassie said. She hadn't really thought about specifics, she just knew she would have to talk to him soon. 'I hope he calls this afternoon,' she prattled on.

'He will.' Maria patted her friend on the shoulder. 'So what do you want to do?'

Without waiting for a reply, she jumped up. 'I know, my brother bought me the new Bob Dylan album. Do you want to hear it? He gave me his old record player and it's in my room.'

'Fabulous.'

Cassie got up and followed Maria through the hallway.

In Maria's room, Cassie felt another wave of nostalgia. How often had they sat here gossiping and sharing their favourite things? They were such beautiful, innocent memories. For a moment she was in limbo again, caught in that vacuum between the past and the present.

Maria pointed over at the desk to a large pile of LPs. On the top was Bob Dylan's 'Nashville Skyline'. Cassie picked it up and handed it to her friend standing by the stereo. Maria slid the record out of its plastic sleeve and placed it on the turntable. Then she switched on the record player. Bending over, tongue out in careful concentration, she lifted the tone arm and gently lowered it, making sure to get it exactly right.

'My brother tells me this is very delicate and I have to be careful. He goes ape when I get it wrong.'

Bob Dylan crackled into life.

His dulcet tones permeated the room and the girls smiled at each other in shared pleasure. Maria picked up the pile of LPs lying on the desk and plonked them on the shaggy rug. They both flopped down, cross-legged and content.

Cassie immersed herself in the moment. School was finished for the year and on Monday, she was due to start a new job at the local shop. It was only a few hours each day, but it would mean some pocket money while waiting on her senior results. She was surprised she remembered all these details, but somehow the pieces just seemed to fall into place.

Walking home alone with the day fading fast, the plaguing thoughts returned.

She quickened her pace, her footfall became more determined. She had come here on this quest and she couldn't afford to panic. She would call Scott when she got home, organise a doctor's appointment as soon as she could and get back to Holt Street and the people she loved.

So successfully had she talked herself into a stronger frame of mind that she almost sashayed into the kitchen when she got home, spurred on by renewed spirit and boldness.

'I'm home, Mum; I'm going to my room.'

Her mother was in the living room reading the *Woman's Weekly*. Cassie walked past quietly, not wanting to be caught up in a conversation, and called over her shoulder as she went.

Her mum didn't look up. 'Did you have a nice time, dear?' and left that hanging in the air, totally engrossed in some article.

Cassie stopped just outside the kitchen door, picked up the phone and dialled Scott's number. She tapped the wall with her index finger, listening intently to it ringing at the other end. Someone answered. It wasn't Scott.

'Hello, it's Cassie here. Is Scott there?'

'Nah, not sure where he is, but I'll let him know you called.'

CHAPTER 23

2013

Katy sipped her tea. Her dad sat opposite, picking at the crumbs on his plate.

'I don't understand why she didn't leave a note. All this cloak and dagger stuff is doing my head in,' Jeff exclaimed.

'At least we know she didn't plan to stay away, Dad; that's encouraging. I'm going to ring those numbers first and see if that shines a light on anything. I can't bear to start calling hospitals.' Katy said. 'I keep telling myself if something terrible had happened we would know by now.'

Jeff pulled over the basket with the stuff they'd collected. He played with the phone, rifled through the bits of paper, and got up and went off to the bedroom. A minute later, her father came back. 'What day was it that I came home and found Mum passed out in the office?' His brow wrinkled and he squinted as he tried to remember. 'I recall I had a work meeting and I was late home. That should be in my diary.'

He disappeared again and came back with his laptop. Scrolling through the last month's entries, he examined the screen. 'Here it is,' he said. 'September 2nd. I had a meeting at 6.00 pm which meant I was home late. I remember that day. It's the same day Cassie fainted and I found her on the floor.'

'It was about then she became withdrawn,' Katy added.

'You're right. She wasn't herself after that.'

'All this has to be connected, Dad. I still feel uneasy about that scanner.' Katy was already dialling. She looked over at her father. 'Scanner lady.' She flicked a pen back and forth and stamped out a tattoo with her feet. She brightened when the number answered.

'Hello ... Anastasia Pendle speaking.'

'H-h-hello,' Katy blundered, 'my name is Katy Foster. Did you sell my mother a scanner?' Fatigue and worry gave her voice an edge.

'Maybe I did, dear.'

'Is there anything we should know about it? Mum's gone missing and we think that scanner has something to do with it.' She stopped abruptly. It sounded stupid. 'I'm sorry.' She ended the call.

Meanwhile, her father was on the phone to Emma. His face was serious. When he finished, he sat down again, massaging his eyes with his thumb and forefinger, head bowed, as if trying to hide.

He'd done it. Now it was concrete—set in stone. Cassie was missing. Katy could see that telling Emma had been hard for him.

'She offered to come up, but I said there wasn't much point right now and tried to reassure her. She's agreed not to tell Gran and Pops just yet, and I guess she needs time to process things herself. '

Katy paced wildly, a spinning top of energy looking for focus, back and forth, back and forth across the room. Her voice jumped up to a crescendo, her arms flailed wildly as she poured out her anguish.

Her father grabbed her firmly by the shoulders. 'Calm down. We'll get through this.'

She threw herself at him with such force he almost lost his balance, but he wrapped her tightly in his arms. Her father spoke calmly. 'We need to control ourselves, for your mother's sake, otherwise we can accomplish nothing.'

Katy broke down, pushing back sobs of frustration. Once she'd regained control, she slumped into a chair, her eyes puffy, her cheeks shiny and swollen. She stretched her neck and rolled her head, eyes closed.

Her dad disappeared for a few minutes, then returned and placed a steaming cup of coffee in her hand.

'I think I'm all right now, Dad. I'm sorry.'

He reached across the table and laid his hand over hers, weathered fingers like bands of hope over her pale, creamy skin.

Katy's phone rang. She took a deep breath and answered it in a dull monotone.

'Hi, Aunty.' She braced herself, forcing back the sob pushing at her chest. 'I am so sorry; I'm out of my mind with worry.'

'Do you want me to come up?' Emma's tone was soothing.

'There is nothing you can do. Uncle Rod and the girls need you there. But maybe you have some ideas?'

'No. But I had a thought, and it might mean something. Your father said Cassie has been out of sorts for a while, and he traced it back to when she fainted. When I was up, we went and had a massage and a reading with a spirit medium on the Saturday before the picnic. Anyway, Cassie was quite shaken by the experience; the psychic brought up a painful incident. Then a few days after I got back here, she called to say the old woman who did the reading was the same person who sold her the scanner. It distressed her. Could they be connected?'

Katy felt a hint of satisfaction as this random loose thread found a hold. Her intuition was right. She hadn't proved it yet, but this fitted. This felt right. 'Yes, yes ...' she squealed into the phone. 'I've had a feeling that your visit and the scanner were somehow connected. 'Oh, yes, this is definitely good news. Thank you. It does help. I'll call you back.'

'You have to call the police, Katy ... and the hospitals. Don't put it off, please.' Emma paused, but Katy was silent. 'And Maria. Have you spoken to her friend Maria? From what your mum told me they spent a bit of time together; perhaps she knows something.'

'We tried, but she couldn't tell us anything.'

'Well perhaps you should give her another go, and tell her what I just told you.'

'Yes, I'll do that. Anything at all to make some progress. It's not like Mum, Aunt Emma; she wouldn't pack up and leave us like that. Did Dad tell you she went without taking her phone or her bag? That's not something Mum would do, is it?'

'Oh, darling, I wish I could be up there with you. Are you sure you don't want me to come up?'

'No, two of us stressing here is enough. We'll keep you up to date with any developments. Just knowing you are there for us means a lot. I feel a bit better.'

'Stay strong. Bye, bye darling,' Emma said.

The minute the call ended, Katy redialled the number on the yellow card.

'Hello, Anastasia Pendle speaking.'

'I called before; I think you sold my mother a scanner.'

'I wondered when you'd call back.' Her tone was terse.

'I'm sorry I hung up on you but I felt so stupid ... feel so stupid.' She corrected herself. 'This probably sounds ridiculous, but that's my mother, the lady who bought the scanner off you. I'm assuming it was you. It was, wasn't it?' Katy garbled on. 'She's missing.'

'I think so. She replied to an advertisement I put on the notice board at the shopping centre.'

More composed, Katy went on, 'We found a yellow card with your number on it. It sounds crazy, but she's disappeared, and we think it's something to do with the scanner.'

The silence was ominous.

'Hello, hello ... are you there, Mrs. Pendle?'

'Yes I am, dear. What do you want me to do? I'm afraid that what happens in your family is none of my business, and if your mum hasn't told you what's going on, it's possibly because she doesn't want you to know. I'm not prepared to betray anyone's confidence.'

'So you agree. There is something going on then?'

The universe hummed with dead air.

'Hello, hello, are you there?' Katy was getting impatient.

'I'm sorry, dear; I really can't talk about this.'

The screen dimmed and the call was gone. Katy dropped back in the chair in amazement. What was that all about? Was this woman being deliberately obtuse?

She wasn't going to let this go.

Jeff came out of the bedroom, clean-shaven, ready for work.

'I just have to go in to check on a few things.'

Katy blathered on about the weird call she'd just had. He didn't react. His features were drawn and tense; too deep in thought to respond.

She watched him for a while as he pushed bits of paper aside; impatient, focussed on whatever it was that was churning him up. He dashed here and there looking for something, reefing up scatter cushions, shoving plates out of the way

Then, a sudden outburst. 'Where are my bloody keys? I have to get to the office, I have stuff to do. And there's nothing here, is there?' His shoulders slumped. 'She's gone. Cassie's gone.'

Katy ran over to her dad. It was her turn to mollify him.

'We'll find her. We will. We haven't had any calls from the hospital or the police. That's got to be good.'

He cried. 'Well, we wouldn't, would we? All her bloody identification is right here. She could be lying dead somewhere, or unconscious in some medical ward. How would we know?'

'I need you, Dad. Please, please. You said yourself, we need to stay cool-headed, or we'll accomplish nothing.'

Katy felt her throat tighten. She'd never seen her dad like this. If he lost control, she'd never manage. A hiatus of silence hung in the air.

He peered at her with haunted eyes. His skin shone with sweat, his breaths burning from him like a cornered dragon.

'D-don't do this. Don't lose it, please Dad.'

He stared at her.

At last, he dropped his chin and closed his eyes. His shoulders heaved as he struggled to find the strength she so needed from him.

A minute went by before he looked up and spoke.

'I'm sorry. You're absolutely right. I'm just worried. We have nothing.'

'But we have, Dad, we have. I just got off the phone to that scanner person and I'm sure she's not telling me all she knows. She was very cagey when I asked her about it. I'm sure she has something to do with Mum's disappearance.'

'What sort of fairy dust are you sprinkling around exactly to get Cassie back? I don't think so.' Her father's words burned.

'Okay. You go off to work for a few hours, and I'll call all the hospitals and police stations to see if they have picked up anyone matching Mum's description.' She was being patronising and she knew it, but she had to placate him somehow.' She wasn't going to get anywhere this way.

Her dad shrugged. 'Help me find my keys, and I'll get away from all this for a while.'

'Done.' Katy took off and started searching.

His features had settled; the fire had left his eyes. Much to Katy's relief, he was in control again.

Five minutes later, he walked out of the study dangling them on his forefinger.

She picked up his laptop and handed it to him, reached out and gave him a hug.

'Call me if you hear anything,' he said on his way out. 'And don't waste any more time on that scanner nonsense, please.'

The house was suddenly dead quiet. Katy ran her fingers through her hair in frustration. She had no choice but to start making phone calls.

CHAPTER 24

1969

It was after nine and still Scott hadn't called back. Cassie lay willing the bell to break the silence. She had to talk to him. She had been replaying their lovemaking, consumed by the exquisite but disastrous liaison. One minute, feelings of bliss washed over her in self-indulgent pleasure, the next she fell into a dark hole of self-recrimination. She'd almost given up when the hallway phone trilled. She leapt off the bed so fast she stumbled getting to the door just in time to see her dad pick up the handset.

'Bit late at night to be calling, don't you think, son?'

He didn't look happy when he passed the phone to his daughter. 'Keep it short,' he mouthed as he turned and went back to his television.

'Scott. I'm so glad you called. I feel awful about what happened ... no, no I meant it was lovely, but I hadn't wanted for things to go so far.'

'It was amazing,' Scott murmured. The silence was a symphony between them.

'Yes it was,' she said at last. 'It was lovely, but it mustn't happen again, Scott. We had no protection. I'm due in about a week's time, and I'm telling myself I'm safe, but I'm worried.'

'You'll be right.' He was almost dismissive.

'We don't know that, do we? I'll spend the next week worrying and waiting for my period.' She was whispering too loudly. 'Please ask your mates tomorrow if they know a doctor who'll prescribe the pill. Please, Scott,' she pleaded.

'I will.' He was suddenly brusque. 'I'll call when I can.'

'I'm starting my new job in the morning, but I'll be home about five. Bye.'

She leaned against the wall for a while. *If it was so good, why am I feeling so rotten right now?*

She said goodnight to her father, apologised for the interruption, and headed back to her room. Her mother was just coming out of the shower, her white chenille dressing gown swirling around her, hair wrapped up in a towel like a giant meringue.

She hugged Cassie as she came by. 'Night night, love. You okay?'

'Yeah, Mum, I'm fine; just a bit tired.'

Cassie peeked into Emma's room. Her sister lay sound asleep, hugging her pillow. She noticed a bold white strip of skin on her shoulder where the strap of her swimsuit must have been. She grimaced. Sunburn.

Alone in her room, she had to fight not to let her thoughts become melancholy. She had tomorrow to sort things out, but even in her most optimistic mood, she knew that was impossible. Her family would be worried. Why hadn't she told them? Why had she not written them a note? Cassie crawled into bed and wrapped herself into a tight cocoon of self-pity until at last she fell into an exhausted sleep.

When her mother rapped on the door at 8.00 am, it took her a while to stir and remember what day it was. The job—she was going to be a shop assistant today. It was only a tiny shop, but she felt a small rush of pride. She wanted to make a good impression on her first day.

She rummaged through her wardrobe and pulled out a navy shift with a little white Mary Quant collar and hoped it wasn't too short. She threw it on the bed, grabbed some underwear, and tiptoed into the shower. Afterwards, she pulled her hair in a ponytail, put on her white sandals and was ready to face the world.

'Morning love. You look pretty. I'm sure Mr Fieldham will be kind; there's a bit to learn. Don't forget your manners,' her mum fussed.

'How hard can it be serving people? I think it'll be interesting.'

'You'll be right, love, just as long as you are polite and cheerful. I'm sure it will go swimmingly,' her father added.

Later, in the warm sunshine, she revelled in the quiet, simple world of 1969. No mobile towers, ordinary-looking houses; kids playing in front yards. Cassie lapped up the atmosphere with unbridled greed. She was young and fit ... except ... then dismal deliberations would ruin the moment again.

She mused and fretted all the four blocks to the shop.

It was a small timber building with a bullnosed, corrugated iron roof jutting over the footpath. Over the door was the familiar Bushells Tea sign. Mr Fieldham was somewhat of a local icon, but these days his little business was very quiet. Not far away, a new Four Square store had opened, and customers preferred the concept of self-service, choosing their own products from the well-stocked shelves in bright new surroundings.

Cassie had been going to Fieldham's since she was a little girl. She didn't much care if it was busy or not; he was going to pay her ten dollars a day and she was excited about earning a wage of her own.

Mr Fieldham was a kindly, gentle man with unruly salt and pepper hair, and big, bushy grey eyebrows framing his weary eyes. She was rather fond of him.

He showed her where everything was, explaining this and that as he went around. Then he retreated to the little storeroom at the back and settled into an old swivel chair to sort out some paperwork.

Cassie enjoyed serving people. She loved whipping up a milkshake or counting out lollies for the little children who came in, but she wasn't fussed on diving into the great cylindrical tubs of ice cream that was rock hard and unforgiving to her contrary scoop. Handling the cash made her a little bit nervous, but the old man helped her until she got the hang of working the register. When it was quiet, her time was taken up filling bags of lollies, restocking empty shelves in the storeroom, or cleaning. The day flew by.

She was home just after four-thirty, tired but satisfied. Her mum made her a cup of Milo and asked her about her day. It was easy chatting about such inconsequential stuff, the big things tucked away for the time being.

Afterwards she had a shower, making a mental note that tomorrow she would wear more suitable clothes. It was very dusty in the storeroom and handling groceries and produce all day was quite filthy work. Washing off the day's grime, she cupped her hands under the shower; the warm stream of water was comforting. Her breasts were firm, her belly and waist trim and taut. No cellulite; no loose skin folding in undulating waves; the purity and perfection still sent a shiver of delight up her spine. Cassie tried to recall her aging body that had been left behind and couldn't. Her ponderings about the future were like some distant memory of a vacation—a slightly blurred image of another lifetime. Then Jeff and Katy came into focus and a melancholy overtook her. If only she could explain to them that she needed to tie up some very loose and fraying ends before she could leave. The tap clunked off, and she reached out and grabbed a towel, patted herself dry, then wrapped it around her body and trotted into her bedroom.

The phone rang. She raced out to get it, anticipating good news from Scott.

'Hi Scott, how are you? Thanks for calling. So what did you find out?'

'Well, nothing much. It turns out it was mostly hearsay. I did manage to get the name of one doctor though. She practices on the other side of town but I could drive you there. There were a couple of other names, but I couldn't get any details.

'Good grief, I need to see someone soon, and I can't think of anyone. Anyway, give me her name and I'm sure there'll be a bus I can catch if you can't drive me.'

He hesitated. 'No, I'll come. Have you got a pencil and paper?'

'Just a sec ...'

Cassie left the phone dangling and returned in a flash, clutching a pen and pad. 'Okay. What is it?'

'It's Doctor Clarke and her number is 92 0012.'

'Thank you,' she said. 'I'll give her a call tomorrow morning and let you know when I can get an appointment.

'Bye.' The line went dead, and Cassie stood there still holding the phone, suffocated by her secrets, swaddled in her towel like a helpless infant.

CHAPTER 25

The following morning Cassie scrambled out of bed and hurried through her routine, eager to get to work. It was a great diversion.

Today she should be sitting at home with Jeff and Katy, with a clean slate and a clean conscience, savouring a sweet reunion.

It wasn't going to happen.

Thanks to her own impetuous weak-mindedness, she was stuck here. It was a bitter pill to swallow; but swallow it she had to. She was determined to make the best of it.

She tucked Doctor Clarke's number into her wallet, together with some loose change. She'd call first thing.

There was a telephone box not far from Mr Fieldham's shop. On the way, she rehearsed what she would say to the receptionist. By the time she reached it, she was shaking. She pulled the door shut behind her, took some twenty cent pieces from her purse, and picked up the phone. She listened for the dial tone, inserted her money, and waited for someone to answer. It rang out. She cursed, but then realised it was only 8.00 am; it was probably too early. She would have to try again at lunchtime.

Her second day in the shop was easier. She could remember where most things were, and she was getting used to the till and reading the scales. The morning dissolved in a haze of activity, and it was one o'clock before she could go on lunch break. Cassie dashed out to the phone box and tried again.

This time a woman answered. She quickly pressed button A. The coins clattered through the system, and the call was connected.

'Doctor Clarke's surgery. Good afternoon. Tricia speaking.'

'H-h-h-hello, my name is Cassie Truscott and I need to make an appointment to see Doctor Clarke as soon as possible.' Her voice was shaky.

'I'm afraid the only time she has available in the next few days is Thursday afternoon at two o'clock.'

'All right,' Cassie whispered.

'We'll see you then.' The receptionist ended the call.

Well, that's just ducky. After work, she approached Mr Fieldham in the back room. He sat hunched over some papers, shoulders rounded, deep in concentration. She knocked on the wall to gain his attention.

'Mr. Fieldham?'

'Yes, Cassie, is anything wrong?'

'Oh, no, not really, but I have a doctor's appointment on Thursday at 2.00 pm. It's a fair drive, so I was wondering if I could come in early so I can leave at one, or I can make it up another time if that suits better ...' she trailed off.

'That's fine; these things happen, but perhaps when it gets busy closer to Christmas, I'll get you to come in on Saturdays.

'Thank you so much. I am sorry to ask.'

'I understand.' His face crinkled into a benevolent smile. 'Now, you go on home to your family; thanks for your efforts today, you're picking things up very quickly, it's a big help.' He gestured towards the door and turned back to the papers lying on the desk.

The first chance she got, she rang Scott.

As soon as he answered, she blurted out. 'The only appointment I could get is on Thursday at two; can you take me?'

'Yeah, no worries, dad won't mind. I can pick you up from work. It's about half an hour's drive if there's not too much traffic. What time do you finish?'

'Mr Fieldham said I can go at one.'

'Okay, see you then.'

'Thank you, Scott.'

He responded with a non-committal 'Hmmm.'

On Thursday afternoon, she excused herself and left. Mr Fieldham didn't seem to mind, but she felt guilty just the same.

Scott was only a few minutes late, and by ten to two, they pulled up outside the surgery. Scott waited in the car and she went in alone and spoke to the receptionist then sat down. She felt dirty and uncomfortable. Common sense told her this was no big deal but the young girl in her felt the eyes of the other patients resting on her in mute accusation. She wanted to run.

'Cassie Truscott?' A crisp voice reverberated in the small room.

Cassie ambled towards the door being held open for her, not daring to look at anything but the floor.

A middle-aged, no nonsense woman with grey hair cropped neatly to frame her sharp features, sat in a big leather chair at the desk. Her thin, pink lips curved into a smile as she looked kindly at Cassie through ebony eyes. Cassie felt a little easier.

'What can I do for you, young lady?'

Cassie gaped. Nothing would come out. It was awkward; this situation was awkward. How does one go about asking for the pill?

'W-w-well, I accidentally had sex last Saturday night and I'm scared I might be pregnant. I want the pill. My period is due this coming weekend, I think.' The words fell out in a torrent.

The doctor arched one eyebrow quizzically. 'Let's just examine you first. When was your last period?'

This flipped out easily; she had recounted the days to herself oodles of times.

'All right, so your last period was on the eighth, correct?'

'I think so, I'm never sure of the exact date. I usually spot a day or two before so I don't know whether to count that as day one or not, but I think it's due this coming weekend.'

'Are you in a relationship with this boy?'

Relationship, relationship. Who said anything about a relationship, Cassie thought?

'He's my boyfriend.'

'All right, this is the drill. I am risking my licence doing this, but I firmly believe you young girls need to be aware of protection early. Do you understand? You must not tell anyone. And by anyone, I mean, not your girlfriends, not your parents, not anyone. Do you hear?'

Cassie nodded.

'This is what I am going to do. Given what you have told me, your period should be here by Sunday. If not, I want you to take one of these pills on Sunday night and the next one the following morning. She indicated a tiny foil strip she was holding between her thumb and forefinger. All being well, this will bring on a normal period and you can start taking the oral contraceptive I'm going to give you now.' She took a small, rectangular packet from the top drawer of her desk and opened it, pulled out a strip of tablets, and ran a knobbly finger along a pink section of the silver foil, indicating the days to take the pill. 'It's most important you don't miss a single day. I'll give you a prescription for six month's supply before you go.'

She winked at Cassie, patted and stroked her on the arm—a show of compassion and support which gave Cassie a modicum of comfort.

The doctor got up and pulled the privacy curtain around the couch. 'Now hop up for me and I'll give you a quick examination, just to make sure all is well.'

Cassie did as she was told, shivering in the cool of the air conditioning.

The doctor put on a pair of sterile gloves in a much-practised, smooth manner.

It was horrible; this violation of her privacy, and Cassie clenched her teeth not to shout in protest.

At last, it was over.

'You can get dressed again now,' the doctor said as she pushed the curtain aside and went back to her desk.

'Your cervix feels quite soft but that's probably because your period is due, but should you not have a bleed in the next fortnight, I want you to come back. Tell the receptionist who you are and the reason you are calling, and she'll squeeze you in somewhere.'

Scratching away at a prescription pad, the doctor went on.

'Just to recap, take the two pills I gave you, one on Sunday night and one the next morning. This should bring on your period and then you can start the contraceptive pill as I explained. And here's that script for a six-month's supply for the future.' She handed her the prescription and continued. 'If it doesn't, you need to come and see me again, understood? But give it at least a couple of weeks. And remember; don't tell anyone, not even your closest friend, is that clear?'

Cassie, red faced and silent, nodded, then walked out, paid the receptionist, and hurried from the surgery clutching her salvation.

Everything had to be all right.

CHAPTER 26

2013

Katy doodled on the pad. She sat looking at her phone unable to start making the calls she knew she had to make. Coco meandered about her legs, occasionally rubbing herself against them, mewing softly for attention.

'You miss her too, don't you, darling.' Katy leant over, heaved the cat onto her lap, and stroked her as she contemplated the situation. The birds chortling outside were a comforting background to her worries. She needed one optimistic thought, one encouraging piece of information, and she wasn't going to get that by sitting on her butt doing nothing. Doggedness at last kicked in. With a pat on the head, and a gentle shove, Coco was back on the floor.

She started with the hospitals. *Her mother could be dead.* The thought fluttered, but was unthinkable. Katy refused to give it wings.

Beginning with the major hospitals, she worked her way through the list, making notes as she did so. Mostly the answer was the same: 'No unidentified women had been admitted since Monday'. One sounded possible. Katy's heart sank until she was told it was a young woman who collapsed while jogging in the park. It took her a couple of hours to contact them all, and it was fruitless, which was oddly comforting. She sent a text to her dad, hoping it would lift his spirits as well.

The police. Should she call the police? Katy thought about it and considered the ramifications. Once the police were involved, it would set up a string of enquiries and actions they had no control over and that scared her. Then, tossing vacillation aside, she elected to call the officer who had come to the door before; he seemed nice and might understand she didn't want to make a formal statement. She found the card and dialled the number.

'Hello, Ashgrove Police. Constable Monk speaking.'

'Oh, oh, hello. It's Katy Foster here, I was hoping to speak to Constable Burwood. We've spoken before.'

'I'm afraid he's not on duty until three. Can I give him a message?'

'He called on us yesterday; I just thought it might be easier to talk to him.'

'I take it this is not an emergency.'

'Oh. No. No. No. Don't worry, I'll call back later.' She was getting flustered. 'No, I mean, yes, it's fine, I'll catch him later.'

The minute the call ended, Katy realised she hadn't really wanted to call the police at all. The voice in her head was more powerful. She wanted to give it her full attention, run with the signals it was sending her—that the answer lay close by. There was more to this than the police would understand, and she wanted to try herself first. She considered what they already knew, inspired by the hunch that the solution would reveal itself in time. Mum was not dead. That was at the root of her conviction; she felt it in her bones.

But where was she? Of course she could call Maria again. She should do that. *What am I afraid of? That it might lead to nothing?* While her mum's friend hadn't been exactly cold over the phone, neither had she seemed warm and friendly. There was something about Maria's manner that was troubling. That thought gathered strength; it grew from a small seed of disquiet that she hadn't recognised at the time, to a ripened kernel of misgiving.

Maria had been evasive. That was it. She was vague; she hadn't elaborated nor shown any desire to get involved. It was worth another call. Maria knew more than she was willing to admit.

Shivering against the unpleasant realisation, she stood up, debating whether she should call now to get it over with or procrastinate.

Procrastination won. She picked up her mother's phone again and started to call the other numbers that seemed unfamiliar. It didn't take too long. Most were perfectly innocent; none alerted her to anything untoward.

Only the niggling, nagging conviction that Maria could help stayed uppermost in her thoughts.

'Bahhha.' She exclaimed aloud. Fatigue, worry and frustration all swirled around in relentless circles.

Katy changed, picked up her satchel and flicked through her timetable to see if she had any lectures in the afternoon, but there was nothing pressing. On Monday she had an exam and another on

Tuesday, but that was it for the year. She decided to trot off to the library in the hope that the change of environment might be more conducive to getting a bit of study done.

When she got back home, her dad was waiting for her.

'Where the hell have you been?' He was tired and angry.

'I needed to get away from all this.' She swept one arm around the room, pushing past him to get to her bedroom.

'So did you find anything?' he called after her.

'No, I would have rung if I had.'

Katy closed the door to the bedroom. She threw herself on the bed, buried her head into her pillow, and surrendered to her tears. Melancholy and exhaustion conspired to tranquillise and before long, Katy drifted off to sleep.

She was woken by a soft knock on the door.

'I'm sorry, love. Come out; I've made you some dinner.'

She groaned. 'Coming.'

When she opened the door, he was waiting, arms outstretched.

'It's all right, Dad. Let's just eat.'

She gave him a peck on the cheek as she walked past, went to the bathroom to wash her face, and joined him a short time later, slightly refreshed.

They sat down together, and Katy picked at the bowl of pasta her dad had made. For a while, they just sat staring into space, saying nothing. They had run out of conversation, having nothing new to add to the enormous, empty sphere of not knowing that surrounded them.

At last he spoke. 'Maybe tomorrow we should go to the police.'

'I'll give Maria another try. I've got a feeling she might be able to tell us more,' Katy said.

Her father shrugged. 'Anyway, we can't put off calling the police any longer, and Gran and Pops need to know, though I'm loath to worry them; the shock won't do them any good. We can ask them about the photo I guess.'

'What about Gran's heart?'

'They're tougher than you think, Kitten.' Jeff chewed, staring into the distance, and said nothing more.

Katy mentioned that she had called the police, but that the officer she wanted to speak to wasn't available. She promised to follow it up the next day.

CHAPTER 27

1969

For Cassie, the way forward, although rough and craggy, was a little clearer. By Sunday, her period would arrive. She'd end it with Scott, and return to 2013. That was the prize. She had to push herself through the worry and the angst. Tears and regret would have to wait until later.

On Saturday morning, she wandered up to the shop at her usual time. Her first week had gone well; she was comfortable with Mr Fieldham, and the majority of the customers were lovely. She felt guilty though; it hadn't been right to leave early on Thursday, and she wanted to make up for it. Besides, it helped to take her mind off the waiting. The old shopkeeper was surprised but pleased to see her. The morning flew by.

Scott came over on Saturday afternoon, and they drove to the creek for a swim. The weather was hot and sticky; the humid, heavy air clung to her like oil and small beads of perspiration made her skin sparkle. They found their favourite water hole and chose a shady spot under a big she-oak to spread out a rug. Cassie was shy about taking off her shorts and top in front of Scott, even though she had her bathing suit on underneath. Absurd, she thought, after what they had done. Before Scott could reach out and hold her, she spun around and jumped into the water. Her body was crackling with anxious sexual tension. She wanted him and seeing that beautiful suntanned young body drove her to madness, but it would be ridiculous to allow it to happen again. In a few days' time, she'd have to do the hardest thing, and it was not fair to go all the way again now.

Scott was hot on her heels, and the moment they plunged into the water she knew it was not going to be easy. She pretended she wasn't aware of the effect his strong arms wrapping about her had as they circled her possessively. She broke away and swam off. The mixed signals in her brain were confusing. She really didn't want him to get closer right now; she *couldn't* get closer right now. When he lunged again and tried to embrace her, she stiffened, her arms pushed rigid against his shoulders.

'We can't do this, Scott. Not now. I just can't, please. All I can think about at the moment is my period.'

His face fell in a belligerent frown. 'Why not? You've got those pills, you'll be fine now.'

'That's not the point. I'm uncomfortable. I feel guilty about sleeping with you. I've deceived my parents, and I'm worried sick. It's been awful. I just want to wait. Can't you understand that?'

He pouted at her. 'Sorta. Come on, let's go home.'

The afternoon was ruined. They drove in silence, the distance between them more than the two feet on the car seat. She was miserable that night, and when she woke up on Sunday morning, and there was still no sign of her period, she felt totally depressed. Wasn't it enough that she was caught in this nonsensical time warp—that her whole family was probably frantic with worry in some other dimension? What if she was pregnant? During breakfast she was grateful that her job gave her something to talk about.

Just before slipping into bed that night, she took the first of the two little pills the doctor had given her.

Monday morning. Nothing. Bitter and tense, she took the second pill, praying it would work, but she could hardly think. She'd have to call Scott and the doctor if it didn't. Oh my God, what was she going to do? She stood under the shower until her father banged on the door. Towelling herself dry, she noticed the soft skin of her rounded belly and hated it. Having the curse was a miserable experience; not having it when you were waiting, a million times worse. Was the sex worth it, she wondered?

Since the duplicitous time travel had begun, she had learnt to squash her instincts, push the improbable events around to become manageable, clamber over those shitty hurdles and encumbrances without losing her mind, but this was the last straw.

Wedged in between a mammoth rock and an unforgiving hard place, she had no choice but to keep moving forward. *Forward.* That was a joke. She'd moved back in time for one thing. She'd exploded the theories of relativity, all in an effort to heal the past, and now this. It was incomprehensible. *I can't be pregnant, can I?*

Anxiety got the better of her a number of times until she realised she had walked to work in a daze, putting one foot in front of the other, had taken all those steps, and all the time her head was stuck in another place. What would she do? She cradled her belly, knowing that having a baby was not an option. Her parents would be dreadfully disappointed in her. Besides, what sort of a beginning would that be for a child? No income, no way of supporting it. This was 1969; there was no support at all for a single mum. How could she possibly be a good parent when she was still a teenager herself? She also knew she wouldn't cope with giving birth only to have her baby taken away for adoption, even if that was selfish. That scared her most of all. And then beyond all of that was the even bigger impact. If she had a baby now, there was no way she could have the family she had left behind in 2013. It would ruin everything for everyone. Her thoughts crept to the little soul that might be inside her. What of that? She squeezed her eyes shut, forcing big tears into her throat, pulsing with fear and suffering. If only she hadn't tried to come back and fix things. If only. Wishes like feathers, wafting away on the breeze.

Mustn't panic. Mustn't panic.

Arriving home that afternoon, she dodged the Milo with her mum, dodged Emma who wanted help with some homework and went straight to her room and curled herself into a miserable ball on the bed.

Her mum knocked on the door at teatime.

'Sweetie, come on, come and have some tea.'

'I'm not hungry.'

'I've made you some grilled cheese on toast, your favourite. You have to eat.'

The door opened gently and her mother smiled down at her kindly.

'I'll leave it here for you, and here's a mug of tea as well. You seem out of sorts, baby; what's wrong?'

Heaving herself up, a mess of tangled clothes and dishevelment, Cassie gingerly took the mug. Her mum put the plate on the bedside table. Seeing the concern in her mother's eyes just made her feel worse.

'I'm sorry Mum ... it's just that time of the month and I feel yukky.' The guilt corroded her. She was almost tempted to confess, but that would break her mother's heart. She couldn't do that to her, not to this beautiful woman who already had and would guide her through so many difficult times in her life. They sat together for a little while. The secret hovered between them, but never made landfall. This was something Cassie had to deal with on her own. It was her mess; hers to clean-up. No one else deserved to suffer, except maybe Scott. She'd saved his life, which was all she had come to do, and now he was behaving as if something had been taken from him. Perhaps she should just tell him everything—the whole damn lot. That'd make him think. Stuck in her misery, Cassie had forgotten her mum was there, and was startled when she got up, kissed her on the forehead, and left the room.

For just a moment, Cassie felt safe.

She fixated on that word. Safe. She realised she hadn't felt really safe for such a long, long time. No such thing as security or knowing. The only moment she had was now. That's all she could deal with. She could plan her little heart out, make all the assumptions and projections she wanted, and it would mean nothing.

Cassie had been so consumed by her own torment that she had forgotten to call Scott. Ironically, that was the one thing she could actually do. How could she forget to ring Scott? She leapt from her bed, running into her father in the hallway.

'Hello poppet, how are you doing?'

'Just feeling a bit nauseous,' she said. 'I just remembered, I promised to call Scott.'

'Shouldn't he be calling you?'

Cassie ignored the remark and loitered by the phone, hoping he would go away.

Her father shrugged and went into the living room.

She dialled Scott's number, praying he would answer.

'Greetings kind caller ...' Damn, it was his housemate being stupid. Cassie cut him short. 'I need to talk to Scott right now. It's important.'

There was a grunt at the other end of the line. Then silence. She waited.

Presently Scott spoke. 'Yeah?' He hadn't thawed much.

'My period didn't come Scott. I'm scared.'

'Don't worry; it must have been late before.'

'I guess so,' Cassie was disappointed.

She hung up and went back to her room, peeled off her clothes, and crawled back into bed.

CHAPTER 28

2013

The morning sun threw long, lazy shafts of gilded light across the rug, bathing the room in a soft glow of promise for the day ahead. Katy massaged her temples trying to stave off the headache waiting to drop its hammer. Saturday. Her Mum had been gone for three days, six if she counted the time she was supposedly at her retreat. Worst thing was it started to feel ordinary, she was getting used to the feelings of worry and anxiety.

She thought about her mother's friend, Maria. Her mother had hardly mentioned her. What role had she played in her past life? Were the memories too painful to talk about? Either Anastasia Pendle or Maria held the key to unlocking this mystery. One of them knew where Mum was, she was sure of it, but if she focussed all her attention on them she might miss something else. What if neither of them revealed anything?

'I'm calling her today,' she exclaimed aloud.

'Who?' said Jeff, stacking last night's dishes in the dishwasher. His morning coffee sat cold on the table.

Katy sat slumped in a chair, sipping at hers. 'Maria. I'm convinced there's something she's not telling us, but I'll do that after we've seen Gran and Pops.'

'If we leave here about ten, they'll be up and about and the roads shouldn't be too busy,' her father said.

'In that case, I'll pop over and see old Mrs Parker before we go; perhaps she's thought of something else. Besides, it will kill some time.'

***

Jeff was left with his thoughts as Katy disappeared into her room. He picked up the photo of Cassie and Scott. Wistfully, he wondered who seventeen-year-old Cassie had been; for that matter, who she was now. He had no idea. It occurred to him standing there, that he hadn't actually checked the scanner. What if there was something to Katy's theory? He turned on the computer and watched as the icons starting popping up on the screen and the beast came to life. When he switched on the scanner everything appeared normal. He placed the photo of Cassie in the machine, chose the destination file and pressed start. It whirred away sweetly and a moment later, it appeared on the computer screen. *There goes that theory*, he thought.

He felt listless. The fire in his belly lay smouldering and there was nothing to do but wait.

***

When Katy knocked on the door at Mrs Parker's, it took a while before it opened.

'Hello dear, any news?' The old lady's wrinkled smile greeted her warmly.

'Nothing, I'm afraid. Just popping over to say hello, take my mind off things.'

'I saw the police over there. Have they been able to help?'

'No. I was going to ask you about that. Was it you who called them?'

Mrs Parker's cheeks turned a rose pink. She shuddered and turned away. 'I'm sorry about that. I panicked, you see. I'm sorry I forgot to mention it to you when you were here.'

'We haven't lodged an official report yet. We're convinced there is a logical explanation for Mum's odd behaviour. Perhaps that's naïve, do you think ... ?'

'Something is amiss, Katy, that's for sure, but if you don't want them involved, I'll respect that. I think you should consider it though. After all, they have the expertise and manpower to do the job more efficiently.'

'Do they though? I'm not so sure.'

'Sit down; I've just made a pot of tea.'

Katy chose the chair furthest from the window. 'I don't suppose you've thought of anything else have you, Mrs Parker? Something you might have forgotten to tell us? We can't make sense of the few bits of information we've got.'

'No. I've given it lots of thought, but nothing else springs to mind.'

'What about her visitors? Can you think of anyone who stood out?'

'No, not really. I don't see everything that goes on in the street.' She gave a little snort of mild disgust. 'But now you mention it? Who was the lady who came to stay with you for a few days? I noticed two young girls. Any relation?'

'Yes. That was my Aunt Emma and my cousins, Evie and Tamara. They visited us from Tamworth.' Katy smiled.

'There was another lady that came to visit while they were here. I noticed her because her car was quite shabby and old; she had a young girl with her too. She was there again the week after. A friend?'

'Do you know what sort of car it was, it might shed some light on her identity; I'm not dismissing anything.' Katy asked.

'It was an oldish red one, one of those small hatchback things. It looked old, anyway.'

'I have no idea,' Katy said, surmising that Mrs Parker pretty much did see everything that was going on in the street.

'That's the only one I noticed.' Mrs Parker said.

'It doesn't matter. It might be nothing, but I'll bear it in mind,' Katy replied.

She listened while Mrs Parker told her about her own family. Ada's eyes glistened with delight as she described the grandchildren, chatting with great animation—on and on about their lives and their achievements. So much so, Katy got a shock when she realised it was already nine thirty. She hurriedly made her excuses and left.

Katy tucked the photo that her father had found in the scanner safely in her wallet and mentally prepared herself for the difficult task of telling her grandparents. Neither spoke a word. When they pulled up, the house looked quiet, but the door opened as soon as they got out, and Katy stiffened, dreading the conversation to come. She sensed her dad, too, was bracing himself for their reaction.

'What a lovely surprise! Why didn't you call? Where's Cass?'

Gran stood in the doorway, wearing a big smile and an aqua tracksuit.

Katy lunged forward and hugged Gran; Jeff put his arm around them both.

'We should go inside. We have something to tell you. Is Pops home?' Katy asked.

'What is it? What's wrong? Katy, what's happened?' She threw a frightened look at Jeff.

Gran pushed Katy away and rested her hands on Katy's shoulders, her face now a mask of concern.

Katy hung her head, pushing back tears, not wanting to make things harder.

The three of them huddled together—a confused cluster in the doorway as her grandfather approached.

'What's up?' the old man croaked.

Katy saw her dad take a deep breath, lift his shoulders to the ceiling and look at her before he spoke. 'Cassie hasn't come home from her trip. She's been missing for three days.' He reached over and held his mother-in-law's hand before going on. 'We've checked with the police and the hospitals, and we are one hundred percent convinced she's not hurt. We think she's been delayed or stuck somewhere. She left her phone behind so she hasn't been able to call us. It's going to be all right.'

Pops spoke. 'And what are the police doing?'

They moved into the living room where Gran gestured for them to take a seat.

'Yes. What are the police doing?' she echoed.

'Well,' Katy said, sounding sheepish, 'we haven't made an official statement. We're convinced she'll turn up.'

'Surely you need to report it to the police, son.'

Both of her grandparents sat there looking at them, stunned. Gran chewed at her fingernail. Pops looked down, fidgeting with his sleeve, not wanting to meet their eyes. He knotted his eyebrows in alarm.

'And we will,' Jeff said, 'we just don't want to panic and start a search and waste everyone's time unless we have to.'

'Does Emma know?' the old lady butted in.

'She does,' Jeff replied. 'Emma offered to come up, but we've reassured her there's nothing she can do. We're keeping her in the loop. Besides, she has her own family. I promise you, Katy and I are confident she'll turn up.'

'But what if you're wrong?' Gran said, choking back a sob. 'You have to call the police.' She buried her face in her hands.

'We will. We just don't want to jump to conclusions. Right now we don't believe she's in danger; she's just been held up or something.' Katy changed the subject as she pulled the photo from her wallet. 'Perhaps you can help us with this.' She glanced at her father for reassurance. 'We think something really odd is going on, and this might have something to do with it.'

Gran bit her lip and looked away. 'What on earth has this got to do with anything?' Irritation and impatience had crept into her voice.

'We don't know, but its story might give us a clue.' Katy said.

The old lady rubbed her face, then reached out, took the photo and studied it.

The room was still; just the lonely cry of a crow outside pierced the air. The old woman looked into the distance; a veil of sadness in her eyes.

Pops reached over and took her hand.

'You've seen this photo, Jeff. Cassie's told you, hasn't she?' Gran said.

He raised his eyebrows in question. 'That was taken just before a school dance, wasn't it?'

Gran spoke softly. 'This is a photo of Cassie with Scott, her first love. She was only about seventeen at the time. A few hours after this photo was taken, Scott was killed driving her home. Cassie survived, but she never forgave herself because she thought it was her fault. She told the police what she could remember at the time, and she was cleared of any blame, but it nearly destroyed her. It was all very painful; it took years for her to come to terms with it. It wasn't until she met you that things started to improve.'

Katy's dad shook his head. 'I vaguely remember Cassie telling me about Scott and that he'd died. The only time she talked about the accident was when I asked her about the scar on her arm, and she said she'd gashed it when she was thrown from the car. She didn't want to elaborate, and I didn't want to push her. She never told me he was killed in that accident. I didn't know the two were connected. You're telling me she's been carrying this grief with her all these years and I didn't know?' He ran his hand through his hair.

'She wanted to bury it Jeff,' Pops said. 'You were the fresh start she needed. I don't think she was deliberately withholding anything from you. She just wanted to put it behind her, that's all.'

'I don't know what to think. Thank you for telling me.' He was visibly shaken. 'Perhaps I don't know her at all.'

Katy looked at her father incredulously, then turned to her grandmother. 'Did she ever mention Maria to you, Gran?'

'Maria?' Gran jerked to attention. 'Why, Maria was her closest friend all through that time. They went to school together, but I thought they had lost touch ages ago.'

'I think you should just call the police right now. Let them sort it out,' Pops demanded.

Her father appeased him. 'We'll contact them first thing Monday.'

It was settled. They'd said what they needed to say, and a short time later they left, leaving behind two distraught parents worrying about their daughter.

On the way home, Katy looked at the photo again, dwelling on the fact that she knew so little about her mum's past. Her father looked straight ahead, stoic and closemouthed.

As soon as they were home, Katy grabbed her mum's phone and dialled Maria's number. She waited as it rang, and after a few moments, Maria spoke. 'Hello, Cassie?'

'No, it's me again, Katy. Nothing's changed, but can we meet for a coffee this afternoon, if that's convenient? Please. I'm worried about Mum. If I could just talk to you, I think it would help. I found out today that you were good friends at school. Perhaps you can shed some light on a few things.'

Katy could hear breathing, but Maria didn't speak.

'Please, Maria. We are going crazy with worry, and I just need to talk to someone who knows her history. Please.'

Finally, Katy heard a very reluctant 'all right then' from Maria.

'I've got to pick up my grand-daughter, Hannah, early and take her to ballet classes at two o'clock on Wednesday. I could meet you then for an hour, but that's the best I can do,' Maria said with a resigned sigh.

'Great. I can meet you then. Is there a café or something nearby?'

Maria gave her some particulars and the appointment was settled. Katy made a fist and punched the air as she hung up.

CHAPTER 29

1969

Cassie sighed. She'd taken the pills just like the doctor said and nothing happened. The novelty of time travel was eclipsed by the situation in which she now found herself. Inside the anxious teenager there was an equally anxious adult. The images of her future family started to fade, and she got into the habit of writing down things. She was afraid of losing it all.

Scott still called but Cassie sensed his resentment. All that tied them together now was mutual fear.

Her parents tried to reach out, but she wanted none of it. She preferred to cry herself to sleep in the sanctuary of her bedroom rather than let on how stupid she had been or confess the very deep trouble she might be in.

She anxiously waited for the days to pass until at last she could stand the suspense no longer and she called the doctor again. She explained the situation to the receptionist, who asked her to hold. The phone crackled and then she heard the woman speak. 'Doctor can see you tomorrow first thing at 8.00 am. That's before surgery, can you manage that?'

'I don't think so, I work.'

There was a pause.

'Well, the only one other option is 5.00 pm tomorrow. That's after her last appointment. Will that do?'

'It'll have to, thank you,' she said.

***

When Scott pulled up outside the shop the next afternoon, Cassie was shaking.

'Hi,' she whispered, sliding into the seat beside him. 'Thanks for doing this.'

He was angry. 'Don't have much choice, do I?' His hands gripped the wheel tightly, and he swung away from the kerb with a jerk.

It was a long drive in stony silence, but at last Cassie was sitting in the surgery. The receptionist had closed the outside door and the waiting room was empty. When Dr Clarke herself came out and called her, Cassie jumped. The tension in her snapped like an elastic band. Reluctant and afraid, she approached the consulting room, step by anguished step.

The doctor frowned. 'I'll examine you again, though I doubt anything much has changed. 'Could you wee into this for me please, and then bring it back?'

She handed Cassie a tiny jar and directed her to the toilet.

Cassie screwed up her nose as she took the bottle, pleased there was no one around to see. The deed done, she took it back into the room where the doctor was seated by her desk, waiting.

'Hop up on the couch and I'll have another look.

She seemed oblivious to Cassie's anxiety; instead she concentrated on the examination. She bent over Cassie's naked tummy gently exploring and feeling, her face a practised, serious mask of mystery. Cassie stared at the ceiling. She thought of leaving this body right now, right this instant. She could just bolt and leave the past to look after itself, but obligation and love bound her.

At last, the doctor was finished. The thwack of a glove being removed pulled Cassie back into the present. 'It's hard to tell, but you might be in the early stages of pregnancy. I can refer you to an obstetrician if you like, though I would suggest waiting for the test to come back, and that will take about two weeks.'

Words were jumping in the air, but made no sense. Frozen in fear and shock, Cassie stared into the empty space around her, unable to respond.

'Did you hear me?'

Cassie nodded sadly.

The doctor went on, 'I'll send this off to the lab and give you a call as soon as I get the results.'

'Oh, no, no,' Cassie uttered, her voice shaking. 'My parents don't know anything about this. Can I call you before then?'

The older woman gave her a look of sympathy. 'All right dear, but you know there won't be any point calling for at least a week. I won't know anything before then.'

Out in the hall, she waited for a long time. She had to keep herself together. She didn't want to face Scott like this. *It's not definite*. She pulled her shoulders back, held her head up and headed out to the car.

'I've got to wait for a test.' She slid in beside Scott.

That was it, then. The long drive home was once again spent in silence, each wrapped in their own version of misery.

CHAPTER 30

2013

It was Sunday, and both sat picking at their lunch half-heartedly.

'You realise we have to go to the police tomorrow, Dad?' Katy said.

Her father looked away, rubbing his chin in thought. 'Perhaps. I still can't believe she would just up and leave like that.'

Katy reached over and put her hand over her father's, protectively. 'Don't you think something would have surfaced by now? Besides, we made that promise to Gran and Pops.'

'I know, but if we do that, it's one step further to admitting the truth. It makes my heart ache. Surely the police can't do any more than we can,' her father said.

'Maybe not, but it might bring some comfort; and what does it matter? The more heads we have working on this the better,'

'Speaking of getting others involved, did you call her friend again?'

'Maria you mean?'

'Yes, the one who spent time with Mum a few days before she disappeared?' he said.

'I got the impression you were against it but, yes, I did.' Katy wondered if she would get a backlash for following her gut.

He looked down at the table, pushing a grain of rice that had strayed from his plate.

'When your Gran mentioned that Maria and your mum had been best friends, I realised it might be worthwhile. They obviously had a close bond.'

'I arranged to meet her on Wednesday; perhaps we can hold off calling the police till then.'

Jeff stared wistfully into space. 'You know, I thought I knew your mother, and then when we heard that dreadful story about Scott's death, I realised I didn't know her at all. Perhaps she wanted to disappear.' He sagged with the thought.

'I'll admit it shocked me as well, but we have to believe the best. It's hard to imagine Mum keeping any secrets that big from you, though.'

'Yet here we are, confused in her wake.'

He slammed his palm on the table, got up, and paced out on to the verandah.

Coco leapt up in fright, bolted into the bedroom and hid under Katy's bed.

Katy had nothing left to talk him back. She got up too and went to her room, trying to busy herself, but she was restless and fidgety.

***

The next morning, Jeff woke with a start. His phone was buzzing on the bedside table. Groggy from lack of sleep and too many whiskies the night before, he grappled to pick it up. He glanced at the clock by the bed; it was 7.38.

Massaging his cheeks, he stirred himself into alertness and grabbed the phone, fumbling to find the answer button.

'Hello, hello? Oh, Pops, it's you. Sorry, bad night last night.'

'Sorry if I woke you son, but we've been worried. We want you to call the police ... now.' It was a command, not a request.

'Yeah, yes. You're right. Leave it with me. I'm barely awake. Trust me, I'll do it.'

'All right, but if I haven't heard back from you by ten, I'll call them myself.'

'I'll do it, I promise.'

The line went dead.

Feeling older than his years, Jeff teetered to the bathroom, swayed over the toilet, and hopped in the shower. He turned the tap to tepid ... he needed to wake up; he needed to be on his game.

Half an hour later, he was in the kitchen making himself a coffee. Katy wasn't around. He listened at her door for a while but heard nothing and assumed she was getting some much-needed sleep.

***

She wasn't. Katy was pounding the pavement, stepping hard and fast, trying to eradicate the worrying thoughts haunting her. By the time she got back home, she was feeling more positive, her hopes resting on Maria. Wednesday couldn't come quickly enough.

'There you are. Where've you been?' Her father called over his shoulder as she walked in. He was standing by the stove. The smell of bacon hit Katy.

'I went out for a long walk. I was feeling restless.'

'I know what you mean. I was startled awake by a call from Pops. They're panicking, I think. I've been read the riot act, and I don't think we can do this on our own any longer. Do you still have that card the officer gave you? We have to call the police.'

'It's here somewhere,' Katy rifled through the basket of bits and pieces and pulled out the card. She placed the card on the table by her phone.

As her father spooned scrambled eggs and bacon onto plates, Katy lingered by the kettle, waiting for it to boil, then made herself a cup of tea.

Mumbling between mouthfuls, her father said, 'Perhaps we should call after breakfast. I don't like it though—all those questions. I hate the thought of them digging into our lives.' 'If I can get hold of that friendly constable who was here the other day, I think it might not be so bad. He seemed pleasant, and perhaps he can help us without going through all that formal stuff. That way, we aren't lying to Gran and Pops, and we aren't giving up all our control either. It's worth a try, isn't it? If nothing else, it might buy us more time.'

Katy sensed how hard it was for her father to ask for help; that wasn't who he was. He fixed things, he sorted things out, and he protected his family. Calling the police was like admitting defeat.

Her dad chewed his lip as he mulled it over. 'Let's do that. You're right; he seemed a reasonable young chap.'

She nodded and picked up her phone, glancing at the clock. 'I hope he's in today.' She started punching in the number, watching her dad as he pushed the last bit of toast over his plate.

'Oh, h-h-hello. My name is Katy Foster, I wonder if I could speak to Constable Burwood if he's there, please.'

'I can help you ma'am, unless it's personal.'

She hesitated. 'Well it is, sort of.'

Her father frowned at her.

'No worries, I'll see if I can find him.'

The line rolled over into a recorded message, reminding callers of the need to be aware of home security. Katy sipped at her tea, listening intently, praying he would be there.

After a few minutes, the officer returned. 'Putting you through now.'

She heard the clicking sounds as the call was diverted.

'Constable Burwood speaking. How can I help?'

'Hi,' Katy pushed lightness into her voice. 'It's Katy Foster here. I don't know if you remember, but last Thursday you came round to see us about a mysterious light in our study.'

'Ah yes ... I do remember ... you were with your dad. The neighbour thought something funny was going on. What can I do for you?'

'Well, actually, I was wondering if we could talk to you again, off the record, as it were.'

He replied, 'It's not customary. Is it because you don't want to make a formal statement?'

'Yes, it is.' She paused, thinking about what she was going to say next. 'The thing is, we have a bit of a situation here, but we really don't want to make a fuss. What's the procedure?'

'Well, you can tell me your problem over the phone now, or you can come down here to the station and we can have a chat. It's up to you. We can't go ahead with an investigation unless you make a formal report, or if we know the perpetrator, then we can use what you tell us as evidence. What would you prefer?'

'Oh, there's no crime been committed; it's just an enquiry really. Could we come and see you? When can we make an appointment?'

'I finish at three today, if you come in at two forty-five, I'm available. Of course I can't guarantee that, but I should be here.'

'That's perfect; we'll see you then. It's Katy and Jeff Foster.'

'I'll remember. Cheerio.'

That was it then. She gave a sigh of satisfaction as she put the phone down, smiling at her dad. 'So, we can see him at 2.45pm today.'

'I'll let Gran and Pops know. They'll be happy to hear it. I'd better ring work as well; I won't go in.'

CHAPTER 31

At 2.45 pm, Katy and Jeff were seated in the small reception area at the local police station. The walls were a faded green, dark and dull. There was a notice board plastered with brochures and telephone numbers on the wall opposite. Next to it was a big poster. Across the top in large letters was printed in bold blue capitals,

HAVE YOU SEEN THIS MISSING PERSON?

The second 'I' in MISSING was replaced by a white silhouette of a man, an empty space as it were. Below it was a selection of grainy photos, enlarged snapshots taken by loved ones. Katy stood in front of it and started to read, becoming engrossed in the short, poignant stories of last sightings and personal details underneath each photo. It was heartbreaking—every face represented a gaping hole left in a family, in someone's life.

That's not us, is it? It can't be us. She wiped away a tear threatening to spill from her eye.

A door slammed, breaking her concentration. Behind the enclosed glass counter, she saw Constable Burwood approaching. Her father heard it too; he got up and came over, reaching for Katy's elbow.

'Hi, Katy and you must be Jeff Foster,' he smiled and shook hands with each of them. 'Sorry to keep you waiting. I was held up with some paperwork.'

The constable had a light sprinkling of freckles over his perfect nose and a friendly, open expression. Remembering her manners, Katy responded. 'Yes, we have a problem. Is there somewhere we can talk?'

'Yes, of course. Follow me.'

He led the way back through the passage and opened the door he had just come through. 'There's an interrogation room here we can use.' He gestured them inside as he held the door open.

Katy shuddered. 'Oh, I don't like the sound of that.'

It's all right; nothing has to go any further. Take a seat. Now, what is the issue here?'

The constable sat down and pulled out a notebook and pen, ready to start writing.

'It doesn't matter. I think we've made a mistake, I can't do this. I can't.' She tried to get up.

Katy chewed her lip. Her mouth had gone dry. The atmosphere in the room was oppressive, as though laden with questions and suspicions. She was losing her nerve.

'Don't worry, darling, I'll do the talking. It'll be fine.' Her father reached out and grabbed her by the arm.

'A week ago my wife went away on what we thought was a three-day break. We both left together early as I had to go to Perth on a business trip and she was going to head up north as soon as she had dropped me off at the airport. There was nothing untoward about that; we scheduled it that way, but whereas I came home on Wednesday night as planned, she did not.'

The officer scribbled on his pad.

'What's concerning is that she left behind her personal things. Mum didn't take anything,' Katy added.

'What kind of things?' Constable Burwood cocked his head to one side, trying to understand.

'Her handbag and her phone were at home. We figured out that she had left the car at a long-term car park from a receipt we found, but after that, nothing.' Katy leaned forward as she was telling the story. 'The overnight bag she packed for the trip was untouched on the back seat of her car.'

'So your mother has been gone since last Thursday; is that what you're saying?'

They both nodded. 'Yes.'

'Do you want to file a missing person report or not, because by all accounts, she is missing.'

'Yes, well, no.' Katy answered.

'The thing is, it's not like my wife,' her father said. 'We didn't argue or anything. Everything was normal before we left last Monday. There was no reason for her to leave.'

'She could have been taken against her will,' the constable suggested, frowning.

'That's just it.' Katy had found her voice. 'We've been asking around and, well, you heard what the old lady said.'

The policeman gave them a blank look. 'What old lady? You've lost me.'

'That's why we're here. You remember coming to the house, don't you? You said you did on the phone,' Katy said.

'Ah, yes. Was that the one with the weird 'blast' that one of your neighbours reported?' Constable Burwood made air quotes with his hands as he spoke.

'That's it. Mrs Parker's her name. She sees everything that goes on. She came over to see me on the Tuesday after Mum left to tell me about it.' Katy bowed her head and mumbled. 'I didn't take her seriously at the time, but when I realise how little we know, it seems she was the last one to see her, because Mum actually came home in a taxi that Monday morning, and then there was the blue flashy thing Mrs Parker saw, and we haven't seen her since.'

'So you don't want to make a formal report, but your mother's disappeared into thin air?' His keen blue eyes looked directly at Katy. 'What exactly do you want me to do?'

'We're not sure,' her father said, 'but I guess we are wondering if there is a way you can find out more than we did.'

'Without making it official, I'm afraid not.'

Jeff looked at Katy; his lips pursed tight, his arms now folded over his chest. 'All right then, we'd better do a report,' he said at last, transferring his gaze to the floor.

The constable rested his fingers on a keyboard and waited.

They gave him all the necessary information and what they had discovered, and by the time it was finished it was well after five o'clock. Katy rang her grandparents straight away to let them know. On the way home they picked up a pizza, and it wasn't until Katy recognised the young man who served her that she remembered she'd had an exam today. It troubled her all the way home. She was relieved to learn it was only a small part of her overall score, and if she didn't mess up tomorrow, she would be all right, but she'd have to spend the night swotting. It had been nearly a week since she'd had her head anywhere near a book, and it would be hard to concentrate.

***

At midday the next day, Katy drove home after the exam, thankful it was over.

She thought about Maria and their meeting the following day. An idea hit her. There might be a photo of Maria in the box of old photos. After all, she was her mum's best mate, and if Scott had been around then, who knows?

At home, she plonked the box on the sofa and sat down. One by one, she pulled out a photograph, peering at the images. A lot of them were taken long before she was born. She wondered what it was like living in those simpler times. There were lots of photos of her mother when she was still quite young, and Katy was intrigued by the resemblance to herself—the same dark hair; the same heart-shaped, angular features; the full lips. Her mum had aged, but she was still beautiful in a matronly sort of way. She ached to give her a hug.

That single thought led her down a dark path of melancholy. Nevertheless, she pressed on, confident that there'd be a picture with Maria in it. Just as she found what she was looking for, she heard the front door open.

Her dad walked into the living room. 'Hello, what are you up to? How did your exam go?'

'Exam was fine; I don't want to think about it anymore. As for this,' Katy gestured to the photos scattered on the sofa beside her. She handed a small square print to her dad, and he studied it closely. 'I figured there might be a snapshot of Mum with her friend Maria, but I forgot there weren't many photos around in those days. Well, I mean there were lots, but nothing compared to nowadays. Look at this.'

He peered at the picture of the two young girls, slightly blurred and faded with age. 'I've never seen Maria, so I don't know, but perhaps you could drive over to see Gran and Pops and ask them; they'd remember, wouldn't they?'

'Good idea. I haven't that many left to go through, so I'll see if there are any others, and I'll go straight over. I should be able to do that before dinner.' She blew him the sweetest daughter kiss she could muster and turned back to her project.

'I guess that means I'm doing dinner then.' Her father wandered off, carrying his laptop, his jacket thrown casually over his shoulder. 'Suppose you want me to feed Coco as well.'
Katy beamed at him when he looked back.

CHAPTER 32

As her dad had predicted, Katy's grandparents were able to identify Maria. She was pleased.

When she got home, her father dished up a stew he'd concocted from leftovers. Afterwards, she showed the pictures to her dad. She was almost happy, buoyed by the fact that showing them to Maria would soften their conversation a little, perhaps leading to more information.

'Here they are. I'm not sure what to expect tomorrow. I'm hoping these might break the ice. This meeting is important to me, but it might be nothing. Anyway, I have all my fingers and toes crossed.'

Her father grunted. 'I think it's a bit of a dead end myself, but I'm prepared to try anything. Have you thought any more about the scanner? Do you still think it's connected?'

'I do, Dad, but I have nothing to back it up. It's just a theory based on zilch, only a hunch really.

Wednesday morning dragged. She toyed with the thought of calling her aunt, eager to have a sounding board for her ideas, but decided against it. Instead, she jotted down some questions to make sure she didn't waste any time she had with Maria.

Her phone buzzed.

'Hello, this is Constable Burwood. Is that Katy Foster?'

'Yes, any news?'

'That's why I'm ringing. We've lodged the report and I'm calling to give you the heads up.'

'So what can you tell us?'

'We've started some preliminary investigations, but when an adult goes missing it's usually on purpose. They might be running away from something, and it's been over a week already, so you might not hear anything for a few days.'

'That's not Mum,' Katy said, her voice low.

The constable went on. 'Anyway, someone from the missing persons unit will contact you in due course. They may ask you to surrender anything they might need as evidence, anything of interest. I'm sorry I can't guarantee a date and time for you, but I'll ask them to give you a call before they come. They might also question your neighbours or anyone who may have had contact with your mum in the days prior to her disappearance. Unless there are suspicious circumstances, there isn't the same sense of urgency as there would be with a child, so things may happen a little slowly for your liking, but I assure you, these people are highly trained and we'll do our best to find her.'

To her surprise, Katy started to cry—whimpering tears of disappointment and desperation.

'Are you there?'

'I-I-I'm sorry; I just can't talk about it now. I'm so sorry. I'll call you back.'

'No, I'm sorry. I didn't mean to upset you—.' Katy hung up. She didn't wait to listen to his apologies.

She rushed into the bathroom and leaned over the sink, turning on the tap as she did so. She splashed her face with cold water. The tears flowed freely, lost in cool clear pools, swirling into oblivion.

Panic crept into her, her throat tightened. *Don't lose it, not now.* She needed to keep herself in control if she was going to confront Maria. She corrected that thought. *Confront?* No. *I'm going to talk to her about my mother, that's all. Mustn't get my hopes up. Stay cool. I'm no good to anyone like this.*

She wandered on to the verandah and sat staring into the back yard. Coco took advantage of the vacant lap and jumped up lightly, ready to settle in for a snooze, but Katy wasn't in the mood and pushed her off.

At last it was time to leave for her rendezvous with Maria. It wasn't a long drive, and Katy battled to conjure up the right frame of mind. By two o'clock, she considered herself able to manage a calm conversation.

***

She found a little table near the door and the moment she saw the old red Pulsar pull up she knew it must be her. When Maria entered, she stood up. 'Hi, thanks so much for meeting me.'

Maria shoved her keys into her bag. She took off her sunglasses and rubbed her eyes, Katy could tell she was exhausted.

'Hello, I recognise you now. I was at your house when your aunt was visiting from Sydney. We weren't introduced. Anyway, I'm Maria.' She said, as she brushed her hair back.

'Sorry to drag you here, but we are worried. I thought talking to you might help. I know you are one of her closest friends.'

'Yes and no; we were inseparable at school and for years after, but life took over and somewhere we lost touch. For the last thirty years I haven't seen her. It was only recently our paths crossed again. I don't know how I can help.'

Katy was surprised. 'How did you reconnect?'

'We ran into one another in the city by accident. We were both in a hurry, so we quickly exchanged numbers and that was it. I heard nothing for a while and then, unexpectedly about a month ago, she called me. We've been making up for lost time ever since. I last saw her a couple of weeks ago.'

'How was she when you saw her? Oh! And I almost forgot ...' Katy plucked an envelope out of her bag, took out the photos and handed them over.

Maria's work-worn hands quivered slightly as she took the photos. She studied them; her expression revealed nothing. But when she looked up at Katy, her eyes were moist. Distant mists of memory softened her features. 'Can you believe we were ever that young?' She said.

'I guess I'll be there one day, and you don't look bad for, dare I say, a sixty-something?' Katy smiled, now feeling more comfortable.

'It seems so long ago.'

Katy chose her words with care. 'I understand you might not be as close as you once were, but did you think Mum had changed when you were reunited?'

'Not really. The years just dropped away. It was wonderful to hear her story and be able to tell her mine. It was like picking up the loose threads of a much-loved worn-out rug; we wove our history back together. It was great. At first.'

'What do you mean 'at first'?' Katy sat upright.

'Well, she had just been retrenched when we met. It didn't seem to worry her that much. In fact, the next time I saw her she was positively revelling in her freedom. We had a lovely time when Emma came up. My grand-daughter, Hannah, got on well with the girls, and we had a fabulous afternoon. But after that, her mood changed, and I started to wonder.' She looked at her watch. 'I'm going to have to leave soon, I'm sorry.'

'Just a few more minutes. What do you think was wrong?'

'I don't know, but there was a time she came to see me after she'd bought a scanner from an old lady in the hills, and she was quite shaken.'

'I knew it!' Katy clenched her hands and banged them on the table.

Maria looked startled. 'Knew what?'

'I've thought all along Mum's disappearance had something to do with that damn scanner. You've just confirmed it. Anything else?'

Maria started hedging and looked away. 'Erm, uhm ...'

'What, Maria? What is it? We need to know. If you don't tell me, I have absolutely no idea what to do next. And there needs to be a next, or I'll go crazy.'

'I don't know how to say this. You'll think I'm mad, or that your mother is a lunatic.'

'I promise I won't. I know there is something weird going on. Any information is good information right now. I'm frantic. I don't care how crazy it sounds.'

Maria wriggled in her seat. She rubbed her chin on her shoulder, looked back at Katy, and squeezed her eyes shut tightly. 'Not long ago she called me one morning and she sounded awfully distressed. She asked me to come straight over, said she had something important she needed to talk to me about. Of course, I went and when I arrived she was a real mess ... that's the only way I can describe it. I thought she'd lost it and I was worried. She was so unlike the Cassie I knew. I encouraged her to talk, but when she did, it was gibberish. I think I was shocked; I couldn't make any sense out of it, then or now. She was spurting forth all this rubbish about time travel and the old lady. She claimed the scanner was magic. She said she wanted to try to save Scott's life. I suppose you know that story?'

'I didn't, but we found out from Gran and Pops last Saturday when we showed them the photos. She never shared it with us. We were dreadfully upset to think she'd never said anything.'

'Look, it's getting late; I have to go and pick up Hannah. I'm sorry to distress you, but this is why I was so reluctant to get involved.' Maria was fidgeting with her sunglasses. 'I really am sorry; it must be shocking to hear. If it's all too much, call me. We can talk again.'

A moment later, she was out of the café and on her way.

Katy sat in stunned silence, trying to wrap her head around what she had just heard.

It wasn't until the waitress reminded her that they were closing that she stirred.

CHAPTER 33

At home, she called her aunt. It wasn't long before Emma picked up.

'Hello, it's Katy. I met up with Maria.'

'Just a minute, I'll turn off the TV. The girls left it blaring in the other room and I can't hear a thing.' There was a brief interval and Emma was back. 'All right, what have you found out?'

'It sounds unbelievable. Maria said Mum was very anxious the last time she saw her. Reckoned she was talking about the scanner having some special power and she could travel back in time. Maria thought she'd lost it.'

'What are you saying? My sister time travelled?'

There was a dramatic pause.

'Yes, well, no, I'm not sure. I'm not game to tell Dad; he'll just laugh at me. It shook me, and now I don't know what to do. Did she say anything to you?'

'No. I would've told you. It's ridiculous though, isn't it? It's impossible—not unless your mum has stumbled on a real TARDIS somewhere. No, Katy, relax. It can't be true. Maria must have misunderstood.'

'Yes, I thought the same, but she was very upset, and she said Mum sounded serious. It rattled her. She said she was stunned when Mum told her and she had no idea how to respond. That's why she was so cagey. She knew no one would believe it.'

'So how did she respond? That's a hell of a thing to tell someone! Your mum is so level-headed. What would possess her to come up with that rubbish?'

'Exactly. She thought Mum was either insane or deluded. But here's the thing that astounded me and gave it credibility.'

She went on. 'Mum indicated to Maria that she'd been given the chance to go back and save Scott.'

'What? No! Unbelievable. Golly, that was all so long ago, I've forgotten the details. What was I? Thirteen, fourteen maybe? I only remember the police coming to the door and telling us there had been an accident. The rest is a blur. Scott was killed and Cassie was grieving for a long time. I think he was her first real boyfriend.'

Katy continued. 'This is where it gets really creepy. We found a photo of Mum with Scott taken the night he was killed. It was lying on the scanner bed.'

Her aunt gasped. 'Oh my God! I see what you mean.'

'What'll I do? I can't tell anyone this. They'd think I was mad. I'm so confused.' Her voice started to tremble. She bit her lip hard, not wanting to upset her aunt any more than she already had. 'I'm sorry to call you. I didn't know who else to turn to.'

'Would you like me to come up?'

Katy hesitated. 'Um ... No, no, you have your own family to think about.'

'Listen, Katy, you're my family. Cassie is my sister for heaven's sake. I'm coming up. The girls will be fine with Rod for a few days. I'll call you back as soon as I've organised some flights.'

'Sorry to lay this on you.'

'It's fine. I'm glad you called me. I'll be there as soon as I can. I have an idea where I can find that clairvoyant. We'll tackle this together.'

When the call ended, Katy hovered in a vacuum, buffeted by her imagination. She distracted herself by making a lasagne, one of her father's favourites. She wanted to butter him up, stall him. Somehow, she had to deflect him from asking too many questions, knowing she'd buckle under scrutiny if he pushed her. There was no way she was ready to try to explain the inexplicable. She muttered to herself, replaying her conversation with Maria until the story started to feel true. Every logical bone in her body denied it, but Maria was genuine. Whatever her own opinion was, Maria fervently believed that her mum was sincere.

It was well after half past nine when Jeff finally walked in.

'Where've you been? I've been worried about you.' Katy hugged him.

'Sorry, I should have let you know. I just got caught up with one of the directors from down south. He turned up unexpectedly this afternoon and I couldn't get away.'

'You could've texted or something. Anyway, I made you a lasagne. It might still be warm if you want some.'

'I've already eaten, I'm afraid.'

'It's bad enough having one parent missing,' Katy complained.

'I'm sorry. It was thoughtless. I'm pooped. Did you hear from the police by any chance, and how did you get on with Maria?'

'Constable Burwood called this morning. We're to expect a visit from some detectives from the missing person's unit, but he said it could take a while.' Katy was pleased she could avoid telling him about Maria and instead expanded on the issue of the police. 'Apparently it takes longer when adults go missing.' She didn't add the implication that her mother might have gone by choice.

'What about Maria? What did she have to say?'

Katy had her back to him as she placed some cling film over the pasta dish and popped it in the fridge. She made light of it. 'There you go, tomorrow's dinner.'

'Katy ... what did she say?' Her father asked again.

'It's complicated, Dad. I'm too tired now. Can we talk about it in the morning?'

'Sure, but I have to leave early, so don't sleep in, hey?'

She walked over and planted a kiss on his cheek. 'Night. I promise I'll be up. Oh, almost forgot. I spoke to Aunt Emma, and she's going to fly up. It's hard on her too, she wants to be here.

***

Katy was up with the sparrows the next morning. She'd hardly slept. The heaviness of the day ahead and her mental and physical exhaustion almost overtook her. It was only 4.00 am. She got up, put on her runners, and snuck quietly out of the house.

The morning air was humid, heavy with the scent of jasmine. It had rained overnight, and the earth rested in satisfied peace, basking in its rich bounty. The grass glistened, renewed and refreshed by a deluge the night before. The birds sang their gratitude, filling the air with calls and chants that drowned out the traffic hum from the highway.

Katy strode beside the creek. The sky was orange and, along the path, tiny spider webs clung to the shrubs like delicate silver stars. The only sounds were her steps crunching into the gravel and the twittering of the birds.

Maria's words resonated in her mind. As preposterous as it was, she believed her. At least she believed Maria was being genuine, and she believed her mum was telling the truth, as absurd and crazy as it might sound. Aunt Emma was right, that weird woman who'd sold her the scanner was at the root of all this. No wonder she'd been so evasive on the phone. What hocus-pocus was she up to, for heaven's sake? More importantly, where was her mum? Questions hung in the air like drones, menacing and mysterious. How was she going to tell her dad? He was pragmatic and stubborn; he'd mock any suggestion of alternative realities. He had no time for magic, not in his world. He was the most logical, grounded person she knew and there was no way he'd buy into her theory.

Daylight was seeping into the morning and the sky washed into the palest of blue. Dark stringy clouds hung on the horizon and in a few hours the sun would be high, scorching the land again, resting against its azure curtain. Katy took a deep breath, immersing herself in the raw, natural smells wafting around her.

When she wandered back inside, it was well after five. She heard movement in her parents' bedroom and assumed her dad was stirring. She put down a bowl of cat food for Coco, made two cups of coffee, and knocked gently on the door of the bedroom.

'Helloooo. Dad, you up?'

The door burst open. 'Good morning, I was just about to come out.' He kissed her lightly on the forehead.

He followed her into the kitchen. He'd already had his shower and was half-dressed, wearing only a t-shirt and slacks and padding around in his socks, his hair shower-messy. 'Thanks.' He reached over and took the mug. 'So, what's this complicated conversation you had yesterday?'

She glanced away, her tongue massaging her upper lip as she picked her way through her words. Her response began with a sigh. 'Dad, promise you will hear me out before you start poo-pooing me, okay?'

'All right then, spit it out. I'm intrigued.'

'Here goes.' She wrapped her fingers tightly around the coffee mug. 'I swear that Maria was serious. She told me she spoke to Mum before her disappearance. One day, Mum called her sounding anxious and said she needed to talk. Of course, Maria came straight over, and when she arrived Mum was in a right state. She told Maria the scanner had special powers and she could travel back in time.'

She carefully avoided the word 'magic', knowing that would set up an immediate barricade, yet the facts as she told them were no more palatable.

Her father just sat there, silent, incredulity etched all over his features as though he were an ancient carving. He looked dumbfounded.

The questions clattered about in the silence.

'That can't be true,' he said at last. 'Why would Maria, and Cassie for that matter, sprout such rubbish?'

'For what it's worth,' Katy said, 'I believe it. Or at least I believe that Maria was being honest, and she believed Mum was. She's her oldest friend, Dad. Remember that photo we found on the scanner? Well, Maria said Mum told her she wanted to go back and undo the events of the night when Scott had his accident; she wanted to save him. That makes a bit of sense, doesn't it? Doesn't it? Mum wasn't deranged or anything. Granted she might have been sucked in by some hoax the old woman had in mind, but she's not stupid. I have no idea how it works, but I believe she believed it!'

'But it's nonsense. Impossible! There has to be another explanation.'

'But what if there isn't, Dad? What if there isn't?' Katy left the words hanging in the air, praying her dad would open his mind a little. 'Anyway, I was really blown away by what she told me, and I rang Aunt Emma as soon as I came home.'

'What did she say?'

'What does anyone say? The same as I did, at first, and what you're saying now. 'It can't be true'. But I think she could tell how worried I am, and so is she, so she's coming up. There is something freaky going on, and we plan to go and see this woman to get to the bottom of it.'

Jeff snorted.

Katy leapt up and went over to the sink with her mug. 'To be honest, right now I don't care what you think. I'm convinced we have to keep an open mind and explore all possibilities.'

She stalked into her room and slammed the door shut.

***

Jeff sat alone in the kitchen, staring at his coffee mug, deep in thought. The bleak stillness hung for a little longer until he set down his cup and moved to hover outside Katy's room. 'We should at least call the police and let them know,' Jeff said as he leaned against her closed door.

'I don't care what you do. Your stubborn scepticism stops you seeing what's right in front of your face. If you think it's going to help, fine,' she shouted back at him.

'Don't be like that, Katy. You have to admit, it's far-fetched.'

She burst out of the room. 'Of course it's far-fetched. It's stupid, but at least it fits!' Her eyes bored into him, fierce and confrontational. 'Do you seriously think the police will do any better?' She turned away from him again, buried her head in her hands, rubbing her face in anguish. She turned back. 'Listen, listen. Just pretend for a minute that it's true. It makes the pieces fit. You can't deny that.'

'How, for God's sake! How?'

'Her mood changed after she bought the scanner. That could be because she was trying to deconstruct the enormity of it. She needed time alone. She *wanted* to get away. Really, Dad, have you ever known Mum to be like that? Then 'poof', she disappears without taking a single personal item with her. The most glaring evidence of all—that photo stuck in the machine. And then there's Mrs Parker's observation—'

'I get it, I get it,' he interrupted her. 'So you're expecting me to forget logic and go along with the story that your mother is, as we speak, in some alternate reality. Don't you think it is all just a little bit implausible?' He craned his neck as he spoke, the veins large and exposed.

Katy was on a roll. 'What about the photos, Dad? Why would Mum cut out little tiny images of our faces? She wanted to carry them with her, that's why. Forget about logic. Forget about certainty for a moment. At least think about the improbable.'

'I still think we should call the police and let them know'

'I can't stop you, can I? But consider this, and I know it is a ginormous if. *If* this is true, they're not going to find anything here, and telling them will only raise suspicions. Would *you* believe it if you were them? We might open ourselves up to scrutiny ...' She trailed off, leaving him to think about it.

Jeff threw his hands in the air, exasperated by her fervent response. 'So how long do we wait, hey? When she's been gone two weeks, two months? We'll have to face the truth sometime.'

'Yes, we will.' She said no more, calm now, pulling herself into check, trying to stay rational. 'How about this?' Her voice was calm again, the words measured and deliberate. 'Emma is coming up tomorrow and she has an idea about how to track down this woman who sold her the scanner. When we do, and you can come if you like, you can hear whatever we hear. In fact, would you like me to call Maria and arrange for her to come over for a coffee so she can tell you what she told me?'

Jeff shook his head, glanced at the time. 'Shit, I have to go.'

Ten minutes later, he was out the door.

***

Katy wondered how the day would unfold. Now she'd voiced her feelings, she felt less confident. It sounded ridiculous.

It crossed her mind to call the old witch. If she knew where to find her right now, she'd be off like a shot, give her a piece of her mind and worm the facts out of her. Stupid, evil woman!

But she daren't. Better to wait. Ideas and theories floated back and forth like flotsam in a running stream. Every time she dared her mind to embrace the idea, the tangibility of the real world blockaded her meanderings.

A knock on the door interrupted her thoughts.

Not sure who it could possibly be, she opened it just a tiny crack and peered out. The first thing she saw was the distinctive chequered band on the cap and she immediately jumped to the conclusion that her father must have called the police after all. At first she was angry but then she relaxed, recognising the fine, chiselled features of the officer they had spoken to at the station, Constable Burwood. He was smiling.

'Hi, I was concerned after I called you yesterday. Is everything all right? You hung up on me.'

She softened. 'Oh, I'm sorry. I'm fine. I was just upset that's all. It looks as though Mum is really missing and we're beside ourselves. Come in. Can I make you a coffee? Is that allowed while you're on duty?'

'No, I'm afraid. I was on my way back to the station and I was passing by. So I thought I'd just check everything was okay. Another time maybe.' He threw her a look she couldn't read.

'Yeah, sure,' she heard herself say.

'Are you sure everything's okay?' The young policeman asked, but not getting an answer, continued. 'All right then, but please call. Let me know how you go.'

'Okay. Thank you.' She closed the door gently and leaned against it for just a moment.

Her phone rang and she picked it up from the kitchen bench. It was Emma. Her flight wasn't coming in until five o'clock so that would work well. She let her dad know and he told her he'd be home late again. He suggested she take Emma out for dinner.

She rang her grandparents and told them there was no news. They were both distressed but appeased for now. Emma had agreed it was best not to tell them about her meeting with Maria. Let them believe the police were doing their job to bring their daughter home safely. It was the best narrative to run with, until they knew more.

Exhausted, Katy took off her runners, set her phone alarm, fell on the bed, and sank into the pillow. Images of her mother danced in her imagination—her mother the way she had been and the way she was just before all this happened. Why hadn't she listened more closely, asked more questions when her mum obviously needed to talk? She remembered the phone call to the old witch, Constable Burwood's smile, Maria's distress. Pictures and words, like floating clouds, wafted over her until she dozed off.

***

The airport was busy for a Thursday; movement through the traffic near the pick-up area was slow and tedious. Katy could see her aunt waiting on the footpath long before Emma realised she was there, but at last she was close enough to pull in.

Emma's face lit up the instant she spied Katy, and she hurried towards the spot where she was parked.

Emma wrenched open the door. 'Boy, am I glad to see you.' She threw her overnight bag on the back seat and flopped in beside her niece.

Katy leaned over and gave her aunt a quick hug and a big kiss on the cheek. 'Me too. Thank you so much for coming up. I feel better already.'

'So how are you all bearing up?'

'You just get on with it, don't you? Gran and Pops are worried sick of course, but we try to reassure them as best we can. We're all anxious, but at their age, and with Gran's heart issues, it's probably worse for them. And Dad, well, you know Dad—stoic and intensely private. Actually, I shouldn't say that. He has talked about it but isn't prepared to listen to anything except logic and fact. Right now both are in short supply.'

'I can imagine. He was never one to lose sight of the data, but it's good he's staying calm.'

'Yes it is. His job is demanding. He's taken some time off, but he still goes in every now and then. At least he has that to sink into'

'And you? What about you?' Emma reached over and brushed away a lock of hair that was hiding Katy's face. 'How are you managing?'

Katy's eyes were shining pools. A single tear escaped. She snorted before pulling in a deep breath. 'I'm good, really I am.' She glanced quickly at her aunt to reassure her. 'Honest. I have my moments, but so far I've managed to keep myself occupied and, for the most part, rational. I wish Dad was on the same page though, that's all.'

'Yes. I can imagine that's hard, but what we're suggesting sounds pretty unlikely, you have to admit, though I had a thought on the plane. It might be nothing, but given what you've told me, I thought I'd mention it. Not long after I was up, I did get one strange call from your mum. She asked me about my eighth birthday present. At the time, I assumed it was just because she was looking through those old photos, but now I wonder.'

Katy brightened. 'Hmmm. Why would she bring that up? I'm so glad you're here. At least now we can follow this hunch, ridiculous or not, together. She reached over and laid her hand on Emma's knee.

The little blue car zoomed up the highway until the turnoff, where Katy took the exit towards home.

'Are you hungry? There are some lovely little restaurants where we can have dinner. Dad said he'll be home late. We can drop off your bags at home and you can freshen up first.'

'That'd be great. I'm glad to see you're still eating.'

'I couldn't for the first couple of days, but you know, you get used to the horrible reality. Isn't that weird? You can't function when you're in shock, and then after a while, the harshness of the situation becomes a routine, and then you realise you still need to eat. Life goes on around you as normal. Does that sound weird?'

'Well, we all manage our grief in different ways, don't we?' Emma said.

CHAPTER 34

1969

Cassie pondered that there were about two hundred and forty hours to worry about the test results, and worry she did. Scott was not particularly sympathetic, there was no comfort there.

When at last it was time to call the doctor for the results, Cassie's chest felt tight and her finger shook, barely able to find the right digits on the dial.

She waited an interminable time before she heard the doctor's voice.

'Hello Cassie, your test came back positive this morning. I'm sorry; I know it's not what you want to hear. If you come back in, I'll give you that letter to the obstetrician I promised.'

Cassie stared out at the busy street in stunned silence.

'Cassie ... Cassie. Are you alright?'

'Y-y-yes.' Cassie shuddered. Everything slowed down; all she could sense was the buzzing in her brain. The news hung somewhere outside herself, suspended by threads of recrimination and remorse.

Dazed and shocked, she left the phone box, the door slamming loudly behind her.

On the way home, she went to a different box and called Scott. 'I'm pregnant,' she sobbed into the phone the minute she heard his voice.

'That's stupid! We only did it the once!'

The wretchedness bled from her. The pain, the regret, the fear— all poured from her in a deluge of tears.

Scott huffed as he let out his annoyance. 'I don't believe it.'

Cassie fumbled in her bag for a tissue and tried to blow her nose to stem the flow that threatened to drown her. 'I need to think. Can I come to your place? I'll call Mum and let her know I won't be home for dinner; I can't bear to face my parents right now.'

'Where are you? I'll pick you up!' He waited just long enough to get her instructions then hung up.

Later, at his place, he left her sitting alone on the sofa and started to make her a coffee, then changed his mind and instead poured a small amount of brandy from a leftover bottle into a small glass. He handed the tumbler to her. Cassie glared at him, then at the brandy. Without a word, she lunged out and took the glass and gulped it down in one hit. It made her cough, but she wanted oblivion right now.

Scott flopped down on the seat next to her. 'So what are ya going to do?'

Cassie glared at him. 'What? This baby is as much yours as mine.' She placed her hand protectively over her belly.

'There's no way I'm gonna take responsibility for a kid.'

'Do you think it's what I want? You've got no idea have you?' Tears stung her eyelids. 'Okay forget it, I wouldn't want you as its dad anyway. I'll sort it out myself.'

'I'll help you find a doctor who can get rid of it.'

'Just get me out of here. I want to go home.' She was disgusted.

Without a word he picked up his car keys and headed to the door. Cassie followed and daren't look at him again.

As soon as she was home, she hid in the sanctuary of her room, struggling with the prospect of facing the reality and dealing with it. It was impossible to reconcile the feelings of dizzy euphoria of those reckless moments with Scott, and her bitter anger now.

It wasn't fair. She bit her lip so hard she tasted blood. Damn!

I'm not strong enough to give up my baby. She knew a girl who had done it once under intense pressure from her parents, and it broke her heart. Besides, she was still so young and had no faith in her own ability to nurture and protect a baby either, but having got herself into this mess, it was up to her to sort it out. *Why did I ever come back?*

From her brief and limited experience of time travel she deduced that the passing of the hours pretty much ran parallel to what she remembered as home, and she tortured herself as the hours melted into days then into weeks, knowing how worried those who loved her and waited for her in 2013 must be. But she had to make a decision, and driven by a need to resolve the dilemma, she made the only one she felt she could.

Her parents worried and fussed about her, knowing something was dreadfully wrong but powerless to help. Emma gave her a wide berth, unable to deal with the intensity of her moods. Jeff and Katy sank into obscurity as she battled with her conscience, and the longer she battled the more distance stretched between them. She had trouble remembering their faces and their mannerisms, and yet she ached to be back in that secure, comfortable world.

She was lying on her bed agonising over her situation when her mum knocked gently on the door and came in carrying a cup of Milo, as if that would solve anything.

'What is it dear? What is so terrible that you won't let us help you? You know we love you no matter what, but we are afraid for you right now. What's worrying you so much?' She looked away, unable to hide her pain. 'One day you'll have children of your own and you'll understand. We want to help. Please.'

Cassie did understand, more than she wished she did. 'Mum, I just can't. I will get through this, I promise. I am going through an awful time right now, but it's my awful time, my problem, and I need to fix it. I will, I promise. I love you, Mum. Please don't worry about me.'

Her mother sighed and turned away, closing the door softly behind her.

Not long afterward the phone rang, and she heard her name mentioned.

'It's Scott for you, Cassie.' Her mum called out.

'H ... h ... h ... hello.' Cassie spoke softly, and looked over her shoulder to see if her mum was within earshot.

'I was in shock ... I didn't know what to say or do.'

That's his apology? 'I don't know what to do either, but if you can help me find someone, that would be a start.'

'Okay, so do you want me to try to find a doctor who will do an abortion?'

Cassie realised she was in no position to reject his offer of help. 'Yes,' she whispered, and hung up.

On her way to the shop the next day, Cassie was lost in deep thought as she kicked pebbles along the path. Her hand found its way to her soft belly for the umpteenth time and the tears welled in her eyes.

It had been six weeks and the last couple of days she had put all her energy into trying to find a doctor who would perform an abortion. It was such an ugly, despicable word. Just thinking it made her feel dirty and disgusting. She knew she'd get through it, but her judgement was clouded and emotional.

Scott had come up with the names of three doctors who might be able to help her. As soon as she finished work in the afternoon, she gathered up all the change she could and walked a few blocks from old Mr Fieldham's to another telephone. She started dialling, not quite knowing what to say, praying that the doctor or receptionist might know what she was asking.

What she was planning to do was immoral, illegal and very sleazy, but she felt trapped.

The first doctor was out of town. The second was no longer practising. The third name filled her with dread. He was a last resort. Even she had heard stories. He was a backyard operator. The thought made her feel ill. She couldn't do it. She slammed the door of the booth behind her and headed home. She hoped she would have some horrible accident and lose the baby, then immediately felt guilty.

After two days of putting it off, the pressure to do something became unbearable. Hanging over her was this most horrible of horrible choices to make, but she was carrying the responsibility for everyone's happiness, not just her own. She still had a whole life yet to live. Then there were her parents, her sister and, of course, the family which technically did not yet exist, and a tiny baby wanting to.

She doubted whether she loved anyone at all. Not Scott—all the romance and glamour had been flushed down the toilet. Her future family? She could hardly visualise them. Maybe the thought of disappointing her parents was the biggest driving force. She couldn't tell anymore. Least of all she loved herself. Every time a small wave of tenderness for the little being inside washed over her, she pushed it away bitterly.

She avoided family time; her distressed parents had called Maria trying to find out what was going on. Cassie hated deceiving them all this way, but she believed the alternative was not an option. Every decision she made was a bad decision. There was only the choice of taking the one with the least catastrophic consequences.

The following Monday it was arranged, more or less. The first call had been the hardest. The doctor answered, spoke in riddles, told her to come to the surgery that night. Scott picked her up from her home and they drove in silence to the address he had given. It was in a rough part of town, and when they reached it, she saw the 'Surgery' was literally a room under his house. She was horrified.

He was an abrupt, no-nonsense man, swaying his big frame around like a prize fighter, and all he did on that first visit was lay down the ground rules. Cassie heard everything, but his words just bounced off the walls. Her body was no longer her own, it was as if she was floating above it. It was a criminal cloak-and-dagger process. Every day she rang the doctor and he'd give her a pre-arranged code word as to the likelihood that it would happen that night.

Scott managed to raise the $250 fee. She daren't ask how he got it. It was more money than she had ever seen in her young adolescent life. He assured her he would be there on the night when it was finally going to happen. The plan was to drop her off and wait in the car outside. Even this had sinister undertones. It had to be done very discreetly for fear of encountering a police patrol.

The following Wednesday, she got the green light.

The critical night arrived. A week after making the first call, almost seven weeks after that first fateful day she had catapulted into her past. She'd lied to her parents and told them Scott was taking her to visit friends and it was a bit of a drive so she would be home late. Her father simply reminded her of her eleven o'clock curfew, oblivious to the truth of her mission.

Cassie waited in the dingy outer room, devoid of patients. It enveloped her like a putrid smell. After several hours, the doctor came out and told her it was just too risky. He couldn't do it.

It was awful, to come this far, to slay all the demons and then be turned away.

It was all too much. She broke down in agonising sobs as she hopped into the car next to Scott. He tried to comfort her, but it was much too late for any of it, and she pushed him away angrily.

The horrendous process started again. Call in the afternoon, code words and innuendo. It coloured her existence. At last it was another yes. That night. It was Saturday. How could that be? Other girls her age were getting ready to go to the pictures or a party. She had to make more excuses to her parents and was crushed when Scott told her he couldn't be there, because it was his mother's birthday. He promised to meet her back at his house as soon as he could and they arranged for her to catch a taxi to his place as soon as it was over, hopefully giving her some time to rest before he would take her home.

Suddenly she realised she could not do this on her own, and in desperation she headed to Maria's place. In her room, safe from prying adults, Cassie broke down and confessed all to her closest friend.

'I'm terrified. I don't think I can do this,' she said.

Maria put her arm around her, tears of commiseration and empathy running freely down her flushed cheeks, re-assuring her and telling her it was the only choice she had.

Having Maria there steeled Cassie for the night ahead. Maria asked her mum if she could go out with Cassie for a while and told her she might be late. Her mother hesitated and examined her daughter's face. She asked a few questions, curious, but mercifully, just hugged Maria and asked her if everything was all right. Maria assured her she just wanted to be with her friend because she was going through a tough time. No more.

Scott had agreed to take her before he went to his parent's place, and he was surprised and annoyed when Cassie instructed him to Maria's house to pick her up as well. The three of them drove in tense silence to the quack's surgery.

The two friends waited and waited and waited. Periodically the doctor would come out to offer a few abrupt words, urging them to be patient. The evening melted into night, and unable to wait any longer, Maria turned to Cassie. 'I'm so sorry, but I have to leave. My parents will be suspicious if I'm home too late. Do you think you'll all right?'

'I'll have to be. It's okay.' Cassie hung her head and began to cry.

Maria hugged her girlfriend tightly. 'You are doing the right thing. It's hard, and it feels wrong, but it truly is best for everyone. Just keep remembering that while you wait. Stay strong, my friend.'

With nothing further to say, Maria got up and quietly walked away, leaving Cassie with her own hideous thoughts caught in a hellish purgatory. Alone with the night, everything pressing on her like a mighty anvil, she started to shake uncontrollably. But she sat frozen in her seat. The clock on the wall showed 1.00 am. She was scared and tired. Her parents would be frantic. The place was disgusting. Occasionally she would see a beam of light travelling slowly across the closed window blinds of the pathetic little hole he called a surgery. She assumed it was the police

Just then the doctor came out. 'Come in,' he said.

He was a creep—big and slimy, moustached and menacing. The surgery was darkish, presumably to evade attention, only a bright light sat arced over the operating table. There was someone else there but, by then, Cassie had lost all sense of reality and the room was spinning around her. She smelled the disinfectant, heard the clunking of metal instruments, but it was happening somewhere else. Things moved rapidly. There were voices echoing around her, a sense of doom and urgency pervading the room. Someone pushed her legs apart. Instinctively she tried to fight it, only to be met with a malicious retort. 'You should have kept your legs closed before.'

Oh, God! It was happening.

She couldn't see for the tears and sweat drowning her. As if to give the knife a sinister twist, the butcher dangled a tiny morsel of a human being in cold steel forceps. Was this how it ended? She screamed in horror. She pleaded with the tiny soul for forgiveness, trying to reassure it and herself that this was the only way. She moaned, she cried, she hurtled abuse into the dispassionate room, and then it was over.

She was pulled roughly up off the table. The abortionist gave her some rudimentary instructions for the next few days. The person with him, whom she now saw was an older woman, gave her a huge pack of what looked like sanitary pads. She took them without a word.

'You'll bleed; a lot ... use these to stop the flow. You must rest tomorrow and once the bleeding has stopped, don't lift anything for at least a week.'

Dazed and disoriented she fell into the lonely night, staggering in pain and disbelief and begging her God for forgiveness.

She had no recollection of how she got to Scott's place. She banged on the door loudly, desperately. At last he arrived, half asleep. He hadn't been there for her. She was all alone in this, but she couldn't possibly go home. He took her onto the verandah where there was a day bed and asked her to sit. He gave her a drink of strong, sweet tea, trying desperately to calm her down. She was still shaking uncontrollably and unable to speak, frozen in shock. Scott got a blanket and wrapped it around her, then sat down. They clung together for a long time, scared and confused.

At last she blurted out. 'Call mum, she'll be out of her mind with worry.' She continued, her shoulders were heaving. 'There's nothing we can do, Scott. It's over, it's over.' She sobbed, burying her face in her hands—tears of loss, relief and shame. When she calmed down, she asked Scott to leave her alone.

There was more blood than she'd ever imagined. She curled up in the bed in a foetal position, clutching a thick towel she'd found draped over the railing between her legs like a life raft. She tried to cling on to consciousness and begged for the release of sleep at the same time, only aware that nothing would ever be the same again.

CHAPTER 35

2013

When Katy opened her eyes the next morning, she felt different. There'd been a shift. Talking with Emma had been cathartic because she seemed so much more receptive and understanding. It was as if her fantasies started to take form. Putting their stories and clues of the last weeks together, a picture was emerging. It was a fantastic, surreal, chimerical, freakish picture.

Why would her mother bring up Emma's birthday which happened over forty years ago? Then there were Mrs Parker's observations. When she talked about that light explosion, she'd expressed wonder. That was it, wonder, and she said the phenomenon was almost celestial. She couldn't wait to get the day started. Katy felt optimistic.

It was Emma who broached the subject of the paranormal with her father. He stiffened visibly, and threw her a look that said, 'Not this again'.

Katy reached over the table and put her hand over his. 'Just listen, Dad ... please.'

Emma told him about the visit to the psychic and the strange phone call from Cassie after she bought the scanner, which in hindsight suggested that Cassie was reliving an event that happened when they were kids. The shreds of conversation took on a complex structure of possibilities.

Katy's dad sat there, saying nothing, his expression vague and disbelieving. But he listened.

'I don't suppose you can remember the exact day she asked you about the ballet shoes, can you, Emma?' Katy said.

'Golly no ... I don't think so. Wait a minute. It was a Tuesday night. Why did I remember that? Oh, yes, I'd only just walked in from dropping Tamara off at basketball practice; that's on a Tuesday.'

Katy gave her dad a pointed look. 'Dad, remember the night you came home and found Mum fainted on the floor? That was a

Monday, wasn't it? 'It makes sense; it fits. I'll bet if we can check the dates, it'll work.'

The three of them sat, staring blankly at each other.

The shadow of silence grew longer. It stretched into the corners of the house. Neither Emma nor Katy dared say anymore, sensing Jeff had reached the limits of affability.

He surprised them, blurting out, 'Okay. Supposing you are on to something, and supposing the scanner has these 'supernatural' properties, and supposing the dates align. Where does that leave us?'

The women exchanged a look of satisfaction.

Emma said, 'I suggest we track down this psychic, witch, shaman, whatever it is you want to call her, and find out what she told Cassie. I have an idea where I can find her but not where she lives, and Katy, you have her phone number, don't you? Or ...' She looked at Katy's dad. 'You could try calling her, Jeff, to see if you have any luck.'

'No, no, no, no. Keep me out of this altogether. I'm no good at that shit.'

'Alright then, it's settled. Katy, you and I are off to see the weird old witch.'

Katy couldn't move for an instant, dumbfounded her dad had pivoted. But now she jumped up to join her aunt.

'Right then, let's do this.' Emma linked her arm in Katy's.

'I'll leave you girls to it,' Katy's father said. 'I'm going to work.'

Katy rummaged through the basket and found the yellow card advertising the scanner and showed it to Emma. 'This is her number; do you want to try to call her? She might be more responsive to you.'

'No, I've got another idea ... we'll catch her at work. I think it was the Being Centre. I'm certain Cassie had a purple card when she came out.'

'Is this the one? I found it in her wallet.' Katy handed her another card that she'd picked up off the bench.

Emma read it out loud. 'Anastasia Pendle. Phone 0432 786 499.'

'It matches the number on the yellow one; that's how I worked out it was her.' Katy's voice grew louder with excitement.

'I'd like to face her in person,' Emma said.

                    Ineke van Os

Katy was already searching 'Being Centre' on her phone. Her eyebrows were knotted in concentration as her finger slid down the possibilities. 'Nothing under that name I'm afraid. I'll try something else. Can you remember where it was?'

A moment later, she found a website. 'Could this be it?' she handed her phone to Emma.

'Hmm ... 'Soul Centre'. It's in McDowall. The address doesn't mean anything, but it could be the one; it was a short, snappy name like that. I'm sure I'll recognise the place when I see it.'

'Let's go then.' Katy said.

They were ready to go just after nine. Katy knew the suburbs well, but when they reached McDowall, she was at a loss, so she pulled over and checked the map.

The minute they pulled into the street, Emma smiled. 'This is it, I'm sure. I recognise that huge fig tree.'

They pulled in. It was well back from the road, and the traffic hummed softly in the distance. The sweet fragrance of jasmine mixed with wonderful aromas wafting from the old house, and as they made their way to the entrance, Katy felt its healing aura. It was hard to imagine this was the source of their worries.

As they entered. Emma said, 'It feels just as sublime as last time, though I doubt your mum would agree.' She glanced sideways at Katy. 'It seems ages ago; so much has happened.'

'Hello, we are looking for this lady.' Katy handed the receptionist the purple card.

'I'm so sorry, she's not in today ... she might be here in the morning. Anastasia doesn't come in as often as she used to. Can I help you?'

'No, not really. It's a personal matter. I don't suppose you know where she lives?'

'I'm afraid I can't give you her address. I'm sure you understand.'

'Yes, we do.' The disappointment in Emma's voice dripped on to the rug.

But Katy wasn't prepared to walk away. 'It's terribly important. Can we make an appointment to see her in the morning please?'

The young receptionist looked at them both, her big hoop earrings wobbling as she shook her head.

'Please ... we just want to ask her a few questions. We promise not to take long,' Emma said.

Stalling again, the earrings hung lifeless as the girl looked down. 'I'm sorry, she only does the readings once a week, and she's fully booked tomorrow.'

'Well, what time does she come in?' Emma persisted.

'Early. Her first appointment is at eight. I'm not sure she would take too kindly to being ambushed.'

'We won't.' Emma took Katy by the elbow and turned to leave. 'We'll be back.'

They decided to go and visit Gran and Pops. Katy dialled their number to let them know, but there was no answer.

'That's funny, but we can try them again later. Maybe they can't hear the phone or something. I've got another idea. Let's go and visit Maria. Do you remember her?'

'Of course, we were reunited when I was up with the girls last time.'

When Katy called, she was pleased to hear a much warmer tone than last time. Maria invited them for lunch. It was a bit of a drive, but they didn't mind.

Maria was more relaxed than when Katy last saw her. She was less inhibited and seemed happy to talk without reservation. The conversation revolved around Cassie's disappearance. The three of them dissected and analysed the information, each contributing their own theories to the mystery. The older women reassured Katy that her mother was no fool, that wherever she was, they were certain she was alive, and she would find her way back to them.

The time whizzed by, and they had to leave. 'It was great to see you; thanks for coming. Don't forget to let me know the minute you hear anything. I'm curious to find out what happens when you talk to that psychic.' Maria said.

'So are we!' they shouted in unison as they drove off.

Katy tried to call her grandparents again, and this time her Gran answered. She arranged to call in on their way home.

Visiting Gran and Pops was more difficult. They were waiting for them, looking stressed and anxious.

Pops hurried to meet them. 'Any news?' he looked at Katy. 'Your Gran's been getting quite agitated. She's convinced Cassie is in trouble.'

'No Dad, I'm sorry. I'm glad I'm here though.' Emma gave him the longest hug, and then reached for her mum who appeared, wringing her hands.

Katy hugged them both and they went inside.

The house was untidy. There were dishes in the sink, the bench tops hadn't been wiped, and there were bits and pieces of clutter all over the place. That was not like Gran. It made Katy feel sad.

'You and Dad sit down; we'll make you a cup of tea,' Emma said.

They disappeared into the kitchen. Once alone, Emma turned to Katy, her brows knitted in worrying lines. 'Oh my, I had no idea anyone could age that much in just a few weeks. Did you notice the mess?'

'They look awful, don't they? Did you see Gran's eyes? They were all grey and rheumy. This is terrible; I've been so selfish, totally wrapped up in myself. What can we do?'

Emma put her arm around her niece. 'We need to be mindful of their feelings. Remember, we know more than they do, and we have activity to keep us occupied. They have nothing; only each other to lean on and I doubt Dad would be a pillar of strength right now.'

Katy hung her head and cupped her face in her hands, rubbing her eyes. 'I feel awful, like I've been neglecting them. Do you think we should tell them what we know?'

'I'm not sure they could handle it. It's hardly comforting, is it? No, I think we'd best keep them focussed on the fact that the police are doing their job.'

Back inside, Emma set down the tray and started divvying out cups of tea. Katy put a plate of biscuits on the table. She leaned over to Gran and hugged her, then turned to Pops and planted a kiss on his cheek.

He reached out and threw an arm around his granddaughter and whispered, 'Your grandmother's been acting strangely; I'm worried about her too.'

'I just know that Cassie is in trouble and needs me, and I feel so useless.' Gran grabbed a tissue from the box beside her and dabbed at her eyes.

'Mum, Cassie will be all right,' Emma said. 'We have to have faith and patience. I'm glad I came; it's much better being close to you all. We need to be here for each other.' Trying to lighten the mood, she changed the subject. 'Where were you this morning?'

Pop answered. 'At a Seniors Citizens meeting. My friend, Frank, picked us up; I don't much like driving these days. It was a diversion.'

'Are you sure you've nothing else to tell us?' Gran looked at Katy expectantly.

She bit her lip. 'Actually, it's very low key. We haven't heard anything from the police yet.'

'Well, why aren't you badgering them?' Pops sounded grumpy.

'We can't. They warned us it might take a while. Katy tried placating him. 'I know you're worried, Pops, but we have to let them do their job. We honestly believe she is alive and well. There has to be a reasonable explanation.'

Emma and Katy stayed long enough to clean up the kitchen and tidy up a bit before they left, making sure there was a meal in the fridge for the evening.

Katy sighed as they left. 'That was terrible. I wish I could have told them more.'

Emma took both Katy's hands in hers and looked into her niece's eyes. 'Darling, everyone is on edge right now. I think you did the right thing. We have to try to be more inclusive with them though; we'll tell them all we know as soon as we can.'

'Yes, I guess so. But what happens if we've got it completely wrong and we're wasting our time.'

'But imagine if we're right? We just can't possibly blabber our suspicions to the world right now. Who'd believe us?'

Katy's dad was sitting at the computer when she arrived home. He'd checked the dates and they did in fact align with the events they had discussed. It was another tiny piece of information that supported their theory. In turn, the women filled him in on the day's events, adding how shocked they were to see Gran and Pops in such a dreadful state. Clearly the anguish of missing Cassie was hitting them hard.

Just before heading to bed, Katy plugged her phone on charge and noticed a missed call. She didn't recognise the number, and it was late so she dismissed it. If it was important, they'd call again. She thought no more about it. She said a silent prayer for her mother and fell into an exhausted sleep.

CHAPTER 36

1969

The world blurred. There were no straight lines or edges. Cassie didn't know where her body began and the air around her ended. She couldn't remember where she was and her limbs were like jelly. Had she really done it? Really? This horrific thing that defiled all she believed.

It was done. But what had she done? The burden of guilt and shame weighed on her. It was as if she was dead, and all the earth had buried her, pressing her into obscurity. She was gone.

Dragged into some living hell, young Cassie grappled with sensibility. She was only vaguely aware of her surroundings. Every now and then, Scott's voice reverberated in the distance. Murmurings of concern. She didn't know or care. She hated Scott, bitter at everything he had taken from her. She hated everyone and everything. She imagined she heard her mother's voice too; it was soft and kind, but seemed far away.

It was in the afternoon when she first perceived some tangible part of the world around her. She lay on the bed groping for clarity. She could barely make out the wooden blinds rattling gently in the breeze. A gentle hand caressed her forehead. And there were words. She could hear words ... not all of them, but they were loving and tender.

Her mother leaned over her, wrapping her child's body in her own. 'Oh, sweetheart. What have you done? It doesn't matter. Never mind, all that matters is that you are alive. I'm here. I'm right here; you'll be all right. You *have* to be all right. Why didn't you come to us?'

Everything was bent out of shape, not only time. Had her mother sat there for hours or days? She didn't know, but eventually the haze in Cassie's brain started to lift. The pain eased, though she couldn't stop herself clutching her tummy where her baby had been. *My baby! Oh God.* The truth kept slapping at her. What she'd done. What an unholy, miserable mess she'd created.

She looked at her mother, whose eyes were red from countless tears, but in them there was also a softness. 'I'm sorry, I'm sorry, Mum. I didn't know what to do. I'm so sorry.'

'Shhhh ... it's all right darling, you need to rest. We can talk later. I am staying right here with you. I love you, and I'm here for you, as long as you need me.'

Cassie was sobbing, her face wet, a deluge of regret glistening on her feverish skin.

Her mother fussed and fretted, brought her hot drinks and nourishment, laid warm towels on her pain, listened when she needed to, and chased Scott away when it was too much. Each moment was fermented in love and concern.

After a time, Cassie was stronger, sitting up, able to talk without breaking down. For the first time since it happened, she was able to think of someone and something else besides herself and the baby she had murdered.

They were alone on the verandah at Scott's place.

'Oh, Mum. I'm so sorry.'

'Darling, I'm just pleased you're alive. It's so good to see the colour coming back into your cheeks.'

'How long have you been here?'

Since the wee hours of Sunday morning. Scott called me, he was afraid you were going to die. We hadn't slept a wink—we were out of our minds with worry. Thank God it was me who answered the phone; I was so relieved you were alive! I explained to your father that you were okay but in trouble, and that I needed to be by your side right now. He took a bit of convincing, but I think he understood. I came straight over and I've been here ever since.

'So what have you told him now? How long have I been here?' Cassie asked.

'You've had a rough couple of days. I called your father and explained you'd be alright but had taken ill with girl problems, and that I'd stay with you at Maria's for a day or two till you were better. He didn't want to know any more, but I could tell he's worried.' She sighed and went on. 'Then I rang Maria. When I found out she knew, I was very angry, but once I calmed down, I realised she was only trying to be a good friend. Then all I wanted to do was protect you from any more pain and letting you rest here seemed like the best option. The boys here were kind enough to drag a mattress onto the verandah so I could stay with you, and I've done my best to keep out of their way.'

'Oh Mum, I've made such a mess of things.'

'It's done; we can't undo what's happened.' Her mother frowned. 'But I want to know who did this. Who butchered my little girl?' There was a tone of acerbity and anger Cassie had never heard before in her voice.

'Please don't ask me, Mum, I can't say. He was a creep, but he did what I asked him to do, and if I report him, it means there's no way out for all those other girls who have nowhere else to go.'

'I'll find out anyway. You know that,' her mother said, and Cassie was too weak to argue.

Instead she said, 'I can't imagine what you've been through. I'm finished with Scott. What did you tell Mr Fieldham?'

'Hmm, I said you had come down with glandular fever and wouldn't be able to come to work for quite a while. He was very understanding, and said he hoped you'd be back when you were feeling better.'

'Oh, Mum, I've made such a mess of things.' Cassie dropped her head in her hands. A sob escaped, but she managed to pull herself together.

'Come on, it's time to go home, you've been away too long, and your father and Emma are worried about you. I can't make excuses for you any longer.' Her mother was firm, but placed her hand over Cassie's as she spoke.

Cassie shook her head vehemently. 'I'm not ready. I'm not brave enough to face them.'

'Listen,' her mother shook her index finger at her, 'you were brave enough to search out a doctor and brave enough to wait in that filthy surgery, so you're brave enough to get on with your life now. It's not over, you know. You're young and, God willing, you will heal and have a beautiful family of your own one day.' She dropped her hand, her tone tender again. 'Come on.' She stood up, took Cassie by the arm and pulled gently to ease her off the bed. 'We can work through the coming months together ... one day at a time, one foot after the other. I'll take you to the doctor to make sure everything is all right, but we won't tell Emma just yet; she's still so young. When the time's right, we can explain it to her together.' She leaned over and squeezed Cassie's hand.

Cassie gathered the few belongings she had and shoved them into a string bag her mother handed to her. Finding a pen and a piece of paper, she scribbled a hurried note to Scott. She couldn't face him again; of that she was certain.

The door creaked softly as she pulled it to, and she prayed she was closing it for the last time. If only it were that easy, if only all the misery and heartache of the last few weeks could be left behind that timber barrier.

Once in the car, the surroundings were less oppressive; things looked as they always had. Her mum was right. She needed to get out of there. 'You know, I went to the doctor straight after it happened and got myself a six months' supply of the pill. I was just really, really unlucky,' she said.

'That's something, I suppose.' Her mother checked her rear-view mirror as she backed into the garage. They were home.

Cassie was relieved to see there was no welcoming committee.

'I told Emma I was bringing you home today, but that you weren't yourself yet, and you needed some space.' She reached over and gave her daughter a big hug. 'We don't have to tell her at all if you don't want to.'

When they got inside, Cassie walked into her bedroom and dumped her stuff. It was like greeting an old friend; here she was safe, wrapped into its comfortable familiarity.

Her mum brought her a big mug of Milo—fixer of all things, and put it on the bedside table.

Once she was alone, Cassie was left with her demons. They sat in the corners, on the desk, perched on the end of the bed, menacing and haunting. The house was quiet and she had no choice but to lie still and allow her thoughts to crystallise.

She must have dozed off, for when she opened her eyes again, the light had changed outside. The western sun was beating down and the room felt hot and humid. Cassie heard footsteps coming up the hallway towards her. There was a light tapping on the door and it opened. It was her father.

'Hello, princess. It's good to see you.' The warmth hit him, and he reached up and switched on the fan. 'It's stifling in here; why didn't you turn this on? That's what it's here for.' He leaned down and gave her the biggest hug. He wasn't usually one for sentimental outpourings of affection. 'I'm glad you're safe.

'I'm fine, Dad. It's good to be back.' She smiled and kissed him on the cheek.

'You just rest and get better soon, okay?' He turned and left the room, mercifully closing the door behind him.

CHAPTER 37

Alone in her bedroom, Cassie had time to think. Gradually her thoughts started to become more coherent. Scraps of images started to resurface. Images of loved ones—her family far away, her real family, her family in the future. It didn't make sense. This was real too. *Now* was real. Intuition gave way to reflections which formed a picture of the magnificent whole. She was here, she knew that for sure, but there was something poking at the veil of her consciousness. Beyond the trauma of the abortion was another layer she'd pushed so far to the back of her mind, she'd almost forgotten it.

Almost ... but not quite.

She got up and rifled through the papers on her desk. The only thing that caught her attention was a number written in the back of her diary. It was significant, but she didn't know why. It was important; something in her gut told her so. She scribbled the number on a piece of paper and lay back on the bed. Holding it up, she stared hard at it.

'XPR 2000079.' She said it softly to herself and pondered the possibilities.

Suddenly she saw it. A picture as clear as a teardrop. She had a vision of Katy and Jeff. Her family, her own family, somewhere a million miles from here, in a place she couldn't see. A cocoon of warmth enveloped her; a feeling so familiar and welcome that her eyes started to water. Her skin tingled and the warmth crept through her body like a blush. She could see her family!

It was as if all the horror of the last few weeks were the illusion. But that wasn't quite right either. That had happened. Scott had happened. The abortion had happened. Then another picture, more perplexing, but every bit as real as the one before emerged. She saw a machine; one she couldn't identify. It looked so detailed it was almost tangible. Cassie was mesmerised. She lay there allowing the images to appear, frame by incredible frame.

Horror and awe mixed together and landed on her like a meteor shower, busting the myth of her existence. She remembered! She had another real family to go home to. It was where she wanted to be more than anything. She was straddling a time warp. The tiny fragments and flashes of recognition became clearer. It was an unimaginable truth.

In the hours that followed she finally understood. There were two separate entities existing inside her. The vivid memory of a life somewhere in the future became clearer, but she knew with absolute conviction that this life was real as well. There had been purpose to it all. The numbers had prompted her, and she resolved to go back as soon as she could. She understood how she had arrived in the first place. She even visualised the old lady and the scanner. Those numbers were her passage home. Repeat them three times out loud and she could end this nightmare!

***

For most of the day her mother had let her be, giving her the space and time to process what had happened. Occasionally she would check on her daughter, bring her a sandwich or a cup of Milo—whatever she felt was needed. Her quiet confidence that her daughter had the resilience to get through this was a safety net. It made Cassie feel protected and loved.

She was overcome with a feeling of wistfulness. She hated the thought of leaving, but now no other path presented itself. Cassie understood that was the only way forward. There was no excuse to stay. She'd saved Scott but killed a baby. A life for a life. It was a shitty deal, but for the first time since her nightmare began, Cassie slept a deep and resigned sleep.

On waking the next morning, she'd found some balance. The truth was more fantastic than she could ever dream. She had got it wrong, and heaven only knows the damage she'd done to herself and all those around her, but she was filled with a new hope. She knew what she had to do. As miserable as her life was in the present reality, she understood that wounds heal, time heals, and that we can't begin to imagine the future that awaits us unless we embrace it.

Her priority was to prepare her young self for the rocky road ahead.

She had the tools to make things easier. Wisdom and experience were on her side, even if she hadn't used those gifts wisely. She had to comfort her seventeen-year-old self, convince her that whatever had happened did not define her. It did not make her a coward or a murderer. She did what she thought was best, even if right now, none of it made any sense.

A new determination set in; she would try to instil in her young heart the courage and confidence to face the future with strength and purpose.

What kept her awake that night were the repercussions of her foolish behaviour. Would the future change? Would the family remember? How had all this affected their evolution? For every question she contemplated, a million others cropped up. Surely this would change everything? Or maybe not. Logic dictated that everyone's futures had changed because of her stupidity. How would this scar an older Cassie? Would her mother look at her differently? The harsh interrogators hung there, hovering in the abyss of the future she had to go back to.

It was 2.00 am. There was no point in just lying here. She padded over to her desk and took out her Snoopy notepad, and by the pale-yellow light of her desk lamp started to write ...

Friday, 19th December 1969
My darling Cassie,
Nothing will prepare you for what I am about to write, but please don't dismiss it, for this is absolutely true.

I am Cassie. I am you. I am you in heart, soul and body. As incredible as this seems, I have come from your future, and I will go back there. I am you in 2013. Through a miracle of time warp I travelled back.

Right now, your world has fallen apart, but I promise that you will never, ever have to experience something as horrific as this again.

I'm ashamed to confess that this is my fault. In a moment's act of selfish disregard for the fallout, I put you into an intolerable situation. For that I am so, so sorry. This knowledge will be a burden I will carry with me for the rest of my life.

This is my story ...

In an alternative reality, Scott was killed in a car accident the night of the senior formal. It haunted me. I felt to blame, and when I was given the opportunity to make amends, I grabbed it. I wanted to save him, that's all.

I was hypnotised by the phenomenon of time travel. The concept is inconceivable, don't you agree? Yet here I am. I never meant to stay. If things had gone as I'd planned, you might never have been aware of that short period I was living your life being you, inside you—experiencing all the emotions and impressions you are living now. I was so intoxicated by your youth and beauty that I lost control.

I know you are at your lowest point. You feel dirty because you have committed an unspeakable act and you can't forgive yourself. You are so filled with self-loathing and regret, that the pain is unbearable. You think you don't deserve to live.

But darling, you do, you really, really do. There are many wonderful things still to come.

Your life has changed inexorably. I cannot undo what's happened, but you can change your attitude to it.

This is the lesson I take back with me. It was a mistake coming back in the first place.

However, I did, and now I have to leave you to deal with the outcome. Remember, I am you. I have every confidence that you will be strong and resolute enough to pick up these broken pieces of yourself and keep going.

Trust me when I tell you there is a time ahead when you will shine. When the decision you had to make will no longer be a crime, when society will be more tolerant, when women are given the right to choose their own course of action. They will have dominion over their bodies.

All this lies ahead for you, and with it, promising opportunities to grow and learn without prejudice or restriction. Your amazing inner strength and beauty will guide you, and you will be part of a new and powerful generation. A generation of women that, step by tiny step, change the world. You will be part of a revolution. Trust in your courage. Take comfort in these words. You will shine.

One day you will meet the man you love and have a beautiful family of your own. The woman in you will rise from the ashes of this experience.

I am leaving, and I sincerely hope you have no lingering awareness of this huge, improbable episode that has made such an impact. You will always be me; it's a deep and irrefutable truth. Love yourself, treasure the time you have and don't waste it on regrets and guilt. You made the only decision you felt you could. In the greater immensity of your life, it's one tragic event and you will heal.

You are loved so very much.

Please keep this letter, keep its secrets, for nothing can be gained by sharing this with anyone. Carry the sentiments in your heart. Keep it as a talisman, a reminder that life is ever changing. The only constant is your soul. Nurture it, Value it beyond all else and live in the present always.

The past can have many demons. Let them rest in peace.

Eternally with love,

Cassie.

Carefully she folded the note into three, then crept into the kitchen, opened her mum's junk drawer and found a good sturdy envelope. She slid the letter inside and crept back to her room for fear of waking anyone. Closing her eyes, she sealed and kissed it. Then she copied a small 'Love is' image from a little book she had onto the back of the envelope—two identical girls holding hands— and circled it with red love hearts.

The cloak of guilt she was wearing was a little lighter. Writing that letter was cathartic for her. She hoped that when young Cassie read it, she would be motivated to move forward. When she went back to bed she fell into a fitful sleep.

CHAPTER 38

2013

Katy and Emma were up early and didn't dawdle over breakfast. Instead, they went through their routine with military precision. At 7.30am, they were sitting in the car outside the Soul Centre, staring at the house like stalking detectives focussed on catching their suspect.

They had no idea what car Anastasia Pendle would be driving, but Emma was confident she would recognise her. A short time later, a little grey van pulled in and parked around the side of the house. From her vantage point Emma was just able to peer around the corner.

'That's her, that's her! Come on, let's go.' Emma leapt out of the car and an instant later bounded up the stairs and straight into reception, Katy trailing behind her.

Emma placed both her palms firmly on the desk. The young girl looked up, startled.

'Yes ... it's us again!'

'W-who?'

Katy had caught up and was horrified to see a different girl at the desk. She was mousy and lacked the confidence of her colleague.

The girl blushed. 'I'm sorry, I don't know you. Can I help you?'

Emma backpedalled. 'Oh, sorry to pounce on you like that, but it's a matter of life and death. We have to talk to Anastasia Pendle. We saw her arrive. We know her first appointment isn't until eight; it's only just gone seven-thirty ... please.'

Katy glanced behind her to find an early client's curious eyes upon them.

The young receptionist bit her lip. 'W-W-Well, I'll see what I can do, but I'm not making any promises.' Regaining her composure, she rose from her chair and stretched herself to her full height and marched off down the hallway.

Katy fiddled with a pen on the desk while they waited.

The girl was back in seconds. 'Ten minutes max. I'm afraid that's all you have.' She pointed down the hallway. 'Third door on the right.'

The two women almost fell over each other in their haste to follow her directions.

The door to Anastasia Pendle's room was ajar. She stood just inside, a deep purple smock hanging loosely over her skeletal frame. Her features were thin and gnarled. Katy understood immediately why her mother must have been intimidated. She looked creepy. The psychic's dark eyes gazed at her and Aunt Emma with suspicion. It was unnerving.

There was an awkward silence for a moment, but then Emma spoke. 'I'm Cassie Foster's sister, Emma. We came here about a month ago, do you remember?'

The old woman's face softened a little and she gave a polite smile. 'I see so many people, dear.'

'I understand, but you sold my mum a scanner and now she's disappeared,' Katy said. 'Please, we are worried about her. You have to tell us what's going on.'

Her tiny body stiffened; she squared her shoulders and said through tight lips, 'I don't have to tell you anything.'

Katy drew closer, her eyes narrowed. 'No, you don't. But if you don't talk to us, we have no choice but to get the police involved, and I'm not sure you'd enjoy the publicity.'

There was no response.

Emma entered the discussion. 'Our family is worried sick. Why wouldn't you want to help us? Surely you are in the business of helping people?'

Cornered and almost beaten, the old lady spat back, 'Yes, but what's said is between me and my clients; it's private.'

'Mum's already blabbed to a friend, so we have an idea what's going on.' Katy crossed her arms. 'You have a choice here, Mrs Pendle. You can give us ten minutes of your time or we'll call in the authorities.'

The frail little lady glared at them both, then suddenly, her features crumbled and her shoulders slumped. Her pale lips trembled and she collapsed into a chair, clutching at her chest.

What are we doing? Katy thought. Her grandparents would have been ashamed of them. 'Look,' she said more gently, 'I'm sorry, okay? We didn't mean to intimidate you. We came because we are frightened for Mum. We just want the truth. You can trust us with your secret. We just want answers ... honest.'

Emma placed her hand on the old lady's shoulder and almost flinched; it felt as small and fragile as a finch's wing. 'We've calmed down, promise. We are just two very worried relatives, and we believe you can help us.'

'I didn't mean any harm ...' The words floated from the old woman in a whisper.

'Sorry? What did you say?' Katy asked.

The medium lifted her head, her hooded eyes intense and dark. 'I said, I didn't mean any harm. I just really don't want to talk about it. It's done. Your mother made her decision, and I had nothing to do with that.'

Emma wasn't convinced. 'That's all very well, but from what we've heard, it was you who enabled her by providing her with the vehicle. You gave her the opportunity. How does that not involve you?'

'All right, all right. Wait here a minute ...' She pushed them aside and shuffled back to reception.

When she returned, she led them into her room.

Once inside, both women gawked at the surroundings. They had entered a fairy cave. Candles and lights and crystals of all shapes and sizes glimmered in the windowless space. And there were books, lots of them; they took up almost an entire wall. It was quite enchanting and seemed incongruous with the seriousness of their objective. Yet the dour expressions on all three faces bore testimony to the fact that it *was* serious.

Mrs Pendle sat down in an old office chair next to a desk and gestured towards a tired sofa up against the adjoining wall. It was draped with colourful scarves and in the soft rose glow that lit the room, it blended nicely with the rest of the clutter.

Subdued, and with a degree of circumspection, Katy and her aunt sat down. Both leaned forward towards Anastasia, giving her the floor. Her eyes were bright; clearly she was in her element.

'All right then, what do you want from me? It seems you know the crux of the matter already.'

Katy fiddled with the frayed edge of a scarf on the armrest beside her. 'Well, our friend Maria told me that Mum was extremely agitated because she had found a way to travel back in time and put to rights a mistake she had made as a teenager. Maria was her closest friend in their youth and knew something of the history, so I guess Mum trusted her.'

'But I specifically told her not to tell anyone. Why would she betray me ... and herself for that matter?'

'We have no idea,' Emma said, 'but we are guessing that she was overwhelmed and decided to share it with someone she trusted.' She glanced sideways at Katy for reassurance. 'All this came to light only a few days ago. She's been gone too long, and we've only had a handful of clues to go by. We've been worried sick.'

'You don't think your mother has just gone off to gather her thoughts?'

'No!' Katy exclaimed, too loudly. 'Because it doesn't make any sense. Mum is usually pretty grounded, but she behaved differently after she got that scanner, and everything we have discovered since points back to that.'

'Very well, then.' Anastasia clasped her hands together and nestled them on her lap. 'Here goes.' She leaned forward and took on a conspiratorial tone. 'When I was young, I realised I'd been given a very special gift. I was given the power of teleportation. Growing up, I practised on everything I could find. It was a toy—a skill I had, that no one else knew about, and it made me feel special, though I knew instinctively that it was my secret and mine alone. As I grew older, I realised I could use this power to travel back into my past, and at first it was exciting and intriguing, but then as I learned more about spiritualism, I realised I'd been given this gift to help others, not for my own amusement.'

Katy and Emma exchanged curious looks.

'That brings me to the present. Driven by this divine power, I was able to persuade anyone I felt inspired to. I could give them the ability to travel back in time to relive precious moments in their life or visit deceased loved ones, that sort of thing.'

'And how did that work for you? It sounds kind of interfering and manipulative to me,' Katy said.

'Fine at first. I built a set of emotional and practical boundaries and safety nets, as it were, and managed to convince myself that I was helping people.' She looked away, gazing into some distant, unknown point.

'So, what? You got greedy, ambitious. What did you get out of it?' Emma gave her a stern look that suggested she was an interfering old fool.

'Nothing. I wanted to do more and I started suggesting people might actually change elements of things in their past that were haunting them.' The set of her angular jaw showed her determination. 'You know, as a kind of therapy.' She was almost haughty now.

'What made you pick on Mum?' Katy asked.

'Well that was interesting. By then I had done it quite a few times. I was always very careful to choose the subjects. I had to make sure they could actually rise to the occasion—people I felt confident would be trustworthy, of course, but also those I was drawn to because I could sense their secret burden. I'm very intuitive, you know. Weeks before your mother came, I'd been having visions—visions of a life lived under the mistaken belief that a crime had been committed. That life that was tormented by the past. I felt compelled to help. I'm sorry.'

'Didn't you recognise that it was incredibly meddlesome?' Emma stared at her, wide eyed in disbelief.

'Well, no, I thought I was helping.'

'In what way did you think dragging up the past and putting her in that position was 'helping'?' Katy made air quotes with her fingers.

'Well, the first time you both came in,' she looked directly at Emma, 'I knew she was the one. You see, I'd never tried anything quite like this before.'

'That's obvious,' Emma snapped.

'With telepathy and willpower, I enticed her to notice that card. The scanner was my prop, you see, and the rest was entirely of her own free will.'

'Oh, yes.' Katy grimaced sarcastically. 'I can just see Mum going out shopping for a time machine.'

'I begged her to listen so I could explain everything in detail. I wanted to prepare her properly, and I wanted her to know the power she was dealing with. I was giving her a gift. Can't you see that?' she said, shrinking into the chair, diminishing before their eyes.

'I can see your thinking is severely skewed.' Emma folded her arms in contempt. 'You stupid, stupid woman. You tell us that you found a way to travel in time, and you expect us to believe it.' She'd had enough.

'It's not rubbish, and I'm not stupid! I never told anyone because I knew that's how they'd react, just like you now. I've been called an old fool and many things worse. But it's true. From my point of view, the only way I could use it for good was to single out deserving people and discharge the power one human being at a time. I'm sorry, I truly am. I realised the moment I saw how agitated Cassie was, that I'd made a mistake. I'd misjudged her. I tried to talk sense into her, honest I did, but by then it was too late. I'm not even sure if she understood everything, or if she processed and remembered any of it.' She bit her lip and started to make horrible whiny noises, and tears welled up in her eyes. 'I'm so sorry; I had no idea.'

'So what you're saying is that Mum could be out there somewhere,' Katy swung her arms around in a dramatic arc. 'She might not even know how to get back!' She leapt up and ran towards the door. 'I can't take any more of this.'

Her aunt caught up with her, grabbing her roughly by the arm and pulled her close, holding her tightly. She turned around to the old lady, now a weeping, purple heap melting into her chair, and pointed. 'You, stop crying, please.' Then to Katy, 'And you calm down. I understand how you feel and I'm angry too. This is horrible, but we have the information we came for.' Gesturing towards the old woman, she added, 'This misguided witch did a really dumb thing, and unless you want to report her to the police, we just have to do our best to come to terms with it. We can't change anything this instant, can we?'

The mystic whimpered. 'I would if I could, really I would. Ever since your first call, I've been trying to use my powers of telepathy to entice her home. She will return. She has to.'

'Do you have a time frame on that?' Katy's tone was bitter.

'No, I don't, but she did tell me that her family was her life, and she would do nothing, absolutely nothing, which would jeopardise their happiness. That was her big dilemma. I don't think she would have risked it if she thought there was a chance she mightn't get back.'

'We have to take your word for that, don't we?' Katy retorted.

'I'm afraid so, dear. It's all we have.' The old lady's self-control had returned.

There was an awkward silence for a while.

'Well, there's nothing left for us here,' said Emma, 'we should go.' Giving Katy a little push towards the door, she looked back over her shoulder at the sad psychic now shrinking into the chair. 'You haven't heard the last of us.'

And with that they hurried away, anxious to get out of the place.

It was already hot and steamy. They sat with the car doors open, oblivious to everything except their own rapid breathing and pounding hearts. Cicadas rattled in the hot air around them. A magpie chattered. Nothing else existed.

It was unbelievable, but they had to believe it.

It seemed ridiculous, but it answered their questions.

Katy was miserable. Emma leaned over and wiped a tear away, sliding her fingertip lovingly over her niece's cheek.

'Darling, I don't know what to believe either, but I'm thinking that we have to let the rest of the family know what we heard, so they can make up their own minds.'

'Yeah, well, we know what they're going to say, don't we?' Katy's voice quivered. 'They'll say it's crazy. And the worst thing is ... it is!'

'I guess we have a choice. There's no point telling the police, unless there is something more plausible that we've missed. They'll come to the same conclusion. Or ... we can be patient and wait.'

Now Katy was sobbing, rubbing her face in anguish. 'But for how long?' she wailed.

'Sweetheart, sweetheart. Come on, you need to calm down; this is getting us nowhere. Listen, listen.' She pulled Katy's face upwards to make her look at her. 'We know she didn't plan to be away for long. Something must have stopped her, and trust me, she would be trying to move heaven and earth to get back. Have a little faith.'

Katy looked back at her, eyes wet with tears, 'But what do we say to people?'

'We tell Gran and Pops and your father. We don't have to tell anyone else. Sooner or later, all of us will have to confront it. Whether it's our crazy theory, or something the police dig up, the truth will out. We let them go through all the motions and perhaps they'll end up with one more missing person on their list. Either way, it's more waiting.' She opened the glove box and pulled out a bag of refresher towels. 'Here, wipe your face with this. We'll go somewhere and have a quiet sit and get our heads together, then go home and tell your dad.'

CHAPTER 39

The cool, fresh sea air was a balm for Katy's bruised soul. The heaviness in her head gradually drifted out to sea with the ebbing tide. Together, she and Emma strolled along the path on the foreshore. Crystal-clear swells of sea water lapped at the old stone wall and mossy rocks sat like giant emeralds on the sandy bed below the surface. It was a glistening day, and countless sparkling diamonds danced on the water. Here they could process what was beginning to look like truth to them.

Is Mum out there somewhere? Where? Katy looked at the horizon and thought of the vastness of the Pacific. It was a world she knew; something she understood. A tangible, real thing. Any map would show islands and countries and cities. But this? It was incredible; the stuff of fiction and fantasy. Yet here they were, dissecting what they had learned. It was the only thing that filled in the gaps, incomprehensible as it was.

The thought of transforming the pertinent details into a palatable truth to present to her grandparents was mind-boggling. Katy knew her dad, if not receptive, had at least been primed a little. They had already broached the subject of the possibilities of time travel, and as much as her father mocked the idea, both she and Emma felt that he would be prepared to listen to their story. The grandparents were stuck in a different mode altogether.

Just then, Katy's phone rang. She pulled it out of her bag and checked to see who was calling. She didn't recognise the number and rejected the call. She had no desire to talk to a stranger right now.

They had walked for over two hours and were depleted and spent, regurgitating the same narrative repeatedly, wanting a different solution. Reluctantly, they headed towards home, the unpleasant conviction that they had somehow failed dragging along with them. They wanted a solution, not a fairy tale.

When they walked in, Jeff looked up eagerly to hear what they had to say. 'And?' A half smile danced on his lips.

'Dad, it was horrible. We managed to talk to the old lady, and I still don't know what to think.'

'Why, what happened? Tell me.' He got up slowly and looked his daughter squarely in the face. 'What did she tell you?' He glanced at Emma. 'You both look miserable.'

Katy couldn't find the words and dithered. She pressed her hands to her cheeks. 'Oh Dad, she basically confirmed everything Maria told us. She orchestrated this wizardry of time travel, convinced she was doing Mum a favour!' She let out a high-pitched wail, 'And she has no idea how to get her back!'

'What do you mean, back? Where is she, then? Where is she?'

'She thinks ...' Emma clenched her fists, 'she thinks Cassie has travelled back in time, and she's not sure if she knows how to come back.'

'That's ridiculous. I don't believe you.' He ran his hand through his hair in exasperation. 'It's absolutely ludicrous.'

'We know,' they said in unison.

'But it's all we've got.' Katy hugged him. 'What do we do?' She burrowed into his chest.

'We tell the police! This woman is a charlatan and she's managed to dupe you. What she told you is not possible, do you hear?' He held his daughter tight and stroked her hair as she clung to him for support. He looked over her head at Emma. 'Do you believe this rubbish as well?'

'We've got nothing else ...' It sounded feeble. Emma grimaced.

The three of them stood there in the study. Katy clung to her dad, Emma beside them, patting her niece on the back.

Just then, there was a firm rap on the front door.

'Oh, God that's all we need.' Katy rubbed her eyes with the heels of her palms.

'Don't answer it,' her father said, but she ignored him and headed up the hallway.

'It might be important.' Katy was still pushing the remnants of her anguish away when she placed her hand on the door latch. Hesitating, she inhaled deeply and sighed, then put on a brave face. She flung open the door to find a complete stranger standing there. She blinked, then as her thoughts crystallised, she realised it was none other than Constable Burwood—out of uniform. She took another sharp intake of air, for out of police garb he looked completely different.

His eyes emanated calm concern. 'Hello, am I catching you at a bad time? I tried to call you, but there was no response. You seemed quite upset when we last spoke and I just wanted to check you're all right.'

Katy bit her lip and shrugged. 'I don't really know. I don't know what to tell you.'

'About what?'

Thinking the better of it, Katy composed herself. 'Oh, it's nothing, but we haven't heard anything from you lot; do you have news for us?' She tilted her head sideways, fixing her gaze on him. 'It's not a great time.'

'I know, but perhaps I can help, off the record as it were. I'm happy to listen, honestly, just try me.'

'Thank you. I'll think about it.' She stepped back into the doorway and reached for the door, ready to close it and end the conversation.

'Wait, wait, don't dismiss me like that. You haven't given me a chance. I'm offering to help.'

'That's very kind of you.' Katy stepped back from the door.

'Listen,' his tone lowered and took on a new seriousness, 'I'm not going to pretend I'm not attracted to you, but I understand this is not the time. What I am offering now is some help and support as a friend. You are worried about your mum, I understand that, and I think you could use some outside help, that's all.'

'I'll bear it in mind.' She managed a warm smile.

He just nodded, turned his back on her, and headed towards the gate.

'Who was that?' Emma was behind her, and placed her hand on Katy's shoulder as they watched him drive away. 'Want to tell me what's going on?'

'Nothing important.' Katy spoke through gritted teeth. 'Anyway, we have to go over and tell the oldies, don't we? Did you and Dad decide anything?'

'Nope. We have absolutely no idea. I vote we put it off till the morning. Who knows, after a bit of sleep we might feel better,' Emma said.

Katy found her father in the kitchen. 'What do you think, Dad? Can we put off telling Gran and Pops until the morning, please?'

He turned to her, wiping his hands on a towel. 'Okay, but we have to tell them this weekend, and on Monday it's the police. Hopefully we can talk to that police constable who we spoke to a few weeks ago. Burwood, wasn't it? He seemed like a nice chap.'

'That was him just now. There's no news, Dad, but maybe he can tell us more on Monday.'

Katy's head was so full of thoughts that her brain spun. 'I'm going to lie down.' She closed her bedroom door and threw herself on the bed. *Fancy Constable Burwood coming to see me.*

CHAPTER 40

Emma knocked lightly on Katy's door. She understood the solace found in sleep, but it was getting late. The sun was fading, and long shadows played on the verandah heralding the twilight.

'Are you awake?' Emma whispered at the door and tapped gently for a second time.

Something resembling a moan escaped the room. Perhaps she was stirring.

'Yeah, what?' Katy growled.

'I have an idea I want to discuss with you. Besides, you've been in there for hours, and I think it's high time you came out. As it is, you'll have trouble sleeping tonight.'

A dishevelled, untidy Katy opened the door. Her eyes were puffy, with dark circles that belied her age. Emma greeted her with a hug, and gently stroked some of her errant locks of hair out of her eyes.

'Come on, go and wash your face or have a shower. Your dad and I are taking you out for a meal; no one feels like cooking.'

Katy meandered over to her wardrobe, opened a drawer, and pulled out some fresh undies. Emma threw her a pair of jeans she'd picked up off the chair.

'Here, get these on; you've got 15 minutes. I'll feed Coco. Your dad's changing, okay?'

'Okay.' Katy's voice lacked conviction.

They drove towards the city, not with any particular plan in mind, just hungry and lazy. Everyone was subdued, like an antique painting in poor light—all browns and blacks.

Jeff pulled into a parking area set back from the main road and brought the car to a stop outside a Vietnamese restaurant. It was a family favourite. A string of fairy lights hung around its perimeter, and beside it, a huge fig tree cast a canopy over the outdoor eating area. Its trunk was dressed in a swirl of coloured lights, creating a festive atmosphere. Chatter from other diners greeted them.

'I figured we could use a little break,' he said, closing the car door. 'Tomorrow we'll talk to Gran and Pops and no doubt we'll have to deal with the fallout, so let's try to enjoy a meal out, hey?'

'We haven't been here for ages.' Katy linked her arm through her father's. Emma followed a little behind; she hadn't had a chance to talk to Katy about her idea, but it could wait until later.

'It's a long while since I've had this sort of food; I'd forgotten how delicious it is.' Emma mumbled between mouthfuls some time later.

'We come here often, the food is great and a lot of the locals eat here. I wish Cassie was here with us,' he said wistfully.

With the dramas of the past few days, they hadn't talked of much else.

Katy steered the conversation on to more general, topical things, anxious to avoid turning the evening into another worry fest. By the time they had finished their banana pudding and drank a cup of green tea, their moods had lightened considerably.

'This was a great idea, Dad, thanks for suggesting it.' Katy seemed brighter.

He just nodded. 'I confess I'm hanging out for a coffee, though.'

***

Katy flopped onto the sofa and dragged Coco onto her lap. They chatted for a little while longer, then Jeff announced he was going to bed.

'Big day tomorrow girls ... don't stay up too late.'

'Night, Dad.' Katy lunged at her father as he strode past, grabbed him round the neck and kissed him on the cheek.

Emma came and sat down beside Katy. 'So how are you feeling?'

'I don't know, still awful I guess. We can't possibly tell people this story. It's so far-fetched and we've wasted so much time on this witch-hunt.'

'I have an idea.' Emma said. 'How well do you know this police officer ... what's his name?'

'Burwood, Paul Burwood, I think. Not at all ... well, not well.'

'I saw the way he looked at you today. I think he's ... interested in you, you know what I mean? Don't tell me you didn't notice. How much do you trust him?'

'No, I'm not going there. Mum's missing.'

'I don't mean that. He's a police officer, isn't he? You don't have to charm him or anything, but from the bit I heard he was trying to be helpful.'

Katy gave her a disapproving glare.

'Come on, I think he wants to help. Isn't it worthwhile chatting to him? You might be surprised to find that he can be supportive without getting the whole police force involved.'

'I don't know. I'm not sure I'm ready to share this with anyone. I feel such a fool for dragging you on this wild goose chase. For a little while I was starting to believe the whole story myself. Maria was so convincing, and so was the old woman. I've just always thought that all the new-age stuff was bunkum. The story sounded plausible coming from her though, sitting smugly on her witch's throne with her crystal ball and all.'

'Don't. Don't punish yourself like this. We're all lost and confused right now, and it's not just your load to carry, do you hear?'

Katy didn't seem convinced.

'Anyway, give it some thought. Talk to your dad, but I'd suggest you take this Paul into your confidence; tell him what you have so far and let him help you. That means not lying to Mum and Dad. We can tell them what we know, and that we're sceptical and Constable Burwood is helping us. I think it will make things easier for them. He seemed nice, and if you trust him, I'd give him a call and meet him for a coffee. It can't do any harm, can it?'

Katy bit her lip.

Emma went on, 'Like I said, give it some thought. Sleep on it tonight. I love you, darling. You'll see, your mum will come home. Maybe not soon, but I'm convinced she's just as anxious as you are to be back here. We need to stay strong and be patient.'

'I can't deal with this now.' Katy threw up her arms.

Emma shrugged. She shook her head, rummaging through her hair with her fingertips. 'Fair enough, but think about it.'

Katy kissed her aunt on the cheek. 'It can all wait until the morning.'

CHAPTER 41

1969

Cassie had hardly slept, but in the end sheer exhaustion had won. Now, waking up and pulling her vague thoughts together, she was bludgeoned into full awareness.

Tonight she was going home. She'd made the decision when wrestling the sheets in the darkness.

Now fully awake, she leapt over to her desk, grappling for the letter. She couldn't remember any more what had been hallucination and what had really happened. But there it was—the letter, sealed and final.

The future beckoned her like a powerful magnet, just as the past had done in what seemed like a heartbeat ago. She had made such a monstrous mess of everything, and nothing could be undone. Not this time, no second chances. She was outraged and confused, fragile and strong, bitter and hopeful, all at the same time. She would leave tonight when everyone was asleep, when she had taken the day to say her bittersweet farewells to 1969. She tried again to focus on the enormous privilege of the experience, but she couldn't find the capacity in that moment. There was only regret. There was no satisfaction at having saved Scott's life; the price had been too high. With uncharacteristic cynicism, she reflected on the number of hours she might have to spend in therapy to work through this debacle.

Reluctantly, she ventured into the hallway and towards the bathroom, her brunch coat draped over her arm. The house was quiet; no one was up yet. She hadn't even looked at the clock. She closed the door quietly behind her. A moment later, she heard her mum.

'You're up early, is everything all right in there?'

Cassie pinched her eyelids together. She wanted to memorise her mother's young voice, these moments. Tomorrow it would all be over. Today would be a series of last times. The last time she would see her family, young and vibrant; the last time she could share her friends' company; the last time she would savour the world as it was. She dug her knuckles hard into her eyes, willing things to be easier, knowing they couldn't be.

'I'm fine, Mum, just couldn't sleep.' She opened the door. Her mum was waiting, arms open. 'No wonder! You've been through so much.'

Cassie's bruised heart sang out in gratitude. She mightn't be able to share her story—there were deep, dark secrets that burned her soul—but her mum would be there. That lifted her spirits somewhat. She was safe; Cassie in 1969 would be safe. She was loved, resilient and brave.

'Come and have a cup of Milo before everyone wakes up.'

Cassie followed her meekly to the kitchen.

The goodbyes were beginning. Listening to the clock ticking away made her fiercely aware that every single minute was precious. She pledged to make this day one of joy, love, and appreciation. There would be plenty of time to rake over the ashes of her despair later.

Now was all she had.

Mum's soft cheeks glowed rosy in the dawn light. Noticing her flawless skin, still supple and unlined, and her thick mop of curly, auburn hair, Cassie adored her in silence, drinking in her warmth and strength. Wistfully she prayed that perhaps, sometime in the future, she could sit with her again and recall this exquisite togetherness.

'Mum, I'm heartbroken that I let you down so badly; I never meant to hurt you. I'm so sorry.'

Cassie's head drooped, her slender fingers twisting and tugging at the satin ribbon of her brunch coat.

Her mother reached over, gently pulling away the hand wrestling with the ribbon, and took it in her own, pulling it close to her breast, urging her daughter to voice her fears.

'Mum ...' Cassie looked up, just for an instant, to catch a glimpse of the devotion that radiated from her mother

'Sweetheart, accidents happen, and you didn't do it all by yourself, did you? We can't undo it. Dwelling on it will only breed resentment and anger. You are a beautiful, smart, talented young lady. You mustn't forget that. Don't let this fester. Promise me you will give yourself a chance and climb out of this pit of misery. It's not healthy.'

'I know, Mum, but it's such an awful disaster.'

'Listen.' Her mother reached over and held Cassie's cheeks as she looked her into her eyes. 'Everyone makes mistakes, everyone, but we must not let them dictate our whole being.'

A powerful surge of love and respect flooded through her. 'Mum, I'll do my best for you. Without you I'd be walking this tightrope by myself. You are my safety net. I know the sacrifices you have made for me, and a part of me understands—it truly does.'

Her mother's eyes sparkled big and round, amber pools of understanding swirled as her mouth opened, but she didn't speak. Cassie hoped that on some cosmic level her mother's intuition heard all she couldn't say.

Emma, still in her pyjamas, strolled in and looked at them both with curious suspicion.

'So what's this little huddle all about then?' she asked.

'Nothing dear, just a chat. Cassie woke up early and I was keeping her company. Do you want a cup of Milo?'

'Nah.' She perched herself on the chair opposite her mum, and Cassie leaned over and tried to hug her.

'Come here, you. You know I adore you, even though I haven't been much of a big sister lately.'

'That's okay,' Emma said, flipping quickly into a new brightness. 'Hey, today's Friday, isn't it? That means tomorrow is Saturday and Mum, can I go to Julie's place? Her cousin is coming over.'

Cassie lunged at her sister, and tried to hug her. 'I love you, chicken.'

Emma wriggled free.

'Maybe I can take you over to that hamburger joint you love so much for lunch today, would you like that?'

Tomorrow's plans were suddenly forgotten.

'Neat. I'm getting one of those big ones with the works.'

'You bet!' Cassie threw a satisfied grin to her mother.

An hour or so later, the household was bustling about in its normal Friday morning routine. Her mum had a CWA meeting to go to, and her dad was mooching around getting ready to leave for work.

When he came in and sat down, Cassie ached to get close to him, but it would have to wait until the evening. She blinked away the pain and reached over to grab the big box of cereal, ready to throw herself into the morning, relishing the simplicity and banality of the moment.

How she longed to say a proper goodbye. She wanted to explain why she had to leave, but enough damage had been done. With luck, she reasoned, the Cassie she left behind might be a stronger, more determined version of herself. She would guard the truth and tuck it away, keeping the damage and influence on those around her to a minimum. With all that had happened, all the mistakes, the horror, and the misery, at her core was the knowledge that all things pass, and she trusted the young woman she was leaving behind.

CHAPTER 42

Cassie leant against the doorjamb; her hands clutched behind her back. With studied concentration, she watched as her mother preened herself in the hall mirror, ready to go out. She looked so smart, still youthful, unconsciously tucking a few stray strands of hair under her neat little pillbox hat. Her pale-lemon suit fitted her slim figure beautifully. Cassie was proud of her.

As if aware she was being watched, her mum looked over 'Hello darling, how long have you been standing there?'

'Just a few minutes,' Cassie said. 'You look great, Mum.'

'Thanks, sweetie, sorry I have to rush, I'll be home early this afternoon. Have you got enough money to take Emma out today?'

'I should be right. We'll catch a bus, and it won't cost much.'

Her mother leaned over and picked up her handbag from the hall table, tossing the gloves draped over them to the side. Unfastening the clip, she dived in and took out her purse, and gave Cassie five dollars. 'That should do it,' she said, passing the note to her daughter.

'Thanks, Mum.' Cassie was suddenly overwhelmed by a wave of nostalgia. She loved that Oroton purse; it had been a gift from Dad a few Christmases before. These flashes of cognisance had plagued her at the craziest times, without warning, rhyme or reason. Her fingers touched the soft mesh lovingly.

Reading her thoughts, her mother said, 'It's beautiful, isn't it, love, though it's getting a little bit bashed around in my bag. Never mind, it's there to be used. Maybe you'll get one for your Twenty-first' She chuckled as she slipped on her gloves and left for the meeting.

Cassie studied the door. Doors were constantly opening and closing, and tonight this one would be shut for good. She shrugged off the awful thoughts with a shiver and headed to Emma's room.

She peered in to see Emma stretched out on her stomach on the floor blissfully studying her *Ingenue*, gleaning the glossy pages for new ideas. Beside her was the tranny, pounding out the sounds of Gerry and the Pacemakers. Her foot pulsed in rhythm to the music.

Cassie threw herself on the rug beside Emma.

'Look at this ...' Emma shoved the page she was reading up to Cassie's face. 'I'm tired of the bob; I think I'll grow my hair long like yours.'

'But you're cute as you are; long hair is harder to look after.'

'I know, but look at this photo of Ann Margaret. She's beautiful.'

'And so are you. Don't change yourself one bit! Come on, the bus leaves in an hour, and you still need a shower.'

'Yeah. Okay.' She threw the magazine on her bed and scrambled to her feet. Cassie reached out an arm, begging for a hand up.

***

When Emma finally appeared in the living room, she was transformed.

She'd changed out of the dull green and brown muumuu, and appeared fresh in crisp white shorts and a pretty aqua and white checked top. Her hair was neatly tucked under a matching bandana. Cassie was smitten, and told her she looked gorgeous.

Together they walked up the hill to the bus stop. They chatted about all sorts of inconsequential things.

When they got to the café, they found a booth near the back, right under the ceiling fan, lazily churning the warm air around them.

'Right,' said Cassie, 'I'm guessing a double chocolate milk shake and a burger with the works for you, correct?'

Emma beamed.

Cassie went up to the counter and put in the order. She decided on a salad roll and a Coke for herself. She paid the girl and went and sat down opposite Emma. 'This is really special you know.' Cassie left the words hanging.

'Mum told me you've been through a rotten time with the breakup. Are you feeling a bit better now?'

'I'm not sure if better is really the right word. I feel like shit. Emma, I don't want to preach at you, but—'

'I knew there'd be a catch.' Emma rolled her eyes.

'No ... no ... you've got it wrong. I'm not going to tell you what to do. I know I can get bossy, but this is different. This is important.'

Just then the waitress arrived, carrying a tray bearing their lunch.

'Thank you,' they said in unison.

Emma wasted no time in sinking her teeth into the big sumptuous burger.

Cassie eyed it with delicious envy, musing that she wouldn't see a burger like that again. She tucked into her salad roll, relieved when Emma picked up the conversation. 'So what's so important then?' Emma asked.

'Well, you know I told you I'd gone all the way with Scott?'

Emma was slurping her milk shake, chewing the straw into oblivion. 'Uh huh.'

'Are you listening?'

'Uh huh.'

Cassie continued. 'Doing that was really, really stupid. You have no idea of the hell I've been through, and it was all for the sake of losing control for just a few moments. I can't even talk about it; it hurts too much, and I won't feel right for a long time. If it weren't for Mum, I might not be here at all. So, two things, sweet sister...'

Emma was leaning over her burger, wiping sauce from her mouth. 'Yeah, what? I'm listening.'

'Firstly, bide your time; wait as long as you want. I promise you your time will come, and when it does, I want it to be fireworks and rockets, not the dismal, ghastly experience I had. So please, make sure you are with someone special—someone you trust and who genuinely cares for you.'

Emma hadn't looked up; either embarrassed or disinterested.

'Right, now I know this is uncomfortable to talk about, but it's crucial you try to understand. Sex won't always be the taboo subject it is right now. Do you hear me?'

Her sister just nodded.

'Secondly, when things do get tough, and they will, none of us get through without a few challenges, lean on us. Mum is savvier than you give her credit for, and she's no prude either. We're always here for you. No matter how big the problem, how insurmountable it seems, you don't have to handle anything on your own.'

She reached over and put her hand on Emma's.

Emma smiled. 'It's all right Cassie, don't worry about me. I'm not really that interested in boys yet; I'm just curious, that's all.'

'That's normal, but talk to us about things, hey? Don't try to work out the answers all by yourself.'

Having said her piece, Cassie relaxed, and took a sip of her Coke.

Changing tack, she asked Emma about school, and the two girls chatted about boys, the latest fashions, and their plans for the rest of the holidays. Cassie felt strange discussing a future she would barely be aware of. She wanted to tell her sister so much more. Tell her about the exciting time that lay ahead; that the world was evolving in a myriad of ways she could not begin to understand. Instead, she took a few deep breaths, just being, absorbing the atmosphere right where she was.

It was perfect; she savoured her impressions, for they would soon be memories. It consoled her that her family was safe and her biggest hope was that they would be unscathed by this sorry episode. She cursed the pact she'd made with the devil, and the woman in her implored the gods to give them a good life.

Abruptly, pictures of Jeff and her family drifted into the frame. The future had clean fine edges as well; it too was beautiful. This juxtaposition of the past and the future was disconcerting, and now that Cassie was closer to going back, or forward, or wherever it was, the sensations became stronger.

'Helloooo ... helloooo,' Emma was waving her hands madly in front of Cassie's face. 'Are you off with the fairies?'

Cassie snapped back into the present. 'Sorry, I was miles away.'

'You've been acting funny all day; what's up?' Emma said.

'Nothing, I'm fine. A lot on my mind.' It was past two when they left the milk bar, and when they got home, Cassie barely had enough time to race up to Maria's.

***

They listened to records in Maria's room for a bit, talked about mundane things, but eventually strayed onto the hard stuff. The last few weeks had been tough on both of them, and Maria understood.

Her best friend had been through all the miserable days, waiting anxiously for Cassie to come home and calling her on the days she couldn't come and see her. Cassie fumbled to express the depth of her gratitude, and, when she hugged Maria for the last time, her knees almost buckled. To ease her through it, she pictured a future with Maria still in it, resolving to make sure that happened.

Ambling home, Cassie tried to take in all the sights and sounds around her, desperately hoping to place them firmly in her memory. She tried to imagine the future again, but she couldn't see it clearly. Jeff and Katy would be there, and it would be wonderful to see them again, but right now, she couldn't picture it. She kicked a stone into the gutter.

She was thankful she'd at least had closure with Scott. She'd written him a long letter saying goodbye, and he hadn't responded. She had a sick feeling in her gut that the question of whether it had been worth it would haunt her until her dying day.

It was starting to get dark by the time she reached home. She could hear utensils being shuffled around—a tap running, the fridge door opening. The wonderful, delicious and cosy sounds of familiarity. She closed her eyes for a minute to savour the simplicity.

Emma was slouching in a beanbag in front of the television, giggling over the Bugs Bunny Show, and Cassie could hear the shower running. Dad must have just got home from work.

This was perfect. This is how she wanted to remember her family. Contented, secure and without complexity. She wanted to erase the nightmare that was Scott and her own stupidity, but she didn't want to forget this.

Her dad didn't have a clue about the ordeal of the abortion, and yet there was this quiet love. This was how it had to be remembered. A normal day in the Truscott family. She could go if she knew this was what she was leaving behind.

By some glorious serendipity, Mum was dishing up her favourite—macaroni and cheese. A secret celebration. Cassie ate noisily, immersing herself in the joy, although she might have been overdoing it, for by the time the jelly and ice-cream was dished up, her mother stopped and looked at her closely and asked her if she was all right.

Yes she was. It would hurt, but looking at the faces at the table with her now, she was reassured. Dad, bless his soul, might not be privy to her dramas, but she knew she could count on him. Mum, so incredibly strong and supportive, and Emma, switched on and confident. They would be all right.

She helped her mum clear up the dishes, then joined Emma and her dad in the lounge room. Her father had turned on the television and was fiddling with the controls to get a better picture. Her mother brought in a tray with four hot mugs of Milo and some biscuits which she set down on the coffee table. Cassie bit into a Delta Cream, relishing the delicious crunch and its saccharine creamy filling, and found her place on the sofa to enjoy Bonanza. Mother and daughters swooned as their favourites galloped through the burning map and burst onto the screen.

When the show was finished Emma got up and went to her bedroom, and Cassie's mum went into the kitchen to finish off a dress she was making. Cassie and her father were alone, sitting side by side on the settee. He was leafing through the *TV Week*, checking to see what was on next, but the *Graham Kennedy Show* wasn't on until 9.00 pm, and nothing else seemed to take his fancy. Cassie slid along the couch and sidled up to her father, then swung her arm around his shoulder and kissed him heavily on the cheek.

He looked around, startled. 'Hello, what was that for?'

'Aw, I don't know, Dad; I just want you to know that I love you.'

He turned sideways, threw down the magazine and hugged her back.

'I've been worried about you, chicken. You've been so quiet, but I know it's mostly girl's stuff, and I'm not much good in that department.' He pulled away slightly, his moist grey eyes scrutinising her closely. 'Some men can be bastards, sweetheart, and I'm truly sorry you've been hurt. I hope you can put it behind you, and in time you'll feel better. Trust me, one day you'll find someone who genuinely loves you, and I'll be circling with a shotgun to ward off the others.' He chuckled.

'Yeah ... I guess so, but I'm not even sure that's what I want right now,' Cassie said.

'Well, that's good. Find the right fit for you. Spread your wings a little, see the world maybe. Point is, you are young and smart, and the world is a big place. There are so many ways your future can unfold. I know you're tough, so you just go, girl!'

She embraced him again, wrapping him in her love. Her heart felt like it would burst, and she longed to make this last, but her dad was already distracted by something on the television.

The mature woman, writhing inside this slim young girl, understood this is how it had to be; this was as sublime as the moment could get.

She loved him and settled back onto the seat, wrapped her legs underneath her, and nestled close to him, pretending that the television was the pivotal thing in their world.

She could feel her heart thumping out the rhythm of the ticking clock, each beat drawing the inevitable closer, pulling the future towards her.

CHAPTER 43

2013

Breakfast in Holt Street was a miserable affair that Sunday morning. All three were despondent; not knowing what to do with the facts they had and the fantasies they were forced to confront. And they were so tired of dead ends and futile conversations.

'That's it!' Jeff slapped his hands hard on his thighs. 'We have to move, do something. We can't just sit here hoping that the missing person's fairy will suddenly drop Mum in our midst.'

It shocked the women into action. Coco shot out from under the table and disappeared into the garden.

Katy jumped up, leading the way. 'You're right Dad. We'll get dressed and head over to Gran and Pops. I'm fed up with the dithering. Let's just tell them everything.'

But their sense of purpose quickly dissolved when they pulled up outside her grandparents' home.

Emma got out of the car first. 'Let's get this over with.'

The other two sat there like errant drivers waiting for the traffic warden approaching to give them a speeding ticket, unwilling to move.

'Come on you two.' Emma was already up the driveway.

'It's about time you turned up. Any news?' Gran asked. She was clearly agitated.

'We'd better go inside,' Jeff said, not giving anything away with his stoicism.

Katy was bringing up the rear, and she hugged them tenderly when she walked inside. 'I'll go and make us a cuppa, shall I?' she said.

By the time she came back into the lounge room, everyone was settled.

Emma reached over to her mum sitting in her recliner. She laid a hand on her mother's. 'Mum, Katy and I have talked to a few people and the only thing we can come up with is quite fantastic. Now, I need you to have a very, very open mind. There's no easy explanation and in all honesty, we are no closer to having Cassie home than we were a week ago. But listen to this ...'

They started at the beginning, Katy and Emma taking turns covering the details of their quest from the phone numbers that proved useless to the extraordinary conversations with Maria and, later, the weird psychic and her unbelievable confession. Every now and then Jeff butted in with his own observations.

The two aged Trustcotts sat, mouths opening and closing like guppies, their brows undulating in waves of concern and disbelief. Gran chewed her lip and murmured whimpering her distaste.

'So there you have it!' Emma said at last. 'It sounds bizarre, but it's all we have.'

'Whether it's a crazy story or a cover for something more sinister we don't know,' Jeff said. 'But tomorrow we are going to talk to the police again. Maybe they can get to the bottom of it.'

Gran seemed to be mesmerised by a spot on the rug; she sat staring in silence. The tension stretched between them all like a tightrope.

At last, she looked up, her eyes screaming dread. 'Are you saying she's stuck in some other time zone? Is she dead? Is that what you're saying? What exactly are you saying? I don't understand. I just don't understand. What's happened to my daughter? I don't believe you. I can feel her so close; sometimes I think I can touch her.' She raved on. 'Cassie's not dead; she can't be dead.' She looked anxiously at her husband. 'What's going on, Henry? What are they saying?'

Emma got up and held her mum close; they were both shaking. She gently stroked her mother's hair and held her tight and felt the force of her sobs.

The old man sat there, stunned, unable to utter a syllable. Katy went to him. 'Pops, listen. We understand this is too much to take in, and I'm afraid I don't have any answers for that.'. She kneeled down beside him and took his weathered hand in hers. 'Pops, we all believe Mum is alive, and we have to keep believing that. We can't allow the panic and uncertainty to get the better of us. We'll get to the bottom of this. I promise.'

He just looked at her and frowned.

Jeff stepped in, 'Please Pops. We don't ... we can't believe it ourselves, but you must know that we would stop at nothing to have Cassie safely home.

The old lady looked at him, searching his eyes for an explanation. 'So what are we supposed to do?'

'We're frustrated as well, but for now, please trust us; trust our hearts and our intentions. We will find her.' Jeff splayed his hands at them, reflecting his own impotency and irritation.

'I'll stay here with you tonight, Mum,' Emma said.

The shock had been delivered and now the air was thick with unasked questions and as gloomy as an abandoned mine.

Emma drove home to gather her personal belongings. In the meantime, Jeff gave each of them a small glass of his father-in-law's Glenfiddich—the most potent alcohol he could lay his hands on. They were sipping sedately when Emma walked back in. By then, the mood was calmer.

Katy headed to the kitchen to forage for food. It was past lunchtime and they still needed to eat. She found some bread in the freezer and the fridge offered up remnants of a chicken, a few tomatoes, and some slightly wilted lettuce. It was enough to muster up a few sandwiches. There were also a couple of small tubs of yoghurt, and a bowl of grapes, so she took those out too.

No one seemed too interested in the food, but it was there; eventually they'd be hungry.

'I'm so glad you can stay, Emma. It means a lot,' Gran said.

'Well, I am here as long as you need me. Dad, is it all right if I use your car to get some groceries later? I'll cook dinner tonight.'

Katy looked at her aunt to express her gratitude too. 'Yes, thank you. It's wonderful you're here. I don't know what we would have done without you.'

Jeff and Katy lingered for another hour or so. It was late afternoon when they left. On the surface, everything was calm, but they both knew it was an illusion—there was major turbulence swirling away behind those tired old eyes.

As Emma gave Katy a goodbye hug, she whispered in her ear. 'Don't forget what I said last night about telling that policeman. Talk to your dad, and ask him. I think it's worth a shot.'

Katy's dad heard and shot her a quizzical look, but Emma brought her fingers to her lips to prevent him from asking any questions.

On the drive home, Katy shared her concern. 'Dad, I'm worried about them. I think it's all been too much of a shock. Maybe we should have kept quiet.'

'Don't punish yourself, Kitten. They were already extremely anxious before we came. They are elderly; it's hard for them to digest a lot of detail. They need time to come to terms with everything.'

The next morning, Katy broached the subject of her conversation she'd had with Emma.

'Dad, Emma suggested I talk to you. Do you think we should tell Constable Burwood about the psychic? He's been incredibly supportive; he's called around to see how we are going, and he's offered to help us any way he can. I know we're supposed to be seeing him in an official capacity this morning, but I'm not sure how much to tell him.'

'Love, we tell him the facts. The police will conduct their own investigations and maybe they'll reach the same stalemate. Don't go giving them any fodder for conjecture. Let them come to their own conclusions. Let them do their job without any prejudice from us.'

Katy thought about it and decided not to tell the police anything, she wasn't prepared to share her thoughts just yet. She called the station and spoke to Constable Burwood to see if there was any progress, but left it at that.

'So, what's the news?' Pops asked the next day, when they were seated in their living room again.

'Nothing, I'm afraid. It feels awful to be thinking of Mum as a missing person. I can't believe I am really saying it. It feels surreal,' Katy said.

'It is surreal,' her father added.

He repeated that it would take time and to expect a visit from the police over the course of the next couple of weeks, urging them not to tell the officers any more than they had to, especially not the part about a magic scanner and the idea that Cassie had travelled back in time to save Scott.

The old lady's head snapped up; her eyes narrowed. 'Save Scott! What for? That young man wasn't right for her, good riddance I say!'

The others at the table jerked to attention.

'Remember, Mum, you told us Scott had been killed in a car accident. You told us when we showed you that photo. Don't you remember?' Emma had spoken in the tone of someone talking to an elderly person suffering a lapse of memory.

She ran her fingers through her hair in anxious frustration. 'I thought he'd died in the accident as well. I was sure he had. At least I think I was sure. Now I don't know what to think. I'm really confused. It was all so long ago and I was so wrapped up in my own world then.' Emma said.

'Why would I say that if it's not true? Scott was terribly immature and almost ruined Cassie's life. He didn't die; he just sort of disappeared.' Gran replied.

Jeff and Katy were momentarily dumbfounded; they couldn't say a thing. They sat there, blown away by the about-face of her story.

Katy was silent. *Why would they lie?*

Jeff, unable to process the incongruity of the remark, went on, 'Anyway, let the police deal with it. Nothing is making any sense right now. It's probably best just not to mention it.'

They veered the conversation towards other things. Emma relayed a phone conversation she'd had with her husband that morning, assuring her he and the girls were fine. She added with a degree of guilt that she hadn't given home much thought since she'd arrived.

The elderly couple sat quietly, not contributing much to the conversation. Another tendril of tension had developed.

Katy's dad tried to distract his father-in-law. 'Henry, why don't you show me that new stamp you bought?'

The old man looked at him blankly at first; then his expression moved into something softer, something resembling pleasure. 'Yes, son, why don't I?' He unfolded himself slowly from his chair, casting a sheepish look at the girls as he turned around to lead the way to his study where he kept his cherished stamp collection.

Katy threw her father a kiss to thank him for distracting her grandfather.

As they disappeared, Gran turned to the two younger women. 'I've been worried about him. This whole awful business is harder on him, I think.'

Katy and Emma exchanged surprised looks.

'You see, I hate missing Cassie. I hate that she is not here. I hate wondering what's going on. But deep in my heart I know she will come home. I'm not sure he has that same belief. Oh, I'll admit I was in shock yesterday, but Emma has been looking after us so well, and we talked about it, didn't we love? I'm feeling better today.'

'That's great, Mum. I'd stay here with you if I didn't have my own family to go home to,' Emma said.

'I know dear, and it's fine. I think you've reminded me I'm not twenty-one anymore. Truth is, I'm finding everything a bit of chore these days.'

Katy leaned closer to her grandma. 'Tell you what; when Mum comes home, we'll look into getting you more help, or perhaps you might consider a move to a small unit or something. What do you think?'

'Maybe.' The old lady suddenly seemed to drift away from them, going somewhere where she wasn't quite within their grasp. 'It's the strangest feeling ... I just have a sense that Cassie is in a lot of trouble and needs me. I can't pinpoint it, but it's this powerful impression that she is going through something difficult but, you know, I can't help thinking she will just re-appear one day, and then everything will work out.'

She lapsed into deep thought. Emma and Katy looked across the table at each other, alarmed by the change in the old woman's demeanour.

Then Gran seemed to relax a little. 'She'll come home, I know she will.'

Emma smiled. 'Wouldn't that be wonderful, Mum?'

Katy turned to her aunt. 'By the way, we should let Maria know we've talked to the police, they're bound to want to talk to her, and I should go and see Mrs Parker as well.'

Gran's chair scraped across the floor as she heaved herself up. 'I think I'll have a little lie down. I hardly got any sleep last night.' She shuffled off towards the bedroom.

'Did you see that? It's as if she had a vision or something. Anyway, how were they last night?' Katy asked when they were left alone.

'They were a mess and I practically force fed them a meal and huddled them off to bed. I found some sedatives in the bedside table and gave them each one of those. Mum said she used them occasionally when she couldn't sleep. I don't know if they did anything. She was mooching around here at about four this morning.'

'What about you, did you get much sleep?'

'Off and on, and now I'm worried about them as well as my sister. Mum's been weird. Every now and then she seems to have these episodes, as if she's hallucinating or something, and as for denying that Scott was dead, I honestly don't know what to make of it! She comes over all funny and I've no idea what happens. I'm hoping it's just the stress.'

'It's all too much for them, isn't it?' Katy's eyes shone dark as midnight, the azure now imbued with a deep look of concern and heartache. 'Once Mum's back, we'll make some phone calls, but right now, I'm finding it hard to keep myself from cracking up. I don't know what to believe. Do you think Scott died in the car accident?'

'Well, if you'd asked me a few days ago, I would have happily gone along with that angle, but now ... I just don't know. I really don't. Forty years is a long time, and I was just a kid.'

Just then, the men returned, their voices lowered, engaged in serious talk. Noticing the empty chair left by his mother-in-law, her dad asked, 'Where's she gone?'

'She just went to have a lie down, Dad,' Katy answered.

'That's been happening a lot lately,' Pops mumbled.

'I'm sure you'll keep an eye on her, won't you, Emma?' her father said. 'Anyway, we should be getting home.'

'Yeah, I guess so,' Katy agreed. 'I'll give you a call tomorrow, Auntie.' She blew a kiss at Emma and hugged her grandfather, then headed to the bedroom to say goodbye to her Gran.

***

When they got home, Katy called Maria. She told her to expect a visit or call from the police at some point. She urged her not to mention the scanner. 'It's up to you, of course; I'm not asking you to lie, but we figure they probably won't be interested in our fanciful thoughts, and we don't want to open that can of worms until we have to.' Katy then went on to tell her about their visit to the old psychic.

'What about her ... are you going to tell her you spoke to the police?'

'No, I'm going to let her sweat it out; she's done a really stupid thing. If that *is* what she's done. I am still having trouble wrapping my brain around it. When we talk like this, it all makes sense, but then I start thinking and rationalising, and I get lost. I'm so confused.' Katy said.

'I know what you mean. I talked to Cassie; I saw how she was, and I still find it hard to believe.'

'Anyway, I'll leave that with you. I've just got home from visiting my grandparents.'

'Oh, how are they? How are they taking it?'

'How does anyone take it? Stunned, I think.'

'The poor things. I can only imagine.'

'They're better today. Emma stayed with them last night. Gran is acting strange ... waffling on about some connection she's having to Cassie. I imagine that's shock or something.'

The question of Scott was gnawing at her. 'Maria, you did tell me that Cassie told you she was going back to save Scott, didn't you?'

'That's right.'

'Today Gran tried to tell us Scott hadn't died; they reckoned he just sort of disappeared out of their lives. They said the accident never happened. What do you make of that? Why would they tell us one thing last week and a different story today?'

'I've no idea, but funnily enough, I've found myself going over the past as well, it's all very blurry and I don't know what to make of it. I distinctly remember Cassie talking about the accident before she went missing ... she said she wanted to go back to save him. What if...'

'What if she *did* travel back and managed to do just that.' Katy interrupted, her high pitched-voice now shaking with excitement. 'Oh my God! What if indeed? Surely not. If we're right, it would change everything. Oh dear, I don't know what to think.'

'Nor do I but I've got to tell my aunt. I'll keep you posted. Bye.' Katy ended the call.

What if Mum's saved him? She'll have to come home soon won't she?

Katy punched her aunt's number into the phone, tapping her foot rapidly in anticipation.

'Hello Katy.' Emma answered.

'Okay,' Katy leapt into the conversation, 'what if Mum *did* travel back in time and managed to save Scott? Then what Gran said would make sense, wouldn't it? I called Maria when we got home and when I told her she suggested that might be the reason Gran's story changed. She even seemed uncertain about her own memories. Wouldn't that be amazing?'

'It gives us something to think about, but calm down. Let's not jump to conclusions. Let's sleep on it and see how we feel in the morning.'

CHAPTER 44

Katy couldn't sleep, it was 2.30am and Coco lay curled up near her feet, a furry ball, oblivious and serene. Words spun around firing at her from all angles—Scott, accident, photo, crystal balls, coffee, cat food, stamps, things said, things unsaid ... flying around in the oppressive fug of her brain.

Suddenly she sat bolt upright.

Scott had lived!

It was the only explanation that made sense. It also validated Gran's behaviour

Mum had succeeded! It meant the psychic's story was true.

Her breathing quickened. She was wide-awake. The edges of her haze started to clear. It hit her that the unbelievable—the improbable—was true. Her body buzzed with excitement. Her Mum had time travelled, and she'd managed to save Scott.

For the first time, she faced the fact that despite all their scepticism, by all appearances her mother had actually broken the time barrier. It was fantastic. It was awesome. It was incredible.

She fell back on the pillow, her thoughts again diverted. *If her job is done, why isn't she home?*

At first light, she was out the door, breathing in the fresh, cool air as she pounded the road. The thwack, thwack rhythm of her runners on the bitumen created a sense of order in her thinking.

When she got home, her father was already up. Breathless and steamy, she approached him as he stood by the kitchen bench. 'I had an epiphany, Dad! Gran and Pops' story changed because the past changed! It's perfectly clear if we put aside that it is technically impossible.' She slumped down on a kitchen stool, her legs stretched out, her breathing still heavy.

Her dad just looked at her.

'Don't you see? Mum told Maria she went back to save Scott, and maybe she did. Maybe that's the reason their memory of it has changed. It makes sense.'

'Don't ask me what makes sense. None of it does.' He grabbed her by the shoulders and studied her closely. 'Granted, as long as we forget that it's preposterous, it all makes perfect sense. The truth will surface sooner or later. Whatever helps us cope, hey?'

Katy's shoulders slumped; she'd hoped for a more positive reaction.

She was sufficiently convinced to call Emma again, who was much more receptive, conceding that it was the only conclusion that made any sense. Then she called Maria. After talking to them both, she made up her mind to believe it.

Mum would be all right.

It occurred to her that Gran had implied exactly that.

***

A few days later, Katy received a call from Constable Burwood letting her know that the detectives would be there the following morning to interview them.

Her father was home the next morning and just after eleven o'clock there was a knock on the door. He threw Katy a reassuring glance as she moved towards the door. 'Remember, just tell the truth and stay calm, love.'

Two men in suits, both middle aged, clean cut, serious—caricatures of every clichéd cop they had seen on television—stood at the door. They introduced themselves as Detective Sergeant Craddock and Detective Constable Sugden from the Missing Persons Unit, Brisbane North.

Jeff invited them in and offered a coffee. They both declined.

The senior man spoke first. 'We've had a report that your wife, Mrs Cassie Foster has been missing since 23rd September. Can you tell us why it took you so long to report it?'

It didn't look good; both Katy and her dad knew it.

'I know it sounds stupid' Jeff gave a nervous chuckle, 'but we thought she would come home; perhaps stuck somewhere unable to contact us. This is very, very unlike my wife. She's generally very reliable.' He looked from one officer to the other earnestly. 'Oh, and I should have added, we called all the hospitals and police stations to check she hadn't been injured or anything.'

'So what did you think when she didn't come home the first week?' DS Craddock asked.

'Well, by then we had ideas of our own, and to be candid, we were reluctant to involve the police or put ourselves through this.'

Officer Sugden joined in. 'Mr Foster, typically in cases of this type, the person has deliberately gone missing. You told the reporting officer, Constable Burwood, that there were no suspicious circumstances. Perhaps you should run through what you know so that we can establish where best to start.'

'All right then. This is what we know. Cassie told us she was going on a retreat while I was away in Perth on business for a few days. When she didn't come home on Wednesday as planned, we were anxious, of course, and that's when we started making our own enquiries.'

'Don't forget, Dad, Mrs Parker, the old lady across the road, said she'd seen Mum arrive home in a taxi on Monday, and then saw a brilliant flash of light coming from the study shortly afterwards. Being the curious soul she is, she came over to find out for herself and was surprised to find no one home. I knew nothing about this at the time because I was at college.' Katy realised how lame it sounded, especially in the light of her latest insight. 'She came over to see me the next morning and told me. At that point I didn't know what to think. I guess I dismissed her as a busybody.'

'But you must have heard some alarm bells?' DC Sugden suggested.

'Yes, of course I did; it worried me terribly, so I came home early that day and found Mum's handbag on the desk, and the brochure opened at the page where she'd circled the name of the retreat. I called them, but no one had heard of her. That's when I got really worried.'

'Didn't you think to call us then?'

'Well, yes ...' Katy was hedging. 'But I guess I just didn't want to believe anything was wrong. I couldn't accept Mrs Parker's story, and I kept hoping there was a reasonable explanation. Besides, I was on my own. I didn't want to scare Dad, and I knew he was due home the following day. I prayed everything would resolve itself by then; that maybe she had been in touch with him.' The words were coming more easily than she'd expected. She tried to forget who she was dealing with and simply did her best to tell the story as truthfully as she could.

'What happened when you came home, Mr Foster?' Detective Sergeant Craddock directed the question at Jeff, who was pulling at his right earlobe awkwardly.

'I was distressed, we both were. And yes, we did consider calling the police, but we're private people, and we were reluctant to admit it to ourselves. We were frightened of the media, mainly, and this.' Jeff gestured towards both men with his outstretched arm.

'So what did you find out?' the sergeant asked, unperturbed by the implication.

Father and daughter exchanged looks. 'We figured that if we could get into her phone we would be able to find out who she had spoken to in the days before she left. We thought that would lead us to her.' Jeff replied in a soft voice.

Katy spoke then. 'It took me a couple of days, but I managed to work out the pin, and from that and a few scraps of paper we found, we discovered she had parked her car at Ken's Airport Parking on the Monday she apparently vanished. We picked up the car and brought it home. The overnight bag in the boot was exactly as she had left it.'

'And the bits of paper ... what did they tell you?' asked the sergeant.

'Well, the parking ticket was one, and there was a card with a phone number on it—an advertisement for a scanner for sale. We dismissed that, but I did call the numbers I found in her phone, and there was nothing of consequence. A couple of calls turned out to be to her childhood friend, Maria, so I spoke to her. She said she'd seen Mum a few days before but otherwise, nothing.' The words sounded empty, given that Katy's viewpoint had altered quite dramatically since those early days that seemed such a long time ago.

'Is there anything else? This isn't much to go on.'

They shook their heads.

'Could you describe her for us please, and we'd like a current photo if you have one.'

Katy disappeared into her room and returned with a copy she had made.

Meanwhile, her father was doing his best to reduce his wife to a series of statistics. 'Cassie is about 165 cm and she's a brunette—I'd say chestnut brown—with shoulder-length hair. I don't really know how much she weighs, but I'm guessing about average, probably between 55 and 60 kilos ... what else?' He gave them a blank look, but got no response.

'Here you are,' Katy handed over the photo. 'I'm sorry we can't give you more. We are both certain Mum wouldn't take off like that; we really thought she'd be home by now.'

'Can we have her phone and the access code please, and anything you think might be helpful for evidence? You'll get it all back,' Sergeant Sugden said.

'Of course.' Jeff picked up the phone; anything important would be on the sim card. He also gave the officer the code and details of the retreat.

The interrogators got up to leave. 'We can't promise anything, but we'll corroborate the information, make a few calls and see what surfaces.'

'Oh, before you go, could you please not involve the media in any of this?' Katy asked. 'We don't want anyone to know yet.'

Detective Craddock smiled weakly at her. 'No miss, don't worry, you may have seen a few too many crime shows. This will be very low key.'

When they pulled away, father and daughter breathed a sigh of relief.

'It wasn't that hard, was it?' he said, giving Katy a hug.

'No, I guess not. A bit intimidating though. I felt quite stupid at times.'

'Sweetheart, there's no rule for how we are supposed to act. They seem to be experienced policemen; we have to trust the system. I'll call Gran and Pops.'

Katy couldn't resist adding, 'They'll have no chance if she's in another dimension.'

Her father glared at her. 'If that is the case, they'll work it out for themselves.' Then he turned round and headed into his bedroom. On his return he said, 'I'm sorry, but I have to put in an appearance at the office.'

'That's all right, Dad. I'll go see Emma and the grandparents.'

Jeff kissed her on the forehead as he headed off. 'It'll be over soon, sweetheart, just hang in there. Keep yourself occupied.'

It was all a bit of an anti-climax; she'd hoped involving the police might somehow open a magic window of discovery. But nothing changed. The house still whispered with the silence of Cassie's absence. Katy wondered what her mother was going through right now, wondered in what universe her life was unfolding.

There was a knock on the door. It was her friend, Ingrid.

'Katy, I'm so pleased you're home, I haven't heard from you for ages. Where've you been? I've been worried about you.'

'Oh, I'm sorry; I've been so wrapped up in family stuff. Come on in. I'll make you a coffee,' Katy said. Ingrid had caught her off guard after spending the last weeks engrossed in her witch-hunt and processing all the edges and corners of her mother's disappearance, she'd almost forgotten the things that constituted her life before it all happened. She concentrated fiercely on making the coffee, keeping her back to Ingrid, for she was not quite sure what to say. Much as she loved her friend, this was a family thing—a very messy family thing, and she didn't want to go into the details.

She turned to Ingrid and handed her a mug. Coco had settled on her friend's lap and was making herself comfortable.

Katy kept it simple. 'Mum's missing. She's officially listed as a missing person. It's been too long now, and we had to face the reality.'

Ingrid gasped. 'Oh, that's awful.' She hugged Katy. 'I can't imagine how that feels. What did the police say?'

'Nothing much really ... they had a go at us because we didn't report it earlier, but I guess that's understandable, we've spent the last couple of weeks trying to track her down ourselves. Other than that they took down a lot of details. We gave them her phone and a recent photo, and that's it. Now it's back to waiting. I'm fed up. I just want everything to be normal again.'

'Of course. Are you okay? Is there anything I can do to help?'

Katy shook her head sadly. 'Not really, but it's lovely that you're here. It makes things a little more ordinary. I really appreciate your coming.'

'Where's your dad? And how's the rest of the family doing?'

Katy explained that her Aunt Emma had arrived from Sydney, and they were supporting each other.

Ingrid was still there when her father came home. They exchanged pleasantries, but then she made her excuses and left them alone.

CHAPTER 45

The following days passed in a blur. Telephone calls flew back and forth as the tiny bunch of concerned people tried to predict what the police knew, in which direction the inquiry was heading, and when, and if, Cassie would return. Both the grandparents and Maria had already had a phone call, but so far no one else had been subjected to a face-to-face interview. Katy was at home alone, absent-mindedly scrolling through her emails.

That changed when Emma turned up at Holt Street late on Friday afternoon. Dismissing pleasantries, she jumped into her concerns. 'They came today. Two plain-clothed detectives. Mum and Dad were anxious. They said they'd tracked her movements from the airport and back home, and no other leads.'

'Are you all right?'

'Yes, I'm fine. They weren't too interested in me; I wasn't even here when it happened, but Mum put her foot in it, going off on her tangents. She told them all about the scanner. She mentioned the old witch and Maria and everything ... I couldn't shut her up!'

'Oh my God, that's all we need. How did they react?' Katy bit her lower lip.

'I hope they put it down to her confusion and nervousness. We'll know soon enough, and who knows what Maria will have to say.'

'Good grief. Do the police even follow up on that sort of thing?' Katy asked.

'I've no idea. I'm worried though. They'll either dismiss us as a bunch of fruitcakes, or we'll be in trouble because we didn't mention it,' Emma said.

'I wonder if they've talked to Mrs Parker yet,' Katy added as an afterthought.

'Is your dad around?'

'No, I think he's gone off to do some business stuff.'

Emma continued, 'Mum's been strange; she's off with the fairies half the time, and she's muttering to herself a lot. That's got worse. I'm afraid the trauma might have stirred up some mental health issue for her. You know, this morning, she said again that Cassie needed her. She was quite agitated.'

'I'll come over in the morning. Let's take them out for a drive or something, get them away from all the drama for a bit. Maybe it will help.'

'Good idea. Bring your father if he wants to come.'

'I will. Look after yourself. Love you.' Katy hugged her aunt and she left.

***

On Sunday morning, only the four of them drove up to Mount Glorious, and enjoyed a light picnic lunch in the fresh, lush atmosphere of the forest. Recent rains had turned the countryside into a rich verdant tapestry of textures and hues, and it was a brilliant day. The distraction was exhilarating, and they were all in better spirits when they arrived back home late in the evening.

The next day, Katy went over to see Mrs Parker, who said the police had been to see her, but she'd hadn't added anything to her original story. She hadn't heard anything since. They chatted for a while, and Katy sat politely, knowing that there was nothing waiting for her at home anyway.

When she returned, the house was still. Her father had been terribly quiet; he'd not joined them on the picnic. Instead he'd hidden in the study, researching, and examining Lord knows what. He gave no indication what was at the forefront of his introspection. Katy imagined all sorts of things that might be going through his head; everything from grieving for Cassie, which overshadowed everything else, to the stresses of the additional work load and his responsibilities. She wished he would talk about it with her. However, as the day wore on, he just seemed to immerse himself more deeply in his own private world.

Her mobile rang, interrupting her thoughts. It was Emma.

'Hello Katy, can you come over, please? Mum's losing it, and it's upsetting Pops. I think it would help.'

'Of course. They seemed okay when I left last night.'

'Yeah, that's what I thought, but it's coming unstuck now.'

'Be there soon.'

Katy threw a comb through her hair and quickly tidied herself. She relayed Emma's message to her dad as she was heading out the door.

'I'll come too. Give me a minute.' He was ready in a flash, grabbed his wallet and keys off the table as he hurried to catch up to and joined Katy who was waiting on the verandah.

When they arrived at Katy's grandparents' house, Emma was there to greet them. Her face was flushed. 'I don't know what to do. Mum's insisting she needs to be with Cassie, and she isn't listening to me. She's not being rational. I've no idea what else I can do. Dad's not much better.'

When they went into the living room, they were horrified to see the old lady pacing back and forth, clenching and unclenching her fists repeatedly. They couldn't understand everything she was muttering, but it was obvious she believed Cassie was in trouble and she wanted to be with her. She said it countless ways, but always the same message, repeating it over and over, the pain distorting her velvety skin into soft, turbulent ripples. Her body was taut with worry and impotency. Katy wasn't sure if she knew they were there. She wouldn't respond to reason; she wouldn't even stand still long enough for anyone to hold and comfort her. They watched, helpless, no one equipped to give her sanctuary from whatever was plaguing her.

Pop sat in the corner, powerless, small and confused. He ran his hands through his hair shaking his head as he spoke. 'She's been saying the same thing all morning.' His eyes narrowed, carving harsh lines into his sagging skin. 'We all miss her. I want my daughter back too, but there's bugger all we can do about it! Can't see the cops doing much. We've had it up to here.' He jerked his hand up to his chin. 'When's it going to end?' He reached up and put his arm around Emma's neck as she approached. She leant over him, trying but failing to soothe him.

The three of them grimaced at each other, their own pain floating over the agitation the elders felt. What could anyone say? Emma escaped to her bedroom for some respite. Jeff and Katy were left uttering platitudes and support.

Gran's distress was intense, and she had caved in on herself, deeply engrossed in her own nightmare, but at last she stopped pacing. Katy managed to cajole her into sitting down on the settee and stayed close, holding her grandmother's hand. They sat in silence. She groped for a way forward, wanting to pull Gran out of the morass of suffering and exasperation.

They lost track of time, the hours and minutes only distinguishable by the indifferent shards of sunlight piercing the thick air. At one point, Emma appeared with sandwiches. The oppressive atmosphere slowly started to dissolve. Slowly, word by word, sentence by sentence, the tension eased. Gran was calmer; she'd lost the haunted sense of urgency.

Her father started a conversation, and it appeared the crisis had passed.

Later, when Katy was helping Emma in the kitchen, she brought up the possibility that her Gran had some sort of psychic connection to Cassie. 'What if Mum is in trouble in some parallel universe? What if that's what Gran's picking up on? I'm scared Emma; I'm scared Mum's in danger. Who knows what mess she's in?'

'Yeah, it's scary all right. Do you think you could stay the night? It'd be good to have you around. I'm not sure I could handle it on my own if your Gran has another episode like this.'

Her father agreed and he left shortly after.

***

The three women sat on the verandah huddled together in the balmy summer air as the daylight faded. Each clutched a mug of coffee. The old man had disappeared into his den.

The lights from the neighbouring windows threw a soft glow onto the floorboards, and in that calmness, a sort of peace loitered.

Emma sat curled up on the old day bed, the others opposite, moulded into the cane chairs with their flaking paint and faded cushions, comfortable and familiar.

Gran spoke first. 'I'm sorry I alarmed everyone earlier.'

Both Katy and Emma reassured her, telling her they understood she was anxious with all that was going on.

'I think there's more to it,' the old lady said, her gaze fixed and determined. 'I've been giving all of this a lot of thought, especially the fact that I told you Scott had died in a car crash. I can't get it out of my mind. I realised I thought he had. That memory was as real to me as this chair here.' She patted the arm rest. 'Yet it doesn't ring true anymore, and I still have this God-awful feeling that Cassie is going through some terrible sort of crisis. It's not a clear thought, but suppose, *just suppose* that she did go back in time and things changed, that she managed to stop Scott from dying. Wouldn't that change our memories as well?'

Katy took her grandmother's hand in hers. 'I can see what you are getting at, Gran.'

'Moreover, we don't know what happened next. For all we know she fell straight into another disaster. Anything could have occurred. Today was so real. Cassie was in danger; I could feel it pulsing through me like poison. But she's better now. She's going to be all right, and she will come home. I'm more at peace with everything.'

Katy and Emma exchanged knowing looks, but neither spoke. They understood. This wasn't a demented, confused old woman talking. Her mind was sharp. What she said made sense. She hadn't been talking gibberish; she was just overwrought with worry knowing her daughter was in trouble. Her mother's instinct was a strong current, powerful and veracious; it was something they could rely on. Yet again, the improbable seemed the only probability.

They raised their coffee mugs to each other in a toast and chorused together, 'Here's to having our Cassie safely home.'

CHAPTER 46

Early on Wednesday, Katy's phone buzzed. It was Maria.

'Hi, I'm calling to let you know the police were here yesterday. They asked a million questions, and I just crumbled. I gave them the whole story, every little nuance that sprang to mind. They gaped of course, and there was a bit of snickering, but now they know. I'm sorry.'

'Don't worry. Gran's already primed them so it couldn't have taken them by surprise. Did you mention the psychic?'

'You bet. It was sounding like a giant yarn anyway, so I threw it all in. I'd love to be in that station when they scrutinise the report!'

'I don't care what they think anymore, as long as it gets Mum back.'

'That's right. You must be exhausted.'

Katy was becoming frustrated with the mystery. It was almost a relief to dump it on the police. But the constabulary hadn't come up with anything, and, illogical or incredible as it sounded, the time travel theory was still the best explanation.

She tried to let it all go. She was too tired. She told herself that it didn't matter what anyone thought. She didn't care.

Until that afternoon.

Two officers knocked on the door at Holt Street. Katy felt a little shiver of apprehension as she went to open the door. Her dad wasn't around; he'd gone to the work. The young men were polite enough and handed her an official-looking document.

'Hello miss, are you Katy Foster?' She nodded. 'This is an authority for us to take your scanner as evidence in the missing person inquiry. It's all legal; you should read it carefully.'

'No, no way.' The colour drained from her cheeks; her chest was pounding. 'No way, you're not getting it. It's private property. You can't just march in here and take it.'

The police officers were inching forward, intimidating her.

'Please, you can't do this. Please.'

The older of the two spoke calmly but left her in no doubt that they were serious. 'We can and we will. This warrant here gives us permission. Please move aside.'

Katy's body turned to jelly, her knees were giving way and without warning, she slumped into the doorjamb, but she was still pleading. 'Please, please don't.' Bordering on a state of panic, she looked around wildly for support. 'You can't do this to me, to us. You don't understand.'

'Please, you're making this harder on yourself. The machine in question is needed in the investigation. Surely you want to co-operate?'

'You don't understand; it's not that simple. Please ...'

It was useless. She ran out of things to say. In exhausted surrender, she pitched her back against the wall. The officers pushed by gently, found the scanner in the study, disconnected it, and left. One handed Cassie a hurriedly written receipt as they walked out, telling her they would return it as quickly as possible.

Katy felt depleted and her limp body slid down the wall. She slumped over in solitary grief.

She sat for ages but eventually recovered enough to digest what had happened. The one thing which embodied all her hopes for her mother's safe return, the only thing that held the promise of a reunion, was gone.

Her eyes stung with angry, unshed tears. They needed to have that scanner here, just in case it really was the vehicle to another dimension. What if her mother couldn't return? The anger morphed into something resembling action as her mind started to look for ways through it.

The shock settled, her body started to respond, and although her world had stopped turning for an interval, her determination kicked in. She would get it back, one way or another. She would get it back—this afternoon.

She called her father and Emma. Both reacted with equal shock and horror. Her dad said he was on his way home immediately.

Then she made another call. It was impulsive, but it had to help.

She dialled Paul Burwood's mobile. It rang a few times, and she dreaded getting a recorded message; what would she say?

'Paul Burwood speaking ...'

'Oh, thank God, thank God. Paul, I need help; I'm losing it here. Please, please help.' She burst into tears.

'Is that you, Katy?'

'Yes, yes. Can you come over, please?'

'I'll be right there.' The phone went dead.

Paul and her father arrived within minutes of each other. When Paul arrived, Katy sat slouched on the settee, her father beside her, his strong arms wrapped around her tiny, vulnerable frame. Her face was streaked with shiny trails of recent tears, but she appeared calm. Her dad regarded the newcomer with suspicious curiosity.

Paul spoke first, directly to him. 'Sorry to barge in like this, sir. Katy called me. I came straight over.'

'Yeah ... it's all right, Dad. I asked him to come.' Katy threw him a look that said, 'Please don't embarrass me right now'.

The young officer was in plain clothes, off duty apparently, and the fact that he was there spoke volumes.

Katy squirmed a little in her seat, kissed her dad on the cheek, and whispered in his ear, 'Can you give us a few minutes?'

'It's good of you to come, young man; can I get you a coffee or something?'

'No thanks, I'm good.' Paul returned his gaze to Katy. 'Are you okay? You sounded terrified on the phone.'

'I panicked; I didn't know what else to do. I'm sorry. They took our scanner! I need your help.'

'What are our rights are here? Have you got that warrant, Katy?' her father asked, still hovering.

She was sitting on it and it was a mangled mess. Katy hadn't even realised she'd been clutching it so tightly she'd almost destroyed it.

'Here.' She handed the crumpled document to her dad. The receipt fluttered out as she handed it over. He snatched it and walked away.

Katy looked up at Paul. 'I'll tell you everything, but you've got to get that scanner back. It's the only link we have to Mum.'

Paul shrugged. 'I don't know if I can. I'm just a constable in the local station. Missing Persons is a whole different area.'

'But it's all we have, Paul.' She took some deep breaths, her expression grave. *God, how do I say this?* She searched for inspiration, and suddenly the words started tumbling out. 'I don't know what you've heard at the station, but we didn't exactly tell you everything, so here goes.'

Katy looked straight ahead, not wanting to be distracted by any judgemental looks Paul might give her. 'It sounds stupid, but we believe Mum used that scanner to travel to another dimension. We think she's time travelled.' She thought she heard a bit of a grunt from him, but when she looked sideways, his eyes didn't betray his thoughts. 'The scanner is our only hope. If what the old lady said is true, she can't come home without it. Do you understand?' The pitch of her voice rose again as her anxiety reasserted itself.

'Wait a minute ... the scanner? You're telling me the scanner is magic? And who's this old lady? I'm sorry, I don't follow.'

'That's why I didn't tell you in the first place. There's no plausible explanation for Mum's disappearance in the other leads we followed, and now I'm afraid the detectives have reached the same conclusion and they have taken the scanner thinking it will give them the evidence they need. It won't, Paul. The scanner isn't magic; it has no power of its own. It's the old psychic who created this mess. According to her, the scanner was a prop. Because Mum used it to get to wherever she is, it's the only way she can get back. Don't you see? If they keep it, she might not be able to break through the time barrier to get home.' The words cascaded from her in a flurry, tumbling out like debris from an explosion.

'Katy, Katy, slow down.' He took one of her hands in his. It was the first time they'd touched, and she shuddered involuntarily. Paul had crossed a line and it confused her, but at the same time she trusted him.

Paul said, 'Katy, if the police seized that scanner looking for proof, you're saying they'll find nothing, is that right?'

She nodded. 'Uh huh. It's all we have. Please, please get it back for us. What if Mum wants to come home, and she can't?'

'Listen, I don't know what to believe; it sounds improbable, but I can see you are distressed, so I want to help. I just don't know if I can do anything. Before I go to these people and make a fool of myself, I really need to have some sort of proof.'

'Okay,' Katy told him everything: The bits of information they'd gathered, the neighbour's observations, Maria's story, the photo, the crazy question mark over Scott's death in 1969, the weird psychic at Soul Centre. All of it. When she was done, she sat, staring blankly, not sure what else she could possibly say.

Paul sat speechless. His face had taken on the look of someone who had suddenly felt the earth collapse.

Surprise and consternation all at once.

'I'm not making this up. I know it sounds ridiculous. But why would I?'

Paul looked at her, studying her eyes. She was trapped by her own beliefs and circumstances, and they'd swallowed her up like quicksand.

'I'll do what I can, I truly want to help, and I sort of believe you, but if I go to see the people at the Missing Persons Unit to get the scanner back with this story, I'm laying my own credibility on the line. Is there a chance I could talk to Emma or Maria?'

'Yes. I guess so, if that will convince you. I just want that scanner exactly where it was when she disappeared.'

She asked when he was free, fully aware they had to move quickly. Fortunately, he had a late shift the following day. She called Maria to see if she could make it down to meet them in the morning, and she agreed, having already spoken to Emma about the missing scanner. Then a quick call to Emma to ask her if she could get there as well, and it was all arranged. They would meet at Holt Street at 9.30 am.

When Paul had gone, Katy found her dad to update him on the latest developments. He slumped back in his chair, his shoulders drooped. 'The police are within their rights. They must believe the scanner's connected, or they wouldn't have taken it. We can't dispute that, can we? I'll be here in the morning as well. I'm not sure I believe it yet, but I also want that thing back here, just in case.'

Paul turned up early. Katy and Jeff had some time to relax with him before the others turned up. By the time Emma and Maria arrived, the meeting had taken on a conspiratorial tone. Katy noticed Paul fidgeting with his mobile, turning it over and over in his hand as he listened. The conversation was laced with elements of mystery and intrigue. For the next few hours, Paul asked a lot of questions. His demeanour went from good-humoured interest, sprinkled with a healthy dose of scepticism, to intense curiosity, to deep concern. In the end, the consensus was that even though every ounce of logic and reason decreed otherwise, they had to accept it was their truth. It was clear that Paul wanted facts and they had none, but Katy felt encouraged when he spoke.

'Honestly, I don't know what to believe right now, but I can see it's very important to all of you, so I'll do my best. I'll try to find out what I can at the station as soon as possible.'

Maria left and Emma went back to her parents. She hadn't told them about the scanner being taken away, convinced it would only worry them more. Katy's father went off to work, having said little.

Alone again, Katy let the hours passed. All afternoon she moped about the place in a haze of melancholy.

When her father came home, she made an effort to be hopeful.

It was nearly eight o'clock when Paul rang. He sounded tired.

'Hi, sorry it's so late, but it's been a hell of a day. Listen, I managed to get over to the evidence room, but they haven't examined it yet. There was no one there, so short of stealing it, I couldn't get hold of the thing. The best I can do is see them in the morning before I go on duty and try to explain, but I can't promise anything.'

Katy sighed, deflated by the news. 'I know, but I'm going crazy with worry. Thanks anyway.'

'Yeah, I get it, and I'm sorry, but my hands are tied.'

'Goodnight, Paul.' Katy disconnected the call. Her disappointment was palpable. She'd hoped the scanner would be back in its place and the longer she lingered wishing and waiting, the more anxious she became.

She woke up feeling putrid, looking like a fifty-year-old version of herself, but she didn't care. All night she'd been wrestling with her own thoughts, oscillating from one disastrous possibility to the other.

When she ambled into the kitchen, her father looked at her, his own features wilted. He pushed a mug of strong black coffee at her, and she took it with indifference.

They both sat at the table, deflated, unable to rouse themselves to enthusiasm for the day ahead. Her father dithered as he prepared to go to the station. He kissed her on the forehead and held her close as he was leaving. 'Try to find something to take your mind off things today, will you? I hate the thought of you sitting here worrying.'

'I'll be fine Dad; I'll probably go to Gran and Pops.'

'Good,' he said, then turned on his heel and walked out the door.

She wondered how she was going to fill in the whole day. It was Friday morning, and she knew that if she didn't have the scanner back by that evening, they would probably have to wait; it seemed unlikely the police would return it on the weekend.

It was a bit easier when she got to her grandparents' place; they whiled away the hours trying to stay optimistic. But there was no call from Paul and no word from the police.

Just after 4.00 pm, Emma couldn't stand it any longer and leapt up in frustration. 'Damn it, I'm calling them. I can't bear this waiting.'

Katy jumped up and followed her into the kitchen, leaving the elderly couple staring at each other.

'Hello, hello ...' Emma was already talking, her jaw heavy with determination and anger. She threw an anxious look at Katy. 'Yes, your officers came and took away our scanner, and I'd like to know what's happened to it.' She rolled her eyes at Katy and tapped her foot impatiently.

Emma's face lit up; something was happening. A second later, she slumped again; the news was not good. She disconnected the call, threw her phone back on the table and strode back into the living room. She explained to Katy that the clerk had been less than enthusiastic to help and could give her no answers. Apparently, the machine was still with forensics, and they had to wait until it was returned. The officer had volunteered nothing and was unwilling to take any further action.

Katy called her dad to let him know.

CHAPTER 47

1969

Cassie was laying 1969 to rest.

The television was off, her father was digging in the fridge, and she music blared from Emma's room. She loitered in the hallway, postponing the inevitable, then padded back into the kitchen and threw herself against her dad's back, wrapping him in one of her best hugs. How she would miss him, miss them all. He wheeled around and hugged her back, lapping it up, wriggling with delight. Bliss. She said goodnight, worried the quiver in her voice might give her away, but he was already extricating himself to get back to the important job in hand, buttering some crackers.

Heading back towards her sister's room, Cassie could hear the radio blaring out the Beatles and reminded herself again—they were alive and new; this was history. *Why have I spent my time digging an incredibly deep and messy hole for myself when I should have been savouring these precious relics of the past?*

She tapped gently on the door. Emma was lying on the bed, the pink chenille bedspread draped haphazardly over her legs. Cassie tiptoed in and sat beside her. 'If I'm not awake when you head off in the morning—'

'Why, what you got planned?'

'Nothing, I just wanted to say goodnight, I guess. I've been so self-absorbed of late. I love you, Emma.'

Emma gave her a funny look. 'We'll see how you feel next time I want to borrow one of your tops.'

Cassie realised that although her world was changing dramatically, for Emma, life was essentially the same. She leaned over and embraced her, breathing in her delicious scent and touched her flawless young shoulders. 'Night night, sweetheart.'

If only they knew.

As she closed the door behind her, she saw her mother coming out of the bathroom. They had a long, sumptuous cuddle but it was gone in an instant. How she wished she could bottle this feeling –

take it with her into the future which now beckoned her with powerful urgency.

She walked into her bedroom and closed the door. According to her Snoopy calendar today was Thursday, 18th December. She had been here for nearly two months, but it felt like an eternity.

The hard work was done here. A life saved, an innocent life lost; the pain and trauma belonged here ... she did not. The more she dwelt on this, the more distinct the future became. She was compelled to connect with that future. That's where her responsibilities lay now. The thoughts started to become forms, the forms took shape into images and the images became living, cherished human beings. *They* were her family. Whatever she'd had here was behind the door, and now she was alone, perched in the middle, stuck between her past and eternity.

For an indeterminate time, she sat at her desk, the detritus of her teenage life lying scattered around her like wildflowers. She scrutinised every tiny bloom of her experience: the notes to herself; her bed (still bearing the horsey transfers her dad had lovingly plastered onto the headboard); the pretty white kitten-heeled shoes she'd bought especially for the formal. On top of her wardrobe, her old teddies and a few other favourite toys gazed down at her. She jumped up and took each one down in turn and caressed it lovingly with her cheek. It was only when she put one of them back that she realised she'd been crying; the bear's soft brown fur was damp to her touch. She tried to explain to them in whispered tones what had happened, how she had ended up in this crazy alchemy of transition.

Not having shared it with anyone, having carried the heavy burden of her secret alone, she allowed herself silent sobs of regret and pain. They didn't last long; she had expended them on all that had gone before.

Cassie caught sight of herself in the mirror. She inhaled deeply, wiped her eyes and looked closely at herself—the first time since the abortion. The guilt stabbed with sharp blades of self-recrimination, but she persisted. Cautiously she undressed, piece by piece, until she stood naked. For the longest time she looked at herself. She stared at her fine, unblemished skin; the smooth curves and mounds of her breasts; the slim hips; her legs, unmarked and strong. She had to remember this painful moment of rupture from her past. As her hands glided over her flawless skin, she saw the impermanence of everything. In a few hours she would be back to being a middle-aged mum—the sagging likeness of beauty that the future had promised. She understood, standing there naked and vulnerable, that everything would disappear. But it was all right.

She lingered before the mirror while the future prodded her gently and the present absorbed her full attention. It was so hard to leave, and she prayed that her pledge to her fate would become something more solid, something she could hang on to as she stepped back into the abyss of time and space.

Consumed with a mixture of apprehension and excitement, she finally turned off the light and climbed into bed, pulling the covers up high, she needed to feel anchored to something.

In the darkness, she lay there, tense, suddenly stiff with fear, unable to clear her mind of the confusion. *What if it didn't work? What if... what if... what if...?*

She gripped the edge of the bed tightly and squeezed her eyes shut and started to utter the alphanumeric code she had written down. She said it softly but out loud three times, all the while visualising Jeff and Katy, willing them into existence.

'XPR2000079, XPR200079, XPR200079.'

The room exploded in a burst of colour. Cassie plummeted into a vortex of swirling clouds, and it was over. The darkness enveloped her.

CHAPTER 48

Katy and her father rattled about the house, bumping off each other like tenpins. They did necessary chores and the air crackled with unspoken thoughts.

So self-absorbed were they, that they nearly didn't hear the knock on the door.

Katy snapped into awareness and ran towards it. *Please, please, please ... let it be some good news, please.* She opened the door.

Standing there on the verandah, the scanner lovingly cradled in his arms, stood Paul, wearing a grin that stretched from one end of the street to the other.

Katy squealed with delight and lunged at him, threw her arms around his neck and kissed him on the cheek, inhibitions thrown to the wind.

The machine sat awkwardly between them.

'You're amazing. How did you get it? Dad! Dad! Come and see what Paul brought!'

In a heartbeat, Jeff was there. His face lit up. 'Wow! This is tremendous. Thank you, thank you. You're a lifesaver.' Carefully he reached over and took the scanner from Paul. 'Let's get this back where it belongs.'

'Come in,' Katy said. 'I— er—we are so grateful. You have no idea.' She was walking back up the hallway, looking over her shoulder at him, relieved and happy. She showed him to the living room.

'I decided to pop over to the evidence room last night when I finished my shift,' Paul said. 'Luckily the officer there was a mate of mine and he told me they no longer needed it. The report had been done; they just hadn't got around to letting us know yet. So, here I am.' His chest heaved and his eyes shone. Katy felt his exhilaration like the warm breath of spring. At that moment, she adored him.

She gestured to Paul to sit down and grabbed her phone, excusing herself while she texted Emma to give her the good news. Not the best news; Mum was still missing, but this was something.

Jeff came out of the kitchen carrying three mugs.

Katy bubbled with excitement. 'Isn't this wonderful, Dad?' She looked at Paul with admiration. 'I don't know how to thank you.'

'The important thing is finding your mum. When things are settled, I'm sure we can work something out.' He threw her a cheeky grin.

After Paul left, Katy turned to her father. 'I'm so relieved. I know it mightn't help, but I feel so much better knowing the scanner is back where it should be. I might give Maria a call and then head over to Gran and Pops. Do you feel like coming?'

'No thanks, it's been a big week.'

When she arrived at her grandparents' house, everyone's mood seemed lighter. Gran was quite positive and said as much. She was convinced that her daughter would manage whatever dilemma she faced.

'I don't quite understand, Mum,' Emma ventured. 'How you can be so complacent; you were as frantic as the rest of us a few days ago.'

The old woman quipped back, 'A mother knows. A mother knows these things! I feel upset that Cassie is going through some sort of trial, but I also know that she is smart and resourceful, and I have every faith in my daughter. You should as well, young lady.' She pulled Emma close, enveloping her in a motherly hug. 'There is one thing that gnaws at me, though. I hope I am not going mad here, but I can't get that photo out of my mind. I know we said Scott had died, but now I'm almost sure he just faded away, disappeared, leaving something quite disturbing in its place, I just don't know what. I'm a bit confused.'

'Well, that makes all of us!' Pops said. 'But no point my speaking; I haven't a clue about anything anymore.' He threw his hands up in exasperation.

Katy brought the subject up again at dinner with her father that evening, but her father didn't offer an opinion. She wondered if they would ever have the answers.

Sunday eased in through the window. The roads were a little quieter, the atmosphere subdued. Katy had managed to sleep off and on, and she met the day with a pinch of optimism. Her dad was already up. They dawdled over breakfast, recognising that although this was not the ordinary Sunday they were both craving, it was the way things were. Coco had come to terms with the new order of things and lay stretched out in the shade on the verandah. Shadows played in the gentle breeze, the air thick with the fragrance of summer.

It occurred to Katy that she hadn't given Mrs Parker a thought since the scanner had been seized. She cut a few flowers from the bottlebrush in the back garden, wrapped them in some moist kitchen towel, and strolled across the street to the old lady's home.

Ada was delighted to see her and shepherded her inside.

Nestled comfortably in the roomy chair, Katy listened as Mrs Parker recounted the events that had animated her week. Katy was only half paying attention, but the time passed pleasantly enough. When she saw Emma's car pull up she couldn't wait to see her, so she made her excuses and left, abandoning the old lady to her solitude.

'So, what brings you here?' Katy hugged Emma as she stepped from her car.

'I took Mum and Dad out for a drive this morning, but after spending a couple of hours in the car with them, I just needed a bit of space. I intended to head to the beach, but somehow ended up here again.'

'Well, I'm glad you came. Do you want some lunch? We've some leftovers in the fridge.'

Emma nodded. 'Anything sounds good.'

They sat at the kitchen to share some leftover moussaka. Jeff was scraping the last morsels of food off his plate, when suddenly there was the weirdest whooshing sound.

Katy gasped. 'What was that? It sounded like a jet engine. It's coming from the study.'

All three leapt up and bounded towards the closed door. A strip of bluish light crept out from under it, spilling into the hallway. Emma grasped Katy's arm, indicating that she should be cautious, but her father didn't hesitate. He reefed the door open.

They froze, transfixed by the scene in the study. Thick ultramarine clouds of mist enveloped them, making it hard to see anything properly. A haze of glittering, shimmering light danced off the walls and ceiling, and the air fizzled. Not one of them could find a voice. Eyes like huge lunar discs struggled to interpret the scene. The room was silent except for the light swishing sound as the atmosphere started to settle.

A large, dark shadow on the floor began to emerge from the fog, and a mass started to take shape.

Three pairs of eyes were riveted to the spot, too shocked to move or speak.

The shape morphed into Cassie. When the hissing and swirling stopped, and the vivid mist was nothing but a hint of blue floating above them, Katy leapt forward, dropped to her knees, and thrust her arm under her mother's head. Her moans of wonder and delight soon turned into whooping great screams of joy. 'Mum! Mum! Mum! Thank God. Thank God, you're back.' She brought her lips close to her prone mother's cheek, kissing her madly, huge tears dropping on to Cassie's face.

Jeff and Emma joined in with a cacophony of ecstatic noises.

'Cass, Cass ... Oh! My darling girl, where have you been? We've been so worried about you.' Jeff threw his body over her, rubbing his face into her bosom, muffled sobs escaping from his shaking form. Emma pushed around them both and, kneeling close to Cassie's head on the other side, she kissed and stroked her sister's hair lovingly.

Cassie lay unconscious.

CHAPTER 49

They huddled over Cassie's supine form. Jeff shook her gently. She opened her eyes briefly, and there was a hint of a smile, but then she drifted back into her stupor.

'Call an ambulance; I'm not going to lose her now,' Jeff barked, but Katy was ahead of him. She was shouting their address into the phone. Then, with her hand over the mouthpiece, she mouthed, 'I'll let the others know.'

'Tell them we're going to the hospital and we'll meet them there,' Jeff said.

Emma fetched a pillow and blanket from the bedroom, and they made Cassie comfortable without moving her too much.

Jeff had Cassie's hand cradled in his palm.

'Let's hope she's just fainted. Any idea how long the ambulance will be?' He looked up at Katy perched in the doorway, caught between concern and disbelief.

'About ten minutes. They said to watch her breathing and pulse.'

'What just happened?' Emma said.

'Stuffed if I know,' Jeff said. 'She's home and alive, that's all I care about. I'm sure she'll tell us everything when she comes to.'

The ambulance pulled up moments later, its lights flashing. Two paramedics leapt out and Katy went to meet them.

Everyone crowded into the tiny room. Jeff, Emma and Katy leaned against the door frame, saying nothing, intent on what the ambulance attendants were doing and straining to hear the words they exchanged in low voices.

After a time, the older one of the two looked at Jeff and smiled. 'Her vital signs are good, but as she's not conscious, we can't rule out brain injury. We'll take her to St Andrews and the doctors can have a closer look. Right now, she's not in any immediate danger. We'll bring in a stretcher. We've got room for one in the ambulance, so who wants to come?'

Emma and Katy both looked at Jeff.

'I'll go. I'll get my keys.'

The two paramedics lifted Cassie onto the blanket, fixed the securing straps with skilled efficiency, locked the trolley into place, and carefully manoeuvred it outside. Jeff trotted beside them, a concerned frown etching his features.

As they were closing the doors, he yelled out to the girls, 'Bring some fresh clothes, and maybe her purse and stuff.'

The ambulance pulled away. Katy and Emma watched from the verandah and hugged each other. They were both shaking.

Inside, Katy went into her parents' room and packed a small overnight bag. At one point, she collapsed on the bed. Emma came in and held her, and they cried together.

Even though they had both seen her in the study, it seemed unbelievable that with one flash the nightmare was over.

They were fortunate to find a parking spot right outside the main entrance to the hospital. Once inside, they headed to the main desk. Both started talking at once. The foyer was quiet, and the woman at the counter asked them to calm down, so she was able to give them directions to the emergency ward where Cassie had been taken.

As soon as they got out of the elevator, they saw Jeff sitting on a chair beside two huge swing doors with the word EMERGENCY over them in large red letters. He was hunched over, his head cradled in his hands that were nervously working their way back and forth.

'Dad!' Katy called out.

He looked up with a relieved sigh. 'Glad you found us. She's in there.' He nodded towards the doors. 'I think it's been about 20 minutes.'

'She'll be all right though, won't she?'

'Of course she will, Kitten. We've got her home, that's the important thing. She'll need time. Heaven only knows what sort of ordeal she's been through.'

Looking around the near-empty corridor, Emma sighed. 'So we just wait. Mum and Dad should be on their way.'

'Golly, I'd better check. In all the kerfuffle I'm not sure I thought about how they were going to get here,' Katy said.

Just as she spoke, the doors of the elevator opened and her grandparents walked out. She bounded over and hugged them.

'Sorry, I should have picked you up on the way; my head was all over the place.'

'It's fine,' Pops said. 'Our neighbour gave us a lift. Thank God she's safe!'

'Mum's in there and as far as we know there is no major injury, but they need to make sure there's no brain damage.'

Together now, scattered across the tandem seating, the circumstances of Cassie's return were questioned and discussed. No one really had any idea what had happened or how. They were elated to have her back. Here in this place, where lives hung in the balance, she was safe, and they floated on a wave of waiting and wondering.

An hour or so passed. At last, the doors flung open and a young doctor walked out. He was smiling..

He looked at the group, guessing instantly who they were. 'You're Cassie Foster's family, I presume?'

'Yes, yes ...' Jeff said. The others nodded in agreement.

'She'll be fine, but she's still in shock. Some sort of trauma brought on the blackout. We'd like to keep her in for a couple of days, do some tests to make sure, but she's conscious now, and it's fine to go in and spend a few minutes with her. Only two at a time please.'

Jeff shook his hand and thanked him. He glanced at the others and then at Katy. 'Can we go in now?'

Gran flicked both hands at them, gesturing for them to go.

Cassie was sitting up in bed, her hair dishevelled. Her skin looked pasty; it had an unnatural sheen in the harsh fluorescent light.

Jeff rushed towards her with Katy behind him. Both reached out to embrace her. But Cassie was unresponsive, her eyes telling a story they would never understand.

However, father and daughter read each other perfectly well. This woman lying in the bed bore little resemblance to the Cassie they remembered. They saw a shell of someone they once knew. When Katy hugged her, she didn't say a word. An eerie emptiness filled the room, and Jeff sat expressionless beside her, cradling her limp hand. They both uttered words of affection, words of encouragement, words of support, but they floated in the air, never finding their mark. She stared blankly ahead, and every now and then her gaze would rest on a point somewhere they couldn't see.

Jeff beckoned Katy to move towards the corner of the bed and when she came close, he whispered. 'I don't want the others to see her like this.'

She nodded back in agreement. 'We should talk to the doctor, Dad; that's not Mum.'

He turned back to Cassie. 'Darling, we're going to leave you to get some rest, but we'll be back soon, okay?'

No response.

They kissed her goodbye, and a moment later, they stood outside the cubicle, surrounded by the clatter and beeping of the ward.

'Let's wait here to talk to the doctor; something's not right,' Jeff said.

Moving out of the way, they stood close to the wall. They stopped the first nurse who wasn't rushing about, and asked if they could see the doctor in charge.

He was a youngish man with a kindly face, his round, wire spectacle frames sagging low on his nose. He had a full, generous mouth that invited conversation.

'Did you ask to see me?' His dark eyes shot from one to the other.

'Yes, we were told that my wife, Cassie Foster, was fine. But we've just been in there and she's almost catatonic. We're worried. Can you tell us what's going on?'

The doctor disappeared into Cassie's cubicle and returned with her chart. He read it, flipping through the pages to pore over the information. 'Just a moment,' he took off again, back behind the screen.

When he came back there was nothing in his expression that gave them any clues. 'I've checked all the obvious, and there is nothing clinically wrong, but I understand your concern. I believe she just needs rest; she's had some sort of major trauma. We'll send her off for a CT scan, just to make sure there's nothing going on, and we'll arrange for a psychologist to come and have a chat. These things take time; we have to be patient.'

Jeff exhaled loudly. 'Patient?'

Katy broke in. 'I'm sorry doctor. You see, Mum's been missing for nearly two months. You can understand we haven't got an abundance of patience right now.'

'I'm afraid there is nothing further we can do now. We'll keep her here overnight and do the scan tomorrow.' He leant slightly towards them and smiled. 'I understand you are worried. She's experienced a shock of some kind, and she'll need a while to recuperate. Try not to push her too hard.'

'When will they be taking her to the ward?' Katy asked.

'Anytime now, I should think. Hold on, I'll find out.'

Off he went again, but was back before they had time to plan their next move.

She'll be taken to Ward 3F shortly. You'll be able to stay as long as you like up there, and while that's happening, I suggest you grab a bite to eat or something. She's in good hands.'

When Katy and Jeff left her the second time, they felt a little better. Outside, Katy explained the situation, preparing the others for possible disappointment.

They took up the doctor's suggestion and by the time they got to Ward 3F, Cassie lay resting. Speaking in turn, each family member expressed their relief and joy at having her safely home. There was a semblance of something in her eyes, but no show of emotion.

It was getting late. Emma suggested she take her parents home and feed Coco, offering to come back to pick up Katy and her dad later. They declined; adamant that they wanted to stay in case there was a change.

Hours later, Katy sat beside the bed, half draped over it. Her head nestled on the pillow next to her mother as she tried to doze. Her father slouched awkwardly in an armchair, bleary eyed and washed out.

Dawn arrived, bathing the room in a golden glow, and glittering reflections of the morning sun bounced off the windows of the building opposite. The first sunrise with her mother home slid into daylight without ceremony or celebration. Her mother slept on.

Katy roused herself, snapping to alertness. Her father sat up and rubbed his eyes with the heels of his hands.

A nurse appeared and offered them a cup of tea which they accepted gratefully.

They stretched and bent their stiffened bodies. After Katy called Emma, they took turns to go down to the canteen and get themselves something to eat.

The hospital clunked into operation. Staff milled around and the ward became noisy with the beeping and whirring of machines, buzzing phones, and unintelligible chatter in the corridor ... a commotion of healing.

At last, her mum woke up, really woke up. Her father sat beside her, gently squeezing her hand. Cassie looked closely at him, studying his face for a long time, then at Katy, standing close by. She brought her hand up to his cheek and ran one finger lightly over the creases, as if testing to see if he was real.

Her first smile illuminated the room.

'I made it,' she said quietly, nodding her head as if barely able to believe it herself. She beamed at them both.

Katy leaned over and embraced her, the energy of joy and relief fizzed in the air.

'I'm home.' Suddenly she became serious, 'I'm so terribly, terribly sorry for what I have put you through.'

Jeff pursed his lips. 'It's not been a picnic, but by the looks of you I think you've had your own nightmare. We can talk about it later, for now you just need to rest.' He stroked her hand fondly, still basking in the miracle.

Brightening up, Katy joined in. 'Mum, it's been absolute hell for us, but it doesn't matter, you're here now. I can't wait to get you home and safe. I'm calling Emma. She's staying with Gran and Pops, and they will be so relieved. Don't worry about anything other than getting better, okay?'

Her mother nodded and smiled. She still appeared disoriented and distant, but slowly she was filtering into the scene.

Katy blurted into the phone with excitement. 'Mum's come to. She's here, she's with us and she's going to be fine. Everything's going to be fine.'

It wasn't long before Emma and her parents arrived.

Gran almost ran to her daughter's bedside. 'Oh, my darling girl! What you've been through!'

Cassie looked at her intently and in that instant, their eyes spoke of a secret suffering shared.

The others followed. The room erupted. There was an atmosphere of celebration and merriment, everyone chattering around, and over, and beside Cassie, who was drowning in a sea of hugs, doing her best to absorb it all. Bodies shuffled and bumped to move near the bed, tears flowed like wine, laughter jingled. The relief was tangible.

CHAPTER 50

Katy's first call the following morning was to Paul to thank him for all that he'd done. She could tell he was glad she'd called. He suggested that either she or her dad call in to the police station in person to make a formal statement, so they could close the enquiry.

Later that afternoon, Ada Parker appeared, quite possibly eaten up by rapacious curiosity. Her visit didn't surprise Katy. The old lady couldn't wait to tell them she had seen that strange blue light again, right before there was all that commotion and the ambulance pulled up; she wanted to know what was going on.

With amiable cordiality, they invited her in. Katy made her a cup of tea and told the story. It was all a mystery, she explained. They had seen the blue light, and her mother had appeared, without logical explanation. The ambulance had been called as a precaution, but all was well.

No doubt, Ada would take great delight in colouring in the details and decorating the story in the future.

Wednesday sparkled. Cassie was coming home. Jeff had left early for the hospital, anxious to bring her home as soon as he could. Katy and Emma stayed, busily preparing for a small celebration. Katy cooked her mum's favourite food, the house was spotless—they were ready.

***

Cassie could feel her heart beating fast as the car pulled up. Her palms were sticky, her senses on high alert. It was as if there had been a small tear in her roadmap home, for she didn't expect to end up in hospital. This was better. Everything was so familiar and authentic. This is where she belonged. She gazed around as she walked slowly up the path with her husband beside her, his arm protectively around her waist. He was beaming. The sounds of the traffic, the lorikeets, and the glorious fragrances wafted back and forth in the breeze. It all cascaded on her, a gushing waterfall of memories and images, sucking her attention into the now. Approaching the front door, she turned the knob with delicious familiarity and walked inside to greet her family.

'Okay, everyone, I'm so thrilled to be back with you all—the people I love most in the universe. I have a story to tell, and I promise that one day I will tell it, but for now, I just want to enjoy being with my family.'

There was a general hubbub in the room.

'I know,' Cassie said, holding both her hands up in a calming gesture, 'you are all dying to know what happened. But I'm still trying to process it myself, so please be patient.'

She turned to Jeff and kissed him on the cheek. Coco was rubbing back and forth against her legs as she spoke, a whiskered diesel engine. Cassie picked her up and stroked her. She caressed the soft fur with her cheek and relished its normalcy.

Jeff brought out a bottle of champagne, Emma and Katy had seen to it that there was enough food for everyone, and the conversation tiptoed around the important things, keeping the mood light.

They were all chattering like mad when there was a knock at the door. Emma rolled her eyes, but dashed off to get it.

'Katy ... I think there's someone here for you,' she said, grinning.

It was Paul. He was carrying an enormous bunch of daffodils, promising wonderful new beginnings.

'I'm so happy to hear your mum's back,' he said, blushing.

'Thank you, it's so sweet of you to come. Are these for her?' Katy admired the flowers.

'Well actually, both of you. Can I come in?'

She took him gently by the arm, said nothing, but kissed him on the cheek. He responded by turning slowly, wrapping his spare arm around her and kissing her on the lips with divine tenderness. They lingered there in the hallway. It was so much more than a thank you kiss, so much more than a greeting; it was a new beginning kiss.

Reaching for his hand, Katy led him into the living room and interrupted the party.

'Mum, this is Paul; he has helped us so much in our search for you, and I'll be forever grateful,' She gazed up at him.

'Good to see you, son,' her father said. 'What do you drink?'

At some point during the afternoon Maria turned up as well. Cassie was visibly thrilled to see her, but it had been a long day and she was starting to fade. When the shadows lengthened, and everyone was calmer, Jeff chased people out until just the three of them were left. They talked a little more, and then Cassie went off to have a shower and go to bed.

Katy and her dad remained. They toasted each other, glass of wine in hand—a toast to the end of the nightmare and the beginning of recovery. There was no doubt in their minds that it would be a long road, and it would be bumpy and unpredictable. Whatever had happened to Cassie had damaged her; she was not the same. They knew it would take patience and time for her to share her experience, and that they might never hear the full story, but they were content with that.

CHAPTER 51

It seemed a lifetime ago that Cassie had slept in this bed, here in their family home. The room felt intimate and comfortable. She sat there for a while, mulling over the events of the last few days, searching for a way to cross the bridge between past and present.

Something struck her. She leapt up and raced over to her wardrobe. Straining to reach into the back of it, she pulled out a carved timber box. Her mum had given it to her on her twenty-first birthday along with an Oroton purse. Taking a deep breath she slowly opened it. Inside was a collection of tiny treasures that embodied the beautiful memories of her past.

There it was, dog eared and yellowed with age. This was it! She took out the discoloured envelope. On the outside was an image of two little girls surrounded by faded red hearts. In reverential awe, she opened it carefully, unfolded the pages, and started to read silently. 'My darling Cassie ...' She squinted hard to hold back the tears, struggling with its significance. She remembered writing it, remembered the whirlpools in the pit of her stomach. Was it really only a week ago? Yet here it was; testimony to her journey back in time. Still clutching the letter, her eyes wandered back to the contents of the box. There, amongst the keepsakes and bits of paper sat the locket. She folded the letter, slid it back into its fragile envelope and picked up the locket. She pried the tiny clip open and, with a sigh, clutched it to her heart and kissed it lightly before placing it back in the box. It was a relief that it wasn't floating in some corner of cyber space, but questions hung like parachutes in her skies of wonder. She knew she would never have the answers for any of it, and that had to be all right. Maybe she just needed to be happy with what she had in the present moment.

She awoke the next morning feeling confused. After a few moments, she oriented herself again, but the uneasy feeling of being scattered and disembodied clung to her, heavy as seaweed clinging to the shore. Beside her, Jeff snored softly; Coco was curled up on the bed, nestled in the crook of her body. She touched them both, affirming their presence.

She thought of the past months. The memories, the new ones she'd created. The memory of saving Scott's life, the jarring pain of the innocent life she had sacrificed in its place. They were all there, reconstructed to become a part of the whole. This was the whole. She was whole—the grim, bitter recollection of the torturous abortion, letting go of her youth, her family—all of it. Her tapestry had been rewoven into a different, more complex pattern. No better, maybe worse, but these were the only threads and colours she had to work with. When it came down to it, all she had was now. This moment, this place. These were the memories of the future.

Jeff stirred, his breathing slow and steady, his eyelids still heavy as they fluttered to attention. 'Morning, darling.' He inhaled deeply and let out a long dreamy sigh. 'You smell so good; having you home is so good.' He nuzzled into the contours of her body, wrapping his arm around her.

Cassie moved closer to him and stroked his face tenderly.

She would put it all behind her; forget the stellar adventure she'd had. She wanted to believe that the past she'd constructed with so much sadness and loss would wax into the present, that she would forget there had ever been anything else.

All she had been, all she was, and all she would be, existed only in this moment. She had to learn to treasure and protect it; nurture and cradle it. Looking at her husband, thinking of everyone who gathered yesterday to celebrate, she understood how much she had grown. These people loved her. They too had an experience that was a part of this nightmare she had lived through, and now she owed it to them to give them everything of herself, without regrets, without expectations.

She smiled tenderly at Jeff and hugged him, giving all, holding nothing back, satisfied with life in the here and now.

Breakfast was a cosy affair, the three of them around the table like old times, but better. Each was acutely aware that a huge transition had, and was, taking place. Cassie's experiences would have to spill into the open at some point; the baggage had to be emptied out and sorted, but there was plenty of time.

Jeff was going to the police station to make his formal statement to tidy up the investigation. Katy, having put her young adult life on hold, was now ready to step into the future with excitement and optimism, knowing the world was offering up its richness to her.

Cassie had only one very important thing to do that morning, and she was quite happy to share it with them both. Marching towards the study, she emerged with the scanner, stepped outside, and placed it on the concrete. Wielding a hammer she had found especially for the purpose, she took great delight in smashing it into a thousand tiny pieces. The others joined in and bashed it as well, until a fractured mess of metal and plastic was all that was left of the machine.

Satisfied that particular demon had been annihilated they looked at each other and smiled—intimate, supportive, loving smiles.

Emma brought her parents over later in the morning and when Jeff returned from the police station, the family were seated around the table.

'Mum had a craving for Milo. Do you want some?' Katy asked.

He nodded, 'I just told them you were home, but that you'd had an emotional crisis, and needed to get away. In your rattled state, you forgot to let us know. I apologised for wasting police time, and the officer said they would need a statement from you as soon as you felt well enough, but for the now, I think they were happy to close the file.'

'I don't think they'd believe me.'

Katy leaned over and hugged her mother. 'You don't have to go until you are ready Mum, and then just tell them what you want to.'

'Exactly.' Jeff agreed. 'I couldn't resist asking what was going to happen to the old psychic though.' They dismissed her altogether, saying there wasn't enough evidence to go on. I suppose that's a good thing ...'

'It's just good to have everyone together again,' Emma said.

***

Cassie might not be able to divulge her secrets just yet, but she knew they would all be there for her when she was able to tell her story. She looked around the table. At Katy, ready for her own adventure, open to the choices that lay ahead. Emma, who'd been such a tower of strength to them all in the past few weeks, sacrificing her own family's needs to be with them, and dear old Gran and Pops who understood that a parent's love and faith would survive anything.

ACKNOWLEDGEMENTS

I owe my gratitude to so many people; the list is way too long to single out any one individual. I thank my family and close friends—you all know who you are, for the continued encouragement, support, and patience that helped to create this work of fiction.

Thank you to those who help us find our power and the courage to express ourselves in a world where excellence is revered and the accomplished so quickly overlooked.

ABOUT THE AUTHOR

Dutch by birth and Australian by circumstances, Ineke lives in Brisbane with her husband.

This debut novel is the culmination of a lifetime of experiences growing up in the suburbs of Brisbane in the sixties.

She has worked in a variety of roles, which has given her the opportunity to gather an assortment of skills and exposure to people from a range of different backgrounds. Her occupation as a travel consultant, spanning three decades, was both interesting and rewarding and enabled her to explore the world. Her curiosity has given her a robust understanding and appreciation of the planet and those of us who inhabit it.

The Atlantis Short Story Awards granted her an honourable mention, and she won the Eyre Writer's Poetry Competition. Having obtained a Diploma in Journalism, Ineke wrote for her own local magazine, but her preference was always creative writing, and her focus is now on prose and poetry. She enjoys regular meetings with other local authors who inspire, encourage, and review each other's work while sharing their common interest.

To contact the author, please email info@inekevanosauthor.com.au

She will soon have a website at www.inekevanosauthor.com.au

ON A PERSONAL NOTE

This novel is dedicated to all the dreamers, plodders, strugglers, triers, and hopers who want to achieve their own personal goals.

My name is Ineke. I've always written. From diaries filled with all the naivety and passion of a hopeful teenager till now, as I am metaphorically saddling my horse for that last ride into the sunset. However, this is my first novel. It comes after years of life being dictated by all the things that make it so wonderful and fascinating. Growing up, falling in love, getting married, travelling, having babies, watching them grow into the remarkable adults they are, and now, sitting back and enjoying grandchildren.

My working life has been interesting and exciting. I never quite made it to university, but made up for it by exploring any new and captivating adventure I could. I have always had a deep conviction that we have to live every moment as best we can and snatch every opportunity to learn, participate, and treasure. All that life experience has given me much joy and sometimes sorrow, and like so many before me, I decided to write a book. For no other reason than testing myself to see if I could.

It became an incredibly sharp learning curve, not the least of which was finding the discipline to actually finish something.

So here it is; it's been an amazing journey for me, and if it brings you some insights or perhaps pleasure as well, I'll be happy with that.